THE SHADOWS WE MISTAKE FOR LOVE

OTHER FICTION BY TOM WAYMAN

Boundary Country (2007)

A Vain Thing (2007)

Woodstock Rising (2009)

The Shadows We Mistake for Love

STORIES

Tom Wayman

Douglas & McIntyre

Douglas and McIntyre (2013) Ltd.
P.O. Box 219, Madeira Park, BC, V0N 2H0
www.douglas-mcintyre.com

Edited by Nicola Goshulak
Cover design by Anna Comfort O'Keeffe
Text design by Carleton Wilson
Printed and bound in Canada
Text paper is FSC-certified

BRITISH COLUMBIA
ARTS COUNCIL
An agency of the Province of British Columbia

Canada Council   Conseil des Arts
for the Arts   du Canada

Canadä

Douglas and McIntyre (2013) Ltd. acknowledges the support of the Canada
Council for the Arts, which last year invested $157 million to bring the arts to
Canadians throughout the country. We also gratefully acknowledge financial
support from the Government of Canada through the Canada Book Fund
and from the Province of British Columbia through the BC Arts Council and
the Book Publishing Tax Credit.

Cataloguing data available from Library and Archives Canada

ISBN 978-1-77162-095-6 (paper)
ISBN 978-1-77162-096-3 (ebook)

CONTENTS

Dwelling

THE MAN HAD lived for more than two decades in the house beside
the forest. One afternoon when he returned home from skiing he
was astonished to find that snow was falling inside the dwelling.

The man had skied for three hours on a trail that followed the
river. Below the overcast that day, fir and spruce along the route
had clumps of snow on their branches and similarly laden evergreens rose up the mountains that formed the valley walls. On the
mountainsides, patches and striations of pure white marked where
granite outcrops interrupted the mat of the forest that ascended toward the peaks. Snow also coated the upper surfaces of the tangle of
branches of cottonwood and birch that grew at the water's edge and
in stands amid the evergreens in the frozen woods. A scrub of hazel,
aspen and vine maple that lined the trail in places also supported
blobs of snow.

Near where the man had kicked and poled along, a single raven
landed amid the high limbs of a hemlock, sending down a small
white spray. Further on, a pair of the black birds glided west across
the mid-river islands of snow between which the icy water flowed
south. The man could hear the air pushed by their wings as they
flapped overhead through the stillness of the winter day. Occasionally one of the birds cawed, the sound loud below the desolate summits that overlooked the trail on which the man skied.

The exertion that propelled the man forward kept him warm.
Despite the cold air inhaled as he travelled, he felt exhilarated by
the exercise. But when at last he returned to his pickup and had to
sit still in the frosty vehicle while he drove home, he began to feel

chilled. The truck's heater eventually took the edge off his discomfort. Yet when he had swung up his driveway, parked and opened the door to his basement, he was glad to step into an enveloping soft heat.

He had stuffed the basement furnace with split cordwood before he left, and closed the damper. The heater had faithfully poured out warmth during the hours he had been absent. But to his amazement, as he stood just within the door, skis and backpack in his hands, he saw that the air below the floor joists was filled with lazily descending snowflakes. The white particles seemed to be forming out of nothing, the way sometimes outside on a sunny day he had observed snowflakes take shape and descend from an apparently cloudless blue sky.

The man gaped at the scene around him, his mind struggling to comprehend a snowfall in a basement. For a second he was seized by panic at the thought that the main floor and roof above him had vanished—burned in a fire, perhaps. Could he have not noticed the missing upper storey when he had driven up to the house? Then he remembered snow was not falling outside.

Yet already a scurf of white lay two or more centimetres deep on the cement floor, and atop the clothes washer and a table where his ski-waxing vises were set up. Racks of shelves holding an array of extension cords, paint cans, work gloves, gardening hand tools and irrigation nozzles brought inside for the winter were similarly coated. As he took a shaky step farther into the room, the powder covering the floor rose and settled from the motion of his boots, as though he were walking a dusty path. When he glanced back at the door after proceeding several paces, no indication of his passage was visible. The disturbed snow had landed where he had trod and lay as if he had never crossed through it.

With an automatic gesture, he brushed the waxing table clear in order to set down his pack. The snow felt odd, however: cool and powdery against his fingers and palm. The material that comprised the white fluff seemed devoid of water. He observed that the heated metal of the furnace's level top appeared the same as ever. No snow was evident, nor any drops or pools of fluid.

When the man removed his boots and climbed the snow-covered

stairs to the main floor of the house, an identical skiff of white covered kitchen floor tiles, counters, stove and refrigerator tops, and even the flatware and cutlery piled in his dish rack to dry. In the living room, the rug, chairs, sofa and sound system were equally adorned with snow. Though his socks plowed through the layer of snow on the floor as, astounded, he checked each room, the wool encasing his feet never became soaked as would have happened had he walked without boots through snow outside. Nor did the air within the house feel less reassuringly warm than usual despite the flakes drifting down below every room's ceiling.

The man stood in his bedroom, attempting without success to grasp how this meteorological anomaly could occur, and how the indoor snow could be so dry. At last he began to change out of his ski clothes. While he tugged on jeans and a sweater, the snowfall around him tapered off. But even when the air cleared completely, the powdery white that coated each object in the house remained. Hunger drove him to begin to cook supper. As he warmed some soup, he noticed the snow disappeared from the glowing burner and heated stovetop. But as with the furnace in the basement, the snow did not convert to water. He took a shower later, steam filling his small bathroom as always. Yet except for those surfaces on which water flowed, such as the interior of the tub or sink, the layer of snow everyplace remained unaffected.

He considered phoning his nearest neighbours, a young couple, to see if they were experiencing the same phenomenon. But if he was hallucinating for some reason, he thought, he didn't want to draw the neighbours' attention to the fact. They were well-meaning, and likely to insist that he seek medical help. He could imagine them with the best of intentions phoning 911 on his behalf whether he wanted them to or not. Who knew what such a call would set in motion? If others in the valley were also experiencing snow indoors, he reasoned, he would unquestionably hear about it. Somebody would contact him to check if he were affected too, the way people phoned each other when the power went off.

The man did not want to lower his head, still damp from the shower, into snow. So as he prepared to climb under the duvet, he shook the powdery coating off the pillowslip. He also brushed snow from the bedroom chair before piling his clothes on it as usual. Like every night, he opened the window a few centimetres, bending to inhale and savour the thin stream of icy air that entered. But throughout his bedtime routine, his bare feet felt only cool despite being buried in snow to the ankles.

In the middle of the night, he woke once to the distant sound of a plow clearing and sanding the main highway a couple of kilometres eastward across the valley. More snow must have fallen outside in the darkness. He thought drowsily of turning on the bedside light to learn if the snowfall indoors had resumed, but was asleep again before he could act.

When he awakened at first light, snowflakes glittered in the air of the bedroom as they gently floated down. He lay watching their beautiful steady fall. Snow had piled up again on the pillow, and the white on the bedroom rug looked deeper than before. The room was a little chilly, but no more so than any other morning after the fire in the furnace had burned to coals. He tossed aside the duvet, swung his feet over the side of the mattress and planted in them in the white fluff. The snow felt coolly powdery on his skin but not cold.

After breakfast, he shrugged into his parka and pulled on boots. Leaving the house, he walked several metres north to his wood shop. He wondered whether snow had fallen inside that building, too. After pulling the shop door open, he flicked on the fluorescents. Several centimetres of snow cloaked the linoleum floor and his big workbench with its hand tools racked on the wall above. Snow likewise lay on his table saws, band saw, lathe and the lumber stacked on the floor on the far side of the space.

A few minutes later he had changed out of his boots into slippers and had lit a fire in the shop's wood heater. He whisked the snow off his current project, a set of kitchen cabinets for a customer up the valley in Slocan, and extracted the drawings for the cupboards from beneath the powder that coated the workbench. The paper was unblemished. Soon he was absorbed in the day's tasks, measuring and cutting, tacking and gluing and clamping. He had to clear snow off a couple of cardboard boxes beside the workbench before he found the one containing the stain the customer had requested.

All day the snow appeared intermittently in the air of the shop and wafted down, or died away. At times the accumulated snow was a nuisance, as when during a heavier fall of snow than usual he couldn't locate for a minute a pencil he had placed on the bench earlier. Once snow had to be blown off a row of small jars of screws in order to find the size he needed to install some metal corner braces. Yet briefly misplacing items was an ordinary part of his workday. His mind often was focused on the next step in the process of creation. Practical details like where he had deposited a hammer or leaned the remnants of a sheet of plywood would escape his notice until suddenly these items were wanted for another stage in the completion of the project at hand. The unaccountable appearance of snow indoors was simply an irritation, resembling a mosquito loose in the shop in summer or a stink bug suddenly flying past his ear in early fall.

Also, the activities required to construct the cupboards, or indeed tackle any shop chore, mostly displaced the snow where he worked. When he swept or vacuumed the floor at the end of his workday, the snow temporarily disappeared where he cleaned. Only when he returned to the shop after lunch, or the first thing each morning, was the sight of the interior of his shop carpeted with fresh snow a reminder of the extra obstacle he now faced in earning his living.

But he quickly became accustomed to the presence within doors of such odd material, lovely but not chilling. He told no one about the snow. His days resumed their routine, broken only when he drove the sixty kilometres to pick up supplies in Nelson, or by afternoon excursions in the valley to provide a customer with an estimate or to deliver and install a finished project. More common were mornings devoted to his solitary work and afternoons skiing through the forest, sometimes past farmsteads and isolated homes, but often deep in the woods. Occasionally in the growing dark he encountered a fellow skier, and one February day as he neared an intersecting road, a young farmer walking the trail stopped the man to ask if he had seen some sheep that had escaped their pen. Most often he met only the ravens or crows, and more rarely an eagle flapping gravely upriver, or pairs of tundra swans gliding on the water or upending themselves to feed on the river bottom so only their rear ends bobbed above the surface of the frigid stream.

Then, amid snow indoors, the morning would be spent fashioning store counters for a new bicycle repair shop that was scheduled to open down the valley at Playmor Junction in the spring. Whenever commercial work temporarily became scarce, the man crafted from scrap wood cutting boards, bowls and toys such as wooden trains or letters that could be hooked together to spell out a child's name. These products he took to Nelson periodically to offer to a craft store or a particular children's boutique receptive to purchasing his work.

Some afternoons during or following a prolonged outside snowfall were devoted to pushing a snow scoop to open wheel paths up his driveway. Many of his neighbours hired someone who operated a skid-steer loader or a tractor rigged with a plow. But the man felt the hours spent removing snow to enable his pickup to climb the drive helped develop and maintain muscles he used for skiing.

When the midwinter thaws arrived, overnight dumps of snow turned to rain around noon. Then the white that blocked his driveway was wet and heavy, making the task of keeping the drive open exhausting and requiring two or three hours longer than usual to accomplish. Indoors, however, the snow retained its light consistency whatever the weather outside. And the man eventually realized that no matter how snowy the world beyond the windows became, within the house and shop the depth of snow never rose higher than eight or nine centimetres.

By mid-March, fresh snow only fell outdoors late in the evening, and the new accumulation was mainly gone by noon, thanks to a strengthening sun. Now the man's afternoons were busy with pruning his apple, plum, cherry and pear trees, often requiring an orchard ladder with its three supports to be propped into the third of a metre of snow that still remained on the ground. When pruning was completed, the man fetched hoses from storage in a garden shed, connected them to the house's outside taps, and over a couple of afternoons sprayed his fruit trees with dormant oil and lime sulfur.

Each day during this flurry of orchard chores, less snow covered meadows and lawns. One night at supper the man's elbow accidentally knocked his fork off the kitchen table. When he bent to retrieve the utensil, he noticed that spaces had begun to open in the white that covered the floor. A quick check revealed the same change was occurring in other rooms. And where powder lay atop chairs, side tables, lamps and bookcases, its thickness had appreciably diminished.

Within a week, the snow was gone entirely from the house. The man spent an afternoon vacuuming rugs, sweeping and mopping floors, and dusting bookcase tops and chair seats. When he was finished, the snow inside might never have been.

The man's business picked up as the valley inhabitants awoke as if from hibernation and began to plan renovations or new constructions. The phone rang frequently with requests for estimates. Many afternoons now he drove through the valley from house to house, or to this or that store or barn, to listen to people's ideas, then suggest what was practicable and calculate a likely cost. Even merchants in Nelson contacted him with possible jobs. Certain town days became extra-long as he measured and prepared estimates for potential customers, or visited a couple of Nelson's building supply stores to check on current prices for lumber, stain, paint. He was too occupied for weeks to store away his skis for the following winter. Poles and boots and skis remained propped against the wall just inside the basement door, a reminder each time he passed that this chore remained undone.

Outdoors, he lifted the mulch from his vegetable gardens and forked the soil over. He also stripped the mulch from flower beds around the house, exposing crocuses and the first shoots of tulips, hyacinths and daffodils. These had to be sprayed to keep the deer from gnawing them. He saw where the does that lived up in the woods west of his house had attacked a rhododendron bush beside the deck stairs. The animals obviously found the rhodo leaves inedible: individual leaves were scattered around the base of the plant. Yet the deer had tugged leaf after leaf from the branches as if expecting the next leaf to be a delicacy. Cursing the deer's mindless hunger, he sprayed the rhodo to protect it from further predation, and for good measure in the afternoon sprayed every fruit tree that was beginning to leaf out.

That evening the man was dawdling after dinner at his kitchen table reading the valley's weekly newspaper. He thought to glance toward the stove to make sure he had switched off the oven where he had baked a potato, one of the last of the previous summer's. Gazing down the room, he observed that the ceiling, in the glare of the overhead lights, was tinged a yellowish green rather than showing its usual stark white.

He wondered if some flaw in the latex used when the ceiling was previously repainted had caused the colour to vary over time. He was uncertain when the kitchen had last been done. Yet when he went into the bathroom, he saw that the ceiling there was now the exact shade as in the kitchen. The bathroom had been repainted only the year before when he'd replaced tub, tub surround and toilet. A quick check of the rest of the house revealed that all the rooms' ceilings—uniformly painted white—had adopted this new shade of yellowy green. He decided that this shift was related to the inexplicable indoor snowfall. Next morning, he found the same alteration in the colour of the shop's ceiling.

As the weeks passed, however, the intensity of the green in the ceiling's pigmentation began to overshadow the yellow. The man found the colour not unpleasant. But he resolved to add repainting the ceilings white to his list of future household chores. During this period, besides having to adjust to the increased pace of his business, he took delivery of his annual truckload of composted manure. The fertilizer was dumped onto newly snow-free but still pale grass, at a spot about halfway up the drive. For the next few afternoons, the man trundled wheelbarrow loads of manure to his various vegetable gardens and flower beds and turned the former over once again. After a morning spent at precision work in the shop, or carefully measuring and figuring a price at a potential client's home, the afternoon's toil preparing the gardens seemed pleasantly routine. These tasks around the grounds were ones the man had undertaken every year during his entire stay on the property. Returning to the garden shed for a trowel, part of his mind was absorbed in figuring out some intricate rabbeting joins in connection with a chest of drawers he was constructing for a customer at Perry Siding. For a moment at the shed door, the man was confused about whether he was obtaining a tool needed to put the gardens in, or to tuck them away again for winter.

Early May also was when his annual purchase of firewood was delivered. Ever since he had acquired the property, he had bought from the same supplier of cut and split cords. The seller now drove a much larger dump truck than all those years ago. Yet the long association between the two of them meant that the supplier was thoroughly familiar with navigating a heavy truck up the man's driveway and jockeying it into position at the top. Each truckload of winter wood was dumped just past the workshop, ensuring that dimension lumber needed for the business could still be unloaded. As a break from other chores, over the next month the enormous heap of firewood was, wheelbarrow load by wheelbarrow load, partially stacked in the basement before the majority of the fuel was arranged in neat piles behind the garden shed.

Other spring afternoons, the man planted young evergreens, birches and a few new fruit trees. When he had purchased his acreage, the land between the house and the road was open meadow, reflecting the original use of the lower third of the property as part of a farm. That first year the man had begun planting evergreens along the edges of this open space, as well as starting a line of birch to cloak the house and shop from passersby on the road. Now the firs, pines, cedars and hemlock he had planted year after year were shading out some of the place's original fruit trees, so the man was slowly developing a new orchard where his plums and apples could receive more sun.

Meantime, in the forest on the ridge above the house, the deciduous trees' array of leaves thickened week by week. Around the grounds, too, such foliage shifted in colour from a first tentative lime to, eventually, a flamboyant emerald. Indoors, the man's ceilings echoed this transformation. To sit reading now at the kitchen table under the overhead lights resembled, the man thought, spending a sunlit hour below the fully leafed-out canopy deep in the woods.

Then vegetables had to be planted, including both seeds and small pots of already-started kale, tomatoes and peppers the man bought from a neighbour, a woman down the road who operated a seasonal nursery. The nursery owner once pointed to an isolated white clear-cut near the top of the mountain across the river from where they stood. The snow on the area's clear-cuts was the last to disappear each spring. "Keep your tomato seedlings indoors until that area has melted," she advised. The man also purchased small flats of annuals from her.

During the weeks of afternoons required to commit to the earth rows of seeds—radish, lettuce, bean, corn and more—and to transplant all the marigolds, petunias, lobelias, fuchsias and other annuals into their beds, the man worked past his former supper hour, taking advantage of the lengthening period of daylight. As a consequence, he often lacked enough energy after dinner to do anything but drag himself to bed. Late one Tuesday evening, he lingered over the plate that had held a meal of baked chicken and rice while he attempted to summon the requisite will to take a shower before stumbling into the bedroom. Happening to look toward the sink, he was startled when his eyes became aware that the kitchen ceiling now showed large white patches amid the green he had become accustomed to. He realized then that the room's illumination was far more a product of the overhead lamps than of the jade glow that had suffused the space for what seemed months.

Surprising himself by the quickness with which his tired legs propelled him to his feet, he stalked through the house snapping on the lights in each room. Every ceiling displayed the same piebald appearance.

By the weekend, the ceilings of house and shop had returned to their normal condition, much as the floors of the house had when the visitation of the powdery snow had ended. The days began to be hot. The man's afternoons now involved uncoiling and connecting his system of irrigation hoses and activating timers to ensure that before he arose each morning the watering of beds would already be underway.

One early July afternoon, he wheeled his bicycle out of the basement and used a small compressor to inflate the tires after their long winter sleep. He lubricated the chain and wheel bearings. Then he ventured out along some of the trails where he had skied months before. The route was lined with tall dense foliage. The trees on either side broadcast the calls of robin, siskin, nuthatch and jay, plus those of songbirds the man could not identify. Crows and ravens continued to lumber or soar overhead, and to squabble with each other in the uppermost green boughs of fir, cottonwood, cedar and birch.

Each afternoon when the man returned indoors from weeding or other garden duties, or wheeled his bike into the basement weary after a long ride, he looked anxiously around the walls, floor and ceiling to see if the sunniest season would transform his home as well. Day after day he was relieved to see the rooms he lived and worked in untouched by any mysterious changes. As with the interior snow, he had not spoken to anyone about the metamorphoses of his ceilings he had witnessed. He was by nature solitary, although he occasionally invited the couple who were his closest neighbours for supper, and was himself invited a few times a year to dinner parties at the home of the owners of a valley fencing company, a couple with whom he had become friends over the years. Since the snow had fallen inside his walls he had not entertained a single visitor.

After three weeks of good weather had passed without anything odd occurring indoors, a woman he knew phoned him long distance. She was a former resident of the area currently living two thousand kilometres to the east in Winnipeg. His friend was one of the few female woodworkers he had met; their paths had crossed when they both had taken an upgrading course in lathe work in Nelson, sponsored by the provincial apprenticeship board and offered through the trades training division of the local community college. They had been assigned as partners, sharing a machine for the practicum portion of the course. The relationship they developed was easy, even flirtatious. Outside of class they spent hours in coffee shops and restaurants chatting about far more than course material. He couldn't tell how much she saw him as a brother and how much as a potential partner, but he loved spending time around her quick wit and small but shapely body.

Her home was in Manitoba, however. She had chosen to take the course in Nelson because she had an uncle and aunt she was close to who lived up the lake from the town, and she could visit with them for the three weeks the course lasted. The man and she had stayed in touch ever since she had returned home: they emailed frequently, and even talked on the phone two or three times a year, updating each other on their lives. One Christmas she emailed him a photo of herself in a revealing bathing suit. He wasn't sure how to process this gift. But he had copied it to the photo file on his computer, and sometimes he would bring the picture up on his screen and look at it.

She returned to Nelson to visit her relatives every few years, and on the phone now she informed the man that she would be out again at the end of July and would love to see him while she was in the Kootenays. He suggested she stay at his place for a night or two on this trip—he had a spare room, and could show her his shop, which he had expanded since the last time she had been his guest for supper two years before. If she was driving west, he said, she should bring her bike. In any case they could go hiking.

The man's older sister, who also lived east of the Rockies but in Calgary, repeatedly urged him on the phone or via email to become more socially active. *I hear Nelson is a happening place,* she wrote. *Friends of mine who visited there raved about the restaurants, the nightlife, the ski resort. You should be out meeting people, meeting women. Do you want to turn into a complete hermit?* He steadily assured her he had sufficient interaction with other people through his woodworking business, and that at the end of a week, especially if he'd had to deal with a difficult customer, he often felt peopled-out. "One carpenter I know," he told his sister on the phone, "always says, 'People ask me to give them an estimate. What they don't know is that they're participating in an audition.' If the carpenter senses they're going to be trouble, he either never gets back to them, or names an impossibly high price. I wish I could do that. But I worry about money so I'm always nice to people. I bid on everything I can."

Now, though, he had a visitor to look forward to. *Whatever happens between us when she's here, it will be fun,* he told himself. *Maybe I am alone too much.*

In the summer heat, he wore shorts and a T-shirt every day, and often went barefoot indoors or to work in the garden. Every window that would open in his house was screened, as was a sliding door onto his deck, and he kept everything possible fully ajar while the sun blazed down. Electric fans and a couple of screened windows meant the shop was tolerable. Because he lived in the mountains, his home cooled down nights, so he slept well even under the duvet. Yet the master bedroom faced east, and despite the window being wide open all night, once the sun crested the eastern valley wall around six thirty he would be sweaty if he lingered too long thereafter beneath the covers.

One morning he sat groggily at the edge of his bed having just awoken, with the first sunbeams streaming in from above the mountain rim. The sky was a faultless blue. As the fogginess of sleep drained from his mind, he was aware of a peaty odour in the room, a heavy scent as of fecund soil. His house was on a septic system, and once in a while outside he caught a whiff of unpleasant stink from the rooftop opening of the stack. The smell that pervaded the room that morning was, by contrast, earthy rather than fecal: thickly redolent with flourishing life, akin to the odour he inhaled while staking up stems and leaves of tomato vines or when he sniffed the nighttime perfume of nicotiana.

At first he thought the odour might originate with something outdoors. But the scent diminished as he pushed a window screen aside and leaned out into the freshness of the morning. His heart sank, and he turned to scan the bedroom rug, ceiling and walls to see if some manifestation of the season was visible that could account for the smell. Nothing was out of place. To his dismay, however, he found the scent now pervaded each room of the house. A quick visit to the shop revealed that the smell there overpowered the rich odour of sawdust that constituted his workplace's usual olfactory backdrop.

The man acknowledged he was bothered that his house would be tainted during the much-anticipated visit of his friend. *Plus I get to spend several weeks smelling muck whenever I'm indoors,* he raged to himself. He prepared and ate breakfast that morning in a black mood. He took his coffee out onto his deck, where he stood in the sun by the rail and watched the wind rustle through the tremulous leaves of the aspen. *Can these occurrences in the house—the snow, the green light and now the scent—be a delusion? Am I punishing myself for some reason by conjuring these up? Am I losing my mind?*

He had installed bathroom cabinets one Saturday the previous fall at the home of a social worker employed by the regional health authority's mental health division. She had told him, while they chatted as he worked, that the defining characteristic for mental illness was dysfunctionality. *No question I'm functional,* the man told himself as he heard from the porch a flicker hammering at the wooden power pole down by the road. A moment later the bird flapped over the lawn toward the forest west of the house. *I can work, feed and clothe myself. I interact with people no worse than I always have. So unless I've developed a tumour or something, there has to be another cause for what is going on.*

The man admitted part of his feeling of anger had to do with not wanting the unexplainable odour to mar his friend's enthusiasm for spending time with him. *Of course, if she can't smell it, I'll* know *I'm crazy.* Maybe this visit they might finally become intimate, he thought. Each time they parted, they hugged and kissed each other. She was very attractive sexually. *But whatever happens between us,* he told himself again, *having her around will be fun. That's the main thing.*

That afternoon he loaded his canoe into his pickup and drove north a quarter hour to Slocan. From the village's beach, he paddled up the lake through the bright summer weather. To his left the high peaks of the Valhalla Range rose, their granite spires lifting far past the treeline. His route lay close to shore along the west side of the lake. As the craft travelled smoothly forward, his mind was lulled by the lap of low waves against the huge stones lining the shore. The boulders often had good-sized cedars growing implausibly from cracks in the rock's surface. His thoughts, while his arms repeatedly stretched forward in the sun to drag the blade of the paddle back through the water, settled on the impending visit. His sense of agitation about the odour calmed. *Maybe my sister is right,* he pondered. *Perhaps I should be living with a woman.* Among other things, he acknowledged ruefully, he'd know if what transpired in his rooms and the shop was a hallucination.

Long ago, in Victoria, he had been married for a dozen years. When he considered that chapter in his life, he concluded the first four years had been good, and the rest increasingly unsatisfactory.

He didn't like to recall some of his actions, infidelities really, nor how he had handled attempts by his wife or himself to discuss their marriage. Her wish for children. His fear that his woodworking could not support a growing family, that he'd be forced to work for someone else at a job only tangentially related to his love of making things from wood. The beauty of grain in every species. The specific attributes of fir, cedar, oak, pine. Relocating to the West Kootenay, establishing a life alone in these remote mountains, had been a balm to his spirit after the turmoil of his years in the city.

When the man's friend stepped out of her rented car at the top of his driveway, she looked lovelier than ever to him. She was dressed in shorts and a short-sleeved blouse with a plunging neckline, where a pendant hung in the cleavage between her breasts. After they hugged, she exclaimed several times about how beautiful she always found his place. She had forgotten, she said, the way the forest above, and the mountain vista on all sides, set off the house. Behind her, he struggled with her luggage along the side of the building to the deck and then in through the door to the main floor. She stopped just inside. "What is that fabulous smell?" she asked.

"Yeah, sorry about that," he said. "I've been trying to figure out what's causing it."

"Mmmm. I love it," she said. "Very earthy. Very *sexy*." Her laugh tinkled out, and his heart flooded with joy and nervousness.

They spent a couple of hours in the shop, while he showed her his current projects and, heads almost touching, bent to leaf through his ring binder of photos of jobs completed that year, while they talked about the technical aspects of each contract. Later they sipped wine while he cooked a chicken vindaloo, and prepared a salad of fresh produce from his gardens. They ate by candlelight as the evening darkened, and he learned to his surprise that she had been involved with a man for much of the past year, before breaking up in March. After her initial disclosure, she didn't seem to want to dwell on the topic, and the conversation shifted to the doings of her uncle and aunt, plus those of her brother who was working as an engineer in the Alberta oil patch.

With the last of the wine bottle in their glasses, they stood side by side leaning on the deck rail to listen to the valley night: dogs barking away over the hills, and the rhythmic pulses of the frogs in the marshes along the river's edge calling for a mate or proclaiming territory. Overcome by the moment, he leaned down and kissed where her neck met her shoulder. She rested her glass on the railing, and swung around to look up at him, her eyes wide. Their lips met in a long kiss, and then another.

A muted negotiation ensued, as his palms, free now also of a wine glass, traced the sides of her body. She took his hand, snagged her glass with her other hand, and led him indoors, depositing the glass on the kitchen table. She sniffed deeply. "I can't get enough of that smell. It's like that cologne some guys wear. We girls call it 'Sure-fuck.'" She laughed at his startled expression in response to her words. Still holding his hand, she turned off the kitchen light. He felt himself tugged along into his bedroom.

Two mornings later, he watched from outside the basement door as her car descended his driveway, the horn sounding a farewell beep as her vehicle reached the road. A surge of loneliness swept into him. The feeling of loss wasn't just about the sex, he told himself as he trudged around the corner of the house toward the wood shop, although making love with her had been wonderful. She was enthusiastic and energetic, and seemed to enjoy tenderly shocking him with some of the things she uttered in the midst of their coupling. Her presence had filled his days during the visit: having someone else to try to please had been a rejuvenating break from his ordinary concentration on himself and his routines. Now that the interlude was ended, he felt bereft, facing the thin and dreary prospect of paying attention once more only to his own concerns.

Yet at some level the man knew that his too-familiar structure would carry him past this sense of deficiency, of a shallowness to his existence. A phone call an hour later from a client pleased with a dining room table and chair set he had delivered the previous week helped ground the man. He became immersed in the challenges of attaching a Formica countertop, and when later that afternoon he was pedalling vigorously down a riverside trail he experienced satisfaction again with the life he had built for himself. The visit, he perceived, had been as welcome, enriching and fleeting as any season. Except, of course, for the sex, which he admitted was a dimension to existence no season could match. *On the other hand,* he thought as he coasted down a long stretch between the trees, *good sex is temporary. The orderly appearance and turn of the seasons is permanent.*

In mid-August, the low dogbane began to turn brown in the meadows and ditches alongside the road. As did some of the bracken, then more and more of it. Leaves of the hazel, the first deciduous tree to acknowledge summer's end, started to yellow and drop. Daylight diminished in intensity, as though less of it was reaching the dry and dusty earth. Though the days continued as hot as ever, the nights grew distinctly cooler than the sun-filled hours.

The brief stay of the visitor from Winnipeg had left the man in a pleasant mood, overall. Happy memories of her surfaced, and he was cheered by these. Emails were exchanged frequently, and he phoned her every couple of weeks. Occasionally she phoned. Nothing was promised about a more enduring connection; he knew they both had fulfilling lives thousands of kilometres apart. Yet he found himself whistling tunes or even singing half-remembered lyrics as he applied wood stain in his shop or manoeuvred his orchard ladder to pluck the first ripened apples. In house and shop, the scent of fertile soil gradually lessened.

One morning during the second week of September, the man, en route to dumping his kitchen scraps on the compost pile, noticed that the leaves of his cucumbers, squash and peppers had withered overnight. A touch of frost in the early hours of the day had been enough to finish these vegetables. Closer inspection of flower beds that afternoon showed that some frost-sensitive annuals had also shrivelled in the darkness.

Weeks might elapse before another frost struck, but the man knew its first appearance prefigured how the new season would establish itself in the valley. Snow would one day coat the summit ranges, and not long afterwards descend partway down the valley walls. For weeks, winter would loom above the autumnal valley floor: the snow and ice soon to assume dominion over daily life was visible to everyone if they looked up. One midnight the snow would silently lower itself to the valley bottom, but would retreat up the mountainside by mid-morning. Like the first frost, this taste of winter's authority might happen again a day or two later, or might not be repeated for another month. Spring and autumn were forthright about their arrival: each twenty-four hours more changes were evident. Winter, however, toyed with the world like a cat playing with a mouse or injured bird the feline would eventually kill.

Harvesting now began in earnest. Potatoes and carrots were dug, tomatoes were picked and each day ripened apples and pears were gathered in a race against the inevitable looting of the fruit trees by a wandering bear fattening herself or himself for hibernation. The man raked into piles the fallen hazel leaves, and also the first birch leaves that had yellowed and dropped. These were bagged to be used for mulch. A large Japanese maple off the deck displayed a few of the crimson leaves that by late October would transform the tree into a bonfire of colour. Where the contents of a flower or vegetable bed were nearly all wilted or picked, the man stripped it of vegetation and covered the empty soil with a layer of fallen leaves.

Taking down the gardens was as time-consuming as planting them in spring, except the job was a more melancholy one. In May, the chores were full of hope and expectation. Now, as the woods and fields faded into sere yellows and browns, and what greens remained looked pallid, exhausted, the tasks of autumn were, despite the bounty of the harvest, more about loss and memory than promise. Although still cheered by the connection with the woman from Winnipeg, the man at times found his mood dimming. When he feared he was becoming too gloomy, he would abandon the afternoon's planned garden work, and steer his bike through the autumn woods on the trail beside the river. The water was low and the current sluggish, but the riverbanks and the wooded mountainsides of the valley were reflected perfectly in the stream as the man pedalled past. On the high slopes around him, stands of larch blazed golden amid the expanses of fir, spruce and pine.

Guiding his bike tiredly into the basement after one long ride, the man saw that a number of desiccated tree leaves littered the cement floor: he recognized aspen, maple and oak, as well as birch and hazel. He wondered if he had tracked in the assortment of dead leaves when he had fetched his bike earlier that afternoon, then returned inside to fill his water bottle and locate his helmet. After parking his bike in its usual spot, he grabbed the basement broom and swept up the leaves, carrying them out to dump on the lawn. But when he reopened the door to step inside, leaves were again scattered across the floor.

He climbed leaf-strewn stairs to the upper hallway. As he guessed he might find, sprays of dry brown leaves lay on the hardwood. A rapid inventory of the rooms revealed that the leaves had appeared only on tile and wooden flooring. The rugs were unaffected.

The man over the next few days learned the characteristics of this phenomenon. As with the winter snow, his passage across the leaves left them ultimately undisturbed, though unlike the snow the leaves crackled underfoot when he walked on them. The detritus might crumble under his socks, slippers or bare feet, but the resultant flakes and dust did not get tracked onto rugs. The leaves slowly accumulated as the weeks passed. Similarly to the snow, however, the layer never mounted beyond eight or nine centimetres in thickness.

He grew used to the gentle crunching underfoot as he passed through the house. His peaceful toleration of the leaves he attributed to his earlier experiences with snow and green light and fecund odour: the leaves, too, would vanish. He had only to be patient. Yet he marvelled at how, in the space of less than a year, he could accept the unfathomable. When he finished work for the day at the shop, he customarily swept and vacuumed up the shavings, chips and sawdust he had produced. The discarded foliage of course was removed in this process. By next morning, though, leaves entirely concealed the shop floor. He met this fact with an equanimity that at times he thought should trouble him more than it did.

One Thursday when he rose and looked out his bedroom window, the top of the east valley wall was white with snow.

Green Hell

WOULD YOU TWO like to join me? This place gets jammed. It's the only decent restaurant for seventy klicks in either direction. Well, the Crossroads Café just up the highway isn't too bad. There's also a couple of coffee-plus-sandwiches joints farther down the valley, but I wouldn't recommend them. I'm Billy. If you can put up with me, you're welcome.

Good to meet you both. You're from . . . ? Hey, I've been to Regina. Stayed a couple of weeks once. No, born and raised in Ontario. Windsor. I was making my way west. Actually, I was *drinking* my way west. I was a drunk. Five years clean and sober now.

Thanks, but you're never too young to be a drunk. I'm forty. If you look close, you'll see the wrinkles that prove it. What do you do in Regina?

You seem too young yourselves, to be retired. I suppose if you were still on the farm, though, you couldn't take time off in July. What kind of crops did you—

Thanks, Janine. I *will* have more coffee. And these good folks probably will have menus, right? Yeah, they're friends of mine. We've known each other since, oh, a minute and a half.

Isn't she something? She's Al Craddock's daughter, the younger one. A very nice person. Not like her sister. If I can make a suggestion, have the Kootenay Special: best breakfast on the menu. If you like French toast, that is. I've never eaten ones so thick. Airy, yet rich. The cook, Marcel, he's French Canadian. From St. Boniface, out your way. Okay, it's in Manitoba, but I mean the Prairies. I josh him, tell him his ethnic origin is why his French toast is so good. Seriously, he's terrific in the kitchen. Makes the Dog what it is.

Sorry. That's what we call this fine establishment. For years it was just the River Restaurant. Then Dave Verigin and his wife bought it. Fixed it up. They renamed it the Lone Coyote.

Definitely: you can hear packs of them up and down the valley most nights. But you'll see single ones loping along the highway. The locals didn't much approve of the name change, so they started to refer to the place as the Solitary Dog. Or the Lonely Hound. To me, the name is—

No, fine for now, Janine. These folks are ready to order, I think. They probably want, ahem, the Dog's breakfast.

Alright, alright, bad joke. I'll shut up. But tell Marcel he better work his magic. Our visitors are from his old stomping ground, the Prairies, and—

He's not? Who's in the kitchen?

Never heard of him. When did he get hired? Folks, forget what I said. This new guy couldn't possibly have the same knack. Is he even using Marcel's recipe?

Janine, if he used to cook in the thriving metropolis of Castlegar... I better explain to our friends: Castlegar is seventy-five klicks south, with, oh, about six thousand inhabitants . . . he's certain to be a gourmet chef. Entitled to inscribe all the culinary initials of distinction after his name: KFC, DQ, A&W. No, no, don't pour any of that on my head. I just don't want these good people to blame me, after I've given the Dog's cuisine such a build-up that—

Yes, ma'am.

She's wonderful, isn't she? Even her boyfriend is a great kid. Drives a logging truck for his dad, John Poznikoff. To me, Janine is better-looking than her sister, though the official valley verdict is that Natasha, who's three years older, is the gorgeous one. Good-looking on the outside, maybe. Janine is beautiful clear through.

Yeah, lots of spirit, like you say. Their mom is pretty fiery herself. She's a Grainger. You crossed Grainger Creek ten klicks to the north: old pioneer family. Wild, the lot of 'em. But never destructive. Except for Natasha, who—

I wouldn't say I know *everybody* in the neighbourhood. But quite a few. You must be acquainted with most of the folks where you used to farm in . . . Grenfell, wasn't it?

We're not exactly a huge population, either: about four hundred. I'm counting permanent residents, not—

You saw the houses along the highway? Across the river, there's a back road that runs parallel, with more homes along there. People also live down side roads both sides of the river. One starts just north of here, by Perepolkin's store: Paradise Valley Road. It goes pretty far up the ridge you can see out those windows.

Good name for the road? People drive through in summer, and the valley seems so peaceful. Clear blue sky on a day like today, green woods, the river sparkling in the sunshine, mountains covered with evergreens, snow not yet gone from the peaks. Idyllic. People say, "Green heaven." I say, "Green—"

In the Dog right now? Let me look: I guess I know maybe a quarter. Summertime, there's always transients.

Six years. I've been here six years this fall. A year disgracing myself as a drunk, and five since clean and sober. I ran my car into a tree the first month I was here. A few fights: in the bar at Slocan up the highway, and one time outside the Civic pub in Nelson. I'm most famous in these parts for burning down Al Craddock's barn that first year. I—

No harm done, really. He had horses he'd bought for Janine and Natasha when they were kids. And a bunch of sheep. Also a stupid donkey that was supposed to scare off the coyotes when the sheep were in the field. I was hired to muck out the barn in April, so all the critters were in the pasture. I had to shovel and wheelbarrow the goop out. Manure is such lovely stuff, as you know. I took along a mickey to console and inspire me. Mid-afternoon, I sit down in the shade of the barn for a smoke break . . . and of course a rye break. It was a warm day, and I wasn't much used to hand labour. I decide I'll rest my eyes for a minute.

Yeah, woke up and my cig had caught the straw. I tried this and tried that to put the fire out. Wasn't thinking too clear. Nobody was home, either: Janine at high school, Natasha was living someplace else. Al works at a hardware store in Nelson, and his wife had gone shopping to the Co-op in Slocan Park. Eventually I dash over to a neighbour's and phone the fire department. Fire crews in the valley are volunteer. By the time—

Really? You were a fire guy at Grenfell?

Good for you. I've thought about joining, but haven't. At least, not yet. Anyhow by the time the fire crew show at Craddock's, the barn is a goner. It was done. Only thing they could do was keep the blaze from spreading to the house. But I'd left my jacket inside the barn on a hook. My wallet was in my jacket, with all the money I had in the world, plus my ID. I'm standing outside, thirty-five years old, with everything I own on my back. Except my beater Toyota, which I still owed for. I had to phone Al at work and say, "Uh, Al, remember the barn you wanted me to clean?"

I couldn't agree more. Never hire a drunk because you feel sorry for him. You'll end up feeling sorrier. Al was calmer than I would have been, though his wife, Sharon, she cussed me out good. But Al's house insurance paid for a new barn. I figure he came out ahead. It was incredibly dumb of me, just the same. One of the low points of my life. I thought I was down when I was rolling around in a few gutters in Sudbury, Winnipeg and Calgary. Or when I did a little time in the joint at Bowden in Alberta. But burning down Al's barn was the bottom for me. By the time he started to rebuild in the fall, I had joined AA. I went to visit him one Saturday morning. Offered to work for nothing, to pay him back for all the trouble I caused. He says to me—

Jeez, that was fast, Janine. I hope the new guy in the kitchen hasn't sacrificed quality for speed. Now these folks will be needing . . . Did you see that? How she whipped out that maple syrup jug from her apron? She's a pro, I tell you. Not much slips past her when she's . . . Sure, I'll have a refill. Maybe these two also want a top-up, to go with their . . . She's way ahead of me, way ahead. Ouch. Why did you do that? You're not supposed to hit the paying customers. What if I complain to the boss? I'll bet Dave takes a dim view of such . . . What?

Quite the character, isn't she? I like the whole family. Other than Natasha, and I don't know where that comes from. Both her parents are salt of the earth. They've been great to me, considering their barn and everything. They probably could have pressed charges and—

You're right. People are basically good everywhere you go. Of course, we've got our share of screwloosers around this place, same as anywhere. When the Dog reopened, after Dave and his wife had upscaled it, some doofus phoned in a bomb threat. The Mounties raced out from Nelson, and we had fire and ambulance crews from as far as Nakusp. Dave gave a great quote to the paper: "I didn't think our cooking was *that* bad." They never did find who to blame.

Cops? Nearest cop shops are in Nelson, seventy klicks away, and New Denver, same distance the other direction. You drove through New Denver to get here. No cops in sight means some people imagine the law doesn't apply to them. But when anybody believes they only have to think about themselves, that causes trouble for the rest of us. I've been there, done that, got the T-shirt. B and Es mostly. In the old days in Calgary. Never here. Why mince words: I'm ashamed of what I did.

That's exactly right. Some people think if they're in the country, they can behave however they please. You'll hear them: "That's why I bought here. So nobody can tell me what to do." We have this new guy on our water line. From Calgary. He's choked at needing a building permit from the Regional District for an addition to his house. I point out to him he hasn't completely left civilization behind. He drives on the right side of the highway. He isn't exempt from the Criminal Code: he can't murder his wife or shoot me, even if he feels like it. His place is connected to the power grid and the phone network and he—

Good question. Jobs *are* scarce. Biggest employer in the whole valley was the sawmill up at Slocan. It's closed at the moment. But that was a couple of hundred paycheques, plus all the work that fed the mill: logging contractors, truckers. Another couple of hundred. Most people have to commute to jobs in Nelson or Castlegar. Young people mainly leave for the Coast or Calgary. Or they head north to the oil patch: Fort St. John, or Fort McMurray. And we've got our share of folks on welfare. Lots of young single moms, but not just them. If I look around the Dog on your typical weekday like this—

Me? I'm gainfully unemployed. You might say my reputation has suffered since Al's barn went up in smoke. A few other things, too, haven't done me any good when it comes to picking up work.

I had six weeks this spring building a park in Slocan. The village had scuffled up some sort of federal or provincial grant to employ us layabouts. I apply for anything I'd be suited for, though. I've got an interview Friday for a job caretaking the elderly at the Castlegar Lodge. Having been a drunk, I know I can handle old folks. Some of them may be several sandwiches short of a picnic, but so were loads of the people I hung with when I was drinking. I've seen plenty of puke, blood and worse. And I'm a quick study when it comes to the ins and outs of a job. I made good grades in school, before I fell among evil companions. I'm talking about my buddies: rye, rum, plonk and certain contraband herbs and chemicals. All behind me now. I'm clean and sober. Five years.

Today? When I'm between jobs, my girlfriend Joan has a list of chores for me to do while she's at work. She's the receptionist for a doc in Nelson. Today I promised to mow the lawns. Joan has a fair amount of lawn: takes me about four hours. This summer, if the weather holds, I'm supposed to re-stain the siding. Fine with me. She pays the mortgage, so the least I can do is contribute my share by putting my shoulder to the wheel. I have my own little projects, too. I'm seeing how many consecutive afternoons since the first of May I can swim in the river. Coffee at the Dog, mid-morning and mid-afternoon, that's another of my—

Ah, the fair Janine. Sure, everything's hunky-dory. At least I think so. Isn't that right, folks? I mean, aside from me talking their ear off. More coffee from the lovely lady? What's this? A bill? You're charging me? When I'm entertaining your customers? You should be *paying* me. Just put it on my tab, and I'll—

Jeez, just kidding, just kidding. I'll pay on my way out. And your service has been so fantastic, you can look forward to a significant tip from me. And I do mean "look forward": you'll get it someday. Someday soon. Soon as I win the lottery. No, don't do that!

Isn't she too much? She wouldn't really scald me with that thing. Janine is smart as can be. Shouldn't be waitressing. But, like I said, not many jobs hereabouts, especially for young people. And when you got no jobs, no cops and a remote location, you get growers.

I mean pot. Marijuana. Acreages in this area are at best hobby farms. But dope is huge. I've heard people claim one out of three houses in the valley grows. Though I'm not sure how anybody would prove such a number. Still, growing is a real temptation. Every once in a while they bust a person whose age would surprise you. Old fogies, like me. Even the occasional Doukhobor grows smoke, and they're usually straight arrows. More likely to be selling garlic than funny lettuce. They—

Doukhobors? That's why there's so many Russian names in the Kootenays, why you'll hear people speaking Russian. A pacifist sect. Burned their guns back in Russia before the turn of the last century. The Czar was plenty annoyed, but between Tolstoy and Queen Victoria they emigrated to Canada. They homesteaded in Saskatchewan first. I'm surprised you never heard of them. Their motto is "Toil and a peaceful life." Seems perfect for this valley, eh? Except around here they took to fussing with each other. Some felt others were backsliding. In order to show material things aren't of value, a few of them started taking off all their clothes and burning down their houses. You know: *We come into this world naked, with nothing. That's how we leave.* Trouble was, a bunch of them got the idea that they should take off their clothes and burn down *other* people's houses. You bet that plan wasn't well received. By now we're in the 1920s. A train was dynamited, killing the group's big cheese. These battles went on right into the fifties. A power cable across Kootenay Lake running juice to the mines at Kimberley was blown up. The Mounties—

Yes, *pacifists.*

Okay, but from their point of view they had nothing but trouble from the law for their beliefs, whether in Russia or this country. I figure the constant hassles by the powers that be are what caused one bunch of them to go overboard. Why is it a crime not to want to kill somebody? In Saskatchewan, a law said that, after so many years, to gain title to your homestead you had to swear allegiance to the king. The Doukhobors said they only swore allegiance to God. Yet some of them didn't want to lose all their hard work creating a farm from nothing. That law led to a split in the community, which is why a group ended up in the Koots. Not that the BC authorities knew how to handle the situation, once the different factions here began to battle each other. In the 1950s the Mounties raided Doukhobor farms in the valley and seized any kids who weren't being sent to school. Some parents thought the schools taught patriotism and glorified war, which you have to admit in part is true. The children were interned in New Denver, same place where the Japanese were interned a few years before during the war. Meanwhile, the province built a special Doukhobor prison down on the Coast for troublesome adults. Families of the prisoners marched from here all the way to—

Not today, no. Everything's quiet. Most of them weren't like the extremists, just ordinary folks leading ordinary lives. Except they don't trust governments at any level. Can't blame them for that. But they're pretty conservative, otherwise. That's why it's a hoot that some of them have been popped for growing. Whether you're religious or not, a grow show has the lure of easy money. A friend of mine has a rug-cleaning business: one of those truck-mounted systems? He got into the hole financially. Big mortgage, then he had to replace his home septic and the contractor hit bedrock. My friend figured the only solution was a greenhouse of bud. Four days before he planned to harvest, some kids ripped him off. You can't phone the cops to complain. Instead—

There *isn't* always jobs. Not here. Unemployment is—

Sure, okay, people could move where the jobs are. But why should you have to leave where you enjoy living? I'll tell you: the worst effect of growing dope isn't that it's still illegal despite how harmless it is compared to, say, booze. The worst isn't the cops patrolling overhead every fall up and down the valley, either, with their choppers and infrared scanners and spectroscopes. The worst of dope growing is that growers lie. If you're raising weed for a living and you have kids, you either have to keep secret from your kids how the family puts food on the table, or lie to them, or teach them to lie about what you do. You're also teaching kids a person doesn't have to work to make money.

You bet such behaviour affects kids. As well as their parents, and not for the better. Remember, I'm a non-drinking drunk: I know what it's like to connive and pretend and lie and hide your true self. Imagine a community meeting, trying to deal with some issue involving land use or water use, and a chunk of those present can't tell the truth about what they use the land or the water for. Imagine two neighbours on a water line trying to solve a water shortage problem, if one of them has a secret patch up in the woods, or a greenhouse, or a basement full of—

I'm not in favour of ratting anybody out. Basically, we should be able to settle problems among ourselves. The question is how? A lot of the population here are love-peace-good-vibes-organic-granola types. But they can be narrow-minded, too: talk to a logger whose job is being blockaded. How do we work out our differences without bringing in Johnny Law? At Passmore, fifteen minutes' drive south, two guys started running a gravel pit and crusher smack in the middle of a bunch of homes on the back road. More of that attitude: "It's my property, and I can do as I please." The neighbours are being driven nuts because of the dust and racket. Heavy trucks are arriving and leaving, front-end loaders revving and beeping, plus the crusher is churning away. Early morning, late at night, any old time. No bylaws. The neighbours try to reason with the guys. The pit operators say they have the right to run their business and, by God, they're going to. So the neighbours hire a lawyer.

Yeah. Not good. The pit owners find a lawyer, too. Office in Nelson, though he lives down the valley in Slocan Park: guy called Duncan Locke. You'll see him in the Dog once in a while for lunch. He has a reputation for taking the simplest disagreements and inflating them. Naturally, his meter is ticking while he pumps up a simple matter into a complicated one. To make a long sad tale short, Locke manages to inflame the gravel pit situation even more. In court, he calls witness after witness to stretch the trial out, at who knows what expense for both sides. The neighbours' lawyer tells them at one point, "For the money this case is costing you, one of you could have put yourself through law school and acted as your own lawyer." Took them two years to get to court, trial goes for six days spread over six months, and a month after the trial, the judge releases his decision. He says *he* wouldn't want to live with this pit next door. But he rules that the neighbours have failed to prove they've suffered enough for the court to intervene.

"Disappointed" is putting it mildly. I was talking to one of them, and he tells me, "Billy, *never* go to law. It's not worth it, financially or emotionally. Your choice is: eat shit, or shotguns."

I apologize for the language. But I understand the sentiment. The trick is to find that balance between the law on one hand, and solving our own messes on the—

I'm not advocating taking the law into your own hands. That isn't balance, either. It's—

I see you're not convinced. You haven't run into anything like this back in Grenfell?

Pig farms. They can be bad. So what happened?

There you go: an attitude of "me first" sucks, but calling in the law doesn't solve anything either. Remember I mentioned Janine's sister, Natasha? A guy around here got involved with Nate. He'd known her a while, but in March a couple of years ago they hooked up, started getting it on. He's renting a house up Pedro Creek Road, more like a cabin, and after a bit she's always over there. Between you and me, the connection was mostly physical, if you know what I mean. I'd been laid off from the sign shop in Nelson at that point. Time on my hands, and Nate on my hands, too.

No, it *was* me. I don't know why I first talked about some "guy." I think I—

Sorry to be confusing. Anyhow, the relationship with Nate was stormy: lots of big blow-ups, lots of making up, you probably know the tune. You don't? Take it from me, it wasn't pretty. Nate didn't even have a job. She'd been hanging out at the Civic in Nelson: they call that pub the Zoo, for good reasons. Maybe she was dealing. She had been going out with a biker before who drank at the Zoo, but she dumped him. Why she quit him doesn't do Nate any credit, but that's another story. Anyway, after a month I come to my senses, and decide the relationship with Natasha is plain crazy, and we should split up. She didn't want to. We continue a few more weeks, spatting and arguing and carrying on. She was boozing up a storm and, I'll admit it, when I couldn't stand what was happening, now and then I'd grab a bottle of rye and just start drinking.

Hey, I didn't mean to backslide. That's just how bad it was. Except sometimes when two people are fighting, making love is the very best. Have you ever noticed that?

Okay, maybe not. One night, though, I finally decide: enough. Natasha had been drinking for hours, and I'd had one or maybe two. I tell her we're going to break up that very evening, immediately. I'm firm about this. We're done.

Hoo-boy is right. She throws a kitchen chair at me. I grab her, try to settle her down. I manage to sort of push her outside the house, toss her coat after her and lock the door. I thought that was that. But she steams around the back, climbs onto the deck, opens the door there and a moment later she's inside again. I was upset. I explain again that we're finished, that's it, we're done. She smacks me. I try to convince her to stop punching, that she needs to leave, and while we're tussling she lands one right here on my nose. It starts to bleed, and I freak. I guess I twisted her arm behind her back, so she'll quit slugging me. She's kicking and hollering. I succeed in dragging her outside. This time, once she's locked out, I dash over and lock the other door. She spends the next half hour shrieking and hammering on the doors and windows, calling me every name in the book. I tell her she should eff off, and that if she doesn't, I'm going to call the police.

Bad idea, actually. Trouble is, Nate's got street smarts. I don't understand how she got them growing up here, where there aren't streets. But she has them. She eventually leaves. Bright and early next morning, the Mounties phone and ask me to drive into Nelson for a chat. They tell me Natasha has been in touch. I had a bit of a hangover, but decide I'll correct this little misunderstanding. I drive into town to meet with the bulls, and proceed at their invitation to blab who did what to whom.

I see you shaking your head. You can imagine what comes next. They type up my statement and I sign it. With a flourish. Then, on the basis of what they're suddenly calling my confession, they charge me with assault. "What do you mean?" I tell them. "If you're going to charge me, charge *her*. She hit *me*." "Doesn't work that way," the Mountie breaks the news. So I had to borrow money from some friends, significant bucks, for a lawyer. And wait in limbo for months. I didn't know what would happen in court, or how much this was going to cost. Of course gossip has me as the villain: people in the valley are mighty quick to assume the worst about anybody. Luckily Al, Sharon and Janine believed in me. They've had their own troubles with Nate. Finally last fall, October, I wound up before a judge. Natasha is all outraged innocence. A few people testify to my good character. Amazing, really, but they were mostly people I'd borrowed money from. I thought of asking Al to say something positive about me, since the barn thing came up in court, but that was impossible because he's Nate's dad. My lawyer was useless, and given my record, bang! my sentence was a hundred hours' community service, I had mandatory anger management counselling and mandatory addiction group therapy. Now I've got a record for assault.

Hey, I didn't handle things well, I accept that. But the judge's ruling wasn't justice, either. In the eyes of the court, I'm completely guilty, and Natasha walks out smirking. That's why the law doesn't always—

I understand. I've been on the road myself: I know you have to get going. I shouldn't have been washing our valley dirty linen in front of you, especially on such a gorgeous day. Wait until you catch the view of Frog Peak, which you'll see ahead of you in just a few minutes down the valley.

This *is* a beautiful part of the world. Did you stop at that lookout at the top of where the highway climbs up from Silverton? Impressive, eh? But you can tell from what I've been blabbing that appearances around here can be deceiving. It may look like wonderland, but—

Yeah, I better motor, too. I need to start cutting Joan's lawns. If she gets home from work and her grass isn't mowed, there'll be consequences for me you don't want to hear about. I'm off. Janine will take care of you. If you want to attract her attention, all you need to do is put two fingers in your mouth and whistle. Or bang your coffee cup on the table. Oops, you don't think she overheard me, do you? *Ouch.*

No tip for you, Janny, just for that. Nice talking to you folks. I'm glad you like our little bit of paradise.

Clouds

MRS. MARKIN DIDN'T seem to think what had occurred was outrageous. "But . . . but he's an RCMP officer," Mr. Hastings had protested to her, "a constable sworn to uphold the law." Mr. Hastings shook his head in disbelief. "And for him to tell me that I had to . . . " Mrs. Markin, now that Mr. Hastings had concluded his story, failed to respond further. Usually Mr. Hastings could count on her for a sympathetic ear, at least until somebody else came into the little post office with a letter or parcel to mail or pick up.

Of course, even if no other customers were present, sometimes Mrs. Markin was distracted by work chores awaiting her beyond the door into the larger portion of the building, where incoming mail had to be sorted and outgoing mail bagged for collection by the truck that arrived every afternoon from Nelson, sixty kilometres away. Most times Mrs. Markin had to accomplish these tasks by herself, although Teena Shkuratoff helped out occasionally and on Saturdays, while at Christmas Mrs. Markin's niece Julia also was hired. Mr. Hastings guessed a quarter of the population served by this post office—a hundred or so of the people who lived on acreages strung along the highway for twenty kilometres in both directions, as well as along the back road across the river—received their mail in boxes here in the building's foyer. The other three-quarters got their bills, magazines, advertising flyers and occasional letters delivered to compartments in green structures that resembled chests of drawers located beside the paved roads and gravel lanes at a couple dozen locations up and down the valley. A Doukhobor woman Mr. Hastings didn't know, who had a Volvo station wagon he'd often seen at the green mail repositories, handled the daily distribution once the mail was sorted into the various routes. A few people still had old-style rural mailboxes at the foot of their driveways, but these were obsolete reminders of the time before home delivery service was phased out.

Mr. Hastings had remarked to Mrs. Markin a few months previously that the government couldn't make up its mind whether its citizens were individuals or not. "On the one hand," he had said, "the province fifteen years ago made the phone company stop linking us to party lines. Each of us now has our very own individual phone line. When it comes to the mail, though—"

"They got rid of party lines because they want you to be able to use the internet," Mrs. Markin had interrupted. She had grown stockier over the years, as he had noticed Doukhobor women often did, but he still thought she had a beautiful face. So kind. "You can't have a dial-up connection if two or three other people use the same phone line."

He had wanted to ask what a "dial-up connection" was, but persisted in finishing his point. "Your phone line has become your own, but you don't get individual household mail delivery anymore. Instead of mail coming to each of us separately, now we all have to go where the mail is."

Mrs. Markin had nodded. But rather than comment, she had looked past his shoulder and stretched out her right hand. "I'll get that for you," she said. Mr. Hastings's neighbour, Klaus Bergdof, had come in the door from the foyer grasping a parcel notification card. Mr. Hastings asked Klaus about his wife: Margrit was being treated for breast cancer in Kelowna, and Klaus, gloomy as ever, had said she was doing as well as could be expected.

Mrs. Markin had clucked sympathetically. "It's like there's an epidemic of breast cancer around here. There's Judy Johnson, lives on Appledale Lower Road, and Dorothy Leaside by the community hall and Betsy Russell who has that hair salon on Hoodikoff Road." The postmistress vanished through the doorway to fetch Klaus's package. Mr. Hastings had once bought a load of manure for Valerie's garden from Dorothy Leaside, but he didn't know the other women Mrs. Markin mentioned. He had said goodbye to Klaus and left.

Today, though, nobody was in the post office except himself and Mrs. Markin. He thought maybe he hadn't been clear enough in explaining what had just happened, so he began to relate the day's events again. For the second time, Mrs. Markin listened to his story with her head slightly angled to her left, the way she did when she was actually paying attention and not just bantering with somebody at the counter who was commenting on the snowy weather or talking about the first crocuses or daffs appearing in their garden or complaining about the damn deer that were such a menace on the roads when they weren't eating everybody's flowers and vegetables.

To the very end of Mr. Hastings's retelling of his run-in with the RCMP, the postmistress remained standing as she did when he could gauge she was listening intently—not busy in the middle of a conversation with weighing and measuring a package or figuring out the postage to Los Angeles or London, England. She listened as she did that time in November when he happened to be in the post office as Mrs. Perepolkin reported in a hushed voice how the Mortimer kid had spun off the road the night before—probably drunk, though nobody said so aloud—and gone down a bank and headfirst into a tree. The volunteer fire department had gotten him out with the Jaws of Life, but he died on the operating table after the Nelson hospital decided to airlift him to Kelowna where there were neurosurgeons. Or how Mrs. Markin had listened to Mr. Hastings during that awful year when Valerie left him, when he had to learn to live as a bachelor again after more than two decades, and then him finding out from Mike and Andrea Relkoff—who ran into Valerie by chance in Arizona—that she had ended up in a trailer park in some suburb of Phoenix, living with a boy half her age.

Mr. Hastings was older than Valerie—at the time he first met her she was a waitress in the coffee shop at the Lord Nelson Hotel that he and the other employees of the CPR diesel repair shop frequented. When the railway suddenly closed the locomotive repair facility in '84, he had been shaken: a job with the CPR—he had been promoted to parts manager several years before—used to be a job for life. Some of the younger diesel shop guys had moved away from the Kootenays to other CPR jobs they were offered. But Mr. Hastings acknowledged he was too settled on his acreage in Passmore to want to up stakes and take a job in the Vancouver or Calgary yards, let alone head for Edmonton to work for CN the way Bobby McLuckie had done. Luckily Mr. Hastings eventually was hired by Cottonwood Transport, who had a garage outside Castlegar, even though most of their drivers were owner-operators. But he had looked for six months before getting the job with Cottonwood, and had begun to feel old.

"Now's a good time to leave me, Valerie," he had said one night in the kitchen as she was making supper. "I'm washed up. My age is against me when I apply anyplace." She scoffed at his suggestion that she abandon him, yet he realized later he probably had planted the idea. He had always been aware that when he reached sixty-five and retired, Valerie would only be fifty—in her prime. Once retirement was less than a decade away, those numbers meant more than a far-off problem. This September Valerie would be fifty-eight, he suddenly figured: she'd been gone ten years.

"And who do we have here?" Mrs. Markin said as he reached the conclusion of his story for the second time. Mr. Hastings was startled, but realized she was gazing behind him. He turned to see that a young couple he didn't know, with a four- or five-year-old standing between them, had opened the door into the room. The adults both wore hiking boots, and the young man had a sash holding up his jeans as the hippies did forty years ago. The woman's right ankle below her full skirt had a tattoo of some flames, and she had a ring through her left eyelid and many rings in the lobe and along the upper rolled edges of each ear.

The postmistress leaned across the counter, bending down toward the child. "Braydon, isn't it?" she continued. "How old are you now?" The child clutched his mother's leg and turned his face toward her skirt in an ecstasy of shyness.

A moment later, outside in the parking lot between the post office building and the general store, Mr. Hastings checked the sky to the south. That was the direction from where the weather usually rolled into this part of the valley, around the end of the west ridge. Enormous white cumulus mounds floated in the lower portions of the intense July blue. He shifted to glance northward up the highway—the other direction from which weather could appear. The dome of clear sky descended from directly overhead to the summits of the forested valley walls, except where a few cirrus wisps hung in the blue distance far to the north.

Mr. Hastings often noted to himself that, after half a lifetime in the Slocan Valley, he had few friends despite being acquainted with so many people, including having watched kids he'd known since birth grow up and leave for the Coast and, in some cases, return. Clouds, with their odd names, were as close to him as most people. It wasn't always this way: at the engine repair shop he'd had dozens of pals, not just other partsmen but mechanics, brakemen, machinists. He and Valerie and his friends and their wives used to be constantly in and out of each other's homes for dinners and parties. But in all the years he was employed by Cottonwood, he couldn't count anybody who worked there as a real friend.

"Maybe I've changed somehow. People don't seem to want to know me," he remarked to Valerie once. "I've never been employed at a place five years before without having at least one good friend from work." She had dismissed his concern. "You're always comparing Cottonwood's garage to the engine shop," she said. "Lighten up on your complaints, and you'll do fine. Wouldn't you call Arnie a friend?"

In the post office parking lot, put off by Mrs. Markin's failure to agree how very, very wrong the Mountie was, Mr. Hastings's gaze shifted south again. One of the gigantic cumuli drifting above Toad Peak now looked to him to be forming a cumulonimbus tower: the flat-bottomed sign of a thunderhead. The radio was predicting lightning storms later in the week. Maybe one had arrived early.

❧

First chore on Mr. Hastings's list that day had been to drive over to the apartment building he owned at Slocan Park to fix the concrete front steps. He and Valerie had been careful with money, and his brother-in-law had convinced him to buy a revenue property. The brother-in-law was of the opinion that Nelson was their best bet for a rental house. Yet only a few small apartment buildings existed in the whole of the Slocan Valley and Mr. Hastings figured there'd always be a demand for these. The area never slackened in its production of single moms, he knew, and they, plus transient guys working or loafing in the valley for a few months, needed a place to live. Also, apartments were less likely to be used for grow shows: everyone had accounts of rented houses being trashed by responsible-seeming renters who turned out to be only wanting to engage in large-scale indoor marijuana production.

One April years ago, a two-storey apartment building with four units, situated a few hundred metres along the highway from Slocan Park's Co-op store, came on the market. Mr. Hastings purchased it. As his brother-in-law had predicted, the tenants over the next decade had in effect bought the building for Mr. Hastings. While he was employed, he had hired a handyman to deal with any repairs he didn't have time to fix. Now that he was retired, he took care of most problems himself.

This morning he had mixed up concrete patches to replace a few chunks of the building's front stairs that had crumbled away. The job had presented no difficulties. While admiring his work, Mr. Hastings had the notion to check the front porch light and, sure enough, it had burned out. After walking over to the Co-op to buy a new light bulb, he went around the back of the apartment building to the shed where he kept a ladder.

Once the new bulb was in place Mr. Hastings decided, since he had the ladder out, to climb further up and take a look at the condition of the porch roof—really, just a gable-ended projection over the stairs, extending out at the height of the second floor. After he ascended he could confirm the roof was getting on in age, but he judged the asphalt shingles would last a few years yet: none were unduly curling, cracking or missing an excessive amount of their granular coating.

From his perch atop the ladder, he had checked the sky. The valley ran east and west here, and away to the west white cumulus masses were gathering. Eastward, toward Crescent Valley, only an occasional puff was pasted high in the blue, apparently motionless. He was about to back down the ladder when he happened to glance into the front window of the easternmost upstairs apartment.

Rising into view were the trunks and leaves of a row of several sturdy-looking plants that, Mr. Hastings recognized, were marijuana. He had seen enough photographs of the lacy-edged leaves in newspaper and magazine articles about the Kootenays to identify what he could hardly believe at first he was seeing. The plants were set back slightly from the window so they could receive lots of sunlight—the front window faced south—but were invisible from ground level.

Mr. Hastings tried to recall the name of the tenant in number three. He was a young guy who claimed to have a job at the Castlegar pulp mill tending the digester. As Mr. Hastings descended the ladder, he hoped the whole interior of the suite hadn't been wrecked by water damage or mould or worse. He had heard that an entire building often had to be condemned if a grow op was present even in a basement, and that insurance often wouldn't cover repairs necessitated as a result of criminal activity.

In a minute he was in the building. The tenant's name came to Mr. Hastings as he knocked at the apartment door. Then he was fumbling with his master key to unlock it.

Everything seemed normal in number three when he stepped inside, to his relief. Breakfast dishes were stacked unwashed by the sink; a bag of what looked like granola had been left out on the counter. A glance in the bedroom as he strode down the hall showed an unmade bed, clothes tossed on a chair and on the floor, and a guitar propped against one wall. Nothing seemed amiss in the bathroom, at least from a cursory view: one towel on the rack and another balled on the floor against the tub. Mr. Hastings had seen messier tenants. Then he was in the living room, facing the big windows that overlooked the highway.

There were six plants in all, placed in plastic containers about the size in which four- or five-foot fruit trees were sold at Georama's nursery west of Nelson. Mr. Hastings noted that each of the containers was set in a large plastic saucer, which meant any excess water wouldn't stain the rug. So the tenant wasn't a complete slob, even though a criminal. The plants themselves were dense with bushy leaves. The main stems, Mr. Hastings observed on closer inspection, were nearly an inch thick where they emerged from the soil.

Mr. Hastings was aware that, as the landlord, he wasn't responsible for any illegal activity that took place in his building. But now that he knew his tenant was involved in a crime, he didn't want to be implicated, to be an accessory after the fact or something.

Bending down, Mr. Hastings tried to hoist the closest of the large pots. It was heavy, but manageable, and with difficulty he carried the nodding plant out of the apartment and down the stairs. He left the plant on the front stoop for a moment while he descended the porch steps, careful not to tread on the repaired patches. He crossed the yard to where his Corolla station wagon was parked beside the building. His hope was that nobody would walk by along the road and notice a good-sized marijuana plant sitting in plain sight.

He drove the vehicle across the small lawn to stop directly in front of the building. After lowering the rear seats to make the Corolla's cargo area larger, he lifted the plant again and loaded it into the back of the station wagon. He carefully shut the rear door once the plant was inside. Five more times he hauled a pot down the stairs, put it on the ground behind the Toyota, opened the vehicle's rear door and placed a plant into the back with the others. When he was done, the rear windows showed a thick mass of green foliage.

Mr. Hastings's plan was to head for the RCMP detachment in Nelson, the nearest police station, to report the crime and hand over the evidence. As he waited for a chip truck to pass before he turned eastward onto the highway, the thought occurred to him that if a cop should notice him transporting the marijuana, he might be mistaken for a criminal himself. He resolved to flag down any police car he encountered between Slocan Park and Nelson, if in fact he met one.

Until the late 1980s there had been a small RCMP detachment in nearby Crescent Valley. How much handier that would have been, he thought as he accelerated after the chip truck, instead of him having to go all the way into Nelson unless he saw a cop en route and could somehow catch his attention.

At Playmor Junction he steered left onto the Nelson–Castlegar road. The highway here ran alongside the Kootenay River, with its series of hydroelectric dams. This watershed, with its proximity to

Kootenay Lake not far to the north, often had a different weather system than the Slocan Valley. When the highway had descended and risen again after Bonnington, the sky ahead out the windshield showed a thin band of cirrus peeking over the ridgeline on the clear-cut-scarred mountains.

Soon after the Beasley volunteer fire station, Mr. Hastings encountered a police cruiser amid a line of traffic approaching him. But with the low-profile rack of lights atop the vehicle, and with so many other cars being painted white these days, the patrol car was gone before Mr. Hastings realized what it was and could react. He checked his rear-view mirror as he reached the Beasley bluffs in case the cop had observed the marijuana in Mr. Hastings's station wagon, pulled a U-turn and was in hot pursuit. Looming behind him, though, was only some Rocket Rodney in a Mazda sports car desperate to pass, hugging Mr. Hastings's bumper and jittering out a metre or so into the other lane every few seconds to check on oncoming traffic, dying to gun around him and race up the two-lane: obviously some tourist unaware that after Beasley there was no legal place to pass all the way into Nelson.

As traffic eventually slowed to sixty klicks, then fifty, to navigate past the octopus of intersecting roads just outside town, the tailgater screeched off onto Government Road. A pickup immediately in front of Mr. Hastings veered right to take the route to Salmo, so the pavement was empty ahead. Rolling toward him, as he could verify at these low speeds, was unmistakably another RCMP cruiser.

Mr. Hastings began flashing his lights, and, with his left hand held up in front of him in the windshield, pointed toward the right, trying to indicate that he was going to pull over. At first there was no response from the approaching cop. But suddenly the cruiser's headlights brightened and dimmed, and its red and blue roof lights begin pulsing. Mr. Hastings swung to his right and stopped on the shoulder, while the cop wheeled about and halted just behind, roof lights still on.

A surge of nervousness passed through Mr. Hastings. He wondered if the car full of marijuana plants wouldn't look suspicious to the constable, regardless of anything he might say. For the longest time there was no sign of life inside the cop car. At last the driver's door opened and the officer, a stern, burly man who looked middle-aged, approached Mr. Hastings's window.

"Good afternoon. Could I see your driver's licence and registration, sir?" the Mountie began.

"There's drugs in this car but I have an explanation," Mr. Hastings blurted.

A ripple of something close to surprise crossed the officer's impassive face for an instant. He took a half-step backwards and focused on what was visible through the rear windows. His features showed no emotion, however, when he resumed his stance at Mr. Hastings's window. "Driver's licence, please. And your vehicle registration and insurance."

"Look, you don't have to bother about that," Mr. Hastings said. "I can explain. See, I own the Midvalley Apartments in Slocan Park, and I was fixing the—"

"I need your driver's licence." The officer's voice was curt. "And your vehicle registration. You crossed the exit lane to Highway 6 without signalling."

Mr. Hastings felt the cop was missing the point. "Never mind that. I saw that my tenant had—"

"Sir, I need to see your driver's licence and registration. It's an offense to operate a motor vehicle without a valid operator's licence and valid registration and insurance."

"You don't understand. I—"

"Do you or do you not have these with you?"

Mr. Hastings glumly fished his wallet out of his pants and produced his licence. He leaned across the front seat and opened the jammed glove compartment, digging through the stack of maps and repair invoices until he found the plastic folder with the registration and insurance documents.

The cop took them from him and started to turn from the window.

"I need to explain—" Mr. Hastings gestured toward the back of the station wagon. The Mountie was already striding toward his patrol car.

Several minutes elapsed, while Mr. Hastings sat fuming. He couldn't believe the cop was so stupid as to care more about whether

Mr. Hastings's automobile paperwork was up-to-date than about illegal drugs being hauled openly from place to place. Mr. Hastings was impatient to tell where the plants were from, but the officer's apparent indifference to evidence of a crime was unsettling. Mr. Hastings had to admit he hadn't initially handled very well giving the officer the information. But surely the cop wasn't going to issue a traffic ticket when Mr. Hastings was the one who had flagged down the patrol car? Maybe this guy was dumb enough that he wasn't going to listen at all to what Mr. Hastings had to say, and he was going to end up charged with drug possession besides not signalling? He received curious looks from the occupants of several cars that rolled by. What he could observe of the sky overhead at the moment contained a haze of cirrostratus to the east.

Then in Mr. Hastings's outside mirror the cruiser's door opened and a moment later the constable was handing back Mr. Hastings's papers. "Now, you flagged me down. What's the problem?"

Still clutching his licence and other documents, Mr. Hastings poured out the story of how he had only an hour before discovered and seized his tenant's marijuana plants to bring in to hand over to the authorities. The officer's face did not alter while he listened.

Mr. Hastings finished and waited expectantly for praise.

"You can't do that."

Mr. Hastings thought he had misheard. "Pardon me?"

"You can't just enter a tenant's dwelling and remove his things. Not without a court order. Technically, it's stealing."

"But . . . but these are against the law. They're illegal. He can't—"

"You're not allowed to go in and take something from a tenant's apartment."

"Are you crazy?" The words had slipped out before Mr. Hastings could stop them. "You're making it sound like I'm the one who did something wrong. He's the one who—"

"You *did* do something wrong. As a landlord, under the Residential Tenancy Act, you cannot enter a rented premises without providing due notice, and you certainly can't seize goods belonging to your tenant without a court order to that effect. Without such an order, what you did constitutes theft, exactly the same as if somebody broke into the apartment and took something of your tenant's."

"But it's illegal to grow marijuana," Mr. Hastings protested. He felt his face flush. "That's what he's doing, can't you see?" Mr. Hasting flung his left arm up, rotated his wrist, and jabbed his index finger repeatedly toward the rear of the station wagon.

"Doesn't matter."

"It doesn't matter that he's doing something illegal? I thought the RCMP were supposed to—"

"It doesn't matter whether the goods removed are legal or illegal. Growing pot is illegal, yes. You should have just reported the grow op to us and we would have dealt with it in due course. But you can't simply remove items from your tenant's apartment without his permission or a court order. You're going to have to put these back."

"What—?" Mr. Hastings felt he was struggling to speak an unfamiliar language, as when he had tried while on holiday in Montreal many years before to communicate with store clerks or waitresses using what he remembered of his high school French. "What do you mean I have to—?"

"You have to return what you have illegally removed from your tenant's apartment. Otherwise he could press charges against you."

"Against *me*? His *plants* are what are illegal."

"Doesn't matter. You or anybody else, including me, have no grounds to enter a premises for the purpose of taking anything unless a court order is obtained. Is he behind on his rent?"

"No, but what's that got to do with it? These are *illegal*."

"I'll take note of the address, sir, and we'll obtain a warrant and deal with it. But meantime you have to return these to your tenant's apartment."

"I'm supposed to drive back to Slocan Park with a car full of dope plants? What if I'm stopped by another policeman?"

"Just obey the speed limit and nobody is going to stop you. If you *were* stopped, another officer would tell you exactly what I'm telling you."

After another exchange resulting in more of the patrolman's dogged assertions that Mr. Hastings was in the wrong to take the plants, he gave up. The Mountie offered him a grudging acknowledgement that he was right to keep his eyes open for grow shows operated by his tenants, and wrote down the tenant's name and the address of the apartment. But the best Mr. Hastings could get from the officer was that he wouldn't give Mr. Hastings a ticket for failing to signal when he had changed lanes.

When the Mountie finally returned to the cruiser, Mr. Hastings was conscious that his own hands and arms were shaking with frustration. As he carefully steered into town to circle back onto the highway, he wondered if the cop was somehow in league with his tenant, or even with the Hells Angels, concerning growing the stuff. Maybe the tenant was paying the Mounties protection money? Then he recalled that the officer had ordered him to return the plants before hearing the tenant's name and address.

Tufts of cirrocumulus were floating high to the southeast across the river as Mr. Hastings drove back toward the junction. The clouds appeared on the verge of forming into bands of herringbone.

At the Midvalley Apartments again, Mr. Hastings unloaded the plants one by one and hauled them up the stairs. Every trip increased his sense of injustice: it was nuts having to put back what the cops were only going to seize when they got a warrant. Even if he *was* in the wrong to take the plants—which he assured himself he wasn't—the Mountie should have accepted the plants if only to save everybody more work later.

Carrying the fourth heavy plant back to the apartment, Mr. Hastings caught one of his by-now-weary feet on the edge of the hallway's indoor-outdoor carpet at the top of the stairs. The container slipped from his hands and fell onto its side. The accident spilled a mound of dirt on the rug, plus ejected a spray of black particles. After scooping up what he could, Mr. Hastings had to go down to the basement to get the big vacuum and haul *that* up to the second floor to clean the mess.

This tenant has to go, Mr. Hastings was thinking amid the motor noise as he moved the vacuum wand back and forth in the hall. *I won't tolerate criminal activity in my building.* The idea struck him, however, that if he evicted the tenant the Mounties wouldn't be able to find the evidence needed to prosecute. *To hell with them,* he said to himself as he lugged the vacuum down to the basement again. *I gave them their chance.*

Mr. Hastings was aware from the West Kootenay Landlords Association newsletter that legal grounds for eviction didn't include a tenant engaging in illegal activity. The newsletter was full of horror stories of building owners battling to get rid of criminal tenants, especially people who had set up grow ops in rental properties. But he also knew from experience that most tenants left if you gave them notice on an official-looking form. Either they didn't know or didn't care what the Residential Tenancy Act said about eviction, or were planning to leave anyway, or didn't want a hassle.

When the last plant was returned to its original spot beside the window, Mr. Hastings tidied up the rear of the Corolla. Then he drove home to get a proper Notice to Tenant form from a stack in the portable file box that held all the material concerning the apartment building. Mulling over the morning's events, he couldn't wait to tell people about the absurdity of the Mountie ordering him, against all common sense and reason, to return the plants.

Mr. Hastings decided, while he sat at his kitchen table filling in the Notice, that rather than drive back to the apartment in Slocan Park and leave the form, he would send it registered mail. That made delivery of the eviction order all the more official. Then on Saturday morning, when the tenant was sure not to be at work, he'd drop by the apartment and give the tenant what for, as well as stressing that the tenant had to get rid of the plants at once and be out by the end of next month.

When Mr. Hastings took the letter to the post office this afternoon to mail, he could also tell Mrs. Markin about his day. As a sort of government representative herself, she'd instantly see the ridiculousness of what the officer had insisted on. She'd confirm that the cop was way out of line. And just before Mr. Hastings's station wagon swung north through the forest, headed toward the crossroads where the post office was located, huge white mountains were floating in the sky.

What We Know About Our Neighbours

WE ENCOUNTERED THE building that should not have been there about three in the afternoon. The mid-December day had been overcast since we started our ski, snowing off and on in brief interludes. But I had realized a few minutes before we glimpsed the structure that the prevailing light was ebbing, and had been thinking of suggesting to my two companions that we should turn around if we didn't want to finish our return trek in the dark.

A couple of times on cross-country excursions by myself I had skied out in failing light and found the process unpleasant even on a route where tracks had been set. Depth perception is the first to go: as I had poled along, peering ahead through the dimness, a ski would wander out of its slot. Once that happened, I either had to contort myself to avert a tumble, or was forced, after losing my balance and pitching forward, to hoist myself out of the snow. The abrupt break in my progress reminded me to pay more attention to what I was doing, to my rhythm and balance, and less to wondering if the next curve was the last before some landmark I remembered or even the parking lot itself.

Our present day on the trails had begun late. However, I could detect no indication that either Ron or Marci was concerned about the hour. Both displayed plenty of energy, despite the steep uphill sections of the trails we had followed, inclines that I had found increasingly tough to navigate up. Both my companions were in better shape than I, having already skied a few times this season. They were year-long residents of the area whom I had known for two decades, whereas the past six years I had been teaching down on the Coast at Langara College. I rented a pied-à-terre in Vancouver, and only drove the nine hours home to the West Kootenay for the summer, long weekends and the Christmas break.

When we came across the building, we had already skied four or five kilometres through the woods up the Clearwater Creek trail. At one point we had impulsively followed an old logging road higher into the forest. Clearwater is part of the complex of trails maintained by the Nelson Nordic Ski Club, of which I'm a member. The trails radiate out from Apex, the summit area on the forty kilometres of Highway 6 between Nelson and Salmo in the southern Selkirk Mountains.

That decision to strike away from the Clearwater trail to follow the unmarked powder of a logging road is typical of the cheerful anarchy of Ron's and Marci's lives—why I enjoy their company. As a college math instructor I confess I have a fussy side to my personality that I've always tried to fight. When I was hired to teach at David Thompson University Centre in Nelson in the early 1980s, I fell in love with the region upon discovering I could live in a house right at the edge of the woods. I liked having one foot in the orderliness of a mowed lawn and neatly laid out flower beds, and one foot in the neighbouring wilderness. I think being in the Kootenays provided me with the kind of delight I had when I was in Boy Scouts—that mix of do-it-by-the-book and untamed nature.

Ron came on faculty at David Thompson to teach business part-time. He had just purchased one of Nelson's two shoe stores, although these days he's a silent partner in the enterprise. You could say he's semi-retired, despite being a bit younger than I am. He's a history buff, and finds an outlet for that fascination by sitting on the board of Nelson's museum and archives, and sometimes contributing to the BC Historical Federation magazine—he always sends me a copy of his article, invariably about some aspect of the West Kootenay's past. He ceased playing an active role in his store, Stepping Out, when he left his wife and moved in with Marci at her acreage in the Slocan Valley, about twenty kilometres from my house.

When the two of them connected—which happened one fall while I was teaching in Van—I was surprised but happy. I'd never imagined them appearing in each other's lives—they existed in two entirely separate spheres, despite inhabiting the same geographic locale. Yet when they did get together, all I could think was, *Of course*. Each has a similar zany approach to life I admire. Ron's I first observed when I ended up behind him at a checkout in Safeway soon after I had been introduced to him at a faculty meeting. While we were chatting, he unloaded from his cart thirty or so of the small paper bags the vegetable section provides for mushrooms. When the whole array was on the counter, I could see the eyes of the woman at the register grow round with amazement. In his matter-of-fact voice, Ron informed her that a sign by the mushroom display declared that two cents would be deducted from the cost of a bag of mushrooms at the checkout to account for the weight of the bag. He had loaded one mushroom per bag, he explained, and figured with the deduction he should be entitled to obtain the tasty morsels for free.

I had met Marci over our daughters' mutual fascination with horses. For the first few years after my divorce, my daughter decided to live with me. Her choice, I believe, was more about not wanting to leave her friends when my ex-wife's employer transferred her to Cranbrook. Marci boarded her horse at the same stable in Blewett where my daughter and Marci's daughter used to ride. Talking with Marci once while we both stood at a corral watching our daughters' dressage lesson, I learned she lived down the road from me. Marci and I never exactly dated, but got together for dinner a few times— either at one of our houses or a restaurant in Nelson. I'm sure she found me somewhat stodgy. How she made a living was never evident to me. She had been married twice, so perhaps was entitled to alimony, although one of her former husbands—at least, according to her stories—is a former Slocan Valley back-to-the-lander who now drives logging truck at Smithers, in the province's north-central region, and is chronically in and out of work. Possibly she had inherited money; I recall her mentioning that her family in Winnipeg, where she grew up, was comfortably off. She considers herself a fibre artist, mainly producing abstract felted wall hangings offered for sale at craft fairs and at Nelson's Craft Connection, the local artisans' co-op. I doubt her art ever supported her, even though the one piece of hers I bought I probably paid too much for. Yet I like how its design evokes a cluster of trunks from one of our valley's many stands of birch or aspen.

I've always been impressed by Marci's in-your-face response to life, no matter what topic you discuss with her. She and Ron frequently bicker, but their disagreements involve cascades of laughter and non-stop wit that I find a pleasure to be around. That morning Ron had phoned to tell me they would be late for our rendezvous at the credit union in Slocan Park. Marci, he said, had foolishly forgotten she had promised to bake for a Myrtle Creek watershed protection fundraiser. I could hear Marci hoot "Not true" in the background. Ron, in a loud-enough-for-Marci-to-overhear whisper, declared, "I think it might be early onset Alzheimer's. But with luck, it's only age-related MCI: minor cognitive impairment." Marci shouted her mock outrage, and a second later she was on the phone saying Ron had slept in, and that the delay was due to him having promised to return his brother's snow blower, which they had borrowed while theirs was being repaired. "Absolutely false!" Ron bellowed amid laughter behind Marci's explanation. "I can't believe you would boldfacedly tell Alan—" Marci's giggles were in my ear for a moment until Ron took possession of the phone again. Before he was far into his pretend-repudiation of Marci's statements, I suggested as mildly as I could that they just phone me whenever they were ready to depart.

Because it was nearly eleven fifteen before we both pulled in at the credit union parking lot where we were to leave their vehicle, we agreed to eat an early lunch in Nelson en route to Apex, rather than out on the trail as we had planned. The highway to Nelson follows the Slocan River and then the Kootenay River, and the entire distance Marci and Ron continued to joyfully contradict each other as we exchanged news on how our autumns had unfolded while I was at the Coast. I'm always surprised at the strangeness of how lives close around us can go on without us being aware, but when certain information is obtained, suddenly we become conscious of the past or present aspects of another's existence.

Ron has a son, Jesse, who had enrolled as a freshman at the local college and was living away from home for the first time in Castlegar. Marci's daughter, Piper, was someplace in Australia on a trip with her boyfriend. I informed my passengers about the current successes of my daughter, Anna, as a web designer in Victoria. And Anna's difficulties with her boss. As is customary with people our age, deaths and health issues infiltrated our conversation. I learned that one of the valley characters of our generation whom I knew slightly—an inveterate writer of letters-to-the-editor published in our local valley paper—had died in October of a stroke. A young woman prominent in their watershed association had been diagnosed with a virulent form of breast cancer. Ron's routine checkup had revealed a surge in his PSA number, although a subsequent biopsy had been negative. "I'm supposed to eat more tomatoes," he said. "I'll probably die because Marci *abhors* tomatoes. She—"

"Oooh, that is such a *complete* lie," Marci bristled with feigned anger, and the two of them cackled delightedly. Marci bent forward from the back seat to speak into my ear: "It's *Ron* who doesn't like tomatoes. He was just afraid to tell his doctor about his deep-seated *hatred* of tomat—" "*What?*" Ron protested from the seat beside me, launching into an equally impassioned, probably false riposte.

I wasn't entirely immune from their good-humoured confrontational approach. When the bill came for our meal at the Full Circle Café in Nelson, I offered to pay for it. "I'm still working," I pointed out. "You guys are on a fixed income. Picking up the tab is the least I can do."

Without missing a beat, Marci leaned across the table, her face intent, serious. "Alan, what's the *most* you can do?" After second or two, her solemn expression dissolved, her face transformed by laughter.

The piles of roadside snow increased in depth as the sanded highway rose out of Nelson toward the Apex summit. Fifteen minutes from town, we passed the parking lot at the club's warming hut—the space half empty, as usual on a weekday. Less than a kilometre more toward Salmo, we steered onto the access road to the Busk–Euphrates trail parking area, where the Clearwater Creek trail also starts. Once we had arranged and stepped into our gear, I shrugged on my daypack and we began the long climb.

The trail angles steeply upwards from the parking lot, so the first thirty minutes involved considerable slogging effort, at least for me. My skis are the old-fashioned waxable type. Back at the car as I was applying my best guess for the right wax, based on the snow temperature I took when we first arrived, I'd found myself chilled; I retrieved my down jacket from where I'd stowed it in my pack. But once we began to plod up the slope, I quickly started to sweat. After about five minutes, I stopped to cram the garment back in my haversack.

Ron and Marci had more modern, no-wax gear, so had less problem with our ascent. However, when the route gradually flattened, and even offered the occasional short downhill stretch, the smooth glide my wax provided made my progress easier than theirs. Our climb remained a challenge, though, as the opening through the forest led ever higher. The Clearwater trail was originally a logging road, and is wide enough to allow you to slow your descent by stepping out of the tracks when required to employ the snowplow technique—pushing your skis ahead of you in a *V*. Cutbanks and fill were used to create the road, which lifts along the north wall of the Clearwater Creek valley. Occasionally the sound of tumbling water below us was audible, although the profound winter silence was more often broken only by the noises of our skis and infrequent joking comments about how strenuous this excursion was. Now and again a *chick-a-dee-dee-dee* call alerted us to where a bird flitted amid the branches of the trailside firs or spruces that crowd the edges of the route. Once, harsh squawks overhead drew us to halt and observe three crows fussing in the snow-laden top of a pine.

We were the first to travel this way since the previous night's snowfall; the white course ahead of us was pristine. The club's track-setter apparently had not been up the Clearwater trail that day. Tracks previously incised were only evident as two slight parallel depressions in fresh powder, but our skis restored the channels' utility. We took turns skiing point, flattening a passage in the remains of the track for the other two sliding or shuffling behind. Where the grade was sharply pitched, the tracks vanished for several metres, and we had to herringbone up.

Three-quarters of an hour from the car, Ron, then at the head of our file, drew our attention to a string of deer hoofprints that had emerged from the woods and begun preceding us. At this spot, the route traversed a gently rising bench or plateau. We had gained enough altitude that the bottom of the overcast was snagged in the uppermost branches of the trees on either side—mainly cedars and firs along this stretch. The effect of the evergreens disappearing into misty cloud was magical: the tops of the trees surrounding us had become ghosts. We swayed forward through a tunnel composed of a white floor, vaporous grey roof, and walls speckled white and green where clumps of snow adhered to the trees' limbs. Our breaths ascended through the icy air to join the clouds hovering close above us.

The deer prints we followed wavered from shoulder to shoulder on the route, but eventually adopted the snowed-over tracks as their preferred location. "Trust a damn deer to ruin something," Marci muttered, once Ron commented on the deer's predilection for the tracks. "Bad as a dog," Ron concurred; dogs are officially banned from set trails, since their feet mar the integrity of the track walls even as their paws excavate holes in the twin channels' bottom surfaces.

Ron's and Marci's statements prompted a conversational flare in which we all commiserated about the malevolent behaviour displayed by deer during their raids on our gardens. An open-ended greenhouse at Marci's last summer had been visited by a doe who walked down the central aisle taking one bite out of each of the tomatoes growing there. I spoke of my outrage at the quadrupeds' persistent attacks on my roses and hollyhocks, and how they had ripped out my rows of late-season carrots, munching only on the occasional leafy top but destroying the entire patch. Ron told of a neighbour, in despair at the local herd's daily predations against her garden, whose kids burst into the house one evening to report to her that a deer had been struck by a car on the road and had crawled partway up their driveway where it was lying mortally wounded. The neighbour's response to her children's announcement, Ron avowed, was a pumped fist and an ecstatic "Yes!"

The deer prints continued through another bend. We plodded or glided onward, depending on the steepness of the terrain. As we navigated a further curve, I was second in line and nearly collided with Ron as he unexpectedly halted. Ten metres in front stood the animal, head swivelled back over one shoulder in our direction. The rich reddish brown of its coat glowed against the snow.

The deer stared at us. In thirty winters of cross-country skiing, I had observed thousands of deer tracks while in the winter woods. But I had never been face to face with a deer on a trail, despite dozens of eyeball-to-eyeball encounters with them on my property during every season. Now, in the thick silence of the December forest, as a few icy flakes materialized in the air and drifted downwards, we two species who share this geography regarded each other.

To me, the gaze of a deer is unsettling. When I chase them off my lawns or out of the garden, most often they simply bolt. Now and again, though, one will stand motionless and watch me as I approach waving my hands and cursing. The expression in their eyes as they look at me is not describable by any category we apply to humans: not curious, fearful or annoyed at being disturbed. Their eyes beam out a state of mind we have no word for. At such a moment, deer seem not to be native to our valleys and mountains but to be residents of a different planet. Or maybe humans, in our determination to trash the biosphere, are the unearthly species.

On the Clearwater trail, the deer's head suddenly shifted to face front and its tail lifted in a display of white hair. All four legs left the snow at once, initiating a series of leaps that propelled it forward along the route. At the next turn, it bounded out of sight.

When we rounded that curve, the deer was poised several metres in front, head again swivelled to appraise us. It held its stance for a long minute after we stopped. Then it jounced up the trail, to disappear at the next bend.

Yet the creature stood in the near distance, as if waiting for us, when we eventually reached the place where it had vanished. "That deer is leading us on," Ron proclaimed.

We paused once more to observe it. This time when the deer reacted to our presence, it sprang away into the snowy trees.

I was conscious of my muscles tightening each time we halted to appreciate the animal. After ten minutes of renewed travel, I suggested a break. I had brought a thermos of coffee as well as trail mix, mandarin oranges and some energy bars. Neither of my companions objected to the idea of a snack. We ate the bars and sipped the hot liquid. Snow began to waft thinly down as we resumed our trek.

The previously set ski tracks became harder to discern, even as the sprinkling of snow eased. Evidently the overnight snowfall this high up the mountain had been heavier than on the lower slopes. I had taken the lead, and now often was no longer certain whether my skis followed the track or whether I was forging a new course through the powder. My skis and even boots were frequently invisible, submerged in the white fluff.

We pushed on through the forest amid a resumption of the snowfall. After ten minutes, the haze of white particulate dissipated and the air emptied. I was in the lead when I noted deer hoofprints again entering our route. I pointed these out to the others.

"Do you think it's the same deer we already saw?" Marci asked. She undercut her question with a short laugh.

"We'll know for sure if it's waiting for us around the next curve," Ron said.

"Maybe it's following us," Marci responded.

"Or leading us, like I said before."

"Leading where?"

"No place good. Think of all the harm Bambi's evil hordes cause on *our* turf in the valley. Now we're up in *their* country."

"Yeah, right," Marci jeered. "Cue ominous music."

I contributed an observation that had struck me. "The critter must be close. Look how sharp the hoof marks are. These had to be made since we came through that flurry."

"Alan, the intrepid tracker," Marci declared.

We took another breather where our route was intersected to the left by an old road, one of a number of former spurs leading off from the main that had become the Clearwater Creek trail. The deer's hoofprints led up this side road. I handed out the oranges I had brought, and we savoured the juicy segments, cold from the hours in my pack. Marci proposed that, since the set tracks now were more or less dysfunctional, we should explore the branch road, where none of us had skied before.

I was not enthusiastic about her whim, since the white open-ing in the woods led up a significant incline. But Ron seconded Marci's recommendation, and a few minutes later I was doggedly herringboning aloft, pausing every ten steps or so to recover my breath. Where the new route finally levelled out it swung north-ward, and the Clearwater trail below us was hidden by a stand of hemlock.

A sharp descent awaited us, an exhilarating run of perhaps a half kilometre into a draw. The untouched powder provided brak-ing power such that I never felt I was zooming faster than I could handle. The experience was so delightful that at Ron's suggestion we trudged back up the slope to ski down the tracks we had just made—a speedier drop this time, since the packed snow offered less resistance. Flashing down, I could feel the chill air cut through my sweater. I had a moment where I thought I was going *too* quickly, and debated lifting one ski out of its track to form a half-V snow-plow. But I resisted the cautionary urge, and managed to stay suffi-ciently in control to remain upright and almost complete the next bend, well past the finish of my initial run. "What a *rush*," Marci shouted, when she slid alongside where Ron and I—who had des-cended ahead of her—stood. Her wool cap had flown off, and she had to climb a third of the way up the hill again to recover it.

Back on the move, we continued to traverse ascending grades, interspersed with level stretches. Always in front was the evidence of the deer having preceded us.

"I hope this effort is worth it," I panted at the top of a portion of the route more sharply angled than those we'd surmounted in the past twenty minutes. Two-thirds of the way up this rise, the deer prints had braided into the bush to our left. I had managed the as-cent without having to herringbone, but only by stepping out of the tracks of Marci and Ron ahead of me, and shuffling upwards through the powder.

"Imagine how much fun the run back will be," Ron said. "We'll land at the car so fast you'll want to ski up here and do it all over."

"Where do you think that deer went?" Marci asked.

I was about to use Ron's comment to broach the subject of our return. My concern was the definite change in the light I had become aware of, a subtle darkening that I knew heralded the conclusion of the brief winter day. As well, I could feel my muscles in need of another break, and was starting to worry about having the strength to ski back without being exhausted at the end. The first ski of the season can leave me nearly crippled if I don't pace myself. A few times I've pushed my out-of-shape leg muscles past their limit while relishing the year's first taste of employing my slippery slats. At the parking lot again, my thigh muscles have been so painfully stiff as to render me almost unable to lift my feet to depress brake and clutch pedals.

Yet I knew Ron was right to a degree. Our descent would take much less time than slogging our way up. My watch, however, showed 2:55. We had at most an hour of any daylight left; dusk begins to be tangible by three thirty on a cloudless day this close to the solstice. And the sky today was leaden.

Ron took over the lead, though, and we resumed our travel.

"What's *that*?" An urgent tone in Marci's voice, after we had traversed only a few metres, forestalled my intent to call attention to the shortening afternoon.

She gestured to our left through a screen of needleless larch, intermixed with snow-laden fir. I could discern what appeared to be the corner of a tallish structure.

"Can't tell," Ron replied. "Part of an old sawmill?"

"It's awfully big. Should we take a look?" Marci said.

"Why not?"

"We'll have to bushwhack," I pointed out the obvious. "And, you know, we probably should start thinking about heading back, since the—" But the other two had already begun to force a passage for themselves through the underbrush. Reluctantly, I followed.

I was tempted more than once to take off my skis and carry them. Several times, one of my skis became snagged amid the bare branches of a shrub. When I attempted to untangle myself, the rear of my other ski would be caught in a different bushy thicket or the bottom boughs of a small fir. Hoisting a ski over horizontal tree trunks that impeded my passage, I twice nearly fell when the accumulated snow on the far side of the log proved much lower than the level from which I had initiated my attempt to side-step over the obstacle. Jumbles of limbs that tend to cluster alongside such logs also obstructed my progress.

When I broke out of the woods, Ron and Marci were motionless in an open area, gawking up at the structure.

"What *is* it?" Marci repeated.

Across a small field of white soared the featureless grey wall of a three- or four-storey building. Without windows or doors, its height was difficult to estimate, but its flat roofline was elevated above most of the large evergreens that ringed the cleared space surrounding the construction. The wall directly opposite us presented the impression of age: its surface was pebbly concrete, the sort that comprises heritage house foundations, or the abandoned World War II gun emplacements and other military installations—such as the searchlight towers on Vancouver's Wreck Beach—I was familiar with from growing up on the Coast. Another hint of the building's age was five evenly spaced spruce that had been planted close to the wall. These were apparently intended to serve the same purpose as the pyramidal cedars planted alongside factory or warehouse walls to soften the harsh lines of those facilities. Here, the ornamental trees had attained impressive size. Their widest branches, now freighted with snow, splayed out against the wall's cement face. The limbs of the bottom quarter of each spruce's trunk intermingled with those of adjacent trees.

Ron kicked into a glide and veered to his left, sliding until just past the closest corner of the structure. Marci and I joined him.

The expanse of wall visible from our new vantage revealed that the building was rectangular, an extended cube taller than wide. The ancient pebbly concrete we scrutinized offered again neither doors nor windows. The ornamental spruce were not present. High over our heads, however, a shelf-like cement cornice protruded out a half metre from the surface two or three metres below the roof. The feature extended across almost the entire width of the wall. Any function for the embellishment, other than decorative, was not evident.

"Could this have been a mine?" Marci asked. During the West Kootenay's heyday of the 1890s, lead, silver and other mineral deposits resulted in a rash of mines dotting the area's slopes. On the valley floors appeared concentrators, smelters and townsites, plus railways to connect this activity to distant markets. Even today a few small mines are operational, and the smelter at Trail remains the world's largest lead and zinc producer—although its ore is now secured from outside the region. Yet I'd never noticed anything in historical photos of mining operations that resembled the construction we stared up at.

Without answering Marci, Ron dug in his poles and sped back to our right. He paused at the other corner; Marci and I followed him.

The face of the building visible from here resembled the second wall we'd seen. A similar cornice spanned the space far above us. Otherwise, a stark expanse of concrete lifted from snow to roofline.

A shiver swept over me. Physically, I remained warm from our ski and the struggle through the strip of bush. But I was conscious of a sense of menace that seemed to originate from the building itself. I tried to dismiss as ridiculous my perception that my existence was somehow in danger because of this structure. The cause of the feeling, I reasoned, was the sky's greyness, which now the light was waning had started to permeate the entire landscape, even as the overcast once more released infrequent snowflakes to drift toward us. Compounding my resultant sense of trepidation was my worry about the passage of time. Marci and Ron, with their what-the-heck attitude, would adjudge a ski down to the parking lot through the dusk as merely another adventure. But based on my previous experiences, I felt apprehensive about the prospect. My muscles reminded me of how unused they were to the day's exertions. My age no doubt contributed to my out-of-condition body's lack of resilience. Worse would be if the intermittent snowfall escalated in intensity, and we were forced to try to descend the Clearwater trail through a snowstorm.

Marci's voice registered. "Alan, do *you* think it was a mine?"

I managed a shrug.

"Ron?" she asked.

His skis were already pushing ahead through the powder toward this wall's far corner. Gliding after him, I glanced aloft at the cornice as I passed, trying once more to fathom a purpose for it.

The walls we'd viewed represented the very definition of utilitarian. Decoration of an industrial building was unlikely, even if the building dated to the Victorian era, with its taste for ornate architectural adornments.

Where Ron's advance had ceased, he was shoving his Peruvian skiing cap back on his head, a pole dangling from the cord at his wrist. His gloved fingers scratched his forehead. Marci and I slid alongside him.

The now-visible fourth wall loomed above us. As with the other three, its grey surface was entirely without windows or doors.

"But how could anybody get inside?" Marci voiced my own astonishment.

Ron pointed. "Check *this* out."

At approximately the same elevation as the two cornices on the other walls, a row of unpainted, irregularly spaced concrete letters spelled *E S I B U C Y M.*

"Was that some mining company's name?" asked Marci. "I mean, I presume some letters are missing."

"Not a name I recognize," Ron said slowly. "And I've never seen any pictures that look like this place."

"I thought you were the big history expert," Marci said.

Ron shrugged. "The historical record isn't complete. That's what's intriguing about it. We think we're familiar with the past; we're comfortable regarding it a certain way, like the years that came before us are our neighbours. Then we discover something totally new."

"How could anybody *not* be aware of something this big?" Marci demanded.

"We can't be the first people to see this," said Ron. "Someone in town must know what it is."

"Who?" Marci asked.

Ron led us forward without replying, and we side-stepped nearer to the wall. Being in closer proximity to the structure did not increase or decrease the feeling of threat that emanated from it. The building exuded the same insistent prediction of personal annihilation I knew from when dread had taken tangible form before: on a hike along a September trail, I see ahead of me a black bear blocking the path. Or I hear the *whump* of an avalanche starting at the top of a snowfield I and some others are traversing. Or a car I'm steering on the icy highway over the Blueberry–Paulson pass abruptly begins to skid toward a ravine.

We inspected the face of the edifice from less than a metre in front of it. The exercise revealed no break in the concrete. The idea occurred to me, despite my persistent sense of foreboding, that perhaps this structure had housed a hydroelectric generating station. I knew that electric power was in its infancy during the Kootenays' mining boom. And that penstocks could divert water to the turbines of a generating facility. Except that stringing electrical transmission lines from a valley powerhouse to a mine atop a peak was easier and cheaper than dynamiting penstocks through rock for several kilometres to produce power on-site. Not to mention hauling turbines up a mountain. I shared my speculation with the others.

"There isn't a door," observed Ron. "You can't house machinery without access."

"I don't disagree," I assured him. "I was simply thinking aloud."

"Maybe," Marci said, "there's an exterior entrance."

"Okay, where?" Ron asked.

"I mean an outbuilding, with stairs or an elevator leading down into this thing," Marci said.

We glanced around. "Let's find out," Ron said. "I'll cover to the edge of the trees this way"—he indicated the northern half of the clearing. "Marce, you take the other direction. Alan, why don't you nose around through there"—he indicated a gap in the surrounding massed firs and pines that, I suddenly saw, could have been where a road led to the structure.

We glided off to our assigned tasks. Once I had crossed the open area and was amid the trees, I slid forward through forest gloom until a copse of hemlocks and cedars extended completely across the apparent route I was following. Nothing man-made presented itself, except for the parallel lanes my skis had cut behind me into the white ground.

I returned in my tracks. The pace of descending snow had increased; new snow already blurred the edges and bottom of the depressions I had made.

The others had rendezvoused close to the building. I shook my head as I approached.

"Same here," Ron said.

"Not even deer tracks," Marci said.

We gaped at the building in the growing darkness. The temperature was falling toward night; despite the exertion of scouting the road, I felt cold when I stopped. I jammed my poles into a drift, unslung my pack and pulled out my jacket. "I think we should head back," I suggested.

Neither of my companions responded, still gazing up at the wall we were beside. "What could it be, Ron?" Marci asked.

Ron hoisted his shoulders and both arms, poles suspended from his wrists, in a shrug. Snow had begun to accumulate on his shoulders, on our shoulders. "A mausoleum?"

"Ron!" Marci scolded.

But I understood what he meant. The impenetrableness of the huge building—both in terms of a lack of doors or windows, and with regard to its purpose—only added to the aura of menace that radiated from the structure. As Marci had noted, a building this dominating erected on a mountain ridge would constitute a local landmark, widely known among residents of the valley floors like us. The blankness of the construction's form, the absence of information about its presence and purpose, amounted to an overwhelming puzzle.

Marci gave a sharp laugh. "I admit this place is a bit creepy. But how would they get the bodies in, smart guy?"

"Haven't a clue, Marce."

I shuffled my skis back and forth where we stood, to keep the bottoms from sticking. Snow that had coated their upper surfaces was shaken off by my action. If the temperature dropped much further, I knew I would have to change waxes to ski out of there. Since a wax for a warmer snow temperature can be applied atop a wax for a colder, but not the reverse, I would have to first remove the wax I had applied at the parking lot. I was equipped to deal with the removal process, but that would take extra time.

Ron awakened from some internal deliberation. "Alan's right, though. We need to start down."

We swung our skis around through the thickening snowfall. I was nervous about the weather, but relieved to be underway. My wax was still functioning.

The light had considerably dimmed. I halted just before we started to bushwhack out to the road we'd followed, and glanced behind me. Already the structure was partially hidden in the steadily descending snow.

Respect

BE STERN, DUNCAN LOCKE'S mind prompts him as he advances toward the couple. The rough trail he is following emerges from the woods at a small gravel beach, and he estimates that the pair who stand at the river's edge are in their early twenties: less than half his age. Both are in jeans and T-shirt, she not bad-looking in a stupid sort of way; they are staring across the fifty-metre width of the current at a couple of midstream gravel bars with stranded tree trunks, and the forest on the south shore. Duncan catches his left hand floating up to begin to skim the back of his skull, checking the extent of his bald spot. "Leave your hair alone," his wife Anne frequently commands in the midst of their arguments. "It'll disappear soon enough without you fingering it all the time."

Duncan halts where the trail ends amid some scrubby young cottonwood. He can hear the burbling of the little creek that flows alongside the path—the water hardly more than a trickle, even now in late June—and a noisy motorcycle gunning past back on the highway. He interlaces his fingers over his stomach to keep his left hand under control. Waits to see if the couple will notice him.

Get the drop on them, Duncan orders himself. He steps forward. "This is private property."

The young people swing around, cow-like expressions pointed at him.

"Huh?" the male responds. His face begins closing down: a man trying to assess, Duncan thinks, whether the situation calls for bluster.

"This is private property. You are trespassing."

"Huh?" the male repeats. "What do you mean?" Stalling for time.
"We saw the sign." From the female. Defensive.

"Yeah. There's a 'For Sale' sign by the road. How are we supposed to buy something if we can't look at it." The male.

Duncan unleashes The Glare. The Glare is a courtroom technique he has perfected: an intense, disapproving stare. Reliably intimidating, he has decided. The trick is to hold your face, your eyes, directed at your opponent as if overcome by negative, censorious thoughts. And to hold it. Hold it longer than seems natural. Duncan finds The Glare especially useful during cross. But he's learned also to swivel around and direct The Glare at the section of the courtroom gallery where the supporters of the other side are seated. Perhaps while opposing counsel is summing up, or just before court convenes. The Glare lets the targets feel he has utter contempt for their wrong-headedness, for their misguided existence. The act seldom fails to discomfit those who have backed the other side. Which is also a service to the client, win or lose.

The clients get The Grin. The Glare and The Grin: the two sides of the coin of courtroom success. The Grin is reassuring, encouraging. It lets Duncan's client understand Duncan is in charge, in control. Useful in examination-in-chief, as he builds his case with his witnesses. After The Grin they are at ease with him; they are certain they are doing great.

Or, he employs The Grin when an opposing witness says something in cross Duncan needs to demolish. A statement he wants the judge to regard as incontestably wrong. Duncan will stop his flow of questions. Drop his pen on the notepad. Or his notes on the lectern. Give an exasperated sigh and head shake. He stalks across the courtroom and pauses in front of the client and the client's friends in the gallery. Silently counts three. Then gives them The Grin. They know he is on top of it. They know they are getting their money's worth. They realize the opposition does not have a chance. After that, Duncan strolls back to the hostile witness, who during this pause has to wait, nervous in the witness box. Duncan then slowly lifts and scans his notes. He is giving the witness time to doubt: "Gee, was what I said really that dumb?" Invariably, Duncan finds hostile witnesses more tractable after a dose of The Glare and The

Grin. He has planted the all-important seed of uncertainty. Planted it with the judge. Planted it with the other side. With the opposing lawyer, too.

Of course, any strategy can get shopworn. The technique has started to lose effectiveness with some colleagues, Duncan has to admit. But never with opposing witnesses. Never against a new lawyer locally, or one from out of town. As for the judges, Duncan has determined most are not bright enough to identify any specific courtroom methodology.

N v, on the riverbank, Duncan keeps his voice grim, strict. "If   d on this property without the owner's permission, you   the company of a real estate agent."

wner?" The male. Trying to sneer. *He sees me as aging,* *ht, balding,* Duncan guesses. He regrets he's wearing clothes, but reminds himself there was no time t   ething more intimidating to this sort of person.

 d been using the electric Weed Eater at the flower bed by the   ches in front. Anne had nagged him for more than a week to attend to the chore. He had slipped the ear protectors off to go search for more extension cord when he heard a vehicle door slam, and saw the oversized pickup on the highway shoulder and a couple disappearing down the trail. Immediately he had scolded himself for not having already put his plan into effect.

He fights the urge to smooth his left hand over his hair; instead, he points up the trail. "I'm a neighbour. I keep an eye on this property for the owner. I live across the road."

The middle sentence is not true, so the words have to be pronounced in a strongly declarative mode. Duncan is aware that an untruth forcefully spoken in the midst of truth is invariably convincing. The Strategic Sandwich is his name for the technique. Two firm facts bracketing a shakier one, or a white lie.

He takes another step toward the couple. "I'm also a lawyer. If you're present on this property without the owner's express permission, or unless accompanied by a real estate agent, you can be charged with trespassing. That's a *serious,* serious offense."

Fear on their faces. "We were just looking around," the female whines.

The male, though, starts to scowl. Duncan can almost see the poor devil's brain smoking in its attempt to produce an effective counter. Hostility about to surface. *Your goal is not to win popularity contests,* Duncan almost chants the phrase old Robinson drilled into him through Duncan's year of articling, the watchword that has sustained him through the decades of his own practice. *Your goal is to win cases. To win thereby not personal approval, but respect.*

Dislike, even hatred, is the natural response accorded a winner, Duncan has found. Loathing is a form of respect: no one hates a nobody. Besides, he reminds himself, he doesn't need to care what the losers who pass for lawyers around the Nelson courthouse think. Duncan was in the stacks at the courthouse law library last week when he overheard McFadden talking to his new articling student, Denise something, Denise Quan, about the other lawyers in town. Nice-looking Chinese girl, but too timid by far for trial work. "Then there's Duncan Locke," McFadden was telling her. "Dunc's middle name is 'Canyon.' Nobody knows why. He's not that deep."

Har har, old joke: Duncan has heard mockery about his middle name his whole life, thanks to his parents. Beatniks, ridiculous premature hippies, especially his mother. *No question I was the "Boy Named Sue" like in the song by Johnny Cash, where the father says he knew that with a name like that the son would either toughen up or get killed.* Except his parents thought the opposite: that if you gave your offspring a nonconformist name, your child would automatically be hip, cool, with it, non-aggressive. At least, as the eldest, Duncan has a conventional first name. His sister is Juniper Butte. *Poor Juni had to be "Butt" all through school; no wonder she weirded out. I tried to get her to emigrate here too, to start over. But she wouldn't.* Committed and discharged from the hospital in Albuquerque five times. During two marriages. Finally back living in Flagstaff.

And Duncan is aware the clerks in the court registry here refer to him as "Fraser": another hee-haw, referring to the Fraser Canyon, the old route of the Trans-Canada Highway west to Vancouver. "Fraser Canyon Locke" even showed up one day on the courthouse's daily roster of trials and lawyers. He raised hell with Arlene, the registrar. But nobody was disciplined. Arlene claimed she could not get anyone to admit responsibility for preparing that day's list.

Two or three times a year Duncan considers whether his middle name might be holding him back from elevation to the bench. At this point in his career, he should be a judge. He has weighed changing his middle name to Frederick. One of the senior partners in the firm in Vancouver where Duncan articled was named Frederick. That partner became a judge—first provincial court, later BC supreme court. Duncan envied the man's style: cordial enough, but also removed, austere. A natural aristocrat. Nobody ever called him Fred, either. *Mr. Justice Duncan Locke.* He envisions himself striding up onto the dais as the clerk drones out, "Order in court," and everybody stands. He can picture himself seated under the great carved coat of arms—lion and unicorn on either side of the shield and the knight's helmet above it—as his former adversaries have to bow and address him as "M'Lord."

But he realizes that long before he is raised to the bench they will be sniggering behind his back if he becomes Frederick. Everybody practicing in the Kootenays is asked to prepare legal name changes from Debbie to Seagull, or William to Star Seeker. Other people just start calling themselves Osprey or Sasquatch. Duncan will be viewed as one more failure pathetically attempting to retrofit a personality by adopting a different name.

"This is a beautiful piece of land," the female offers, attempting to smile ingratiatingly at Duncan. She's frightened, Duncan observes: a good result. *Keep your expression merciless, unforgiving.*

"Hey, if the owner wants to sell this property, how come he has you kick people off who might wanna buy it?" the male barks. Here's the expected chest-thumping, Duncan notes. He mentally shakes his head at the male's predictability, places a mark in the box of an imaginary checklist. On the other hand, Duncan concedes, the male's question in itself is not a bad one. Duncan raises his estimate of the male's intelligence a notch: up from slug to flatfish, he decides.

"I told you: if you attend on this property without the owner's permission or accompanied by a realtor, you're trespassing. That's the law." *Never retreat, never yield.*

The female tugs at the male's arm. "Guess we better go, hon?" She sighs. "Nice place. We can come back with an agent?" She starts to walk toward where Duncan waits at the entrance to the path.

The male remains rooted, gazing at Duncan through narrowed eyes. "We're within our rights to be here," he pronounces. "It says, 'For Sale.' This guy ain't the owner."

Defiance. Duncan's left hand twitches, but he subdues the urge. *Do nothing,* he instructs himself. *She'll handle him.*

The female is alongside Duncan now. She turns around.

"It's okay? Honey? We'll come another time?" She swivels to flash a tight smile at Duncan: a pleaser's appeal. Then back at her husband/boyfriend. "We're supposed to be at your mother's at four anyway. To pick up Connor?" An additional grimace shot toward Duncan. "We'll be late as it is." She steps around Duncan toward the trail.

The male lumbers into motion, angry look fixed on Duncan. *It is fine if you are not their favourite person,* he reminds himself. Duncan waits while the male steps around him, begins to follow the female along the path. By bringing up the rear, Duncan is escorting them off the property.

He recalls Lisa's advice, offered to him one afternoon during the past month when he had been complaining that at times he believes he is the most detested man in the West Kootenay. He had been accosted in the produce section at the Nelson Safeway by the plaintiff in a civil suit over a water line. Duncan's client owned a well near Six Mile that he no longer wanted to be the water source for a neighbour. The latter had no easement or anything in writing: a slam-dunk case. But during the plaintiff's spit-spraying harangue in the supermarket he had mentioned the names of several other losers Duncan had bested on behalf of clients in the past and insisted they all had nothing but contempt for Duncan. He had refused to be drawn in, and afterwards had torn a strip off the plaintiff's lawyer. *Rules are rules, and if your client chooses to get in the game he can't start attacking officers of the court once it looks like he's not going to win.* Duncan, despite himself, had been bothered by the plaintiff's vehemence, however. He thought briefly of mentioning something to the RCMP in Nelson, just in case.

Lisa put the incident in perspective. She has that way of insisting he open up about himself. His wife Anne never demands he talk about what he feels. Duncan finds Lisa's questions both scary and exhilarating. When she prods him relentlessly to reveal himself, she proves she *cares* about him, unlike his wife. Lisa can be a challenge, but she behaves as though she is truly fascinated by what makes him tick. For instance her reaction to his confession of being widely hated. Her eyes had inspected him in silence for a moment. Then her response, so unexpected: "Hey, get *into* it."

She is so damn *right*, Duncan had responded to himself. Why not *enjoy* the role? His mood of self-pity had vanished and he burst out laughing with relief. They had been up in her bedroom, propped by pillows leaning against the bed's headboard, sipping Lisa's favourite after-sex cooling-out drink: ice water with a slice of lemon. The more Duncan had considered her idea of how to deal with the inevitable consequence of his being a winner, the more pleased he felt. He put down his glass, bent across and kissed her about a hundred times all over her face. Her squeals and wriggles of protest got him hard again. His hand slipped into her open shirt and identified that her nipples had hardened, too. Lisa likes to wear an item of clothing—usually a shirt—when they make love; being partially clothed is more of a turn-on for her than nudity, she claims. On this occasion she purred, "Back off, buster. I've got an appointment in fifteen minutes." But Duncan could see her eyes shining with the fierce soft light he recognized by now as her signal of desire. About two seconds later they had both slid down horizontal in the bed, and he was inside her.

Sex with Anne is entirely different. Lisa is open about what she prefers, is demanding sometimes even in the heat of passion: "Faster; slower; not so rough." Yet she appears to genuinely enjoy the act. Anne mostly submits to sex; her climactic commentary is, "No, no, no," which to Duncan sums up her deepest attitude toward their once- or twice-a-month lovemaking.

Duncan began his affair with Lisa three months before when he was referred for physio. She is one of two physiotherapists he is aware of along Kootenay Lake's West Arm who have converted parts of their homes into clinics, the way other women on that stretch from Nelson to the ferry landing at Balfour operate hairdressing salons in their houses. Duncan had twisted his back forking a load of manure for Anne's gardens out of a neighbour's barn.

His doctor had suggested physio, and Duncan remembered he had processed Lisa's conveyancing when she bought her property not far from town four years ago. He had admired her energy when they spoke in his office; she was in her forties, and listed her status on the documents as divorced. A boyfriend didn't seem to be in the picture.

Duncan's admiration trebled at her clinic as she discussed his diagnosis, examined him and applied ultrasound. As far as Duncan can perceive, Lisa is happy with her job, with herself. Anne, on the other hand, qualifies as a lost soul, incapable of deciding what gives her pleasure in life or what does not. After twenty-eight years of marriage, she still is not sure who she is. She does occasional relief shifts at the Nelson museum, and has a potter's wheel she sometimes uses in a basement room he had built for her when she became interested in ceramics. But he regards her as a chronic complainer, upset most about the hours he puts in at his practice, even though these hours are what make their lifestyle possible. During their frequent disagreements, often initiated by some comment of hers about how little time he devotes to being at home, he urges her to discover some occupation or activity that she finds meaningful.

Lisa is the exact opposite: she delights in each aspect of being alive, sex not the least of these. At her clinic she often wears revealing tops: Duncan found her cleavage almost unbearably tantalizing before they started adding a sexual dimension to their weekly medical trysts. He considered it odd at the beginning that she wanted her deeply cut lace brassiere off but her shirt left on as they tussled upstairs on her double bed. Yet her appetite for sex was such that he quickly adjusted to her whims. The first time she took him by mouth, he tried to stop her before he came because Anne intensely dislikes that experience. Lisa lifted her face up from what she was doing, grinned, shifted over to kiss him, then went back to her task.

Lisa is not Duncan's first affair. He once calculated his success rate as one such episode, usually short-lived, every three years. A client, a friendly witness, a museum colleague of Anne's. He may have put on a little weight, but he is aware his professional success, financial status, boyish looks and sandy hair are definitely a combination women find appealing.

During the days he does not see Lisa, far too often he imagines being with her. The relationship is new, he reasons, so no surprise that he regards Lisa at present as overwhelmingly attractive. He has postponed thinking about whether his excitement at being around her means he wants his marriage to terminate. *Whatever happens, enjoy your time with Lisa,* he tells himself. *You've earned it.*

When the couple and Duncan reach the road, Duncan notes that the absurdly huge pickup is new. Vehicle loan, he calculates, maybe a mortgage, looking for land to put a house or trailer on. Likely the couple owe as well on a snowmobile and power boat, perhaps an ATV, too. They must have relatively good-paying jobs, or at least the male does: telephone company or Nelson City or a journeyman of some sort at Kalesnikoff's sawmill or in the Teck smelter down at Trail.

"Sorry we looked around without permission," the female states, a little breathlessly, from where she has paused by the passenger door. "You wouldn't happen to know what the owner wants for it, do you?"

The male is leaning on the hood beside her. Duncan fields an inquiring look from him also. Time to shift gears, he resolves.

"If *you* owned this property," Duncan says, his voice now a pleasant *I'm-on-your-side,* "you'd *want* me to find out who was wandering around on it when you were absent." He produces The Grin, then names a figure he guesses is more than they can afford, but not so large as to be out of the question. He can see the recoil in their eyes.

If they check with the real estate outfit, Duncan cautions himself, they'll discover the number is much lower. *Cover yourself.* "I could be wrong. That's what I heard."

He decides to launch The Downer: you introduce, then attach, a negative aura to your opponent's idea or position. "You folks aiming to build? If you acquire some property, I mean?"

"Yep," from the male.

"I probably shouldn't tell you this," Duncan begins. Drops his voice to indicate a confidence. "You seem nice folks, though." Stern again: "Of course you shouldn't be on anybody's land without permission." Shifts to The Grin. Then a pause, as if wrestling with conscience. He wrinkles his forehead worriedly: should he betray the owner? Face smooths: decision made in their favour. Leans closer toward them. "At least two previous buyers have been burned by this property."

"Why?" "What is it?" The male and the female in unison. Hook, line and now the sinker.

"Flood plain. You aren't allowed to build here. Folks buy this land, get their house plans together, go the district office for their building permit. *Bam*: permit refused."

More recoil evident. The male initially disbelieving, of course, but the concept percolating in. "Flood plain?"

"What's a flood plain, hon?" The female.

"Government says certain areas are unsafe to construct on. The property might flood every hundred years." Stupid young males, ever a font of practical knowledge: Duncan checks off another square on his phantom checklist.

"Oh. I guess that settles it." The eternally trustful little woman.

"Maybe. Don't look to me like that creek could flood. We're about at the end of the June rise, and look at it: I've seen horses piss more than that. And there's no sign the river ever flooded along here."

"It's been declared flood plain," Duncan responds, his voice cheery. *Don't allow them to associate the negative aura with yourself.* "At least, as far as I know. Still, it's a good piece of land. If you buy it, you can come up summers and camp on it. You have kids? Your kids will love it. Or you could hold the property for investment. Land prices in the valley are only going to rise."

"Not if you can't build." The male: a genius.

"You're right about that," Duncan almost purrs. "But it *is* waterfront. Great holiday spot. Cool out by the river."

A snort of derision from the male. *Let them have their imagined victory, no matter how tiny, in defeat.*

I need to get my plan in gear fast, Duncan thinks. Anne asks him why he doesn't simply buy the land if he wants to keep their privacy. And he does want to, and more: having their own beach has been a real plus, especially since they didn't have to pay for it. He recalls several memorable picnics at the gravel beach with friends, and even with just Anne and him. Someone building on this property—cutting a driveway in, then clearing a site and constructing a house—would amount to a definite reduction in their quality of life: more people around, more traffic and more noise, and especially losing their personal beach.

Yet they knew some day old Ernie would try to sell his place. Duncan has assured Anne he can chase off anybody interested in purchasing it, which is infinitely cheaper than handing Ernie the bag of gold he insists his crummy acre and a half is worth. But, Duncan muses, the male here is capable—remotely—of blundering into the land title office or district office and asking a few too many questions.

Duncan devised his strategy three weeks ago, the moment Ernie's "For Sale" sign appeared across the highway. Events could not have been more fortuitous. Duncan has been smoothing over Peter Geddes's indiscretions. Geddes and three of the other boys in the district planning office were gambling online on their work computers during office hours, particularly on Geddes's computer. Some site where you could bet on horse races, and NFL games. Not only was that activity not too bright. An audit revealed that Geddes had been dipping into district funds to place some of the bets. Incredibly dumb. Geddes so far had always restored the funds on payday, but no question this was breach of trust.

When the auditor notified the Mounties, Geddes denied everything, but eventually hired Duncan. The deal Duncan has proposed is early retirement for Peter—not quite a golden handshake, but not dismissal either—and letters of reprimand for the rest. Everybody but Peter to undergo counselling for gambling addiction. The arrangement saves expense and embarrassment for all parties. He nearly has the district and the union and the Crown convinced. Almost, but not quite. So Geddes and the others are still vulnerable. Geddes will owe him big, too, when everybody signs off on the deal.

Duncan's plan is to breathe in Peter's ear a simple request, achievable before he's officially out of there. But until today, nobody has showed up to gawk at the land. Possibly it's a slow year for real estate, Duncan decides. Or, the "For Sale" sign has drawn fewer looky-loos because this property borders the highway, rather than being on a more peaceful side road.

Geddes couldn't care less, Duncan is sure, if another riverside lot is flagged as flood-prone, unsafe for habitation. Duncan can offer to discount his bill by 10 percent as a token of appreciation. *Get on the phone the instant young Mr. Macho and his consort depart,* Duncan admonishes himself. *This should have been nailed down tight the day Ernie listed the property.*

In a sense, the whole exercise will be doing the district a favour, Duncan reasons. The less people who live right on the river, the less chance of sewage pollution, not to mention shoreline degradation due to tree removal for building sites.

Duncan knows from case law that flood plain designations are pretty arbitrary. A partner he'd had for a few years in the nineties had represented a property owner suing the district for not having so designated his land, and also a couple suing because their land *was* so designated. Testimony in both disputes showed that the engineers' calculations can be based on rather far-fetched predictions. Not that Ernie would sue: the old man is too much of a penny pincher, Duncan is certain, to do anything but complain.

Duncan has revealed his scheme to both Anne and Lisa. Anne had shaken her head. "Do whatever you want to," she had said. "But I still don't understand why we don't just buy the property. You've got the money." He started to explain again but she had cut him off: "I don't want to hear it."

Lisa, characteristically, had laughed when he outlined his strategy. "You're a clever rascal, Mr. Locke," she had said, her eyes twinkling. "I hope you don't outsmart yourself. Flood plain," she chuckled, as if she admired the audacity of his idea.

"We better get going. Hey, man, thanks for the tip." The male's voice is difficult for Duncan to read—he's unsure if the male is convinced. *That call to Peter Geddes is overdue regardless,* Duncan lectures himself. *It may be Saturday but you have his home number.*

"Perhaps we'll see you again," the female says, opening the truck door.

"Nice meeting you two," Duncan uses a sincere tone. "Look me up if you need a lawyer. My office handles property conveyancing. Name is Duncan Locke. I'd give you my card, but I don't have any on me. I'm in the Nelson phone book, though, under 'Lawyers': Locke with an 'e.'" *Stick out your hand to the male.*

"An 'e'?"

What a halfwit. "L-o-c-k-e: Locke."

An arm reaches toward his hand. "Don Barsotti. We'll keep you in mind."

Shake on it, sucker. The pickup's tires spin gravel as it lurches from the shoulder onto the road. Duncan watches the vehicle disappear.

Why did I fail to contact Geddes the same afternoon the sign was posted? Duncan chastises himself as he climbs his driveway. A good lawyer, he knows, cannot be reluctant to make such phone calls. He initiates calls like this constantly, ones that make happen what he wants to happen. To neglect to place even one such call, he reminds himself, is to fumble, is the road to disaster.

Duncan recognizes he has long had a twinge of aversion to using the phone, a failing that he has worked fiercely to overcome. He prefers to observe in person the reaction to what he's saying, which lets him in turn fine-tune his response. Or is the Peter Geddes business particularly difficult, he wonders, because he has a stake in the outcome? He can imagine Geddes refusing, claiming he doesn't want to get into more trouble if anyone finds out. Duncan knows he needs to have his rebuttals ready for that. Worst-case scenario, however, like Anne says he can easily pay Ernie. But why, if there is a more cost-effective way?

He reviews other calls he dreads: phoning his parents, for example. Yet despite the distaste he experiences as he dials their apartment in Phoenix, and his relief when he finally hangs up, he does place the call. His parents complain that Juniper never phones. Duncan isn't surprised. But tough phone calls are one means by which he earns his money. They helped get him where he is.

Duncan removes his gardening shoes at the front door of the house, and passes through the cool rooms to his study. He sits at his desk. Anne is off somewhere—a summer school pottery class? He is grateful that she won't have witnessed the couple's arrival and him charging off after them. Anne can put two and two together, sometimes. His left hand lifts to allow his fingers to inspect the boundaries of the bare patch at the rear of his skull.

Not that he or Juni *owe* their parents any calls, Duncan reflects. Neither their mother nor father was over-endowed with parenting skills. Duncan remembers coming down to breakfast one morning and his mother starting in on him again at the table about his demeanour. He was fourteen. She had just announced that as a special treat the whole family was going to attend a concert that night by some pathetic folksinger. He was pouring cereal when she leaped up, strode around the table and grabbed him by both ears. She started jerking his head from side to side, left to right to left. "Why ...(yank)...can't...(yank)...you *ever*...(yank)...look...(yank)... *happy*?" His sister gaped bug-eyed, open-mouthed, across the table. His father was not yet out of bed.

Small wonder he wasn't interested in having children, as he had told Anne years before. What if, despite his best intentions, he inflicted that sort of disrespect on their kids?

Duncan pulls the Geddes files from his attaché case, finds the home contact information. He catches himself tracing the outline of the hairless area on his head, picks up the phone and punches the numbers. "Is Peter there?"

Many Rivers

PURDUE WASN'T A big man. But he was stocky, squat and held his arms bent at the elbows when they weren't doing anything, as if he was a weightlifter. So I always thought of him as powerful. He projected a no-bullshit, don't-fuck-with-me attitude. Besides a little pointy beard, he had slicked-back hair, and a thin gold chain around his neck. Pictures of Bob Marley were tacked up in his rooms behind the store, and usually heavy reggae fusion was pounding through his speakers. Or old songs like Jimmy Cliff's plaintive "Many Rivers to Cross":

> *Many rivers to cross*
> *But I can't seem to find*
> *My way over.*

I guess Purdue had been to Jamaica at some point; when we were all sitting around on his back deck getting loaded, he'd break into his version of Rasta talk: "mon" this and "mon" that; joints were always "spliffs." "I and I be living in Babylon," he'd say, if Danny was relating how Kootcheroff's grow op was raided by the Mounties, or when Frog was busted that time in the bar at Slocan. "Babylon." The rest of the time Purdue talked with a hint of a southern US drawl. If a woman came into his store, which wasn't often, he was always going, "Ma'am": "Jackets are over here, ma'am."

I was first aware he was around in March, a couple of months before Danny dropped out of school. Purdue's place was on a narrow piece of land between the highway and the Slocan River. The building is post-and-beam, with vertical plank siding. It had been a restaurant for years, then sat empty, then somebody converted it to a house, then a couple of years later it was empty again. I was riding the school bus with Danny when we passed the spot and he started talking about the guy who had recently bought the property. I've lived here most of my life, so since I finished Grade 6 at Winlaw Elementary, I've ridden that boring bus to the junction, where Mount Sentinel high school is, every day of the school year—fall, winter and spring. All that changes about the ride, except for the view and new kids on the bus each September, are the tunes I'm playing through my earbuds.

To be honest, I thought the place's new signs that Danny pointed out were lame: they were hand-painted, crude looking. "Ain't trying to be slick," I heard Purdue tell a customer once when the shopper made some comment about the signs. "We need to prepare ourselves, and we're running late. There's no time for nicey-nicey."

Just north of the building is a small open area, originally the restaurant's parking lot, and along the edge closest to the river a half-size billboard proclaimed in unevenly spaced letters: *PEOPLE GET READY*. And underneath in smaller print: *Hi-tek tools for protekting home, family and busness. Guns, camo, knifes, dried food, more.*

One night around the time I started going to Purdue's, Danny and Frog and I were over there and Danny asked Purdue what his sign *meant* by "get ready" and also what some of the gear in his store—army surplus dried rations, fishing reels, axes—had to do with guarding your crop, which is what we figured he meant by protecting your business. "Men," Purdue said in his slow drawl, "I don't know how tuned in you are to what's going down. But times are coming that will be a trial. Each and every one of us must be prepared to defend what's ours, our way of life. To do that, we must each prepare first of all to survive, to fight for our survival. And win."

"Fight who? Fight *what*? That sounds like a lot of bullshit," Frog challenged. Even then he was prickly around Purdue, though almost every time I was at the store Frog was present.

Purdue's voice kept the same slow, measured pace. "Just because you don't see something, my man, doesn't mean it ain't real. That's one of the first things they teach you in the Special Forces." By now Purdue had let it be known to us, sort of indirectly, that he was a US Army veteran, which was why he was so knowledgeable about firearms. "There's a war coming: a big one, the biggest."

"You mean, like, against the Muslims?" I asked him. War seemed very remote from the scene visible from where we sat on his deck overlooking the river, getting wasted. The nearly full moon shone down on the water, on the forest of firs and pines covering Perry Ridge across the horizon to the west, and on the new leaves of the cottonwoods and aspen closer to us along both sides of the bend of the river. The sound of the water chuckling past Purdue's was about the only noise, except for an occasional barking dog somewhere in the valley, or a huge chip truck or smaller vehicle passing by every so often on the highway on the other side of the house.

Purdue took a hit from the joint that was going around. "A-rabs? Could be."

"You think the Arabs are going to invade?" scoffed Frog. "I fucking doubt it."

"Don't know whether the A-rabs will be involved," Purdue said, unruffled as ever. "But I do know it's going to involve the niggers. Race war, boys, race war. That's what's coming, and that's what you need to, we all need to, prepare for."

"You got pictures of Bob Marley up," Frog noted. "Why would you do that, if you think black people are going to attack us?"

Purdue shook his head, as though Frog's outburst revealed some sad shortcoming in his character. "Know your enemy. Never heard that before? Simple common sense. If I know how my enemy thinks, I can be certain how he'll respond to any situation. And if I know how he's going to respond, I've got the fucker exactly where I want him."

On the bus that first day when Danny drew my attention to Purdue's, Danny mentioned his dad had already visited the store, which had opened on the weekend. Danny's dad said the shop stocked mainly hunting and fishing stuff. I had to admit a new store selling such gear was strange, since less and less people hunt every fall, which accounts for why the deer are taking over everybody's gardens. And fishing is banned in the river, although you *are* allowed to fish in Slocan Lake, or Kootenay Lake north of Nelson, or the Arrow Lakes to the west, plus all the alpine lakes in the high country that Fisheries stocks with trout each year. Yet why open a sporting goods store in the middle of nowhere, sixty klicks west of Nelson? Danny said his dad had the same question. His dad is vice-president of the Riverkeepers, who are trying to bring back the salmon that used to spawn in the Slocan River before the dams were built on the Columbia. He came and talked to our Grade 10 ecology class about it last year. We had to write a report on what he said.

The weirdest thing about the store, according to Danny's dad, was that a supposed outdoors store right on the river didn't stock tubes. Tubing is a big deal hereabouts in summer—you can jump in at the Perry Siding bridge and float all the way down to Crescent Valley, where the Slocan River meets the Kootenay River several kilometres upstream from where it flows into the Columbia. Of course, that float on the Slocan would take you all day and even on a hot August afternoon your ass would be solid ice by the time you arrived—the river is glacier fed. But some people don't seem to mind a numb butt.

Danny's father was a real hippie, which meant Danny and I were lumped together at the Winlaw school. His dad was arrested at two different logging blockades that I know of. The school was split between logger kids and hippie kids, and there was pushing and an occasional punch-out between members of the two groups about once a month. Lots of petty shit, too—flat tires on your bike, or your lunch or gym strip stolen, books scribbled on, anything they could get away with. Danny was the one who the first week of school explained to me what the two sides were, and which I belonged to.

Later on, in junior high at Mount Sentinel, the logger kids realized there were differences between tree-hugging hippies and dope-growing hippies. My dad and his friends just sat around our house all day high, and would never get excited about clear-cuts unless their crop was threatened. Most of the grow shows are indoors now, anyway—refurbished chicken coops or greenhouses or basements or rented houses. The Mounties are airborne too much—choppers patrol the valley, especially in fall, even using heat sensors to spot if some deserted cabin is warmer than it should be. They also have spectrometers calibrated to pick out the exact shade of green in the woods that indicates pot plants. Plus it's a lot harder to guard a crop out in the forest than in a building you can lock and alarm.

By junior high, a lot of the logger kids were into dope, so suddenly the hippie growers weren't so bad, which meant some of us kids were off the hook. My mom was more like Danny's dad: out there protesting if watersheds were being threatened or some other environmental issue was getting people in the valley excited. When she and my dad split up and she moved to Passmore, though, she grew a patch. Mainly for her own use, I think. I stayed with my dad—it seemed too much of a hassle to relocate down the valley with my mom, and my dad left me alone mostly, whereas my mom was always on my case. My dad's girlfriend was into shrooms and coke more than he ever was, so she was usually too out of it to say more than "hi" when I got back from school or whenever I came out of my room. She and my dad, being loaded most of the day, weren't particularly interested whether I was home or not, so much of the time I could come and go without it being a big deal. Unlike if I spent a weekend at my mom's.

When the logger kids suddenly wanted drugs, a few of us went from zero to hero in their eyes. That's how I got to be friends with Frog, whose dad was a faller for years before he got mangled in some accident and took up driving logging truck. I guess I always admired Frog for how he had the confidence to get in the face of teachers or older kids or anybody he thought was acting dumb. Of course he could take his attitude too far. Once in Grade 6 he was suspended by the principal for a couple of days for mouthing off in class to Ms. Cribbs, when she was loading us up with homework right before Hallowe'en. Next morning he rode his bike to school and spent a couple of hours fooling around on it in the parking lot in plain view of the rest of us confined inside, which pissed off the principal even more. But I thought what Frog did was cool.

Frog's family are real old valley people—when one teacher we had did a unit on local history, she was all goo-goo over some photos Frog brought in of his great-grandparents. They had one of the first homesteads, according to Froggie: a dairy farm around

Perry Siding. Later they ran a store in Silverton. But from the pictures and what Frog told the class at Miss Hamilton's urging they did a little of everything to get by—logging, road building, running a small sawmill, hunting, even operating a mine. Everything except grow weed, which I guess hadn't been invented then. Danny told me once that grass was legal in Canada until the 1930s, but I don't know if I believe that.

Since I was friends with Danny, that's how Frog and he started to run together. Plus when Danny's dad and mom got divorced, Danny's dad went out with Frog's mom's sister for a while, which pissed off Frog's dad no end, according to Froggie. So Danny and Frog were practically related while that lasted, which was only six months. But the three of us were hanging together by Grade 8, and stayed tight after that, even when Frog quit school the year before Danny did. He had slowly adopted more and more of the goth look, so by the time he met Purdue he was always dressed in black, usually wearing one of his Deth MakR shirts, with several ear-piercings and a ring in his lip, too.

Frog was the reason we ended up chilling at Purdue's on a regular basis. When we were almost done with Grade 10 last May, Frog's parents split up. He started to have even more attitude than usual, and soon school was "totally dumb" and "a waste of time." Which amounts to "duh," as far as I'm concerned. But you finish what you start, as my mom says; also, you need high school if you want a life outside this valley. Frog's mom moved to New Denver to a nursing job and he went with her, which meant he'd have to do his last two years there at Lucerne School, since of course there's no bus from New Denver all the way to Mount Sentinel. So he said fuck it. We still saw lots of him: after he got his licence his dad helped him buy a little shitbox white Honda, complete with spoiler. You could hear him coming several klicks away, because among other things it needed a new muffler. He worked for a while at the dryland log sort at Rosebery, but after it shut down he seemed to be mainly dealing. He was having coffee at Who Needs Sleep here in Winlaw one morning when somebody introduced Purdue to him as a potential customer for weed. Turned out Purdue didn't mind people he knew hanging at his place, and after a while Frog was over there regularly. Purdue was generous with his smoke, not that getting hold of pot was any problem for Froggie. Once in a while Purdue offered us lines, though never crack, which he referred to a few times as "nigger junk."

One Friday night in late March, Frog and me had been having some brewskis over at Danny's—his mom and her boyfriend had gone on a road trip to Spokane—and Frog suggested we all drop over to Purdue's. No parties were going on in the valley that we knew of, and nobody felt like driving all the way into Nelson to hang. So I figured, why not? I was curious about the place. I'd heard my dad and his friends saying the guy who owned it was trouble, plus I'd overheard a couple of my teachers clucking their tongues about this new survivalist store in Winlaw, which I figured must mean People Get Ready. I vaguely knew Froggie had met the owner, and the whole deal about Purdue and his store seemed enticing: dark and edgy. We had gotten into that frame of mind that if there was something that our parents didn't approve of, like the Walmart in Nelson or the new trash-hop rapper, Jugularz, whose concerts were getting shut down in the States by the cops, it was probably awesome.

Frog led us to a door off the parking lot that bypassed the store area and opened directly into the living quarters behind. Purdue answered Frog's knock. "My man," he said. We followed Purdue through the darkened living room, then the kitchen, which opened onto the deck. Some cane seats with cushions, a recliner and a couple of beat-up side tables were scattered down the deck; later in the spring Purdue also stacked a few folding patio chairs out there. That night, two young guys I'd never seen before were in the cane chairs. Since evenings are chilly in March, after Purdue hauled a couple of kitchen chairs out to the deck, we sat around in our jackets and had a few tokes. The guys with Purdue were from Castlegar. I don't know how Purdue knew them, and I never saw them again.

But we went back lots of times. Purdue always had interesting things to say, though I generally tuned out when he started telling us about the world war against black people that was around the corner. Not that he brought that up too often. But I could see he didn't like to be contradicted on the subject. "It's a free country," he cut off this other guy from our class, Paul, who was at Purdue's one time, when Paul started to argue with Purdue about the race war. "And I don't even hate nigger-lovers," Purdue said. "Hate makes you stupid, and in any conflict you can't afford to be stupid. I'll defend to the death your right to spout your uninformed and ignorant views. But when the shooting starts, if I even sense you're a race traitor, I'll kill you, man."

I'd heard threats like that from my dad's friends when they were all excited about this guy or that who they decided had ripped them off or had tipped the Mounties about somebody's grow op. Once this friend of my dad, Wheelie, was sitting at our kitchen table fucked up on something when I came out of my room to get some juice from the fridge. My dad was off someplace. Wheelie starts this paranoid rap about how if I ever brought the cops down on his or my dad's grow show I was as good as dead, so I should always watch what I said whenever I was speaking to anybody, because my life was on the line. I just ignored him. Nothing ever came of that talk, and I put Purdue into the same category when he was holding forth about the war.

Still, I'd never met anyone like Purdue. I was flattered that he took an interest in me and my classmates. The impression I had most of the time from my parents, their friends and other adults I met was that we were at best a minor irritation, and at worst an annoying interruption in the oh-so-important stuff they had to do each day.

After a while I would drop by Purdue's myself if I felt like it. Purdue knew all kinds of cool details about the ancient Mayan and Egyptian civilizations, and especially knowledge and technologies that we haven't caught up to yet. He could talk for quite a while about the Rastafarians, and explain what dozens of their words meant, and even how their vocabulary originated. Although I didn't swallow everything he hinted about his background, he really did seem to have been on some hairy missions for the American army, unlike my dad's friends who, despite all their tough talk, had never done anything as far as I could tell but grow dope and sit on their asses.

Purdue wouldn't reveal exactly where he had been dropped or set ashore, but it could have been Iraq or Afghanistan or Iran or even Russia. I was convinced when he said he'd killed people, since his voice was different—lower—than when he was bragging about having been an Olympic-level 440 racer and hurdler right after high school. Or about his feats on an NBA farm team somewhere in the South after he graduated, which I found particularly hard to accept given how short he was.

I have to say he seemed to show a special interest in me. Maybe because whenever I thought he was bullshitting I kept my thoughts to myself and didn't call him on it, the way the other guys did from time to time. I figure if you're over at somebody's house, drinking their beer, eating their munchies and smoking their dope, you don't dis them to their face. Plus Purdue and I shared a fascination with classic Star Wars, which everybody else thought was lame. He and I agreed the most awesome device in all the movies was the AT-AT, the huge elephant-like All Terrain Armored Transport machine that stomped relentlessly forward, step after step, to attack. One night out on the deck we were doing "if you could be any animal, what would it be?" Paul, who is one of those ghetto wannabes who wears a toque and hoodie winter and summer, had brought along his then-girlfriend Judy, who was also in our year at Mount Sentinel. Having a chick on the deck was unusual. Girls didn't seem to relate to Purdue so they were rarely over there. I remember when Danny began dating Rebecca, who I thought was cool-looking myself, she only went with us to Purdue's once. She told Danny she thought Purdue was totally nuts.

The night we did the animal game I said I'd choose to be Chewbacca, or another Wookiee. Purdue couldn't get over how that was going to be his answer, too. "We be Wookiee brothers-in-arms, mon," he repeated a few times, in his Rasta mode. We did the homie handshake on that one. When Purdue learned in May that Danny was quitting school to go tree planting, Purdue went on and on about how there was enough uneducated white trash already, and that white kids should get as much education as they could as long as they weren't brainwashed in the process by teachers who are liberal one-world race traitors. "Education, true education, is the path to power," he said. "Quitting to make money is just short-term gain for long-term pain. You and Frog should take a lesson from Evan here, and tough it out. I wouldn't understand half how the world works if I'd been like my brothers and sisters and never finished high school. I'd be glued to the TV set like them, believing whatever the powers that be tell them. It's pathetic."

One Thursday night in the first week of June just me and this older guy Rodney, from Nakusp, were at Purdue's. Rodney was a carpenter who'd just returned home from making big money in the oil patch at Fort Mac, so was driving a new white Chev dually with Alberta plates. His arms were muscular like Purdue's, and he wore a small earring in each ear plus a necklace of big wooden beads. His ball cap read: *What are you looking at, asshole?*

I had a socials quiz the next day, but my dad and his girlfriend were having some sort of party, so I couldn't study at our place. I borrowed my Dad's beat-up Nissan pickup, and drove to Who Needs Sleep for a coffee and looked at my notes and my textbook there for a while. When I figured I was as prepared as I'd ever be, I headed over to Purdue's, since I knew I wouldn't be able to crash at home until things wound down about two in the morning. Purdue had a brand-new chainsaw he had brought onto the deck to show Rodney. The two of them were planning to drop some trees on Rodney's acreage and start getting their winter wood. They began talking about a visit by the cops that day to Purdue's, supposedly to alert him that somebody had broken into a sporting goods store in Castlegar back in March just before People Get Ready opened. The thief or thieves had driven off with a big haul. The horsemen also said they were there to check that Purdue was following all the rules for display and storage of the rifles he had for sale.

"It was a fishing expedition," Purdue declared. "You could see their beady eyes shifting all around searching for anything they could nail me for. They didn't have a warrant so they knew they couldn't demand invoices to prove my wares aren't stolen property."

Rodney drained a beer. "I hope you stayed cool."

Purdue grinned. "I be a serious threat to the status quo, de bald heads, mon. You bet I ain't going to give them any excuse to shut me down."

"Any more of these?" Rodney waved his empty can.

"In the fridge. But let me show you what they *didn't* see." Purdue heaved himself out of his chair. "I wouldn't let anybody else in on this, but I know you and Evan can be trusted." He winked in my direction.

We followed Purdue through the kitchen and living area to the small bathroom. We hung back at the bathroom doorway, while Purdue bent and reached up under the sink. The basin was set into a wooden countertop, and a foot of panelling descended from the counter edge to enclose the sink.

Purdue's arm disappeared under the front panel, and a moment later withdrew clutching a pistol. Rodney whistled. Purdue pushed a button and a clip slid out of the weapon's handle. He passed the emptied gun to Rodney. "Feast your eyes on this baby."

Rodney took the weapon. "How did you get—?"

"Mon, for me to know. De downpression of de govmint be every mon's duty to oppose. Dat right to bear arms be a basic human right. Get up, stand up. You Canadians should get wid de program."

When Rodney finished examining the pistol and passed it to me, I was surprised at how heavy it felt. The gun smelled strongly of oil. I handed it back to Purdue, who reinserted the clip and returned the pistol to its hiding place.

"De govmint can seize all de shootin' sticks in de front of me store," he said, "and I still can defend myself, take care of business. Call me Johnny Too-Bad." He winked at me again.

A week later I was over at People Get Ready on Friday night waiting for Frog to finish work at the store. Purdue had recently hired Frog part-time, despite Frog's attitude. Frequently the two would end up shouting at each other in the midst of some dispute about Iraq War deserters in Canada, or what was going to happen to our area now that so many sawmills had closed because of the US housing collapse. Yet a day or two later you'd hear Frog arguing with another of our friends and taking Purdue's side. Maybe Purdue knew that. Or maybe he hired Frog because of Froggie's bust in the Slocan Inn bar. Possession of herb for the purposes of trafficking wasn't a big deal in the Kootenays: usually a couple hundred dollars fine and suspended sentence—probation, in effect. Even growers ordinarily were just dinged a grand or less, except that their crop and equipment was confiscated: expensive, if you were into hydroponics. In both cases, though, you had a record afterwards. Plus, officially, you could do jail time even for possession; and hiring a decent defense lawyer cost big bucks. We all knew that Frog burned through money as fast as he got any.

Purdue had started keeping the store open Friday nights until nine, but nobody was in the aisles this particular evening. I wandered around, looking at the racks and shelves of gear. Displayed over by the scopes, shooting stands and rifle bipods were these cool new camo T-shirts with the phrase "People Get Ready" across the front. I'd found one in my size, and was up at the counter where Frog was stationed showing it to him and telling him how I thought this would blow them away at school.

"They're phat," Frog agreed. "Why don't you buy one?"

I was tempted, but the tag read $29.95. I could score spending money whenever my dad was flush and in a good mood and his girlfriend wasn't in the room. But I never knew how far what was in my pockets would have to stretch. My mom told me I was supposed to have a regular allowance, so much a week, but I could see that wouldn't fly. My dad alternated between having lots of cash and being flat broke, depending on crop sales, whether his girlfriend demanded he buy her clothes or one of the "cute" stuffed animals that had begun to spread out of their bedroom into the rest of the house, or whether something major needed to be fixed on the pickup again or he needed a new lamp or something for his grow setup in our barn.

I had recently pried a fifty dollar bill from him, which the T-shirt would obviously eat most of. I explained this to Froggie, and was about to return the shirt to the rack.

"Let him have it," Purdue's voice came from the direction of the knife case, where he was arranging new stock that he'd acquired from a Slocan Park guy who fashions incredible blades out of scraps of sheet metal.

"Huh?" Frog said.

"All you have to do is wear it to school. Advertising for me," Purdue said.

"I couldn't just take it," I protested.

"I'm telling you: it's yours. I'm sure some of the little bastards in your class are rolling in dough, and they might as well spend it here. Spread de word, mon."

I was wearing it a month later the night I went over to see Danny when he was home from tree planting for a few days. School was out for the year, and I had a week's work as a labourer on a crew repairing the irrigation system at the Valley View Golf Course. One of my dad's regular customers was on Valley View's board of directors. I thought golf sucked, but a job's a job.

When Danny opened his door and saw the shirt, he made a face. "You know your Purdue is a real asshole," he said.

"Yeah? How so?"

Danny didn't answer as he set us up with a couple of beers, which we took into his backyard. Nobody else was home, and the mosquitoes weren't bad yet in the part of the valley where his mom lived.

"He and my mom have been getting it on," Danny said as we sat down in a couple of lawn chairs.

I was stunned. I flashed on how Purdue never mentioned women, other than to curse an ex-wife, the way my dad and his friends did routinely. I guess I had figured, though I hadn't given it much thought, that the store and his other interests were all-consuming.

"What about Robert?" I asked, referring to Danny's mom's boyfriend.

"That's where it gets icky. While I've been gone, the three of them have started to party together, and I guess it's all okay with Robert."

I was aware that the valley was a small place, and that the various circles within it overlapped and interacted. Both my parents repeated stories to their friends of unlikely couples, and of the twists and turns these people underwent before finally separating. I also remembered plenty of occasions on which gossip my parents had related in front of me was outright denied or argued against by their friends. Certainly at school, rumours about couples among our classmates proved false more often than true. "Did your mom tell you this? Or Robert?"

"Eileen."

Eileen was a close friend of Danny's girlfriend Rebecca. "Hey," I managed, "are you still, like, seeing Rebecca?"

"Yeah, guess so. She's in Quebec for five weeks taking a French immersion course."

"How did Eileen find out?"

"She's Robert's niece."

"I didn't know that." I was familiar with how, since the 1960s, valley counterculture types had incessantly hooked up, had kids, separated and gotten together with other people. Even in elementary school, we would compare notes as to who was related to who by what arrangement—whether past or present, and no matter how temporary—as with Danny and Frog's sudden connection through Danny's dad dating Frog's aunt. The endless rearrangements of valley couples I had heard referred to by my mom and her women friends as the Slocan Shuffle.

Danny offered me a cigarette, although before he went tree planting he hadn't smoked tobacco. I waved off the invitation.

"Eileen joined our crew when we were planting up in the Lardeau," Danny said, blowing smoke from his nose. "She said her mom told her my mom is doing both of them."

"No way," I said.

"Apparently it's cool with everybody. But Eileen said Purdue was trying to talk my mom into convincing Robert to join in the fun."

"You mean—" my mind was reeling, "—a three-way? Like, Purdue's *gay*?"

"Maybe AC/DC, if not entirely a fag."

"I don't know if I believe that," I said. "People in this fucking valley are always making up stories. Anyway, how would Eileen know all this?"

"I told you: her mom is Robert's sister."

"Robert blabs to his *sister* about his kinky sex life? And she tells her daughter?"

Danny shrugged. "*I* believe it. Why would Eileen's mom make up a story that made her own brother look bad?"

"I don't know. I don't have a sister."

"Neither do I. Rebecca didn't like Purdue that time we were over. She thought he was a phony, all full of himself. Have you been hanging there a lot?"

"Some. Have you asked *your* mom about this?"

Danny dropped his butt into his empty bottle. "Sure thing. Would you ask your mom: 'Say, mom, is it true you're doing two different guys at once?' Anyway, I trust Eileen. Your Purdue is a fucking faggot, as far as I'm concerned."

I took a closer look at Purdue when I was next over at his place, yet I couldn't see anything that made him out to be a homo. And once the job at the golf course finished, I ended up spending more time over there. I was scouting around trying to find summer work other than trimming plants for my dad or his buddies—slave labour, more or less. But real paying jobs were scarce in the valley, as always. I found being at home all day depressing: my dad had a list of chores around the place he'd be after me to do, if he wasn't bugging me about looking harder for some kind of employment.

That's why I was at Purdue's on this Wednesday after lunch in late July, chilling on the deck while I gazed out at the river. Occasionally some people floated by on tubes. Instead of using truck tire inner tubes, more and more people buy specially made small rubber rafts, although the water remains just as icy. Some tubers drifted past whooping and hollering, obviously getting bombed on booze or already stoned.

That Wednesday on Purdue's porch I was sharing a jay with Paul and the older carpenter guy from Nakusp who drove the Chev dually, Rodney. I'd gotten to know Paul a little better since I'd seen him a couple more times at Purdue's. He had transferred to Mount Sentinel in the fall, after having been home-schooled. Like a lot of home-schoolers, he had pretty much kept to himself, but was never shy about speaking up in class. I never learned why he started hanging at Purdue's.

Paul and I were lazing in the cane chairs, with Rodney in the recliner, nobody talking much, just kicking back and enjoying the gorgeous blue sky overhead, the green mountains all around, the heat of the sun on our skin. In the front of the building, Purdue that afternoon had Frog helping him take inventory. After I'd been there a while, they joined us on the deck for a break, then returned inside.

Frog must have been feeling owly as ever, because before the break I could hear him and Purdue occasionally yell something at each other. I didn't pay much attention. They didn't say a lot when they were out on the deck, each pounding down a brew and having a few tokes of hash from a pipe Rodney had brought. But Purdue and Frog started to shout back and forth steadily a few minutes after they left us. I slouched down in my chair, head resting back on the siding, more or less nodding off—the warm afternoon breeze that flows down the ridge on hot days was just starting. The sound of the wind in the leaves of the riverside birch and cottonwood, plus the rippling noise of the water flowing over a few rocks directly offshore, were wafting away my mind. Froggie and Purdue's argument was just distant background static, like a clump of motorcycles revving along the highway on the other side of the place.

Then Purdue's voice boomed out, distinct over every other sound, angrier than I'd ever heard it. "No, I want your keys. Give me your fucking *keys,* douchebag."

I straightened up and started to listen, but couldn't catch Frog's reply.

Purdue's voice was hoarse, bellowing with that exaggerated emphasis on each word like my dad uses when he's over-the-top enraged: "Give. Me. Those. *Keys!* Don't make me do something we'll both regret!"

A second later Frog was in the doorway. He nervously snatched a joint out of Paul's hands, just as Paul lit it, and sucked down a couple of hits. "Geez, I'm in the shit now," Frog announced. He was gone inside again, I heard the fridge open in the kitchen, then he was back.

"Been bugging Purdue?" Rodney asked idly, eyes shut where he lay in the recliner, a beer bottle held vertical at his chest.

"He's on my case for sure, man. I think he's lost it. Maybe I should split."

Frog's agitated tone drew me from checking out a couple of bikini-clad chicks floating into view. His arms and legs kept shifting position in a jittery way; his fingers, once he'd handed the joint back to Paul, were scrabbling at the label on the beer bottle he'd scooped. "What was the deal about your keys?" I asked him.

He gulped down a long swallow. "Purdue got it in his head I'm ripping him off. But I'm not, man. I wouldn't do that."

"Sure you wouldn't," Rodney mocked, his eyes still shut.

"I *wouldn't*," Frog exploded. "What? You think I'm fucking ripping him off, too?"

"Didn't say that."

Purdue yelled something from the parking lot, his words obliterated by a wall of noise as a chip truck swung by the place.

Frog seemed to have understood Purdue, though. "Holy fuck. I better get out of here." He disappeared into the kitchen.

I heard the door from the parking area into the living room open, and a moment later Purdue stuck his head out onto the deck. His complexion was flushed. "Where is that little fuck? He's a fucking *thief*."

Purdue vanished. A couple of chairs or something crashed over, then silence, then a door slamming, silence, more bellows from Purdue, and something that sounded like Frog's voice, except pitched too high. Then, impossibly loud, a shot. Followed by a second. And a moment later, a third.

Paul and I followed Rodney's lead and were out of our seats in an instant, peering into the kitchen through the doorway and window. Paul's face was white. "You don't think he . . . ?"

"If he did, Frog deserved it," Rodney stated, his hands on either side of his face as he stared through the window's glass. He stepped back, picked up his beer, sucked on it, and wiped his mouth.

No sound or motion came from inside. The fridge still stood opposite the kitchen table and chairs. Some dirty dishes were on the counter beside the sink.

Purdue walked into the kitchen and stopped. His fists, dangling at the end of his arms, clenched and unclenched. We pulled back slightly from the door and window; I could hear through the screen Purdue inside inhaling and exhaling loudly, as if he'd been running.

On the deck, we glanced at each other, but nobody said anything. Purdue stared at the river but I don't think he saw us looking in at him.

His body quivered once, and his head jerked. He strode forward and onto the deck. We fell back to give him space.

"Frog was ripping me *off*," Purdue announced. His eyes were larger than usual, his expression wild. "Nobody fucks with *me*, man."

"Take it easy, bro," Rodney said.

"What happened?" Paul asked.

Purdue glanced at him, then away at the cottonwoods across the water.

"Sit down, Purdue," Rodney said, motioning toward a chair. "Can I get you a beer? You want a toke of something?"

"Inventory wasn't adding up," Purdue said, turning to face Rodney. "Some of this, some of that, wasn't accounted for. Two-man tent, walkie-talkie, a couple of backpacks. I don't get so many customers in the store at once that anybody could have shoplifted and I wouldn't have noticed. When I ask Frog about it, he starts twitching, man. I figured if he was ripping me, he'd stash it in his car. He's mostly couch-surfing these days, not staying up at his mom's. Sure enough, a pile of my shit was in his fucking trunk. A GPS, one of my Swarovski binos and a thousand-dollar Parker crossbow. He couldn't have bagged it all today, either. Stupid fuck must have been boosting a little every so often and stockpiling it."

"Yeah, when he came out here just now, he—"

Purdue shook his head. "Imagine being so fucking *dumb* as to drive around every day with what you ripped off stashed in your trunk. He's probably fencing it someplace. Did he fucking think I wouldn't fucking *notice*? Nobody, nobody fucks with *me*, man."

"What did you—?" Paul began.

Purdue looked around at Paul and me. "You maggots are accessories after the fact." He broke into a half-chanted, half-sung opening of Marley's tune: "*I shot the sheriff. But I didn't shoot no deputy* . . . Listen up, and listen good, maggots. Here's what you're going to do. You been smoking my dope and drinking my booze. Probably you've been fucking my women. Now it's payback time. First, you're—"

"We *haven't*," Paul said.

"Makes no nevermind. As far as the law is concerned, you're in this as deep as me. Shut up and listen."

My mind was jumping around trying to make sense of the situation. Had Purdue actually shot Frog? I'd heard what sounded like a gun, but no weapon was visible. We had been sitting out on the deck talking. Okay, toking and talking, but not—

"—owes me, and owes me big," Purdue was saying when I clicked back in. "I'm taking possession of his car by way of repayment. Rodney and I will head for Nelson, and he'll be Frog and sign the transfer papers. If we split right now, we can make some Autoplan office in town before they all close. The one in Slocan Park is probably where Frog registered the car, and they may know him. Rodney can practice Frog's signature on the way to Nelson."

Rodney lifted his beer bottle toward Purdue in acknowledgement. "Sweet. That will also put us on the road about the time of the shooting. If it ever comes to that. You can call me Mr. Frog."

"You maggots are going to take care of what's left of our dear departed brother. You've got your dad's pickup, right, Evan? Dude has some messed up my bedroom rug, so you'll wrap him in that. Grab a couple of shovels from my shed, take him up a logging road and bury him good. Bring back the shovels, and after that, make yourself scarce. You haven't seen him, you haven't been here for a week, you don't know nothing. Got it?"

My stomach heaved over at Purdue's words; I could taste copper in my mouth. I tried to say something, but my tongue wouldn't work. Paul got my thought out first, his voice squeaky.

"You *killed* him? *Killed* him? That's *murder.*"

Purdue pointed the first finger of his right hand at Paul. "Overstand me words, mon. He thiefed me. Nobody, *nobody* thiefs Purdue."

"You can't just *shoot* somebody because you think they—"

Purdue stepped toward Paul, his right hand now a fist. "You not listening to me, boy. Steal from Purdue, you *die*. Frog stole. Frog die."

Paul stepped back, colliding with one of the chairs. "This has nothing to do with me, Purdue. With us. We were just out here. You're the one murdered him."

"That's not how it works, maggot." Purdue's face was a few centimetres away from Paul's. "We're all in this *together*. You have your orders." His right hand shot out and clutched Paul's upper left arm. Purdue yanked Paul's body in the direction of the door into the kitchen; Paul stumbled and nearly fell. "We can't waste any time, boy, if Rodney and I are going to get to Nelson before they close.

Now get in there and haul what's left of him out of here." He turned toward me. "Evan?"

My feet and thighs felt as if I were wading upstream against the strong pressure of the river's current beside the sandbars where we sometimes swim. Purdue led the way through the kitchen, followed by Paul and then me. Rodney brought up the rear.

A door led off the living room to the south. I didn't want to look in, far less enter. My guess is that Frog had dashed into the bedroom to hide when he heard Purdue yelling that he had discovered the gear in Frog's trunk. A sealed double-pane window in the room looked south where the river disappears on the westward jog of its bend, with the green woods and riverside brush beyond. A double bed was covered with a rust-coloured spread marked with yellow zigzag designs—Aztec or something. Sticking out onto the hardwood floor on the far side of the bed were two black jean legs from which ankles disappeared into runners.

Purdue stopped at those legs and glanced down. "Can't believe I missed with my first shot. I need more practice." He glared in our direction and beckoned. "Get your asses over here, maggots, and roll him up. Waste of a good rug. I should have thought to stock body bags."

My legs refused to function. Paul hung back, too.

"Get *over* here," Purdue snarled.

Then Paul and I and Purdue stood together in the space between the bed and the room's west wall, looking down at Frog's back, with his face turned as if to see under the bed. His upper torso was twisted toward the west, however. He appeared smaller, as if he had deflated. He seemed absolutely still. I couldn't make out any mark on him, but I didn't look that closely. A pool of red fluid had flowed from under his shoulder where his flung-forward left arm stretched toward the north wall. The glistening colour puddled across a dark brown area rug, nearly as long as the bed, which was scrunched up in places underneath him. The fluid had found its way onto the hardwood, too.

Over the sound of my breathing I heard Purdue order Rodney to grab some rope.

"Where from?" Rodney had crowded in behind us, and was craning over our shoulders to peer at Frog.

"The store, you moron."

Purdue pointed at me. "Take the head end. Pull his arms down alongside his body, so you and Paul can roll him up in the rug." I saw how Frog's left hand, reaching toward the north wall, was palm up, cupped.

Purdue shifted a little toward the wall, to let me squeeze past him. A thick smoke of fear choked my brain and I could feel the vapour scudding down my veins and arteries. I probably *wanted* to obey Purdue, terrified as I was by what he might do to *me* if I didn't follow his commands. But my fear of approaching the horrible thing on the floor was stronger: not one of my limbs was able to function.

"Go on, *move*," Purdue shouted. Something slammed into my shoulder, almost causing me to fall across the corpse. I heard a shriek, and managed to shuffle my feet to stay upright.

"Fucking pussy," Purdue decreed. "Okay, you, Paul. Take the head end."

"You just want our prints all over the body," Paul squeaked. "No fucking way."

Rodney was back. "Got the rope."

Purdue released an exasperated hiss. "What a bunch of useless tits."

"Huh?" Rodney said.

"Not you, dummy. You have a point about prints, though, maggot. Rodney, go score us four pairs of gloves."

"Store?"

"Yeah, they need to be new. Along the wall to the right of the cash register. Cut them free of the packaging. And turn off the 'Open' sign."

We stared down at Frog. Rodney shouldered past me when he returned, tossing a pair of work gloves at me. I managed to catch them; my fingers vibrated as I pulled them on. I retreated across the room to stand by Paul near the doorway where I couldn't see what Rodney and Purdue were doing crouched over Frog, hidden by the expanse of bed.

After a long series of intermingled curses and sharp commands from Purdue, and one thump as some heavy weight hit the floor, he and Rodney straightened, lifting between them a rolled-up carpet tied with new yellow plastic rope.

"Okay, weenies," Purdue said, following Rodney who led past us through the door. "We're loading this piece of shit into Evan's pickup, and then we be off to Nelson. Wid dispatch, mon. You two fucks just pretend you're burying an old carpet."

We trailed the sagging bundle through Purdue's living room and outside across the parking lot. A Ford SUV sped south along the highway. If anybody in the vehicle happened to notice our little parade, we'd just appear to be some guys carrying a rug.

Purdue and Rodney lowered the roll into the back of the pickup. I could see where the stain had soaked through to the outer surface of the fabric. Instructed by Purdue, I went over to a small shed under a mountain ash at the north end of the lot and took out a couple of shovels. I laid them beside the rug. Purdue dragged a blue plastic tarp from his woodpile at the edge of the parking area, and tossed the tarp over the carpet and shovels.

"Stow everything back in the shed when you're done, maggots," he ordered. "If I were you, Evan, I'd hose out the pickup bed once you get rid of your load, just to be on the safe side. Fucking Frog managed to stain my floor, but Rodney and I will take care of that when we get back from Nelson."

"You think you're going to get away with this?" Paul said. I could hardly hear him, but Purdue's face instantly became all scowl. He stalked around the truck toward Paul.

"We should hit the road, Purdue, if we're going to be there in time," Rodney said. "Also, maybe we should burn the gloves in case there's blood on them or something."

"Listen, punk," Purdue punched his right hand's first finger into Paul's chest. "*Nobody* fucks with me. Not Frog, not the cops, not *you*. Do what I tell you, and keep your fucking mouth shut. Or you'll be very, *very* sorry. Somebody will notice Frog isn't around after a while. No loss, but probably the cops will check it out. You haven't seen him, you don't know nothing and what do they have to go on? He's been busted for trafficking before; they'll think he's either away on some drug deal or he's crossed somebody on a score and been hit. But—" Purdue jabbed at Paul again—"don't you even *think* about ratting us out."

Purdue waved his arm toward the back of my pickup. "'Cause if you do, I *promise* you'll end up rolled in a rug like your buddy here. Overstand me, mon?"

Paul did not reply.

"Overstand?"

"Yeah, yeah," Paul said in a small voice.

My hand was shaking so badly I had to try several times to fit the key into the ignition. Purdue and Rodney waited by Frog's car to watch us pull onto the highway.

Neither of us spoke as I drove north. After about fifteen minutes, I steered off the highway into the Lemon Creek rest area. My arms and legs were trembling, and even my teeth were chattering.

"What are we going to do?" Paul asked.

I had fixated on an aspect of Purdue's plan that seemed risky. "You know any spots we can drive to where there's no people? Digging a hole will take a while, and we need to be where nobody's going to see us, let alone stop and ask what we're doing."

"Are we really going to bury him? Shouldn't we go talk to the Mounties in New Denver?"

I couldn't stop my body vibrating. The image of Frog lying beside the bed, and of Purdue's face with his eyes wide after the shots were fired, hovered in the windshield. A man who could obliterate Frog in a rage was capable of much, much more.

"I think we should do what Purdue wants," I replied after a silence. "As he said, we tell the cops that we haven't seen Frog for a few days, and what do they have to go on?"

Paul said nothing.

"I don't want to end up dead, too," I admitted. When I turned toward Paul, he was looking at the floor mat.

His head lifted, and he met my gaze. "This makes us accomplices. Like Purdue said."

"*We* didn't kill him," I protested. "But we're fucked, either way."

Through the pickup's windows, we listened to Lemon Creek gibber and rumble over the rocks of its descent.

I suggested to Paul we head up to Six Mile Lakes, find an old forestry road we could follow and bury Frog somewhere along it. Paul pointed out that the area was heavily used by people gathering their winter wood supply, since the summit, where the lakes are, is accessible from the Nelson side as well as the valley side. Although most people leave cutting their winter wood until September or even October, the keeners were already tackling the chore. He thought we should drive up Shannon Creek Road at the head of Slocan Lake. People got firewood there, too, but the population was much smaller, and on a weekday in high summer likely nobody would be around.

The worst moment up Shannon Creek was when we had to hoist the carpet roll out of the pickup. Hacking a hole in the ground after we stopped far in along some disused logging track was bad enough: where the soil wasn't full of big stones that we had to pry loose, it was crammed with roots. After a couple of hours we only had an excavation two-thirds of a metre down. But the longer we sweated at our task, the more nervous I was that by chance somebody might be up here riding a quad or dirt bike and choose this spur road to explore.

I lowered the tailgate, and stared at the blue tarp covering our cargo. I had a horror the carpet would come untied while we were manoeuvring it out of the pickup, and Frog's body would flop out. I doubted I'd have the ability to wrap it back in the rug or even to lever it somehow across the shrubs, seedling firs and fallen branches to the hole. I figured we'd just leave it where it fell. Maybe an animal would drag it away; also, maybe nobody ever *would* happen by this part of the mountainside. But after I steeled myself and flipped the tarp off, the knots held. We hauled the carpet over to the hole and toppled the thing in, then quickly shovelled dirt and stones onto it. Paul suggested we drag a couple of logs across the spot once we'd filled the hole in. We tried to make everything look natural where we'd disturbed the ground.

My dad was pissed off when I got home, since I guess I'd promised to return the pickup before I actually did. Though I couldn't see any sign of blood in the back, I'd intended to hose the bed out. But he and his girlfriend went charging off on some errand as soon as I pulled in.

I tried for the next few days to keep my mind off what had happened. Yet I worried constantly despite my best efforts. The valley had changed: the mountains weren't the same height or colour as before; the evergreens, hazels and aspens around our place seemed different, foreign. I stuck close to the house, although on Saturday I couldn't stand it any longer and went out to Who Needs Sleep to see if anybody I knew was around. Rebecca was there, back from Quebec. She said Danny was planting east of Prince George, but should be home at the end of the month.

On Monday I had to borrow my dad's truck to go to Slocan Park because a friend of my dad's told him I should put in my resumé for a job through the Recreation Commission. Funding had come through for a crew to build picnic tables and outhouses along the rails-to-trails line between Crescent Valley and Winlaw. As I drove south past Purdue's about ten in the morning, I almost steered off the highway. Three RCMP cruisers and a black van with *Police* in white lettering on the side were in his parking lot, along with two or three other vehicles that looked like they could be ghost cars. I started to shake again. When I got to Slocan Park, I headed for The Beanery to get a coffee to calm myself. They had a copy of that day's *Nelson Daily News* somebody had left. On the front page was "Valley Men Charged in Car Theft."

The paper said Purdue had been arrested in connection with the registration in his name of a car belonging to Gaston Albert Brunet, an employee of his, who hadn't been seen since Wednesday morning. Police had received a tip in the case, according to the article. Rodney had been charged with possession of a stolen vehicle, and fraud. Both men were being held, the account said, because the police suspected foul play in Brunet's disappearance. A picture of Frog—I recognized his goofy Grade 10 photo—was on page three with a phone number to call if you saw him.

My head swam. I could hardly swallow the coffee after I went back out and sat in the truck and tried to think. I reassured myself that maybe the tip mentioned wasn't from Paul, but from the insurance clerk. If a database showed Frog's age, the guy might have noticed that Rodney couldn't be Frog. The cops could have put two and two together when they couldn't find anybody who'd seen Frog, even his parents. That would explain why the horsemen appeared to be all over People Get Ready. I couldn't imagine how Purdue could claim he thought Rodney was Frog, since Frog worked for Purdue. But perhaps Purdue could say he thought Frog had sold his car to Rodney, and didn't notice what name Rodney signed on the forms?

I couldn't get my brain to stop whirling. Paul and I would still be in the clear if the focus was on Frog's car, but the reference to the Mounties tying the car to Frog's disappearance was scary. I managed to calm myself enough to drive over to the community hall, hand in my resumé and talk to the guy there about the job for a few minutes. I have no idea what I said to him.

The cops were still parked at Purdue's when I drove home— possibly there were more of them. When I signalled to turn into our driveway, I noticed an ATV and rider parked on the shoulder but saw too late the quad driver had "POLICE" written across the back of his jacket. He followed me along the drive, and when I steered into our yard about eight cop cars and trucks were parked, including a couple over by the barn which meant they would have seized my dad's crop. I flashed on how if Paul had talked to them, they might have gotten a warrant to search our place for evidence, and not much effort would be required to find the hydroponics setup. Which meant I'd have gotten my dad into the shit. He was a well-enough-known grower that somebody would front him the money to replace his equipment, but he'd be major upset with me about having to go through all the hassle and expense of lawyers and court and about the loss of an entire harvest.

I was finding each breath more difficult to pull in than the previous one. I could see in my rear-view the cop on the quad speaking into the mike clipped to his shirt. He climbed off, and came up the passenger's side of the pickup as a uniformed cop stepped out of one of the parked cruisers and walked toward me. I managed to lower my window, and he leaned in. "Evan Jensen?" he asked. I nodded. "We want to talk to you about what you know concerning Albert Brunet."

Ever since I was little, I've swum in the river each summer. I remember watching the big kids leaping in from the Winlaw bridge or the Perry Siding bridge. Then I was old enough to jump—frightening the first time, then not so much, although the icy river was always a shock.

Lots of my friends wouldn't open their eyes under water, but I never minded doing it. I enjoyed seeing through a wavering haze a world totally unlike that on the riverbank above in the air. I could smell the minty breath of the cop at my window, waiting for me to speak, the identical scent of my dentist in Nelson when he bent close to examine my teeth, or to drill. Across the yard, a group of cops were bringing my dad out of the house with his hands behind him, and my dad and the men surrounding him and the cop's face beside me shimmered in the fluttering light as though we were all below the surface in some other river.

The Shadows We Mistake
for Love

JUST BECAUSE A STORY is old doesn't mean it can't be sad.

The pain was so severe, each time a contraction hit she could feel her whole body shaking and hear screaming. At the same time, she had the sensation she was floating above the bed gazing down on a body that jerked in agony. From this vantage she could see her friend Jane and the midwife Arachne bending toward her from either side of the mattress. Whenever she was stung by a bee or wasp, as happened nearly every summer, the fiery jolt was so much more harsh than she remembered that she almost laughed because how could she forget a sting was that painful: a relentless searing burn that went on for so long? Today, each surge was a hundred bee stings simultaneously. And the anguish stretched out a hundred times longer than the result of any wasp venom.

She had been in intermittent pain now for nine hours and was weary to the core. During the night she recalled and then lost and then followed again the pain-control lessons of the prenatal classes Arachne had led in the community hall. The baby at one point had to be turned inside her, to ensure it was head-down. She had wanted everything to be natural, but finally had yelled for painkillers when the unbelievable force at one moment sank its fangs into her stomach and back and simply would not let go.

She knew she would be grateful to Jane for the rest of her life because when the intensity of the agony first ambushed her, overwhelmed her, Jane rested a hand lightly on her distended stomach and said, "Breathe. Just breathe." *Of course,* she had thought, and became absorbed in her breathing so that the pain for a minute or two was only another thing in the room, not, as occurred later, all that was present within the room's walls, ceiling, floor. Back at the beginning, when the next wave crashed over her so that she floundered, shrieking—at least, somebody was shrieking—thanks to Jane's reminder she had a sense that what she was drowning in was not entirely out of her control. She could do something other than be tossed in the raging current, fighting for air before she was dragged underwater again, hammered against the slimy boulders below the rapids until she was sure she would die, and then at the last instant heaved above the surface for a blissful second, gasping a sweet breath and even another before she was tugged under again into the pain.

She did not know if she had screamed aloud or only thought, *You bastard, David, to get me into this*—how he had put her aboard this hideous whitewater ride of fear and agony that she knew there was no end to except death or her body finally ejecting the baby. At the start of a bad drug trip, as she was aware from a couple of experiences, once anxiety mounts you can fight it or distract it: think good thoughts, look at beautiful flowers or images, remind yourself this will pass, that there's an end to the path you're on through the frightening forest, with the way forward obstructed by roots and fallen logs, and with menacing beasts pacing in the dark underbrush around you. Except on this birth ride the terror was three-dimensional and already clawing and ripping her insides. And neither she nor anybody else could predict how long she would be borne along, smashed repeatedly against rocks, or where the journey would stop.

I'm never, ever doing this again, she also might have shouted or maybe just imagined saying, for a moment flashing on her aunt having had *two* kids. And those Victorian-era women—Queen Victoria herself—having whole litters. She remembered from her Victorian Studies courses that the monarch had nine children, the way peasant families in Italy or India still did nowadays. *Maybe they didn't or don't feel pain like me,* she concluded.

And where is *David?* she thought or said in a clear moment. Arachne had her back to her, absorbed with something on the low table against one bedroom wall. The candles on the table had been moved to join the others already on the two dressers and the window ledge. Unfamiliar things were piled on the table—a basin and odd-shaped bags and pouches of herbs from Arachne's backpack, which was nearby on the floor. The onset had begun about ten the night before—she had noted the time because she wanted to be able to tell the baby everything about its birth—and later she was aware the room was lit by candles. Weeks before, she had told Arachne and Arachne agreed that candles were a more natural way to greet the baby than the glare of electric lights. David had lit some aromatherapy incense, too, after the first contractions had hit and he and she were waiting for the midwife and Jane. But when the contractions drove her out of herself, she knew only that at some point the first thin light of dawn and then the April sunshine was filling the room, and Arachne was extinguishing the candles. David, who had held her hand at first and let her squeeze when she was swamped by her body, and even once had climbed onto the bed behind her and massaged her shoulders the way he had been taught by the visiting massage instructor in the prenatal classes, seemed to have vanished along with the darkness.

Jane held a glass of water to her lips, and she grasped it thankfully and drank. She even managed to turn to place it on the bedside table when it was empty. "Your mother phoned. She'll be up on the noon flight." She nodded acknowledgement. But the scorching vise of a contraction clamped down again harder than ever, and she was borne away, struggling to swim into air above the agony.

∾

Her parents had been opposed to her decision to move to the West Kootenay. "We didn't spend all that money on your education for you to just toss it away by joining some hippie commune," her mother had exploded when she broke the news. She had returned to Vancouver to give notice on her half of the garden apartment she shared with another young woman on the lower floor of a house in the city's Point Grey area. At the apartment she sorted through her possessions, and boxed up those she intended to store in her parents' basement: the books, clothes, vacuum cleaner, microwave, espresso coffee maker and other household gear she wouldn't need at Earth House.

"They aren't *hippies*," she shot back at her mother. They were sitting at her parents' kitchen table, a steaming tea cup resting in front of each of the three of them. She had dropped by to tell them her plans, her first visit since her return from the Slocan Valley. Her car in her parents' driveway was filled with the initial load of boxes she wanted to leave with them.

"In fact, there haven't been any hippies for decades, or haven't you noticed?" she continued. "And I worked every year I was at university to help pay my tuition."

"You were a part-time waitress in a marginal bagel shop," her mother said. "It paid almost nothing. If it hadn't been for your father and I, you'd be sixty thousand dollars in debt right now. Of course, if you had been going into debt, you might have picked a more lucrative subject to study."

"There are lots of English teaching jobs in the college system. You can teach with a master's. And if I ever go back and get my Ph.D. I'll—"

"If there's lots of jobs, why don't you get one instead of running off to live with a bunch of shiftless—"

"They're not 'shiftless.' They—"

"What do they do that's *productive*? That's what I want to know. I'm sure half of them are on welfare and the other half sell drugs. Or grow it. Or both. You've got brains and a good education and to throw it away on—"

"They're fighting to save the environment, not just wringing their hands and clucking their tongues about global warming while nobody does anything. What could be more productive, as you put it, than fighting to keep the air and the water and the land from being destroyed? You'll be singing a different tune when all the trees are cut down and there's no oxygen for the air. And nothing for you to eat because they've paved over or built houses on all the farmland here and food is more expensive than you can afford because they have to truck it in from South America or wherever the giant agribusiness corporations are still growing anything. You'll be—"

"Act your age. Exaggerating matters won't solve—"

"You'll be saying, 'Why didn't somebody *do* something?' That's exactly what the people at Earth House are trying to accomplish. It's the *best* place to put my brains and whatever I learned at university."

Her father sat silent, as usual. She had fought with her mother through junior high school and beyond: about makeup, about how revealing her clothes were, about how late she could stay out weeknights and on weekends, about her boyfriend Josef's goth T-shirts, piercings, tattoos and use of eyeliner. Her father, if appealed to during an argument, invariably said little more than that he sided with her mother. Sometimes a day or two later when she and her father were alone in the car as he drove her to a school friend's house, or to a Saturday cooking class for teens she was taking, he would present her parents' viewpoint in a manner that seemed more reasonable to her. Of course, by then she had calmed down and had even accepted some formerly contentious stricture or rule.

"You are just, like, so old, you don't have a clue," she had yelled when her mother had outright forbidden her to accompany her friend Melissa to a party at Melissa's older brother's West End apartment. "I don't take drugs or sleep around the way some of the girls in my class do. Neither does Melissa. We both get good marks. You act as if I'm an infant. That's, like, stupid. No wonder your generation has fucked up everything. You're—"

"You watch your mouth, young lady. Fifteen is too young to go to a party where there's no adult supervision and who knows who'll be there."

"Ethan *is* an adult. He's nineteen. He can drive, he can vote. He's smart, too. He's working at Safeway now but he's, like, going back to school. He's going to be a diplomat; he's got these cool ideas about what we need to do to stop wars. We're not going to get into any trouble at his party. Melissa is, like, his *sister,* for God's sake."

"It's not appropriate and you're not going."

"'Appropriate?' Look where being 'appropriate' has gotten the world. The bees and frogs are, like, dying off, the sea is full of plastic, you've used up all the oil, you eat meat, the glaciers are—"

"We'll see if your generation does any better."

"We *will*. It isn't hard to be smarter than you. It's so, like, *obvious* what needs to happen. Everybody who's young knows there's totally—"

"You act as if youth is an achievement of yours," her mother had said. "It's not. Youth is simply something else you owe to your parents. Because of your age, you don't yet understand how complex the world is."

Both of them realized they were no longer disputing about the party. But each for a different reason hoped the other hadn't noticed the shift. Nearly a decade later in her parents' kitchen, she realized she had let her mother push her buttons again. Of course her news about her move to the Kootenays was unexpected, and of course her parents weren't pleased. But they couldn't stop her. And she was at their house, too, to ask a favour: to let her pile her boxes of belongings in a corner of their basement.

To distract herself, she thought of David kissing her goodbye so tenderly as they stood beside her Corolla with the July air cool and still before the sun crested the peaks. She had wanted to get an early start for the nine-hour run west to the Coast. In the beauty of the new day, the forested slopes and summit ridges that hemmed the valley were vivid in the clear light, the mountains looming over the firs, pines and cedars that ringed Earth House's lawns. A hummingbird buzzed inches above where she and David stood; they held hands as they watched the tiny feathered bullet streak toward a feeder on the deck. A flicker hammered somewhere in the stand of aspen across the property's lower meadow. Two ravens alternately floated and flapped overhead, one offering a raucous screech as they steered toward a third raven blundering about in the uppermost branches of a spruce.

In Vancouver, she felt calmed by the thought of what awaited her on her return. The day before she left, she and Bronwen, another Earth House resident, were walking in the tall grass of the upper meadow when a fawn had suddenly struggled to its feet only a couple of metres ahead of them. The women gasped in wonder at the sight of the frail new creature. They had stopped to let it stumble on wobbly legs toward the safety of a grove of birch on the meadow's edge.

She lifted her teacup, sipped, then took a breath. "I know you're concerned, Mom, about me moving away," she began. "I know you want the best for me. I appreciate that. But I'm not rushing into anything. I've given this a lot of thought."

~

A sense of change suffused her, despite the pain, when Arachne reported she was fully dilated. *I can do this,* she felt or said, despite now hearing somebody groan each time she pushed at Jane's urging. Energy coursed through her as she bore down, tensing and squeezing muscles she had not been conscious of before. The sense of being recharged, of a second wind, was like discovering a hope—faint at first, then stronger—that this endless fiery shredding of her body would at some point cease.

"*Push,*" Jane and Arachne said in unison once, and then laughed at the unexpected convergence. She almost smiled herself, but was too busy complying. Taking action like this let her almost ignore the pain, rather than focus on enduring its repeated presence.

"Push," Jane said. She pushed.

Later she was dimly aware of David's presence in the room. He was carrying a Mason jar filled with the first of the daisy-like wildflowers from the meadow and some blue and pink lupines. He was standing beside the bed next to Jane, saying something about having to give Emile a ride into Nelson to see his probation officer. Three residents of Earth House had received suspended sentences from the Chico Creek blockade. David seemed to be talking about how the fight to protect the earth didn't stop even when new lives were taking form. She was gathering strength for the next push, however, and his words faded while she concentrated on the task that would set her free.

She had forgotten about David when, an age later, Arachne declared, "She's crowning."

"Just about there," Jane said, her voice excited. "*Push.*"

She pushed.

~

From the first time Jane had brought her to the Crossroads Café, she found the place intriguing. The floor, walls, tables and chairs were all wooden, unpretentious and homey. Paintings by local artists were hung between the big windows that looked east onto a patio with the highway just beyond. The owner frequently changed the featured artist. Yet whosever work was shown, the paintings were usually scenes from the valley, whether realist or somewhat abstracted: aspen trunks in a glow of background colours, a half-collapsed log barn in a meadow or the sugarloaf of Mount Wilton looming above the winding Slocan River, its banks lined with cottonwoods.

The clientele were mostly young—both men and women frequently wearing dreads above costumes that were a cross between hippie, Rasta and frontier: tie-dyed shirts, multicoloured vests and fringed leather jackets were visible, as well as baggy trousers, jeans, floor-length skirts and blouses woven of coarse cloth in plain shades. Some people sat by themselves behind laptops; cords descended from their earbuds toward invisible iPods, or sometimes they wore headphones. A few men and an occasional young woman wore a broad leather belt to which was affixed a large sheathed hunting knife. Ball caps in a spectrum of conditions from pristine to grimy were a common male head adornment, although imitation-ghetto-rapper toques and broad-brimmed leather hats were also evident.

At one or two tables of the twenty in the large room, middle-aged tourists huddled in couples or foursomes. They had seen the highway signs announcing the café as they drove past and decided to pull over for a break. Sometimes those at these tables wore the leathers of grey-haired motorcycle riders. The tourists sipped at coffee or a beer, glancing from time to time at the scene around them, or one by one rising to use the washroom at one end of the restaurant or to inspect the cakes, pies and cookies displayed in a cooler next to the counter midway along the west wall.

A couple of young waitresses circulated slowly from table to table, chatting with friends or neighbours among the customers, or strode to and from the kitchen carrying full or empty plates. The young employees were dressed identically to the youthful clientele.

Indeed, the staff could be identified only by the small pad of paper they clutched in one hand or tucked briefly in a skirt or shirt pocket when carrying meals or dishes, water jugs or coffee carafes. Many people in the room obviously knew each other, and table-hopped from group to group. Some of this interaction was intergenerational, with older men in jeans, plaid shirts and ball caps leaning over to speak familiarly to tables of younger people of both genders bristling with nose and ear piercings, sashes and wooden necklaces, as well as with arm, ankle and neck tattoos.

But she was most taken with the children: the five- and six-year-olds who scurried around the room in packs, or toddlers who wandered up and down between the tables while their erstwhile guardians were sidetracked in conversation with other seated adults. The children were costumed as miniature versions of their parents: a four-year old in an exquisitely sewn ruffled gingham dress, a three-year-old in velvet button-up overalls, a nine-year-old boy in jeans with a sash in place of a belt and wearing a sweatshirt that displayed a drawing of Mickey Mouse's head and shoulders morphed to resemble a portrait of Che Guevara, complete with beret displaying a red star.

In a play space at the north end of the dining area, a couple of child-sized benches were covered with dog-eared books, battered board games and wooden and plastic pull-trains, pails, balls and other toys. Here, toddlers discovered treasures, and brought their finds back to display to seated mothers or fathers, on whose laps they were continually on and off as the parents gossiped, laughed, ate and drank. At other tables, youngsters were bent intently over colouring books, sharing or arguing about preferred colours while the adult pre- or post-meal talk swirled above and around them.

She was entranced by a six-year-old girl in a sparkly outfit combining a tutu and leotard who entered the restaurant holding her mother's hand. "Look," she drew Jane's attention to the child. "How precious." But Jane, having turned to see, began waving to signal the mother, who headed to their table and, following introductions, began to talk gardening with Jane. The child kept her eyes on her sparkling sandals, and turned her head away shyly when asked her name.

Several people invariably stopped by their table during the times Jane and she went to the Crossroads for lunch or a coffee. In the café she first met Bronwen and Justin, both Earth House residents, when they paused at the table to speak to Jane and were invited to join the two women. "You should bring Shannon to the next meeting," Bronwen said to Jane, smiling, after the round of introductions.

"She's just visiting," Jane said. "Let her enjoy herself and not get tangled up in our dreary cries of outrage and protest."

The couple laughed. "We're *all* just visiting this planet," Justin said with a grin. "You know what they say: 'Take nothing but pictures, leave nothing but footprints.' Trouble is, our footprint is made out of solid carbon."

Bronwen playfully batted his shoulder. "Jane's right. Everybody needs a break from hearing nothing but bad news."

"I'll take a break when the planet catches one," Justin said. But he smiled at Bronwen when he said it. The talk at their table shifted to a planned mass bicycle ride down the valley's former railroad right-of-way, now a linear park featuring a maintained trail.

Whenever Jane and she were at the café, she felt something between admiration and jealousy watching the young mothers coping so off-handedly with a "he-hit-me, she-hit-me-first" crisis involving their children, complete with screaming and tears, or with an affectionate kiss and nuzzle initiated by a toddler who demanded attention in the midst of his mother's narration of some event to a listening table of adults. The women seemed so competent, juggling effortlessly the shifting needs of the children—producing a sippy cup of juice from a tote bag, or leading a youngster to the washroom in response to a request whispered by the child into their ears. They dealt in an equally smooth manner with the demands of their husbands or partners, who evidently also had to be listened to, instructed, cajoled, admired for their achievements and utterances, encouraged to engage with others, and who, like their offspring, suddenly insisted they needed to leave the restaurant in order to pursue pressing matters.

The children at the Crossroads became even more a focus of her interest when she knew she was pregnant. By then she recognized a few of the kids by name, having met them when their parents attended public meetings or social gatherings at the community hall or Earth House. She was pleased when Amber, a five-year-old, came across the café to show her a new doll her grandparents had sent. She hoisted the child onto her lap and they talked for three-quarters of an hour about the doll's name and its behaviour and habits as Amber imagined them.

When the pregnancy began to show, she was proud and excited to think she'd soon be joining the other young mothers: she saw herself serenely dispensing love and care while being admired by her peers, by David and the other fathers, and the young women yet to attain the status of parent. She felt a rush of satisfaction as she manoeuvred her growing bulk into the Crossroads alongside David. Of all the women in the valley, of all the women he had ever known, she was the one he loved deeply enough to bind himself to forever through jointly having a child, and maybe even children, though she recognized that having more than one offspring wasn't good for the planet. She regarded herself as chosen, honoured, adored by David because of the pregnancy—the sweetness of being so re-vered by him compensating for his occasional grumpy outbursts or silences, or her disappointment whenever he had to be absent from prenatal classes because of urgent Living Earth Society duties.

~

She had met David through Jane. Jane and she had become good friends as English honours classmates at UBC, and she had been Jane's maid of honour when Jane and Willy married after gradua-tion. Willy was hired by a West Kootenay accounting firm based in Castlegar, a dreadful pulp mill town according to Jane. The newly-weds looked for a house in Nelson, about a thirty-minute commute away. But prices were high, so they bought a small house and acre-age in the Slocan Valley. Willy wasted no time establishing himself at his profession. Within a year and a half he had his own practice in Nelson and an open-once-a-week branch office in the valley just north of the Crossroads Café amid a row of rustic shops under a single roof. The other little stores offered used clothing, pottery, herbs or candles and incense.

"What do you *do* all day?" she had asked Jane on the phone. Unlike Willy, her Andrew—a fellow master's student at the University of Alberta in Edmonton—showed no sign of asking her to marry him, and she wasn't even sure she wanted him to. He was brainy, but a bit disconnected from any reality other than the literary theories they all had to quote from in their essays. The theories sneered at any notion that there *was* any sort of reality other than how oppressive language itself is, contributing as it does to the oppression of women, people of colour, non-hetero-normatives, the differently abled and the working class. The only acceptable literature was thus writing fashioned by authors aware of language's deeply flawed nature, and especially such literary texts produced by women, people of colour, gay-lesbian-bi-and/or-transgendered souls and the differently abled—literature written in such a manner as to be impossible to understand unless you had read the right critical theorists. This inaccessibility was a good thing because the struggle for a better world would only be won when writing made no rational sense: such literature would compel everyone to rethink everything, thereby adopting an anti-capitalist world view. Sometimes she was doubtful about these claims, since the professors who were so enthusiastic in imparting these concepts nevertheless insisted that student essays and theses complied fully with the standard rules of grammar and spelling, even though the student papers were deemed correct when they denounced such linguistic norms as the root of oppression. But Andrew could talk and talk, and in the end she guessed he was probably right, that non-linear, non-narrative and non-referential writing really was a blow struck for freedom. Andrew, was, after all, a year ahead of her. He won a prestigious SSHRC graduate fellowship and was accepted to a Ph.D. program at Queen's.

When he had left for Ontario to begin work on his doctorate, the thousands of kilometres separating them meant the bond between them became more tenuous. There were some flights back and forth, but when she visited Kingston his friends apparently didn't think she was even worth talking to at the bar. When he spent a long weekend back at her apartment in Edmonton, he seemed far more *eastern* with each visit, disparaging everything Albertan, even though he had been born and grew up in the province in Carstairs, north of Calgary. He decreed that Maritime, Prairie and BC literary scholarship should best focus on issues "necessarily regional in scope," leaving any English, American, postcolonial or diasporic heavy lifting to the academics in the nation's centre, Ontario, who naturally had a broader and more international outlook.

Both years she was at the U of A, Jane urged her to visit, to detour south from Revelstoke when she was en route by car to see her parents in Vancouver. But although Jane and she emailed almost daily, spoke by phone frequently and Skyped occasionally, their reunion was planned and cancelled several times. Edmonton to Vancouver or vice versa was a sixteen-hour drive, done over one or two days, and adding additional time with a side excursion to the West Kootenay seemed more than she or her old Corolla could bear. Only when she had finished her master's course work, and had returned to Vancouver to live on the last of a scholarship and whatever part-time college teaching she could pick up while finishing her thesis—"(Un)conscious Patriarchal and Speciesist Perspective in William Morris's *News from Nowhere*"—did the trip east to see Jane seem possible.

"What do I do all day?" Jane had laughed from the other end of the line. "You'd be surprised how busy you can be without a job. Willy has lots of contacts, so I usually have some editing work: corporate annual reports and such. That work is really *rewriting* rather than editing, but let's not go there. Maintaining a house in the country takes more time and effort than in a city, for some reason. The veggie and flower gardens keep me hopping with spring planting, summer tending and putting the beds away in the fall. Then the snow shovelling starts, so our altogether-too-long driveway is open when Willy gets back from town in the evening. We could hire somebody to plow, I guess, but that's expensive and I don't mind the exercise. I also—"

"You never were into *gardening* before," she interrupted. "But I imagine it keeps you in shape. There probably aren't too many stretch classes out where you are."

Jane chuckled. "Stretch? No. But lots and lots of yoga classes. Here in the valley and in Nelson, yoga is practically a religion."

"It's a religion here among some people. I try to go once a week, but I'm usually swamped with—"

"I haven't been in months," Jane said. "Too much to do. My neighbour keeps goats and chickens, and I want to learn how to do that, so I'm over there a lot. Although we seem to spend a lot of time just gossiping. I've started to learn about weaving, too. A former one-room schoolhouse down the road is run by a group called the Threads Guild, and they put on classes. I want Willy to get me my own loom for Christmas. Plus we've gotten involved with a local environmental group, since we're only a few kilometres from a watershed that's going to be ruined by logging. Our water comes from a different creek, thank God, but ours could easily be next. Where your water comes from is not the kind of thing we even had to *think* about in Vancouver."

"Wow, you're really into this back-to-the-land, earth-mother thing with a vengeance. You'll be having kids soon, too?"

Jane snorted. "I can tell you're an only child and never grew up with babies. My mother had a kid about every second year, and guess who had to babysit as soon as my mom could trust me not to drown it in the sink or bake it in the oven? I'm in no hurry, and neither is Willy."

When the Corolla navigated the exit past Hope from the eastbound Trans-Canada onto Highway 3, headed at last through the June sunshine for Jane and Willy's, she told herself the trip was a reward for nearly being done with her thesis. Her plan was that the change of scene would prove restorative, would provide the boost of energy she needed to tuck down and complete the final two chapters. She admitted to herself that when it came to the thesis she was dawdling. Once she had settled into her new apartment in Vancouver the previous June, she found she regarded her topic as insipid, although she had been assured by her advisor that dissatisfaction with the subject matter was a common stage when undergoing a thesis. Yet when in the future she underwent her defense—at the end of the approaching summer, she hoped—she knew she would still have to decide where she wanted to go from there. A Ph.D? More courses to take and teach, the latter for very little money as long as she was a grad student? Plus the horror of having to write a *longer* thesis? Yet if not that career path, then what?

Her bleak frame of mind brightened as the road east wound through different ecosystems. From the rainforest of the Coast Mountains, whose higher peaks and ridges still displayed winter snow, she descended into the valley of the Similkameen River, where the strengthening sun shone hotly on sandy fields, many of them converted into vineyards. Then Highway 3 snaked up into low pine-forested mountains before dropping down into the southern Okanagan, where Osoyoos Lake extended toward the eastern horizon. After Osoyoos the Corolla again began climbing, this time traversing up the huge escarpment east of town: a spectacular ascent as the highway hairpinned back and forth across the nearly vertical rise from valley floor to forested plateau above.

She was travel-weary when, four hours later, she saw through the windshield, just as Jane's detailed instructions promised, the numbered sign at the bottom of Jane and Willy's driveway. Despite her tiredness, she felt excited by a sensation she had acquired when the highway over Paulson Pass finally had emerged at Castlegar from densely wooded elevations into the river valleys among which Jane lived: the feeling that with her vehicle's long descent she had entered a hidden, enchanted place.

Nothing Jane showed her or spoke of in the following days shook her enthusiasm for what seemed a magical hideaway. Though Jane and Willy's house in most respects resembled a comfortable suburban dwelling, the building was situated in a clearing in the forest where each day more yellow-green leaves appeared on the birch, aspen and hazel boughs that mingled with pine, fir and cedar all around the lawn. As Jane drove her through the area, mysterious dirt roads took off from paved routes that followed the river—the main highway on one side of the water, and the more winding back road where Jane lived on the other. Everywhere were modest houses with gardens. Several of these properties displayed collections of junked cars and pickups, or parked logging trucks, excavators and other heavy equipment. The dwellings and gardens were glimpsed through the trees and thick underbrush that clung to the routes' shoulders. When the two women drove in Jane's small jeep-like Tracker north toward the hamlet of New Denver, stunning vistas amid the forest revealed the snow-topped Valhalla Range lifting steeply from the expanse of Slocan Lake. Closer to home, they strolled the trail constructed atop the former rail line to the village of Slocan. Back again at Jane's, they sipped tea on the deck or drove the half-dozen kilometres to have coffee at the Crossroads Café.

Adding to the impression of having been transported to a sanctuary of incredible beauty, removed from the concerns of the rest of the world, was the absence of cellphone service. Jane and Willy's house connected to the internet, Jane explained, via a dish beside their porch aimed at a repeater tower on a nearby mountain. But cellphones didn't function once one left the Castlegar–Nelson road.

The dynamic between the two women subtly changed when Willy arrived late each afternoon with his tales of how his workday had unfolded. Yet Willy and Jane's visitor had always found him pleasant company, and he seemed anxious that she enjoy her stay. He told her he was pleased that she had shown up at last, because after a barrage of meeting new people in the valley, Jane had been hungry to reconnect with those with whom she had a longer history.

Jane announced over supper one evening that the Living Earth Society, the local environmental group of which she and Willy were members, was having a watershed action meeting the next night. "Willy and I should probably go, but I meant it when I told Bronwen and Justin at the café that you should just enjoy yourself here and give it a miss."

"I'll go. I'm curious to meet more of your friends."

"They're not exactly our friends," Willy interjected. "Neighbours. Some of them are environmental loonies. But a house has zero value without water, and the group as a whole has been standing up for valley households at risk of losing their water."

"Doesn't the government step in if a person's water is threatened?" she asked.

"Unfortunately, no," Jane said. "The province issues water licences and collects fees for them. But they won't guarantee the water your licence says you're entitled to. The government is more interested in kowtowing to the lumber industry than protecting homeowners."

"It's the wild west around here," Willy said. "If you don't stand up for yourself, nobody is going to do it for you."

With Jane at the wheel of the Tracker the following evening, the two women swung off the highway at the local general store and proceeded along a narrow road that wound upwards between overhanging trees. Willy had been left behind with a briefcase full of unexpected papers he had brought home that he said he absolutely had to plow through before the next morning. As the Tracker climbed, driveways identified by four-digit numbered signs appeared and disappeared. Finally an opening in the woods was marked by both a number and a larger *Earth House. Welcome.* A one-lane dirt track led through the forest for a hundred metres or so, and then emerged onto a broad sweep of meadow. Jane's passenger could see ahead that the drive curved toward a three-storey wooden house. Eight older-model pickups, vans, cars and station wagons were parked in a line, pulled over to the edge of the lane with their passenger-side tires resting on a strip of lawn that paralleled the drive.

She liked the house the moment they entered. The walls of the hallway and large living room were constructed of logs, although the outside of the building was sheathed in more conventional wood siding. A high ceiling gave a spacious feel to the living room, in which an assortment of twenty-five folding wooden and metal chairs had been set out in rows. The arrangement faced three additional chairs that looked back into the room from one wall. Comfortable-looking couches sagged around the rest of the perimeter, with colourful quilts and crocheted wool coverings tossed on sofa backs. Small shelves were attached to the room's walls apparently at random at various heights, displaying pottery, a vase of lupines, a couple of kerosene lanterns, candles stuck in wax-encrusted candlesticks and a couple of jars each holding a burning incense stick that added a faint odour of jasmine to the air.

When Jane and she first entered the room, several men and women were already sitting scattered in ones and twos in the chairs, talking quietly to each other or staring toward the three chairs ahead of them. Among those seated were a stolid-looking middle-aged couple, the man with his thick-fingered hands resting on the knees of his jeans. The majority of the room's inhabitants were younger—a reassembling, she thought, of the customers at the Crossroads Café.

A cluster stood chatting around a table near the opening into the room from the entrance hall. Many of these people clutched mugs; a couple of oversized teapots stood on the table beside an array of ceramic cups, a glass container of honey and a small pottery cream jug in the shape of a cow. A young man detached from the far side of the group at the table and approached the new arrivals where they had stopped just within the room.

Something electric quivered in her as he neared them. He seemed lanky, though not exceptionally tall, but with intense blue eyes that seemed directed at her. His hair and trimmed full beard were brown; the trace of a smile rested on his lips. He was wearing jeans and an untucked, softly flowing pale green shirt with a Henley collar. Thick grey wool socks were jammed into sandals. His walk and bearing radiated a commanding self-confidence, an assurance about who he was and his place in the world that she instantly found admirable.

"Jane," he said. "Welcome." His extended arms offered an embrace. He and Jane clinched briefly, and then he was standing looking openly at Jane's companion, smiling. "I see Willy couldn't make it, but who is this?" He put out a hand. "I'm David."

To her surprise, she felt flustered, although she could think of no reason why she should be. Almost automatically, she noted he wasn't wearing a ring. Jane was explaining that David was the chair and main sparkplug of the Living Earth Society, and a resident of Earth House. Shannon, Jane continued, was her very best friend, visiting from Vancouver.

"Do you all live here?" she asked, looking up to meet David's gaze beaming down at her. *What a dumb question,* she castigated herself. *I saw the parked cars outside that obviously brought people here.* David was answering before she could continue to berate herself.

"Some of us. Living Earth has lots of members in the valley, though, like your friends Jane and Willy. Also several in Nelson, and even down on the Coast. But we needed an office, and some members who had just moved to the area needed a place to stay. So we bought this place. It's a communal house. There's a long tradition of these in this valley, as maybe Jane mentioned."

"How long have you—?" she began, but a shorter young man with spectacles and an officious manner was tugging at David's sleeve. "We should get started," the newcomer said. "The agenda is pretty long."

"Okay, Dewclaw," David said. Still looking at her, he rolled his eyes as if being called away to begin the meeting was ridiculous, a source of humour. He reached forward and touched her upper arm. "We'll talk later. It's great to meet you." He moved off, leaning down slightly to listen to the man who had fetched him. A second later he stood in front of the rows of chairs.

"Take your seats, everybody," he called. "We're about to begin. We've got a lot of ground to cover. *Hey,*" he yelled, as the noise around the tea table showed no sign of diminishing. He laughed at the sudden quiet, and beckoned with one hand. "C'mon. Let's get this show on the road."

Jane and her guest took seats near the front. As people filed into the rows in twos and threes, still talking, she turned to Jane. "Did he call that other fellow 'Dewclaw'?"

Jane nodded. "That's not his real name, of course. Sort of a *nom de guerre.* Or *nom de environment,* or something."

"What a strange name: sort of soft and hard at once."

Jane looked at her. "A dewclaw is that little appendage just up a dog's leg from their paw. Deer have them, too: residual hoofs, or something."

"Why pick such a—"

"Dewclaw's a little odd. I think he said once he took the name because we humans are like that: an evolutionary development that didn't pan out and is in the process of disappearing."

She watched David as the meeting got underway. Bronwen's friend Justin took the seat beside David, and an older woman with glasses sat on his other side—evidently they were elected officials of the Society. Justin and the woman gave reports updating the audience on the group's legal efforts to oppose the logging above and beside Chico Creek, from which twelve valley families drew water. David kept the flow of information and discussion moving easily, with a confident grace, she thought. He cracked jokes to lighten tense moments, and spoke earnestly when seriousness was needed to remind the gathering of the gravity of the situation, of the strength of the powers who they intended to defy. He frequently addressed somebody in the audience by name, water users on the creek, apparently, who hadn't commented on some matter, thus drawing them into the proceedings. He handled deftly a disruption caused by the sole elderly woman in the room, who at one point ignored the agenda item the meeting was considering and launched into a fervent declaration of how water was sacred, vital to all living things, and how on the globe as a whole water was in short supply and thus every drop was precious.

"Not only that," the grey-haired woman said, "but we need to educate people about those planes that fly up from the States every day and seed the clouds above the valley. I've seen them myself, and my friend Marty has photos of them. They take off from that air force base in Spokane and drop aluminum crystals, to reflect more of the sun's rays and slow global warming. That way they can keep right on polluting the planet. But who knows what that aluminum is doing to *our* water. And to *us*. We have to—"

David gently interrupted, and managed to return the woman's attention to the item at hand, and thus into silence. A second later, the meeting was back on track. Yet at times David's own words about an aspect of the Chico Creek issue were a rousing reminder of the big picture, she thought, of how the small local issue the group was responding to was part of a larger struggle to save the earth.

She was impressed repeatedly by his ability to link macro and micro, to never lose sight that, as he said, there was nobody but themselves to take a stand for the woods and water. At one moment he rolled up his sleeves, and something in her chest shifted and flared at the sight of his bared forearms.

The group was planning an act of civil disobedience, she suddenly realized. Another middle-aged man she hadn't noticed before rose to his feet to say he was a logger himself and proud of it, but he didn't believe in ruining people's lives by how he earned his living. He claimed to know the man who had been hired to do the cutting on Chico Creek, and listed three or four examples of poor practices the man's company had demonstrated on other sidehills, other logging shows in the region. The speaker detailed how he had personally confronted the other logger about the threat to the creek's water, and how his views had been brushed aside. "This guy is bad news," he concluded. "The government and our MLA are useless. We have to do something." He received a loud round of applause.

The meeting eventually settled on a date and time for a blockade at the logging site. The group had obviously planned such actions before. David kept the meeting's attention on what had to be done as the gathering worked through a checklist of chores involving media publicity, mobilization of supporters, teeing up legal defense for those willing to be arrested, organizing a sign-making session. Volunteers were plentiful, although they mainly were the youngest members of the audience, she noticed. Neither Jane nor any of the middle-aged people present committed themselves to working on the advance preparations for the blockade, except for a mustachioed, balding man who had spoken from the back row on some arcane aspects of the group's legal brief opposing the logging. His right hand, in a nervous gesture, touched over and over again his thinning hair at the back of his head while he talked. She concluded, due to his confidence discussing such legal matters, that the man was a lawyer.

Eventually David adjourned the meeting with a flourish. Yet after the audience had stood up and stretched, they were slow to dissipate. Small groups of people formed around the room to chat energetically. More tea was produced. A few people were holding beer bottles and cans, although she couldn't see where these had originated. Meanwhile, two audience members started busily folding up chairs and, skirting the clumps of talkers, carrying the chairs into another room. She thought about joining the people clearing the space, since Jane had been snagged by an overweight woman and the two were deep in a discussion of whether certain covers for tomato plants were worthwhile. All but a few of the chairs were removed, however, before she could act. She threaded her way between the various conversations to inspect framed pictures that had been hung on the walls amid the shelves. A couple of sepia photographs looked like somebody's ancestors. Other photos were of demonstrations in front of a turreted building that Jane later informed her was Nelson's courthouse. People also posed hoisting picket signs on a road through the woods someplace. A shot showed a group of young people standing on the front steps of what she realized was the house she was in. Some charcoal sketches of wildflowers, and an oil of a valley scene of river and mountains were also displayed.

Her tour of the pictures ended at the table where the teapots were. She asked a young woman who had just poured a mug whether the tea was herbal, and learned that it was a ginger zinger. After securing a mugful and dripping honey into it, she turned. David was standing smiling in front of her.

She felt herself flush. "Hello," she managed.

"How did you like the meeting?" he asked.

"I really did," she said. "It was terrific. I think you're doing exactly what needs to be done." *I sound like I'm gushing,* she admonished herself. *Stop it.*

He didn't seem to object to her enthusiasm, however, and she asked a couple of what she hoped were intelligent questions about water flow down the valley walls, and about other threats to household water use in the area. Almost immediately, though, she was answering questions about herself. Embarrassed by what she suddenly regarded as a rather self-indulgent life so far, she tried to redirect their conversation to *his* background. He had a master's in Environmental Studies from York University in Toronto, she learned, and had travelled west to work with the Western Canada Wilderness Committee. But he had friends in the West Kootenay, and one trip to visit them and he was hooked.

She laughed. "I'm beginning to feel that way myself."

He wanted to know how long she planned to be around, and she heard herself promise to accompany Jane to the blockade the following Monday. She also accepted an invitation to be shown around Earth House and its gardens the next afternoon. "Tomorrow is about the last chance I'll have for free time before the countdown to the blockade gets underway," he said.

"I'd love to see all you're doing here," she said. Jane materialized at her elbow. "We don't have anything planned for tomorrow afternoon, do we? David has invited us to tour Earth House."

"I've seen it," Jane said. "But you go ahead. I wouldn't mind an hour or two working on that contract for the rails-to-trails society annual report."

After lunch the next day, in the guest room at Jane's she spent twenty minutes agonizing over what to wear to meet David. Something sturdy to demonstrate that she was seriously interested in the outdoors, the environment, gardens and all that? Or something skimpy and flirty, given the warm weather and that she was on vacation, just passing through from the big city? She settled for her tightest jeans, and a plaid shirt that she unbuttoned rather far and set off with a bright blue scarf.

As she walked up the steps of Earth House, she wasn't sure if one knocked at the door of a communal house, or just opened the door and stepped inside. Again she decided on a compromise, and knocked a couple of times before pulling the door ajar.

The house was dimmer than the night before, the large main room gloomy without the lights and people filling it. Nobody was in sight. Should she shout to notify David that she had arrived? He *had* invited her. Down a hallway she saw the kitchen, and stepping in that direction she spotted with relief Bronwen at a counter stirring something in a bowl with a large wooden spoon. Bronwen glanced up as she entered.

"Hi," the visitor said. "Is David around? He said I could come by this afternoon and he was going to show me the place."

Bronwen resumed mixing. "He did, eh?"

"Yeah. Did he have to go somewhere? Maybe he meant later in the afternoon?"

"No, he's here." Bronwen beckoned. "Take over the stirring, will you? I'll go see if I can find him."

As the spoon circumnavigated the mixing bowl, the visitor took a closer look at the kitchen, with its brightly painted cupboards and ranks of carefully labelled jars and canisters arrayed on shelves and against the wall at the rear of a wide counter. A small toaster oven was visible on a shelf, but no microwave was evident. She realized there was no dishwasher, either. Then David walked through the doorway, trailed by Bronwen.

He beamed a smile at her. "Shannon. I'm so glad you stopped by." She felt a little breathless in his presence, but diverted herself by the business of returning the spoon to Bronwen. Then she swivelled and melted into David's proffered hug.

His hand lingered for a few seconds on her back. "We'll take a quick walk-through of the house before I give you the garden tour," he said. "It's too nice a day to spend indoors."

When late that evening in the solitude of her room at Jane and Willy's she reviewed her time at Earth House, she was still happily jangled by how the experience had gone, how enticing the hours with David were. At first, as she was led through the upstairs of Earth House, peeping into people's bedrooms, she had felt herself stiffly trying to make a good impression. She recalled facts and attitudes from her teenage obsession with ecological perils, and hoped she didn't sound like an idiot as she threw in prompting questions while David described in detail the founding, growth and present activities of the Living Earth Society.

Outdoors, she had oohed and ahhed at the vigour of the veggies already growing in the greenhouse. Some other Earth House residents were introduced when David and she encountered them rototilling and manuring the extensive gardens, although except for Dewclaw and the woman with glasses from the night before—who called herself Osprey, and seemed a little unfriendly—the people she met were a blur. The tour ended with a beer on the Earth House deck, which looked across the gardens past massed trees on the property's edge toward the ridge that formed the valley's western wall. The conversation took a more personal turn: she inquired about his parents' attitude toward his ecological activities, and that topic led to each of them describing their families. His parents and most of his siblings still lived in the Leamington area of southwestern Ontario. She found herself enjoying watching him talk about his brothers and sisters and their lives.

About five she said she should be going, and he invited her to share the communal supper. "Bronwen's the chef tonight, and I can promise you a culinary delight. She's good."

"I'll have to check with Jane. I mean, I'd love to stay, but I need to let Jane know I won't be there for dinner. And I didn't bring anything to contribute."

"That's okay. Next time you can bring something."

Nine people including her were seated around a large wooden table in the dining room for Bronwen's meal—a veggie stew accompanied by a spiced rice dish and fresh-baked bread. No tablecloth covered the scarred wood of the table's top, but a multicoloured woven placemat was set out for each diner, and the effect was pleasing to her, suggesting a rustic comfort. A vase displaying a mix of purple and white lilacs, which were still in bloom in the valley, provided a delicate scent to the room discernible despite the odours of the tasty food. She felt abashed eating with these committed ecological campaigners, and said little as the residents discussed household issues, the state of the garden, new developments in the Chico Creek fight and in a province-wide coalition against a planned enormous ski resort in the Purcell Mountains of the East Kootenay. She was grateful when David made an effort to include her in the ebb and flow of talk.

After coffee, she offered to help with the washing-up. Bronwen and David immediately declined her aid, pointing out her status as a guest. Justin made a joking comment about him being behind anyway in his house responsibilities. She wondered if he was trying to spend more time around Bronwen. David accompanied her to the door when she announced she should head back to Jane and Willy's.

"I enjoyed getting to know you a little today, Shannon," he said. His right hand reached out and smoothed her hair. Ordinarily, she would have regarded such a gesture as offensively presumptuous when made by a man she hardly knew. But her knees trembled when David touched her: his act seemed a tender acknowledgement of a real connection between them.

"I'd very much like to spend some time with you again," he said. "As you know, I'm pretty tied up now with preparations for Monday's blockade. And who knows how long that action will last, unless they simply bust us on Monday. You'll be heading back to Vancouver soon, I guess?"

She murmured something about enjoying meeting him, as well.

"Can you come to the sign-making session here Friday night? It should only last a couple of hours, and then we can hang out. Living Earth tries to have a social aspect to everything we do. There's usually a bit of a party after a work meeting. The idea is to not lose sight of the better life we're fighting for."

She agreed to participate, and then he enfolded her in his arms. He didn't try to kiss her. When she reported in detail to Jane about her day, her hostess was noncommital. "Sounds like you had a good time," was Jane's only response.

Jane had more to say on Saturday morning, however. Claiming she wanted to work further on editorial jobs she had been neglecting, Jane had decided not to take part in the Friday evening sign-making bee. Her friend also figured that since she had been monopolizing most of Jane's attention since her arrival, Jane could probably use some time alone with Willy.

In the living room at Earth House, the gathering to create picket signs and a couple of big banners had been as pleasant as David had predicted. Besides the communal house residents, more of whom she was beginning to recognize by name, six other Living Earth Society members were there. As before, most were young, except for the balding man who had spoken at the planning meeting on legal issues—she discovered his name was Duncan Locke, and he *was* a lawyer, as she had surmised. She was flattered that he seemed to want to be engaged in the same tasks she occupied herself with: part of a group cutting cardboard for picket signs and stapling already-lettered signs to wooden stakes. A couple of times David called her away from where she was working with the lawyer to ask her advice, on the basis of her English academic background, about the wording of a slogan he and two other Earth House residents sequestered in the dining room had concocted.

When the sign-making was declared complete, beer and wine were produced along with tea. People sat or sprawled on the living room floor, and as at the Earth House dinner table, conversation ranged from House and Society internal matters to gossip about valley individuals to condemnation of a dam project planned for north of Revelstoke designed to stockpile the huge quantities of water necessary for the energy corporations' new technique of fracturing rock deep underground to access oil and natural gas. After an hour and a half, the lawyer was the last of the non-residents except her who hadn't departed. Some of the Earth House inhabitants had retired to their bedrooms, and eventually even the lawyer announced he had appointments the following morning.

Everyone left in the living room stood when the lawyer did, and the lawyer insisted on hugs all around.

"I should be going, too," she said, as the door closed behind him.

"First come out on the deck and look at the stars," David suggested. They passed through the house and into the chilly evening. On the deck they were silent, heads tilted back to take in the vast array of dots and clusters of light that arched far above. The stars were infinitely more abundant than she was used to seeing, their plenitude luminous and daunting in the night sky. She was aware of David's presence close beside her. Then he broke the stillness by asking if she was familiar with the stars, and when she admitted she wasn't, he began to point out some constellations.

"You're shivering," he noted after a minute. He pulled her into an embrace, and her hands went around his body.

"You're nice and warm," she said. She rested her head against his shoulder. "Doesn't the cold get to you?"

"You're so very special, Shannon," he said. "I'm very glad we met, and I really like getting to know you."

His hand tilted her chin up toward his face, and they began to kiss. She was shaking in part because of the temperature and in part from excitement. After a minute or so, his tongue touched hers, and their two tongues started to caress and probe each other.

He pulled his face back from hers at some point. "You're cold," he announced, concern in his voice. "We should go inside." She had no words, but managed to nod. His arm wrapped around her back as he conducted her into the darkened living room. No one was around. They collapsed onto a sofa and resumed kissing. After a time his hand began to travel over her body. He began to undo her clothing.

She didn't return to Jane and Willy's until eight the next morning. Twice in the night she sat up in David's bed, intending to get dressed to head back to her car. But each time his fingers and lips and tongue had traversed her vibrating skin and she had lain back "just for a minute" before becoming lost again in the pleasures he evoked in her body. She suddenly awakened in the dawn, and slipped out from under the blankets where he was asleep. Dressed, she kissed him awake and thanked him. He mumbled about breakfast, but she assured him she needed to go in case Jane was worried about her. He was unconscious again before she found her shoes.

Out the door, she stood on the house steps and breathed in the cool freshness of the country morning. A rooster crowed from the chicken coop, and an answering declaration or challenge resounded from a neighbour's rooster somewhere beyond the surrounding trees. Crossing the dewy lawn to her Corolla, she realized she was a little sore. David was an ardent lover. She felt suffused, however, with joy at David's regard for her, and with delight at thoughts of their lovemaking and the promise of a new day.

Jane and Willy were just getting up when she entered their house. "Let's walk down to the river," Jane said once the small talk of a rather strained breakfast was over, and Willy had taken his coffee to his study. Nobody had mentioned her absence overnight. "There's some things I want to speak to you about."

"I know I should have called," her friend blurted. She flushed with embarrassment and guilt. "I do apologize. I never intended to stay over. One thing led to another and it was too late by the time—"

"Let's go get ready."

She felt awful about her failure to notify Jane she wouldn't be home. But as she pulled on and tied her hiking shoes, she acknowledged that she also floated in a pleasurable daze. *He loves me. I know he does. He is such a beautiful man.*

"We knew where you had gone, so I sort of figured what had happened with you," Jane began as they followed a gravel road that left the pavement not far from Jane and Willy's driveway. "But this is the country. There are bears, not to mention drunk drivers and—"

"I really, really am sorry. It was the middle of the night and I knew you'd be asleep and, to be honest, I didn't know how to stop things long enough to—"

"How much sleep do you think I got?" Jane said. "On the one hand, you're a big girl and can do what you want. But on the other hand, I feel sort of responsible for you here. You can wander off on your own in the city. But here, how was I to know a bear or a cougar—?"

"Not letting you know where I was is inexcusable," her friend said. "Although I didn't see how to at the time, I absolutely should have—"

"David knows you are staying with us. If he'd been thinking about you at all, he'd have suggested you call us at some point. But it's not just you not checking in." Jane stopped on the road and turned toward her companion. "I don't know how much what just happened means to you. But if it's more than a fling, I need to tell you: David has a reputation."

They resumed walking in silence. As she stepped along beside her host, she recalled David's head between her legs, his tongue and fingers unhurriedly, languidly sending repeated jolts of ecstasy coursing through her. He would pause only to kiss her mound and inner thighs before returning to the task of driving her mad. "A reputation?" she managed.

"He's an excellent organizer. But he's a womanizer, too. New recruits are his specialty. Since we've known him, he's been with four or five different women, that we're aware of. Three of them were new to the Society. And that's only the ones who have stuck around long enough for the rest of us to meet them. Honey, I just don't want you to think more is going on than maybe is."

~

Bradley Newcome Dunn was so tiny and so perfect and she instantly loved his smell and his exquisite toes and fingers, how he wriggled and thrashed his new arms and legs as if trying them out, and how he stared around wide-eyed at the world. At her breast, once he caught on to the good thing the nipple promised him, how content both she and Bradley were while he greedily suckled. How wise and yet vulnerable he looked when he slept.

But she was exhausted. The last part of labour drew more energy from her than she had known she possessed, and when Bradley was put into her arms the enormous responsibility for keeping this minuscule creature alive was immediately as tangible as the blanket that wrapped the newborn. She craved sleep, yet Bradley was insatiable in his needs, whether by day or night. Rest was available only when he chose to sleep. She had been warned that the first weeks would be a trial, but she was not prepared for the constant pain—healing was very slow. It was hard to walk.

She existed in a haze. Bradley was often wakeful after she had nursed him in the middle of the night, and she spent endless groggy hours by herself in the living room, either pacing, as best as the pain allowed, with Bradley in her arms, or sitting bouncing him on her lap while he peered at the fascinating things visible in the semi-darkness on every side of them. At first David was intrigued by Bradley—she loved the sight of David holding and admiring his son. Yet she realized David was increasingly withdrawn from her and Bradley. Partially he was busy with crafting Living Earth's presentation to a touring government commission charged with rewriting the province's water strategy. Living Earth wanted to show how local issues like resource extraction's impact on domestic watersheds was interconnected with larger hydrological issues brought on by climate change. David's excited talk about what their presentation could communicate—aided by a planned large demonstration in support of Living Earth's ideas at the commission hearing in Nelson—seemed distant and abstract to her world of diaper changes, nursing sessions and the omnipresent desire to sleep. Partially she realized David was overwhelmed by the baby's presence in their lives. But she needed more involvement from him.

"I'd do more, but I really don't know what to do around Bradley," he said during one of their arguments.

"You think I know? All I'm asking you to do right now is look after him for a few minutes while I take a quick shower. I stink and my hair's a mess. I'm thinking of having Jane cut it all off. I don't know how you can stand to be around me."

He kissed her. "You always look beautiful to me. I'd love to look after Bradley, but Duncan is coming over any second, along with that forest hydrologist guy he says is sympathetic, to meet with me and Osprey and Alexander. In a couple of weeks the commission will have come and gone, and I'll be able to give you more of a hand. But we're way behind on getting our act together about what to say to these clowns if we're going to make an impact."

Her anger flared when she had to drag her aching, tired body in repeated trips downstairs to the laundry room, lugging both a baby that howled when she tried to put him down for a moment and a basket of all she could carry of the mounting pile of soiled towels, sheets, baby clothes and their own jeans, socks, underwear and shirts. At the same time, she felt guilty for asking more from David when he was tearing around trying to meet impossible deadlines, herding the crew of sometimes-reliable, sometimes-not volunteers toward completion of Living Earth's latest project.

Yet he was capable of trying to add to her guilt. If David and she were scheduled to cook the communal meal, or to do the cleanup of the common rooms and hallways, he was obviously resentful if the demands of the baby limited her ability to help prepare a salad or vacuum the upstairs bathroom. Worse was when he claimed the baby was responsible for his default state of being overextended. "I really need your support right now," he emphasized when she tried to talk to him about doing more of his share. "I thought when we got together I'd have a partner, someone to help me plan my time better, to carry some of the load. Since the baby came, it's more work for me, not less."

"That's what having a baby means," she said, trying to remain calm. "We both—"

"Plus I feel you're very distant from me right now," he said. "There's lots going on that I want to talk to you about. I value your opinion, your ideas. But you're so absorbed with Bradley I feel like I'm intruding, like I'm a fifth wheel, or a hired home support person or something. Don't you *want* to make time for me as well as the baby?"

I don't have a single minute for myself. How can I make time for you? she thought. "Having Bradley was a decision we *both* made," she said, attempting to keep her voice firm but not accusing. "We knew it was going to be extra work. We even talked about it, I remember. Of course I love you very much, but I am sooooo tired. It seems like years since I had more than three consecutive hours of sleep. If I had more help from you, I'd have more energy to *give* you. A baby changes things. We knew that. You even told me that a baby would help you better prioritize your work, focus on what's important and not get sidetracked in stupid stuff. That you'd—"

"That was before we even knew about the commission. I heard yesterday from Duncan a film crew is accompanying these guys, so what we say to them could be part of a movie if we can make our presentation hard-hitting enough. That would get our message out even further. Dewclaw thinks we should raise money and have our own film made. There's enough wannabe filmmakers in Nelson that we should be able to find somebody who—"

"We were talking about you and me and Bradley," she reminded him.

"That's exactly what I mean," he exploded. "You're not interested anymore in what I'm doing, what we're doing. It's all about the baby."

"It *is* all about the baby right now," she snapped back.

~

As Jane and she had trudged up the logging road toward the blockade, she was glad Willy had insisted they bundle up against the early morning chill. She was wearing a heavy sweater of Jane's, and Willy had loaned her a bulky down vest to wear over her jacket. The sun was just cresting the valley's eastern wall by the time they started to drive toward the Chico Creek protest. But once they crossed the river to the highway side of the valley they were back in shadow.

The windows at Jane and Willy's had shown nothing but darkness when Jane awakened her Monday morning. Despite the ridiculously early hour, Willy was already busy in the kitchen making a thermos of coffee for them to take in a backpack along with various power bars and trail mix. He was adamant they write his office phone number on their arms since, he said, the cops often confiscate any paper you might have with you if you're arrested. "I'm in Nelson today so I'll come over to the cop shop and bail you two out," he said, grinning at them.

"We're not going to get busted, Willy," Jane reminded him. "We're just going to be there to show support and bear witness and all that."

"Doesn't hurt to be safe," Willy said. After filling the thermos, he topped up the two women's cups where they sat at the kitchen table.

"Never mind safe. Why does this thing start so early?" Jane's friend mock-complained. Jane had explained earlier in the week that the protesters wanted to be in place before the work crew arrived at six thirty.

"It's not much of a blockade if everybody's already at work before we show up," Jane said. "Most crews will respect our line if there's enough of us."

"Until the company gets an injunction, or the cops decide you're trespassing," Willy said.

Despite Jane's plan, they didn't leave the house until six fifteen. After Jane steered her Tracker off pavement onto the Chico Creek road, they jostled and bounced along a ribbon of gravel winding uphill through forest. She watched Jane concentrating on the track ahead and began to wonder if her friend had made some error and was headed up the wrong logging truck route. But as they climbed around yet another bend, she saw a cluster of pickups and cars parked single file where a cleared area of stumps and slash piles bordered the road.

They left the Tracker with the other vehicles, and continued upwards along the lane on foot. While they plodded forward, she could hear the vibrato roar of a creek through the trees down a slope to her left, more audible at some times than others. The parked vehicles were a couple of hundred metres behind them, invisible now that the track had curved up a steep incline, when they came upon a television news van and an Explorer SUV whose sides advertised the hosts of a local radio station's afternoon music program. Both the van and SUV were pulled over as close to the edge of the narrow road as possible. Not far past the evidence of media interest, four white RCMP cruisers sat parked along the shoulder. Ahead of them was a brown Crown Victoria bristling with extra antennas that she suspected was a ghost car.

"Looks serious," she panted to Jane.

"We should already be there," Jane wheezed back. "Let's hurry."

"I thought we *were* hurrying," her friend tried to joke. Her stomach had knotted at the sight of the massed police cars. Clearly, the blockade was an important matter if it brought this many police so far up a mountain in the middle of nowhere this early in the morning.

Around another turn, they heard the indistinct sound of voices, and then the route angled into a surprisingly large cleared area in the forest. Opposite them, on the far side of the opening, a clump of men and women stood under a banner she recognized from the sign-painting session at Earth House: "Our water, our homes, our life: save Chico Creek." The banner was strung between two trees so it hung across where the road they were on wound higher into the woods from the clearing. Several of the two dozen or so people beneath the banner were carrying picket signs constructed that same evening at Earth House. She spotted David next to Bronwen and Dewclaw, his face angled to speak with someone behind him. A few others she recognized from her visits to Earth House, but many of those present she had never seen before. Stacked picket signs leaned against a tree nearby. Some people in the protest group besides David were chatting to each other, and one man she didn't know had stepped forward and was crouched in front facing the blockade to take photographs of the assembly. He called out imploring certain individuals to smile, and a moment later asked them to look resolute. Nervous laughter greeted his commands. But most of the blockaders' eyes were steadily aimed across the uneven ground at a second group, this one entirely male.

Two large trucks pulling low open trailers were parked in the clearing; she wondered if the rigs had enough room to turn around in the space, large as it seemed compared to the narrow opening between the trees Jane and she had followed. She couldn't imagine even a skilled driver backing the big vehicles all the way down to the bottom of the logging road. A massive bulldozer rested on the trailer behind one of the trucks. The other trailer was empty, but beside it on the ground was a smaller yellow vehicle. This one ran on big tires swaddled in chains rather than on caterpillar tracks. A short stubby crane rose behind a metal and mesh cage surrounding the operator's seat, and three cables dangled down a foot or so from the end of the crane.

Beside the trailers several RCMP in peaked caps and uniform jackets with "POLICE" across the backs stood talking easily to a dozen men, some wearing or carrying yellow hard hats and a few in reflective vests. A number of the loggers were smoking cigarettes. Not far from them, a pile of gear included five chainsaws, gasoline cans, ropes, axes, folded tarps and three large tool boxes. The crackling sound of walkie-talkies the police had clipped to their upper chests resounded intermittently. A constable occasionally would bow his head toward his chest as his right hand adjusted some control while he spoke into the device.

Muted cheers and called greetings were directed at the two women as they stepped into view, picking their way unsteadily toward the protesters across churned-up soil. David stepped forward to meet them and hugged Jane. His face lit up as he swivelled away from Jane and held out his arms. "Shannon," he said. A second later he was embracing her. They kissed briefly, in front of everybody.

He kept his arm around her waist, as he swept her into the ranks of the blockade. "Sorry we're late," she panted, a little overwhelmed by his enthusiasm. "We were slow getting—"

"You're here," he said, looking directly at her, his voice tender. "That's the important thing."

Then Jane was asking for an update, and David was telling how the Earth House bunch were still rigging up the banner when the first of the trucks pulled into the clearing, followed shortly by the cops. More protesters and loggers had trickled in over the past half hour. Bronwen chimed in to say the police seemed to be waiting for something, and hadn't even approached them yet.

"We know they have an injunction," Dewclaw said. David mentioned that it was a sign of Living Earth's past successes that the contractor could obtain an injunction even before anything had happened, based on Living Earth's announcement that the blockade was planned.

"Duncan doesn't think their injunction will hold up in court," Dewclaw said. "It was essentially *ex parte,* and before the fact."

"That won't stop them arresting us today and dismissing the charge in court later," David said.

"And meantime, the logging will be underway," Bronwen said.

"Where *is* Duncan?" another protester asked.

"Had to work," David said. "But he's standing by, just in case."

"Like Willy," Jane said. "Shannon, are you warm enough?"

In fact she had felt herself trembling uncontrollably, but thought it had to do not so much with the chill air as the combined excitement of actually being part of a protest where she could get arrested, and of David holding her body next to his.

He bent to kiss her forehead. "Do you want my coat?"

She blushed at the attention suddenly focused on her. "I'm fine," she insisted. "I think I'm just scared about what might happen."

"Don't worry," Bronwen said. "These blockades are more or less a ritual. We show up, they either have or get an injunction, the cops give you a chance to step aside, some of us get arrested and the boys with their toys get on with the job." She nodded toward the heavy equipment resting opposite them across the clearing.

"It isn't always that way." The voice was that of the elderly woman from the planning meeting at Earth House, who had spoken about US planes seeding the area's clouds with aluminum. She clutched a feather of some sort in her left hand, and waved it around as she spoke. "At the north end of Perry Ridge last year there was that encampment that set back road building for weeks."

"For *two* weeks, Violet," Bronwen noted. "In the end it was the usual: the contractor got his injunction, the teepees and tents came down, seven people were arrested and the logging road got built."

"If you think like that, why are you—" the woman began.

"Here they come," somebody yelled.

The squad of policemen, eight in all, had begun walking abreast toward the blockade. Jeers sounded from a couple of sources among the protesters. Trailing after the officers were three civilians, one man hoisting a television camera and one waving a microphone boom.

"Now don't worry, Shannon," David said. "It's a peaceful protest and the Mounties know it."

He dropped his arm from around her. Jane reached for her friend's hand.

~

It was early afternoon before those arrested at Chico Creek had emerged into the reception area of the Nelson RCMP building through a door marked *No Admittance* and protected by a lock activated by a punch code. She had glanced at that door repeatedly, hour after hour, once the receptionist—a woman in her forties in civilian clothes—said their friends would be released through there after they were processed. Long hours of sitting on an uncomfortable metal chair, speaking occasionally with the three other protesters waiting with her, or walking outside to pace back and forth in the parking lot for a breath of fresh air.

A middle-aged man came in to report that his car had hit and killed a deer at Six Mile east of town, and the receptionist duly filled out a form on her computer. A young couple showed up to ask how to contest a roadside suspension that the baseball-capped male had received the previous evening for driving over the legal limit for alcohol. He was full of indignant bluster, but the receptionist kept calmly advising him to speak to a lawyer. The pair eventually left. The clock on the wall above the counter where the receptionist interacted with the public advanced its minute hand with incredible slowness.

An hour and a half after she had arrived at the wheel of Jane's Tracker, after travelling to town with three other vehicles driven by blockaders who had also volunteered to pick up those arrested, Duncan Locke bustled in. He wore a suit and had an attaché case in hand. They all stood to meet him, and he explained that he had begun the process of getting everybody out of custody. Because so many had been busted at previous demonstrations, and because the cops considered this to have been a violent demonstration due to Violet's actions—technically, she had been charged with assault on a police officer and interference with a police officer in performance of his duties—the Mounties were reluctant to release anybody on their own recognizance. The lawyer said he had arranged for bail money if necessary, but wanted to try to convince the authorities to reconsider, at least for some of those arrested. "Canadian law doesn't recognize guilt by association, except for gang members," he declared. When the flurry of blockaders' questions subsided, he spoke to the receptionist and was buzzed through a different door in the wall alongside the counter, and disappeared.

He was gone a long time. The group from the protest had fallen silent, although Rodney—an Earth House resident she recognized—went on a coffee run at one point and came back after forty-five minutes with sugar-free spelt cookies from the organic bakery, besides the hot drinks. She found the confection tasteless, but the others devoured them with gusto.

At noon the receptionist lowered a metal shutter over the counter. A sign on the shutter announced that reception was closed between twelve and one, and listed a number to call for non-emergency matters. Fifteen minutes later the lawyer appeared through the same door he had entered. They all rose, and he announced he had been partially successful and that everybody would be out soon except for Violet. She insisted the state was illegitimate, due to its failure to protect water, and was refusing to be bailed out, at least for now, since release was contingent on a promise of lawful behaviour. Duncan said he would wait with them until one PM, after which, if those in custody hadn't been released, he would have to leave for another appointment. It was impossible to tell, he said, how soon their friends would be freed.

When the group resumed sitting, Duncan lowered himself into the empty chair beside her. He asked after Jane and Willy, but was soon talking about himself while she half-listened, wondering how David was faring, glad that he wasn't going to stay behind bars over some principle. Duncan was explaining, she realized suddenly, how he had become aware of the vital mission of the environmental movement after his wife divorced him for no apparent reason. He had indulged her throughout their marriage by supporting her ever-changing interests in pottery, weaving, acrylic painting and then watercolours. Out of nowhere his wife announced she needed to leave the marriage to find herself. He confessed her departure had thrown him into a spell of feeling lost, of re-evaluating who he was and what was he doing with his talents. That had resulted in him beginning to accept more pro bono cases, which in turn had introduced him to the Living Earth Society, Earth House and the environmental movement generally, whose ideas he now felt were central to his life.

He asked her what led her to become involved with Living Earth, but before she could reply they were startled by the metal shutter over the counter being raised. Duncan glanced at his watch, and said he needed to leave but that he had enjoyed speaking with her and looked forward to them talking again. At the door into the parking lot, he called out that somebody should phone him if those arrested weren't released within two more hours.

~

The RCMP officers had formed into a line opposite the blockade. One of them with grey hair showing under his cap had stepped forward and taken eyeglasses and a piece of paper out of a pocket behind his bulletproof vest. After carefully attaching the glasses to his face, he read out a court order declaring the blockade illegal. Before he finished, boos erupted from behind and on either side of her where she stood between Jane and David. As the Mountie raised his voice to be heard over the interference, three vehicles emerged at the entrance to the open area—two black RCMP vans and a small yellow bus. They slowly proceeded toward the tractor-trailers, lurching and jolting over the rough ground, and halted just behind the bulldozer. After a moment, the bus door opened and a dozen police wearing riot helmets with lifted visors filed out and formed a line alongside. Unlike the Mounties directly in front of the blockaders, each of the newly arrived officers stood with a club held in his right hand, with the body of the weapon angled across his torso and the free end cradled in his left.

Someone had handed the grey-haired Mountie a bullhorn, and over shouts and catcalls he began reading the injunction again from the start. When he finished, he removed his glasses and tucked them and the paper into his shirt once more. Lifting the bullhorn another time, he ordered all those present not wanting to be arrested to move away from the blockade and to leave the area. He pointed past the line of riot police to where the logging road led down the mountain.

She was aware of the protest thinning as several people besides Jane and herself detached from the group and started to walk across the clearing toward the road. Each step she took felt like she were in a dream. From behind she heard a shouted order: "Everybody down." She thought she recognized Justin's voice. Stopping to glance back, along with the others withdrawing with her, she saw the remnants of the protesters had seated themselves and linked arms, except for the old woman.

Shuffling forward toward the wall of Mounties, the elderly blockader held up and waved the feather she carried, launching into a tuneless hum. As she approached closer to the row of RCMP jackets, she began chanting mumbled syllables.

The elderly woman halted just in front of the police and extended one quivering arm so that her lifted feather jounced down the line inches from the officers' faces, and started back. One of the cops suddenly jerked his head back as the feather travelled past. His arm shot out and grabbed the woman's. She unleashed a scream, surprisingly loud.

"Violet!" the voices of David and a couple of others responded. He and two other men, as well as Bronwen, were on their feet and striding toward where the officer and a partner were attempting to pull the shrieking woman's arms behind her back and handcuff her. The feather lay on muddy ground. The remaining blockaders stood uncertainly.

Immediately, at a shouted command, three members of the riot squad lowered their helmet visors, and jogged rapidly toward where the dozen departing protesters had bunched. The three riot cops were yelling at them, "Move! Go!" The officers gestured with their clubs as they neared, pointing toward the road into the clearing. A gloved left hand grabbed Jane's shoulder, heaving her forward so that she stumbled into a middle-aged woman next to her with the force of the push. "Clear the area, clear the area," one of the other riot policemen commanded repeatedly. He and his two colleagues impatiently urged the former blockaders into motion, waving with their free hands, brandishing clubs and shoving at any dawdling protestors' backs to hurry them to the clearing's entrance. Once on the logging road, the group` was harried downhill and around a curve past where the police cruisers were parked. Then the three visored officers halted, forming a line across the track. A dozen metres beyond the constables, those who had left the protest milled around in a clump, talking to each other.

The former blockaders were buzzed on the adrenaline of the morning's events. People spoke quickly, in spurts, speculating about what might be happening back up the mountain. The slightest attempt at a joke provoked nervous laughter. Forty minutes later, after a few of the group had drifted off toward their cars, those protestors remaining were ordered by the riot cops to clear the route. First the

Mounties, then the former blockaders stepped to the sides of the lane as the two RCMP vans holding those arrested inched slowly past. Behind them came the patrol cars, each with one or two people in the back seat cage. She tried to see where David was confined, but caught no glimpse of him.

Since the police vehicles were travelling at a walking pace, some members of the group tried to stride beside the vans and cruisers, dodging the tree boughs and other foliage that edged the road as the vehicles descended the track. The protestors shouted encouragement and slogans, and flashed V signs and clenched fists at the prisoners inside, with the ones confined in the cruisers responding in kind, until the procession reached the blockaders' own parked cars. The rest of the protestors followed behind the motorcade. A couple of times en route, the officers used their vehicles' PA systems to order people to keep back. One of the patrol car drivers activated his siren briefly to warn off a small group that darted toward the rear of the van in front of him. The sudden whoops of the siren startled the convoy's entire escort. As the procession descended, visible behind them until the first bend were the three riot policemen still blocking the emptied stretch of logging road.

∽

David had seemed to her almost manic when at last the arrested blockaders appeared through the door in ones and twos and threes—like airplane passengers exiting through a security door into an arrivals waiting area, she thought. Accompanied by Dewclaw and a bearded man she hadn't seen before, David stepped into the reception lobby after most of the others had been freed. He bore down toward her with a determined tread, ignoring questions and shouts of praise and welcome. In an instant she was in his arms and he was kissing her all over her face. "Shannon," he said repeatedly. Later he told her she was all he could think of in the holding cell. In the lobby, though, she felt a little embarrassed by the intensity of his public display of affection.

He seemed on a talking jag as she steered him and three others in Jane's Tracker back up the valley. His excited topics ranged from the publicity the morning's confrontation was sure to receive, thanks to Violet and the police overreaction, to the need for an immediate statement from Living Earth and plans for a public meeting within a few days. Fourteen people had been arrested, with much more serious charges laid against four of them, including David, although he was confident these would be reduced to the more usual ones once Duncan got to work. From the back seat, Dewclaw and the two others—a pretty young woman, Jennifer, who said she had never been to a demonstration before, and an Earth House inhabitant, Alden, who clearly had his eye on Jennifer—could hardly interrupt David's speculations about press coverage and ideas of how to capitalize on the arrests. Yet he kept his hand on her right thigh the whole way back to Earth House, where Jennifer had left her car early in the morning to travel to the protest with the others.

People seated around the Earth House living room broke into applause when David walked in. Justin said there had been eight calls from the media David needed to reply to. But David took her hand and pulled her to sit beside him on one of the couches while he talked energetically to the group, pausing only to swallow beer from a bottle somebody had given him. She shook her head when a beer was offered her, though several people around the room were eagerly consuming them.

David's ideas about the next steps Living Earth needed to take in defense of Chico Creek were interrupted several times by joking and laughing whenever something he said reminded one of the group of an incident from the morning's confrontation. For the first time, she heard David cut off somebody else's spoken suggestion as a new idea hit him, as if he would lose his train of thought unless he uttered his brainstorm right away. The other people present seemed to accept David's cranked-up mode good-humouredly; she wondered if this post-demonstration behaviour was familiar to them.

During a lull in him holding forth, she managed to tell him she really needed to return Jane's Tracker. He walked her to the hallway. The murmur of talk from the living room, interspersed with bursts of laughter, was audible behind them as he gathered her into a fierce embrace. A long session of kissing ensued, with an array of coats and jackets hung on hooks witnessing their passion from either side of the hallway. "I want to be with you tonight, Shannon," he whispered in her ear at one point. "I want so much to be with you. All the time." His hand stroked firmly down her back, then pulled her against him with both hands cupping her buttocks through her jeans. Holding her there, he began kissing where her neck joined her shoulder.

"I'm . . . I should get the Tracker back to Jane," she managed. His evident urgent need for her was arousing, she had to admit. He was kissing her face again, and she put up one hand to gently touch his lips. "I'd like to be with you, too. But Jane might be wanting to use her car. I should have thought to leave her the keys to mine. But it seemed important that we follow right behind the cops into town, and when we were sorting out who would go and who would drive Jane home and everything, I was a bit dis—"

His hands were smoothing her hair down either side of her head. "Maybe Jane doesn't need the car right away and you could get it to her later? Can you phone and ask?"

Jane was glad to hear everybody arrested was out of custody, and said she was fine with her friend keeping the Tracker a little longer. "Promise me, though, that if you stay over, you'll let me know. I don't want to put in another night like the last time you were there, worrying about whether you're in the ditch or whatever. I have to run some errands in the morning, too, so bottom line is be back by 10 AM. God, I feel like your mother."

Seconds after the door to David's room closed behind them, he had her shirt pulled up and her brassiere undone and was nuzzling and licking her nipples. His lovemaking was rougher than she'd experienced with him, as he tugged her free of the rest of her clothes and half-lifted, half-pushed her onto the bed. His frantic desire was contagious; he dispensed with foreplay, unlike the previous time they had been intimate, but she could tell her body was slick with excitement as he entered her and began to thrust with frenzied determination. She was dimly aware at that moment both of them were vocalizing cries she had not heard before.

When his head had collapsed against her breasts, and she was stroking his hair, the thought occurred to her that they hadn't used a condom. She had stopped taking birth control pills when Andrew moved to Kingston. Though he complained, she had read of the health hazards involved with long-term birth control use, and insisted Andrew use a condom during their subsequent trysts.

At Earth House, with David's welcome weight atop her as he gently snored, she calculated and recalculated the days since her last period, and realized she was on the cusp of a dangerous time. When David woke from his doze, and resumed kissing her while his fingers started to lightly stroke between her legs, she reminded him that they should use protection if they were going to make love another time. They were both startled awake when the dinner gong rang on the floor below them.

David brought back to the bedroom from the celebratory supper a half-full bottle of wine. They were both a little giddy, sitting with their backs against the headboard while they finished the bottle. She had felt shy being with the others at the meal, since she knew they were aware of what she and David had been up to in his room. Mostly she listened to the continued replay of the events of the day and their impact for the Chico Creek and other Living Earth campaigns. But back on David's bed, she found that she could tease him, perhaps because he so clearly was enamoured of her.

When David had her bare from the waist up and was suckling on her breasts, she remembered in time to stop him. "I take it from your attention to my girls that you'd like me to stay the night?"

"More than that," he slurred, "I'd *love* you to." Then, suddenly serious, looking at her intently: "I love you, Shannon. I—"

She leaned forward to kiss his nose, then wriggled out from under his arms and perched on the edge of the bed, retrieving and buttoning her shirt. "Be right back. I promised Jane I'd phone."

"You're right," he confirmed. "I forgot we were going to do that. I was having too good a time, I guess."

When she slipped back into the room, he was propped up once more against the headboard with a wineglass in his hand, staring across the room at nothing. She quickly shucked off her clothes and climbed naked under the covers.

"Shannon," he said, still sitting atop the duvet. "There's something serious I need to ask you."

"You want to ask me for a blow job," she said, mock-serious, looking up at him from where she lay with her head on a pillow. "Well, I'll have to see what I can do."

"No!" he seemed scandalized. "I'm *serious*. This is a big step for me. But I . . . I want you to move in with me. I know we haven't known each other all that long, but I can't stop thinking about you. Like I was telling you, when I was in the lockup and should probably have been considering how Living Earth could best make use of the arrests, or what to do about crazy Violet, all I could focus on was how good it feels to be around you. How good it is when we make love."

Her stomach had tightened when he spoke about them living together. She remembered Jane's question about what her connection with David meant to her. His offer seemed awfully sudden. "Sounds to me like you're in lust with me," she kept her tone bright.

"Shannon." His voice was reproachful, crestfallen.

She sat up and turned to face him. "It's sweet of you to ask." She kissed his cheek. "But I think we need to know each other better. Let's just enjoy the time we have for now, and see what happens."

"You'll head back to Vancouver soon," he said. "I don't think I could bear that."

She started to tug at the buttons on his shirt. "Unless Jane and Willy kick me out, I'm not leaving tomorrow. But unless you take those clothes off, I don't see how I can give you that blow job."

"I didn't ask you for—"

"Shhhh." She pulled his arm out of his shirt. "You don't understand. I *want* to."

～

In public, she tried to keep from showing the resentment she felt at being left to look after the baby more or less on her own. Although she made a point of always being civil to David when they were around others, especially at each night's communal dinner if he was there, she wondered sometimes if Earth House's inhabitants sensed the tension between herself and David. She could express some of her frustration to Jane whenever she loaded Bradley into his new car seat and steered the Corolla over to Jane's for tea. But she didn't want to bother Jane unnecessarily: Jane had unexpectedly landed a big contract with the Columbia Basin Trust, a public granting agency for community projects. The work was a rush job to edit a series of position papers on waste recycling in the area; Jane's contact at the Trust had implied more contracts would be available, perhaps even steady employment, if Jane did a good job with this initial assignment.

Still, Jane offered to take the baby overnight to provide a break for the new parents. "It'll be an experiment: practice for Willy and me in case we ever decide to have kids. Plus I'm curious how Willy will react to looking after Bradley." The proposal was tempting, since Jane's ability to calm and soothe the baby when he acted out during visits was impressive. Jane attributed this knack to her childhood spent tending younger siblings. Still, the thought of leaving Bradley with someone else—even someone as remarkable with babies as Jane—was upsetting. The baby was extraordinarily precious, even if how to cope with him was an exhausting puzzle, and she couldn't yet imagine passing Bradley over to someone else for a whole night. She wondered, too, if at some level having Jane help her let David off the hook. She wanted David to *want* to help her with Bradley.

Besides, the day-to-day chores were what she needed David to participate in, and that problem wouldn't be solved by an occasional overnight respite. She desperately wished for someone to look after Bradley so she could have a moment to clean herself, tidy up the bedroom, catch up on laundry and maybe even return some of the mounting pile of emails from her thesis supervisor, friends and her aunts and other relatives. Or even snatch a nap between feedings.

One Wednesday she was attempting to simultaneously change Bradley, put away in the closet and chests of drawers a basket full of David's and her clean clothes that had sat on a chair for nearly a week, and iron a shirt preparatory to driving down to the Co-op in Slocan Park to shop for staples since the house duty roster had assigned this task to the couple. David had left right after breakfast for Nelson to take Living Earth's proposal for action to an all-day meeting of the coalition of groups opposed to the gigantic ski resort scheduled to be built in the Purcell Mountains.

She answered a knock on the room's door, while Bradley behind her on the bed screeched his displeasure about some discomfort even a changed diaper hadn't resolved. Bronwen stood in the doorway. "Would it help if I looked after Bradley while you go to the Co-op?" she asked.

Bronwen's offer startled her, and she burst into tears of gratitude. Once the initial novelty of having an infant living at Earth House had worn off and the residents had ceased pausing to coo and make faces at Bradley whenever they saw him, she was sure the inhabitants had begun to secretly resent having a crying baby on the premises. Yet, at least in public, everyone at the House only said laudatory things about him if she had him in his car seat on the floor beside her at dinner. Or, if he began to fuss and she was attempting to eat with one hand while dandling him with the other, somebody was sure to ask to hold him, bouncing him up and down for a minute or two before passing him back.

In the end Bronwen accompanied her and Bradley to the Co-op, since the idea of leaving him with Bronwen bothered her as much or more as leaving him with Jane. Bronwen continued over the following weeks to assist with the baby, however, minding him for a few minutes several times a day if not occupied with some chore in the garden, the house or the Living Earth office. Bradley's mother was grateful for the moments she could give her full attention to some horribly overdue task. The baby was always at ease around Bronwen; his face would light up if he saw her. And she sometimes seemed to have a sixth sense about when Bradley's mother was at her wits' end.

Why Bronwen stepped forward to aid in this way wasn't clear. In the bedroom one night, David denied having specifically asked her to intervene, but went on to laud her thoughtfulness and devotion to the environmental cause. "Her help is right in the spirit of the environmental community, after all. The whole idea is to look after each other. In the fall, say, if somebody has to go into town to confront Forestry over a new timber licence that threatens people's water, the rest of the people on that water line will help get in that person's winter wood."

Watching Bronwen amuse Bradley with a rattle the next afternoon, his mother, as she worked through a list of phone calls she had put off for days, questioned how strong her own commitment to Living Earth really was. She wondered whether David wouldn't have done better to have a child with someone like Bronwen, an uncomplaining adherent who would have been glad to mother his child single-handed, or indeed shoulder any burden if it freed the most articulate and knowledgeable spokesperson for the group to carry on the daily struggle on behalf of the planet.

~

She had driven back from the doctor in Nelson both ecstatic and apprehensive. Her three weeks living at Earth House since her return from Vancouver had been an unblemished joy, despite her initial qualms. David was tender and considerate, if a bit moony sometimes—seeming to never be sated with staring at her, touching her, talking by the hour with her, making marvellous love to her. He rearranged the bedroom to make space for a small IKEA desk she brought from Vancouver so she could work on her thesis in the quiet of their room. And while she hadn't yet started to make progress on the remaining chapters, she had taken time to review everything she had written so far and had produced a page of detailed notes on what the thesis's final portion needed to cover.

David arranged with Alden, who David said probably possessed the most carpentry skills of anybody at Earth House, to extend the room's closet so she could hang her clothes. They cleared out David's winter jackets and ski gear from the closet and packed them into boxes that he slid under the bed, making more space for her skirts, dresses and shoes. At a garage sale in Slocan one Saturday they found a chest of drawers they placed alongside his to hold the rest of her things.

When David didn't have a pressing morning engagement, he seemed to like to slip downstairs to bring coffee up from the kitchen for the two of them to enjoy in bed. They sipped the hot drink leaning back on pillows, chatting of this and that or just smiling at each other in silence in the room filled with summer light. From outside were audible the hammering of flickers and calls of jays and robins, or the occasional distant voices of house residents already at work in the garden. Then David's hands would caress her thigh or ribs or breasts, their lips would meet, coffee cups would be set down on the floor or table beside the bed, and a few moments later they would be naked in each other's arms.

At some level she knew these days and nights with David constituted an idyll, a honeymoon, but she could think of no reason not to savour it. And to want it to continue. Now, though, she was returning from Nelson with news that could threaten all this happiness.

Or add to it, she had reminded herself as she slowed past the clump of houses, the large Co-op store, credit union branch, repair garage and a few other businesses along the stretch of highway known as Slocan Park. The pregnancy was certainly not planned. Yet she was glad to carry David's child. Her parents would be thrilled at the idea of a grandchild, she reflected, though they would put pressure on her to be married to David before the baby was born. She could deflect her parents' insistence on marriage, but what if David didn't want a child? Demanded she not go through with having the baby? Did she want to give birth to a child by herself? She had always assumed that she would have a child or children one day, that she would want this when she found a man, a partner, a husband she would be willing to raise a child with. Without doubt David was such a man. On the other hand, they hadn't lived together for even a whole month. She had never heard David speak about children one way or another, let alone marriage.

As she signalled to turn onto the road to Earth House, she told herself not to anticipate. She had thought of talking her situation over with Jane before informing David. This would probably be the most rational approach: to sort out her feelings with Jane's help before she spoke to David. But she acknowledged that more than anything she wanted David to be the first to know.

She patiently waited until David had returned from a legal strategy meeting at Duncan's office and reported to an informal gathering in Earth House's living room about the lawyer's plans for defending the blockaders. Duncan's idea was to use a hydrologist friendly to Living Earth as a witness at the trial. The scientist would explain the potential danger logging posed to the hydrological cycle, and hence human existence. Duncan intended to argue that the protest, and even Violet's over-zealous opposition to police attempts to curtail the blockade, amounted to acts of self-defense. The announcement was met with cheers.

At last she drew David away from the others for a walk. He was still pumped at the lawyer's willingness to use the courtroom to stress the seriousness of what the small logging job up Chico Creek represented to the planet's ability to sustain human life. They strolled hand in hand through the forest north of the house, following an overgrown cat trail left over from when the grounds of Earth House were clear-cut by the dwelling's original owner.

David initially seemed unable to comprehend what she was telling him. He pulled his hand back from hers and halted on the brushy track beside where the corrugated trunk of a huge cedar rose from the underbrush. His face aimed toward her was twisted into an expression she had never seen him display: shock and fear replacing the usual self-confidence he radiated. He started to utter several words and choked each of them off before trying to speak another. He looked miserable.

Her stomach spasmed. She was terrified of his reply, and simultaneously hated to cause him such distress. Yet she needed to learn how he would respond. She reached out to touch his arm.

"I think it was the day of the blockade," she heard herself say. "We were both pretty wrought up. I never thought something like this would happen. But we love each other. At least, I know I love you, and I think you love me." She could see his face loosen a tiny amount.

A thought struck her she hoped might catch his imagination, reconcile him to what had happened, intrigue him even. "So it's a blockade baby. A little warrior for the earth."

"A blockade baby." She noted a change in his eyes—a slight easing of their tightness, though the trepidation in them was still evident.

She nodded. "A blockade baby. Something wonderful that appeared when we least expected it, that happened as a result of taking a stand for Chico Creek. A green being that showed up to cheer us on."

He tried to grin, though due to the tension still obvious in his face his expression resembled a grimace. But he stepped toward her and embraced her, kissing her lips.

His arms stayed around her. "It's just . . . unexpected," he managed.

"For me, too." She kissed him, then pulled her head back to stare into his eyes. "You don't have to have anything to do with us, you know. The baby and me, I mean. I won't hold you to anything."

His eyes glistened. "I love you, Shannon." His voice wavered. "I guess I hadn't thought too far ahead about you and me. I love being around you, and I guess I was just enjoying that." He took a breath. "I'm scared."

"You think I'm not?" she said. She smiled at him and kissed him again. "But as long as there's two of us, if you're with me on this, it's not so scary. I think we can—"

"Three," he said.

"Three?"

"You, me and the baby." He took a deep breath. "I can't help it." His voice sounded bewildered. "I love you."

They kissed for a long time.

The Earth House crew appeared thrilled when, at dinner that evening, David tapped on a glass, stood up and announced that the following April someone else would be moving in. Cheers, hoots, shouted congratulations, hugs and high-fives for David and her greeted his explanation of who the scheduled inhabitant would be. She felt a bit like a celebrity, and thought she saw David's enthusiasm for the baby notch up with each positive response from their fellow residents over the course of the evening.

His self-confidence seemed nearly restored when, after his hesitant question when they finally retired to their room, she assured him they could make love as usual.

"No need for a condom, either," she said. "The only catch is, in about five months I'll be fat and ugly and you won't want to have sex with me. So we better make up for the lost time we're going to have."

"I can't imagine that. You're awfully sexy."

"Trust me. Plus I'll be throwing up in the mornings, which is probably also a turnoff."

"Not to me."

"Yeah, right." But in fact there was an urgency to his lovemaking for weeks afterwards, an added forcefulness that she found arousing, as if he indeed regarded her as overwhelmingly desirable, irresistibly alluring.

The Living Earth members seemed to treat her with added respect, once the news of the pregnancy spread through the organization. If she ventured an opinion on some topic, whether at a formal or informal gathering, the voices present were either full of positive response to her idea or vague in their disagreement. Women she hardly knew hugged her and spoke as though growing a baby—or maybe growing *David's* baby, she was never sure which—was a significant accomplishment on her part.

Jane, however, was less of a cheerleader. A long silence ensued at Jane's kitchen table when, over tea, the news was transmitted.

"I'm going to say this once," Jane eventually stated, "and then I'll drop it. You know you're a very important person in my—"

"I think I know what you're going to say. But I'm not doing this lightly. Neither is David. He and I have talked. We—"

"Please, let me finish," Jane said. "You're probably my dearest friend, Shannon. But I'm going to repeat what I said when you told us you were going to move in with David. And then I promise you won't hear it from me ever again, no matter what happens." She lifted her mug of tea. "I didn't think moving in at Earth House was a good idea. David has real skills as a leader, but you haven't really known him long enough to know how committed he really is to—"

Jane held up her free hand to ward off the objection being launched from the chair opposite her. "Willy and I have known him longer than you have. We've seen how he behaves in his relationships with women. Going through with a pregnancy, intending to have a child with him, is ten times the bad idea that moving in with him was."

Jane took a sip of her tea and lowered the mug to the table. "That's that. Now I'll support you fully in whatever you decide. I know Willy will, too."

"David really cares for me," her friend said, her eyes suddenly teary. "Once he got over the shock, he's wild about the idea of us having a baby together."

Jane moved around the table and held her while she cried.

"I wa-want you to be happy for me. For us. I've really, really g-given this a lot of—" Sobs overrode the words.

Jane stroked her hair and kissed the top of her head. "What do you think you'll call it?"

∿

The shock to her parents when she had informed them on the phone she was pregnant was predictable, but more difficult to handle than she had anticipated. When she had made the decision to move in with David, after two days considering his offer and two additional nights of bliss in his bed, she told her parents only that she was relocating to the Kootenays, to Earth House. So on the phone now, scant weeks later, she pretended that shortly after she started living at Earth House she had fallen in love with David. She admitted having a child with him so soon was a risk, but stressed how much they loved each other. Her father, in one of his rare interventions, wanted to know what David did for a living. The explanation was greeted with silence.

In the end her mother extracted two promises from her before her parents would let her off the phone. First that she would bring David to Vancouver soon for them to meet him, and second that she would finish her thesis before the baby was born. "You won't have a moment to yourself once the baby arrives," her mother cautioned, adding, for the sixth time, "You don't know what you're getting into."

David's call to his parents had gone more smoothly. His mother and father, along with his youngest sister, were spending three weeks at the family cottage near Owen Sound on Georgian Bay, a property they had purchased in the 1950s. "My folks already have three grandkids," David explained. "So another one isn't as big a deal. My brother has two by two different wives, and my oldest sister has one." David's parents told him they were looking forward to meeting Shannon, either at Christmas when a family rendezvous was planned in Florida, with tickets for everyone who was going to attend paid for by the parents, or on a trip to the Kootenays the parents said they would make once the baby arrived.

"They keep talking about visiting my cabin in the pines," David reported. "I've sent them photos, and keep insisting it's a *house*, a communal *house*. I can't tell if they're simply being dense or are trying to give me a hard time."

"Did they ask to see a picture of me?" she asked.

He kissed her. "No. But I can't wait to send them one. They'll never believe I'm with someone so beautiful."

"Flatterer."

"If flattery has gotten me you, it's obvious that flattery really will get you everything."

"How corny can you get?" she asked, her tone mock-dismissive. But she kissed him back.

Her parents and David's poured advice and gifts for the baby on them. David's brother sent a portable crib and car seat that his youngest son had outgrown. The demand her parents had made to meet David was fulfilled in late August when he decided to travel to Victoria for a provincial strategy meeting called by the Green Party. She and David drove to the Coast, where after a couple of days with her parents in Vancouver, David took the ferry to Vancouver Island to attend the strategy gathering. Her parents were cool toward him, but she was pleased to see him attempting to charm them, good-humouredly insisting on the value of the work Living Earth was doing, while at the same time listening to her mother's concerns about how expensive children are to raise.

When she and David were back again at Earth House, her mother sent an email politely thanking her for introducing him to them. He did seem an admirable person, her mother conceded, although she couldn't help mentioning how much more relieved they all would feel if David had regular employment.

The pending court case, and monitoring the logging on Chico Creek, occupied a lot of David's time. And a new concern was the mismanagement of a community forest at Kaslo, north of Nelson on Kootenay Lake. Living Earth was following closely a wrangle in Kaslo between two factions in the society overseeing the forest; both factions had elected members to the village council. Residents of Earth House were part of a local coalition planning to advocate for a community forest in the valley, and everyone was anxious to avoid the mistakes the directors of Kaslo's venture had clearly made.

After enduring the bitter cold of two Edmonton winters, she found the snowy season at Earth House temperate and pleasant. The thermometer rarely dipped under four below, and the plentiful snow turned meadow, woods, riverbank and mountains into picturesque Christmas card scenes. As in summer, she was awed by the beauty everyplace around her. Crows squawked as usual as they flew over the white landscape, but eagles haunted the barren cottonwood stands along the river, and she once saw an owl in daylight perched on a snowy power line near the Winlaw bridge. Despite her increasing bulk, she was out on cross-country skis more frequently than ever before in her life—skiing the former rail line with David, or Jane, or by herself. Occasionally a group from Earth House would drive to the Nelson cross-country ski club's trailhead area on the Nelson–Salmo highway. On one of these excursions, she, Bronwen and Justin skied the length of the club's Clearwater Creek trail, which from a parking lot rose high into the backcountry. Portions of the tracked ascent were quite steep, but she managed to keep pace with the others and on their return downhill only wiped out twice. She found exhilarating the descent's repeated drops down a long slope, followed often by a curve at the bottom.

Jane was as good as her word in never again mentioning her disapproval of the pregnancy. The expectant couple was duly invited to Jane and Willy's for supper, and the two women frequently met for coffee or tea, or drove together into Nelson on shopping trips. Jane's friend was alert for any undermining of her relationship with David or her decision to have the baby. Yet all that could be designated as even a hint of negativity on Jane's part was gossip concerning some of the young mothers they saw and frequently spoke with at the Crossroads Café: which one had broken up with a partner or husband, or who was going around with a new man, or who had just moved in with somebody else's ex. Such gossip was as likely to be heard at the Earth House dinner table, however, as from Jane. The longer the mother-to-be lived in the valley, the better she knew the young women and men who filled the café, or danced the evening away at the community hall in Vallican, or who took part in fall equinox or winter solstice celebratory gatherings. And the better acquainted she became with the valley's young people, the more she realized how unstable the young valley families were.

Her pregnancy was used as a small element of the court proceedings when those arrested at the Chico Creek protest went to trial in late January. As Living Earth's lawyer, Duncan wanted her to attend as one of the group's supporters, who he said were vital to show the judge that the blockade enjoyed community support. Also, the lawyer insisted, her presence carrying her unborn child represented the future of the human race, threatened now with ecological peril. In addition, her connection with David demonstrated how normal, responsible, he was.

As instructed by Duncan, whenever there was a formal break in the trial, she would walk forward from the audience in the Nelson courtroom to the table where David sat beside the lawyer along with the three other protesters whose charges the Crown had decided to proceed with. David would stand, and she and he would kiss and confer. Although the judge was almost always absent during such breaks, Duncan claimed the presence of a pregnant partner of David's would be communicated informally to His Lordship by one or another of the court officials. "They love gossip as much as anybody," Duncan said. "I know it's theatre, but that's what court is: theatre." She felt foolish acting the role of the anxious pregnant wife, but did as she was told.

More engaging was when the lawyer, on discovering her background in English, asked her to research legal precedents concerning police activities at blockades and other instances where concerned citizens impeded access to buildings or roads for what they deemed a good cause. Some research she could do online, but she discovered that the librarian at the Nelson courthouse's law library was particularly helpful and friendly. The library was open to the public for certain hours each week, yet almost nobody used the library except members of the legal profession, the librarian told her.

Reading case after case from a list the librarian helped her develop, she quickly became fascinated by how a society adjudicates competing rights: at Chico Creek, for instance, the right of a company holding logging tenure to cut trees conflicted with the right of water users to protect the resource upon which depended the quiet enjoyment, as the term was, of their homes. She found she loved the precision of legal definitions: how burglary was not the same as breaking and entering, car theft was not the same as joyriding. Duncan praised her skill at locating leading cases once she had, with the help of the librarian, grasped the concept and identified those judgements that defense lawyers in similar prosecutions consistently referred to. Her case summaries were pronounced impressive by Duncan, and she began to wonder whether once she had completed her master's and the baby was old enough she ought to consider law school.

Duncan's attempt in court to call the hydrologist, to bring the big picture into the case was denied by the judge, who seemed impatient with many of the lawyer's statements. Several times the judge chastised Duncan for launching into a line of argument the judge declared was serving only to drag out the trial. The protesters had elected, on Duncan's advice, trial by judge rather than jury. The majority on local juries could as easily be forest industry employees, or their close relatives, as environmentally minded citizens.

Various members of Living Earth expressed anger at the judge's rulings, yet she now could see that for him the trial was a matter of law, not justice. Certain laws existed stipulating obedience to legal orders given by duly constituted authorities like the police, and forbidding interference with such authorities as they carried out legally sanctioned tasks. Had in this case such laws been broken? If so, the lawbreaker's intent, rationale, motivation and other fuzzy matters were no concern of the court's. A law might even be a bad law, but to the judge the issue at hand was reduced to whether a law—good or bad—had been transgressed. She saw how the judge's blinkers shut out much, but also found herself intrigued by how the arrangement allowed a society to distribute decision-making. The laws that existed were determined by city councils, provincial legislatures, national parliaments. Whether a specific law had been violated by individuals was decided by a judge or jury. She could appreciate the judge's lack of patience for someone attempting to blur these areas of responsibility, to in effect dispute a law, or aspects of a law, in court rather than to proceed with the court's proper task of determining whether that law had in this particular instance been broken.

She kept these thoughts to herself, though, and joined with the others in a general condemnation of the thick-headedness of the judge in not allowing them to present the *reason* why they had engaged in civil disobedience. The group didn't go around all day breaking laws; *why* they had chosen to blockade the Chico Creek Forestry Road was surely the basis of their case, and it was sheer stupidity or bias on the part of the judge when he refused to let their side introduce such vital matters.

Their lawyer did refer openly to her pregnancy once the protesters were found guilty, and he was allowed to address sentencing. In return for a peace bond, suspended sentence and reporting periodically to a parole officer, all but one of the group were freed. Violet, the elderly woman originally charged with assaulting a police officer, refused to sign to keep the peace. She declared to the judge, her voice rising to piercing levels, that since the survival of the planet, the survival of the whole human species, was at stake, no one of conscience could do anything but fight while they lived with every ounce of their breath for Mother Earth and the bears and trees and lakes and rivers and the entire human family. The judge, Violet stated, should be thoroughly ashamed of himself for aligning himself and the law with the despoilers of the planet, those who hold their fellow humans and the water that nourishes and sustains all life in contempt. After an extended effort by both the judge and Duncan to halt her outburst, she wound down at last and the judge managed to adjourn the court. Neither David nor the others could convince Violet that the peace bond would allow her to fight another day, and she was led off by a sheriff.

When the rest of the defendants and their supporters filed into the lobby outside the courtroom, David very publicly kissed her dress over the bulge in her belly and declared that the baby was already aiding their cause. Cheers and applause from Living Earth members and backers greeted his remark.

The legal research tasks Duncan had set her, plus some months of nausea as the fetus grew, ate into her time intended for the thesis.

Working on Living Earth projects, doing her share of household duties or spending enjoyable hours with David or Jane all meant the weeks spun past without much progress on her academic project. Reading about childbirth and child raising took priority over poring over her notes from more than a year ago on a critical article about the artist Edward Burne-Jones's relation to the rest of William Morris's circle, and trying to remember why she had flagged this paper's ideas as important to her thesis on Morris's novel.

Prenatal classes were eventually added to the week's activities. Still, twice in the fall she sent her advisor a revised thesis completion schedule. She was confident she could finish before Christmas, and defend in the winter before the baby arrived. Yet the university demanded all graduate students without a firm thesis defense date apply for both internal and external scholarships. The application forms were elaborate, and most required her to recast her project to demonstrate her thesis's applicability to the ever-changing scholarly aims of some external funding agency, or to the recently adopted research goals of the university's latest academic plan. She complained to Jane that working on these applications, as well as being time-consuming, made her feel fraudulent since she now doubted she was headed for the academic career such financial support was intended to kick-start. She also increasingly felt her thesis subject was irrelevant, despite having to construct a pitch, in her mandatory quest for grants, that extolled the societal as well as the scholarly virtue of her consideration of Morris's novel. She managed, though, to send one more thesis chapter to her supervisor, and was at her desk scanning his subsequent comments and suggested structural rearrangements when the first contractions hit.

~

After she and Bradley left Earth House they moved to a tiny apartment in the basement of a house about a kilometre and a half down the road from Jane and Willy's. The owners of the house were friends of Jane's, and had a four-year-old boy of their own. The rented space was mainly one room, with its own door at ground level that led into the garden. The room contained a small kitchen, and the apartment had its own minuscule bathroom with just enough room for a sink, toilet and shower.

She could hear the four-year-old racing through the house directly above their heads, but she also knew that the lack of sound insulation undoubtedly meant the owners, Meredith and Jason, had to listen to Bradley when he cried. The advantage of the place, as Jane mentioned when she suggested the apartment might work as temporary housing, was that Meredith and her tenant could share childcare at times, giving each other a break from the constant demands of the boys. She used a breast pump so she could leave bottles of milk with Meredith if she went into Nelson for a morning to shop, or for a job interview. Meredith proved to be a helpful source of information, too, when Bradley seemed listless or feverish or randomly refused to nurse or to eat anything.

David had become preoccupied in March with a website redesign intended to highlight past successes of Living Earth, and to provide information about and solicit donations for the group's current activities. A slender young woman, Lindsey Filipoff, who had recently returned to the valley after some years on the Coast, had attended her first Living Earth meeting. During it she stood to urge the group to update their web presence with not only a more up-to-date site but also integration with social media. After the meeting, David introduced her to his partner and son, and the three adults had a long talk about how Living Earth could better employ Facebook to expand the range of support for their projects. Although cellphone service remained unavailable in the valley, Lindsey had a suggestion about how tweets could be posted from Earth House.

The newcomer described a home-based business in web marketing she had just started, and how she wanted to ensure that as far as possible her commercial work had an ecological slant. So expanding Living Earth's online presence was perfect for her resume. She was intrigued by Bradley, asking to hold him, saying that she had grown up in a big Doukhobor family and missed being around kids. Bradley seemed to enjoy being bounced by Lindsey, but the baby's mother took him back when he eventually grew restless.

She noticed how intently David watched Lindsey's face as they spoke. At one point, Lindsey's hand reached to touch David's arm to emphasize that her comments about the Living Earth website were not meant as a criticism of the very worthwhile work the group was doing, but were intended only to suggest that a wider audience could be engaged if the site was upgraded. When David assured her that he could tell she was with them in spirit, his hand reached to touch Lindsey's hair where an orange streak cascaded down over one ear.

A week later, Bradley was asleep in his little bed, softly snoring, when his mother awoke. She had lain down exhausted when she finished nursing Bradley and had nodded off with the lights still on. She saw it was past midnight. David, who had mentioned a number of times over the past week how with Lindsey's help the group could have a much bigger national, even international, presence, had driven with Justin to the web expert's house right after supper to look at some mock-ups for the new website. A session involving Lindsey and a hastily convened Living Earth website committee had been held at Earth House the day before, and afterwards David escorted Lindsey around the place for a couple of hours to take photos of the building, inhabitants and the still partially snow-covered gardens and grounds.

Bradley was in the midst of being changed when Justin had knocked on the bedroom door about nine PM to say he had come back alone because he was on breakfast duty the next morning. One of Lindsey's website mock-ups was totally awesome, he reported, and they had picked that one. David had stayed on to key in some content changes he wanted, so the home page would look perfect when they showed it to the others at the next committee meeting. Lindsey had volunteered to drive David back to Earth House when they were done.

At one AM he had still not returned. Bradley continued to sleep, and his mother lowered face-down onto the bed a novel whose sentences and paragraphs she found herself rereading without grasping their meaning. She swung off the mattress, and decided to gamble that Bradley would continue to snuffle contentedly while she risked heading for the bathroom. Returning along the hallway, she noticed a light under Bronwen's door. On impulse, she knocked.

The door opened almost immediately. Before she could speak, Bronwen, wrapped in a dressing gown, asked if something was wrong with Bradley.

"No, no, he's sleeping like an angel," his mother said. She apologized for disturbing Bronwen, but explained how David had not shown up. Phoning Lindsey's place at this hour seemed wrong, she said, but she didn't know quite what to do. Justin had said that David would be brought back when they were done, but could the work have continued all this time? Should she worry that they had gone off the road? Or could Lindsey have dropped David off at the bottom of the driveway, as people sometime did, and he'd encountered a bear in the dark? A fresh bear flop had been discovered on the driveway near the house on the weekend, so definitely a local one was out of the den and hungrily prowling around. She didn't want to wake the baby but was it worth someone taking a flashlight and checking the drive?

Bronwen shook her head, stepped forward and hugged her. "Oh, Shannon," she said. "I don't think it's four-legged creatures you have to worry about."

A pulse of fear and anger throbbed in her stomach as, back in her bedroom, she considered Bronwen's words again and again. She recalled Jane's warning about David's reputation. But surely his love for her was stronger than the infatuations he had acted on before. He had been so sweetly vulnerable the night Bradley had been conceived after the blockade, and also when she had informed him she was pregnant, once he thought about it.

Also, he was a father now. He wouldn't throw away their little family just because he thought momentarily he might be attracted to someone. She told herself he wasn't that stupid.

The bedside clock in the darkness read 2:35 when she finally heard David enter the room. He kissed the top of her head when he climbed in under the covers and saw she was awake.

"How's the Bradster?" he whispered. His tone was jaunty.

"Why are you so *late*?" she couldn't help but whisper back.

"Sorry, sorry. I don't know if Justin told you, but the new site Lindsey's come up with is amazing. I wanted to tweak it so what it says is as good as it looks, and the time just flew by."

"Couldn't you have phoned to say you were going to be late? I had the impression from Justin you had just a little more to do and then you'd be back."

"You know how it is when you're editing something. You correct this over here and then realize *that* has to be changed."

"You couldn't have phoned?"

"I kept figuring we'd be done in a few minutes. Wait until you see it. I also didn't want to phone in case you were asleep. I know chasing after the Bradster all day tuckers you out."

She said nothing.

"Speaking of sleep, I'd better get some if I'm going to up and at 'em in the morning. When you check out the fantastic new site, you'll see why it's all worth it." He kissed her hair again, and rolled onto his side with his back to her.

Moments later, it seemed, her eyes opened to the March sunlight and the sound of Bradley beginning to stir, uttering a few tentative cries. She groggily lifted him out of his covers, and after throwing on a robe, took him downstairs to nurse so they wouldn't wake David.

No one was up but Justin, busy in the kitchen, so she sat with Bradley in the living room. *If David is inclined to stray,* she thought, *I'm probably a lot to blame, since I haven't been much a partner to him since Bradley was born.* She knew having basically the whole responsibility for this new being sapped her energy. Yet she probably could pay more attention to what was exciting David or discouraging him with regard to Living Earth. And David and she had seldom made love since Bradley was born. The first time was very uncomfortable for her; she had still felt raw and sore. Then about ten days later David was being very sweet, and although she was fatigued to the point of giddiness and only wanted to sleep now that Bradley was down for a couple of hours, she thought that having sex, since David was being so insistent in a gentle way, would be something she could do to connect a little with him again. Yet with constantly responding to the baby's needs, plus toting him from place to place or otherwise holding him most of her waking hours, as well as providing him with her breasts, the last thing she wanted was to share her body with somebody else. David hadn't asked again. She could recall them making love twice in the fall and once in January.

In the living room, the baby squirmed to be put down, and she fetched his rug and a toy from a small box of baby gear that now was tucked into a corner. She resolved to be nicer to David. A couple of hours later, after having had breakfast with the half of Earth House inhabitants who had risen in time for the meal, she took a cup of coffee for David when she went upstairs to dress herself and the baby.

David was asleep, but seemed grateful for being awoken to coffee and a kiss. He didn't even seem to mind looking after Bradley on the bed while she hurriedly went down the hall for a quick shower.

Bradley had dozed off beside his father when she returned. She descended the stairs again to secure a refill for David and a cup of tea for herself, and they sat together on the bed, a family, the adults leaning back on pillows as they sipped their drinks. She reached out to hold David's hand and listened as he, under the covers, spoke softly, so as not to wake Bradley, about his delight at the features of the new website. A blog there would be linked to a new Facebook page, and Alden had agreed to write daily tweets. "We're going to be so up-to-date I can't stand it," David joked.

She glanced at the clock at one point and reminded David that she was off to Slocan Park shortly for a hairdresser appointment. Jane had recommended the woman, who had a salon in her home. The styling would be her first since the baby had been born, but now she also thought of it as making herself look attractive again for David. *I've turned into quite a frump,* she thought.

She squeezed David's hand and thanked him for looking after the baby while she was away.

In the bed, his legs shifted position. "I meant to tell you, Shannon. Something came up yesterday and I'm not going to be able to have Bradley this morning."

"What?"

"Yeah. Sorry I didn't tell you earlier. I had a call yesterday from Bruce Crocetti, the logger from Passmore that comes to our meetings sometimes? There's a guy, a neighbour of his, who's applied to put a gravel pit right next to their creek, and Bruce wants me to come take a look at the situation."

"David, I checked with you before I made the appointment. You said you were free. I don't ask you to do much childcare, but this is important to me. I look like hell, and it won't kill you to have Bradley for a couple of hours. I'll feed him just before I go, and he'll probably sleep the whole time."

"You look great to me." He leaned over and kissed her cheek. "I'm really sorry. This thing with Bruce just came up. Can't you take Bradley to the hairdresser's?"

"Look, Bradley is a prior commitment you have. Make another time to go see this guy. Or send somebody else. You're not the whole organization, you know."

He shrugged. "Bruce asked for me specifically. We don't have that many fallers in Living Earth, to put it mildly. I figure it's good politics to respond to his request. Today's the only day he could do it. He's starting a job up in the Lardeau that he says will last for a few weeks, so it has to be this morning. The Ministry's closing date for responses to the gravel pit plan is this Friday. Bruce wants to hear what I say and get his written protest in before he leaves."

"In other words, he waited until the last minute to contact you."

"I guess so, yeah. But that's not my fault. Like I say, it's just good politics to keep Bruce happy. If the word gets out that we're not anti-loggers, just anti-bad-logging, that's a real boost for us."

"You made a commitment to me to look after Bradley. Aren't I important, too? To be honest, I was looking forward to a little break from being the one to look after him 24-7."

"Of course you're important to me. Doesn't Bronwen help out with Bradley? Anyway, when I weighed a haircut against a water system that serves nine families, it just seemed what Bruce asked was more important."

"So you're not going to keep your word."

"I'm not breaking my word. Something important came up that is absolutely out of my control. That's not the same thing at all. I'll look after Bradley another day."

She pivoted off the bed and stood. "Yeah, right."

"What's that supposed to mean?"

She busied herself gathering Bradley's things.

"Don't they have childcare at hair salons?" he asked. "You can't be the only client who brings a kid when they want their hair done. Or maybe Bronwen would—"

She was at the bedroom door, the baby scooped under one arm, a tote bag dangling from her shoulder. She turned toward him and interrupted. "I'll see you this afternoon."

The door opened and she was gone. He had to climb out of bed to close it.

Two nights later, David didn't come home at all. The parents had hardly spoken in the intervening time. She vaguely knew he was headed to Lindsey's to drop off a flash drive of photos of Living Earth demonstrations that were to be part of the website. He and Dewclaw had driven into Nelson and talked the local newspaper into letting them have free electronic copies of news photos involving the group. Plus Dewclaw collected and loaded onto the drive other photos of Living Earth activities taken by various Earth House residents.

As she dozed and woke again to check the clock, rose to tend Bradley or lay rigid in bed, she cycled through rage and hurt at David's absence. Hour after hour she considered and rejected whether there could be an explanation for David's failure to return home other than the obvious. He was clearly letting her know he was having an affair. How should she respond? No way was she going to put up with his continued avoidance of his share of looking after the baby. And she absolutely refused to be the cheated-on, long-suffering partner. David might well be the compulsive philanderer Jane had indicated he was. Too bad for him, but what was best for her, for Bradley? She weighed whether there was any reason to stay on at Earth House, and tried to think where else she could go, what she should do.

When the windows began to noticeably lighten, she was suffused with a sudden resolve, tossed aside the covers and stood. Her limbs felt simultaneously buoyant and weighted from lack of sleep, but they vibrated with energy. She fished her suitcases from under the bed, and began to pack.

She worked feverishly—dashing down to the kitchen to secure three cardboard boxes she remembered had been piled by the back door waiting for use in some capacity or to be taken to recycling. Bradley awoke and had to be nursed, and though she tried not to be impatient, she fretted at the time required. If David came home while she was in the midst of assembling her belongings, she told herself, she would simply announce she was leaving and why and continue with the task. But she hoped she would be gone before he showed up again. If he planned to show up again.

Loading the car took six trips tiptoeing through the sleeping house laden with boxes, bags, coats, baby things, suitcases. She was tense with fear that someone would awaken, and she'd have to explain what she was doing. But though the clock moved remorselessly toward 7:00, when whoever was on breakfast duty would arise, she had everything stuffed into her car by 6:40 and lugged Bradley's car seat back to the room to strap him inside. During her second-last excursion to the front door and the chilly morning air, she heard a toilet flush somewhere in the building and stopped for a second in the hall. Then she reminded herself to deal with whatever happened as it came, that she had every right to move out, that she could explain herself without needing to blame or accuse. But no one accosted her.

She had left a piece of paper on her desk when she packed up her computer and thesis material, and shovelled her stationery supplies into a box. Moving to and from the car, she debated whether to leave David a note, and what to write if she did. Eventually she resolved that no matter how thoughtlessly he acted, he was still Bradley's father. And she didn't want to behave the way he did. So before hoisting the car seat containing the baby, and descending the stairs for the last time, she scrawled: *Obviously, this relationship is over. Jane will know where I am. Shannon.* Willy was up making coffee when fifteen minutes later she knocked on their door.

Despite being very aware of the comings and goings upstairs at Meredith and Jason's, she felt a calmness characterized her life in the apartment, a certainty that withdrawing from David and Earth House was the right action to take. When she first left, she half-expected David would show up at Jane and Willy's immediately, begging for forgiveness and asking her to return. She both dreaded and longed for his appearance. But she heard nothing from him in the days that followed. By the time she relocated to Meredith and Jason's basement, she had concluded David probably was glad she wasn't around to constantly remind him he had responsibilities other than the ones connected to Living Earth's agenda.

Willy insisted she meet with a lawyer friend of his in Nelson to establish a separation agreement. She found herself chatting to the lawyer about her experiences doing legal research for the Chico Creek trial, and had started to ask about the process of applying for law school when Bradley awoke and began to cry.

"We never married," she would later joke once the questions of access and support were agreed to by David, "but we did get a divorce." Jane had taken the draft document to Earth House to give him. And Jane, besides finally convincing Bradley's mother to let Willy and her take the baby overnight occasionally, found editing work to subcontract so her friend had some extra income. Indeed, the main time when this work could be accomplished was when the baby was over at Jane and Willy's.

Bronwen dropped by the apartment a few days after the baby and his mother had moved in, to say how sorry she was about what had happened. At Bronwen's suggestion, the two women took Bradley to the Crossroads Café. His mother was nervous about being there, but Bronwen, guessing her discomfort, assured her David was away in Prince George for a provincial meeting between Aboriginal and environmental activists.

The custody agreement allowed David weekend access to his son—short visits until Bradley was eighteen months, and overnight stays thereafter if he could provide suitable care. He showed no inclination to exercise this right. Not long after a phone was connected in the apartment, David called one evening. They had an awkward conversation ostensibly about Bradley, but filled with long silences when neither she nor David said anything. She felt mostly sad after they agreed to hang up. In one nightmare fantasy she had, David and Lindsey would become a couple, and Lindsey would demand the baby for all the court-approved time David was entitled to. But from what Bradley's mother was able to glean obliquely from Bronwen and Jane, whatever happened between David and the web designer was of short duration.

David's parents showed up in June on their long-postponed excursion to the West, so she finally met them. She had been sitting

one hot afternoon outside the apartment door on a garden bench
Jason had placed there for her use, as Bradley played with a wooden
pull-toy at her feet, when without advance notice a giant RV ascended the driveway. The vehicle, a rental as she could see from the
advertising on the side of it, was half the size of the house. The front
radiator stopped just across from where she was sitting, with the RV
filling the drive. A bald man in sporty white slacks and top, and a
well-coiffed woman in a patterned sundress, emerged around the
grille and headed toward her. She invited them in for tea.

Meredith knocked on the door a half hour later and asked
them to move the RV since Jason would be home soon from his
shift at Kalesnikoff's sawmill. Backing the huge vehicle down the
driveway turned out to be a lengthy process, with one or other of
the rear set of wheels repeatedly riding up on the bank that lined
the lower part of the drive. Jason's pickup appeared, and once he
grasped the situation, he left his truck on the road and attempted
to direct the manoeuvre. Finally he persuaded the couple to let
him take the wheel and safely inched the RV down the rest of the
way to pavement.

Her own parents wanted her to return to Vancouver, where, they
said, she would have more opportunities to teach and they could
get to know their grandson. When her parents drove east to spend a
week in May visiting her and the baby, she arranged for them to stay
at a bed and breakfast not far along the road from Meredith and
Jason's. She explained repeatedly that she didn't wish to be unfair
to David by taking Bradley out of the area, that she wasn't sure how
legal such an act would be, and that she wanted Bradley eventually to
know his dad. But one night during her parents' visit, sitting at her
desk, which Jane and Willy had retrieved for her from Earth House,
she thought while Bradley slept how in any case she wasn't ready
to leave. She loved the little daily jolts of beauty living in the region
gave her: a blue butterfly fluttering amid the geraniums she had just
planted outside the door, a rufous hummingbird at the feeder she
had hung by the window, how the sunlight scattered through the
leaves of a young aspen growing along the path between her door
and the driveway. Bradley would attend, when he was older, a valley
playgroup that friends of Meredith took their toddlers to. Yesterday

he even tried to sing along when, once he was in bed, she crooned "Rock-a-bye Baby" to him, their faces nearly touching.

She could hardly keep her eyes open to focus on brochure copy she was editing for a client of Willy's, a Nelson non-profit providing services to children. She had noted a couple of these programs for future use. Her thesis was neatly packed away beside the desk; her supervisor had agreed to her request for an extension, given her circumstances. And she had already read online, when she was supposed to be fact-checking a Regional District document for Jane, how to apply to law schools in Calgary and Vancouver.

She felt blessed, too, by how helpful and uncomplainingly good to her Jane and Willy had been. Why would one not want to live close to such friends? A friendship seemed to be developing with Bronwen, too. And Meredith. When she took her parents to the Crossroads Café for tea, the waitress, Shonna, asked her if she wanted her usual.

Money was going to be tight, but she had lived for years as a student, she reminded herself. David's parents would be good for his contribution to child support, even if he couldn't get it together. Her dad had promised to provide her and Bradley—whether she relocated back to Vancouver or not—a couple of hundred dollars monthly until she found some steady employment. She might be eligible for income assistance from Social Services or the Ministry of Families, Meredith had suggested, given that David's income was so low.

Raising Bradley alone would be tough, she knew, but the envelope of community she sensed forming around her seemed beneficent, supportive, rich with possibility. Willy and Jane had talked her into attending, the Saturday after her parents left, a dance at the Vallican community hall. The event was to be family-friendly so she could bring Bradley; Jane said they'd be glad to look after the baby if a spin on the dance floor appealed. Bradley's mother warned them that she likely would leave early, so would bring her own car. Her friends did not object to that arrangement. But it turned out that a friend of Willy's from Nelson, also an accountant, was the trumpeter in the band that would be playing. "We think you'd like to meet him," Jane said when the idea of the evening out was broached. Bradley was on her lap as they sat around the dining room table after a meal. "He's quite a creative person for an accountant, so don't let that put you off. He's been divorced about six months, no kids, although we know for a fact he and his wife were going to the clinic for—"

"What do you mean, 'creative for an accountant'?" Willy interrupted. He was grinning. "Don't you read the paper? That bozo from Castlegar you met at the last Association Christmas dinner has just been charged with several counts of fraud. Take a look at what they say he did. If juggling funds like he's accused of isn't creative—"

Bradley's mother assured them she was a long, long way from being interested in dating. Both Willy and Jane emphasized that there was no pressure, that Willy's friend was a thoroughly nice guy, and that it would do her good to meet more people than Living Earth types. "Bradley will enjoy hearing some cool tunes, too, and hanging out for a bit with a band member," Willy said, and they all laughed.

Mountain Grown

I'M A MITE afraid nobody will attend the meeting I've organized, plus snow starts falling mid-afternoon and doesn't look like it will ever stop. But the promise of free gourmet beers and the threat of the new legislation south of the border brings them out in droves. By the time I call the gathering to order, more than sixty people in ones and twos have pulled open the Vallican Whole's wooden doors, stomped snow from their boots and brushed the snow off their parkas and ski jackets in the entrance vestibule. The Whole isn't the cheapest venue around—I could have booked something at the Hume Hotel in Nelson, or one of the local community halls. But the Whole's cachet as the hippie community centre is a real plus, considering who I've invited, and the place is large enough to hold everybody, as well as being right here in the valley.

I have Donna behind a table down at the main doors with the list of invitees, for security reasons. Once the arrivals' names have been checked off, and they climb the stairs into the hall, chairs for about seventy-five are set out facing a screen for my presentation. Along one wall I've got two big tables covered with white paper, an array of beers and Charles behind the tables dipping into one of six portable coolers filled with ice and bottles, depending on what brand the arrivals want to try. Stacks of plastic glasses are on the table, though hardly anybody is drinking out of anything but a bottle. On the wall back of Charles is one of my advertising banners from when we have a booth at garden shows or the Nelson street market: WAY TO GROW! GARDEN SUPPLIES. The skunky scent of marijuana, outgassing from the arrivals' clothes and outerwear, starts to fill the hall.

"Eau de Kootenay," as a customer of mine termed it after another customer positively reeking of weed left the store.

Donna thought the meeting was a crazy idea. "Look how much it's costing you: renting the Whole, giving away expensive booze, paying Charles overtime to work the evening. Why not just talk about your crackpot scheme to them one at a time?" I pointed out these expenses are an investment, not a loss. Financial acumen isn't her main attraction. Me, I'm a natural with money, which is how I launched Way to Grow! I'd been at loose ends between girlfriends about eight years ago and had travelled up to Nelson from the Coast for a week-long yoga intensive. I'd seen a poster about the workshop. Ever been to a yoga class? You should try it: chicks dig yoga. After a few days of checking out the talent at the intensive, and meeting a bunch of people around town, I could see that besides boasting some hot mamas, the West Kootenay is a gold mine for growing dope. And if I know one thing, it's that in a gold rush you want to sell shovels, not dig for gold. Most people go broke at the latter. Sure, a tiny number of them strike pay dirt. But like the lottery, statistically, practically, realistically *you* aren't going to win. Plus those who do hit the jackpot generally ruin their lives: they can't handle it. Take it slow and steady, flog them shovels, is my motto. You'll end up rich and by the time you do you'll have learned how to properly handle all that filthy lucre.

After the yoga workshop, I went back to Quadra Island, sold my funky coffee shop and set up Way to Grow! in South Slocan, within easy reach of Castlegar, Nelson, the valley. Hydroponics, grow lamps, security systems, everything for the grower. And enough regular garden supplies to be legit, too. Not that selling grow paraphernalia is against the law. Yet. But you never want to draw too much attention to yourself. If you know what I mean.

That same yoga class is where I met Donna. To this day she's sure that true love is what led me to shut down my old life on Quadra and move to the Koots to be with only her. I wouldn't have her believe anything else. I know that's what she tells her friends, because I had a little number with one of them, Kaycee, a couple of years ago. Spacey Kaycee. What a bod. Actually, Donna's pretty good-looking herself, if I do say so. And she's good with my kids, who are now, what, nine and eleven? I get them summers for a couple of weeks and most Christmases if Donna and I aren't away in Costa Rica or someplace toasty. Donna really plans out the kids' visits: stuff they might like to do, places to go. She's got parenting chops I'll never have in a million years. Even though she's never had kids of her own.

But you've heard of the downward dog pose? In yoga? When it comes to chicks, I'm the original downward dog. Can't get enough of that *mm-mm-mmm*. I'm telling you, garden supplies are almost as good a chick magnet as yoga. In the store, you talk to some honey about nurturing little plants: I mean marigolds or echinacea or cukes, not bud. Their eyes get all dewy while they're clutching their little pots of lettuce starts or foxglove or rosemary. They can tell you're sensitive and caring. That's how I met Marcia last spring. After she'd dropped by the store about four times, I suggest I drive out to her place and see her garden first-hand: conduct a soil test and recommend a fertilizer. A cup of tea later we're in her bedroom going at it like crazed monkeys. She'd like me to leave Donna. Marcia's never said as much, but I know because her best friend is married to a good customer of mine, Bart. He and I used to be in the same men's group in the valley. So when I run into Bart I get all the lowdown. Sometimes this valley is too small. I'm not in any hurry, though, to bail on Donna. Marcia pretty much agrees with everything I say, which is flattering, but Donna is like the loyal Opposition. In business, sometimes you need to consider a different point of view. Think of those young MBAs who ruined Westinghouse, WorldCom, you name it. Idiots who were so full of themselves they couldn't listen to what people who'd been in the business for decades, or the customers, were saying.

Despite Donna's opinion, I knew my night at the Whole was a fabulous idea. Make the pitch where the boys can see others listening. They'll be drinking my beer so at some level they owe me. That's psychology. Then, after my spiel, I'll field all the scoffing questions and negative comments I'm sure to land, since most of these guys are morons. Then they witness somebody step forward. That move is costing me, too, though just some grow lamps. Donna, thank God, doesn't know about *that* expense. Hey, I read once that when Elvis first performed, Colonel Parker paid all these teenage tighties to scream. That got the ball rolling: people are pretty much sheep. And Jordan is a guy I can trust to keep his mouth shut. Still, the bulk of the crowd will go home full of beer, bullshit and bravado about what a dumb plan I've proposed. Then, starting tomorrow, one by one they'll be dropping by my store to sign up.

"Why rent the *Whole,* though?" Donna had asked. "It's more expensive than one of the community halls."

She's right, of course, but Slocan Park Hall or Winlaw Hall have pretty straight contact people, and I didn't want somebody hanging around my meeting who would make the boys nervous. I also had a more grandiose reason, and that's the one I shared with Donna.

"Tradition."

"Tradition? What's this, *Fiddler on the Roof*?"

I reminded her that construction of the Vallican Whole was a significant moment in the valley. In 1971 a bunch of hippies met and decided to put up their own community building on some land in Passmore, modelled after the Doukhobor and community halls all through these valleys. The freaks applied for and received funding from some federal youth program, and as you can guess work proceeded rather slowly since they had no idea what they were doing, other than how to ingest certain illegal substances. For quite a while the only physical manifestation of the hall was a hole dug in the ground for the basement. Straight folks used to laugh about the Vallican Hole, saying that was about the best that hippies could do. But when the freaks got it together and the building finally opened in 1975, they kept the derisive name, only adding a letter to emphasize that, love 'em or hate 'em, hippies were part now of the whole valley community.

The construction of the Whole represented a big change, I told Donna. Before the building went up, people around here maybe thought the hippies, draft dodgers, back-to-the-landers were a bunch of transients, who would blow through the valley briefly and within a few years be back in San Francisco or Toronto or Detroit or Vancouver. The Whole said: "We're here to stay." The paradigm shift I was going to lay on everybody at my event, I assured Donna, was as momentous a change in the valley as the hippies erecting the building. She just rolled her beautiful eyes.

As people climb up the stairs into the hall, I'm over by the beer tables shaking hands, fist-bumping and high-fiving, making sure everybody selects a brew they like. Schmoozarama. Charles is a good worker in the store, and he's just as solid here, going full out dispensing the beer. After a while, a bearded young guy with dreadlocks I don't know approaches me—this was an invitation-only event, but I had told the growers to spread the word to folks they trusted, although pre-registration was definitely required. Beardie inquires if my name is Alan. When I plead guilty, he informs me that the lady down in the entranceway asked him to tell me to go down there, that there's a problem.

I head for the stairs. Nearly everybody who has already arrived is as freaky looking as you'd expect: dreads, sashes, embroidered jeans, toques, long hair, beards, face hardware, tattoos. In short, the swelling crowd mostly sports the official grower look that's a cross between hippie, Rastafarian and wannabe ghetto rap star. A few folks, however, are just dressed country pie: jeans and checked shirt, maybe some chainsaw-maker-branded suspenders.

Two-thirds of the people crowding into the hall are in their twenties and thirties, but there's lots of folks my age, too, or even older: fifties, sixties. Old Man McKay is here with his two sons: all of them drive logging truck, hard-working guys, and they all grow, too. Steady customers of mine, once we resolved that little disagreement about some seeds I sold them they claimed were defective. Dad McKay has a truck and the boys, Donny and Alvin, share another rig: Alvin is a heavy equipment mechanic for the Highways contractor, but drives on his days off. The family are straight arrows: McKay's wife Irene, the boys' mom, is on the credit union board and the school board and was a sparkplug in the group that got the seniors' home built at Passmore. When the family grow op on their land up behind Silverton was busted, and Dad and the boys were popped, some people wanted her to resign. She claimed she had no idea what the rest of her family was up to. That was her story and she was sticking to it. Old Man McKay took the rap himself and got house arrest except for going to work and eventually life went back to normal.

I navigate through the knots of people standing talking and drinking, and scoot down the stairs to see what Donna wants. At the table is a baby-faced guy, stocky, medium height, clean-shaven, late thirties or early forties, wearing sharply creased pants and a V-neck sweater over a button-down shirt. Three metres away I can pick up the sickly reek of cologne, as if he's a high school kid who doesn't know better and has drenched himself in Axe. His appearance just screams *cop*. Donna tells me his name isn't on the list.

"Good evening, officer," I say to him. "This is a private party, but what can I do for you?" He gives a half-hearted laugh and then starts to assure me that he's in the loop, part of the scene, reeling off four names that he says encouraged him to attend—major players. One of his references is already here, so I ask Mr. Green Team, as the Mounties around here like to call their dope squad, to wait where he is. Upstairs among the drinkers I find who I'm looking for, and when I begin to describe the guy who just showed up, his verifier starts to laugh. "Roger," he says.

"That's his name?" I ask. He swears that Roger is a conduit between a number of locals and some coastal wholesalers with a fondness for motorcycles. I ask my informant to accompany me to the door to positively ID the newcomer, which he does.

As the two start up the stairs together Donna gives me a look that says *I hope you know what you're doing.* I shrug: too late now to change course.

The next twenty minutes are more schmooza-palooza for me, lots of laughing and kidding around. I keep one eye on the stairs, though, and people are still trickling in. This is the Kootenays, after all, where a lot of people would be late for their own funeral if they could swing it. Every so often I thread my way downstairs to check in with Donna to be sure she's okay. Once she's chatting with Tricia Olsen, a hard-bitten woman in her fifties, slim as a fence rail with muscular arms and a permanent big grin, whom everybody likes. Tricia runs a small herd of cows on her acreage as well as operating a fence-building business mostly by herself. One of her barns is entirely set aside for a grow show. I get a hug from Tricia that leaves me checking my ribs as I head upstairs once more.

Another time I peek down at the entrance desk, however, and Donna is deep in conversation with my former men's group buddy Bart, whose wife, you'll recall, is the bosom pal of my current sideline, Marcia. Bart has parked his butt on the desk, and the two of their heads are close together as they talk, both with intense expressions. My sphincter tightens right up. To begin with, I wasn't even aware Donna knew Bart, other than me mentioning him as part of the men's group, back when I was involved. Come to think of it, maybe there was a potluck or two that included the womenfolk, but mostly what the group did was strictly No Girls Allowed. Donna and Bart is not a linkage I want to encourage. All I need to hear is, "Bart and his wife want us to come for dinner next week. Sounds like fun." Worst will be if Bart inadvertently let the cat out of the bag with regard to me and Marcia. I'm jolted by the thought that he might have forgotten to associate Donna with me, and could say something that arouses Donna's suspicions. Say what you like about Donna, she's not dumb. I start to sweat, watching them chatter away with such concentration. I tell myself to keep calm. They could be talking valley politics, or road maintenance, or cross-country ski techniques. "The wicked flee when no man pursueth" is one of the few bits of the Bible I remember from Sunday school. But the last thing I need right now on the very cusp of making my presentation is a revelation of my little number with Marcia, accompanied by the loud, histrionic and generally unpleasant domestic fallout guaranteed to immediately ensue.

I square my shoulders, trip down the stairs with a smile pasted on my cake hole and break up Donna and Bart's little party with a big arms-extended welcome to my old amigo Bart. Turns out the duo were exchanging zucchini recipes, not vital data concerning my infidelity, and I break into a sweat again, this time of relief. Luckily, a couple more bozos come through the front door at this moment, and I seize the opportunity as Donna gets busy checking their names to whisk Bart up the stairs with me while I babble on about the thirty-seven kinds of beer assembled for his tasting enjoyment.

I park him in front of Charles and his trusty bottle opener, and return to glad-handing the crowd. While I'm doing so, one part of my brain is whining, "Why do you complicate your life like this? Don't you have enough going on, implementing this project that will make you simultaneously rich beyond your wildest dreams and more popular than John Lennon? Imagine how you'll be rewarded when the grateful populace, or at least the dope-growing portion of it, finally understands what a benevolent genius has been living unheralded in their midst. Why do you also need to get involved with extramural pussy?" And another part of my brain is retorting, "Extra pussy has always been the prerogative of genius. Your ability to juggle successfully an overload of details that would stagger an ordinary person is precisely what defines your genius. Use it or lose it: if you don't have far too much happening, you might as well give up and start watching four point five hours of television a night, or whatever the abysmal national viewing average is."

Spacey Kaycee's term for my inclination to ride the edge was "negative excitement." Some term she picked up from her time in AA, as it turned out.

Eventually the voice in favour of multitasking wins the debate, as usual. But then a face I recognize as an intermittent customer of Way to Grow! interrupts a conversation I'm having with Old Man McKay about the playoff prospects of the Calgary Flames. The interloper asks, "When's this fucking thing going to start?" So I know it's time. I lope down to the entrance again and tell Donna I'm going to begin. I open the front doors where, sure enough, four or five guys on the porch are sharing a doobie. I call them in. Then it's up to the hall, and shout that everybody should grab a seat, we're about to get underway.

People are having a good time with the beer social, so I'm more or less ignored at first. Water has pooled on the floor here and there, having melted from people's boots, but that's normal at a public gathering in winter. I slip between the assembled chairs to where the laptop and video projector are set up, and click them on. A photo of the valley in summer projects onto the screen, a paradisiacal image of green mountainsides as backdrop to leafy birch and cottonwood branches overhanging the lazy river. I chose this shot to put people into the mood of laid-back good-vibe days. Donna, bless her, has followed me upstairs and now flicks the hall lights off and on a few times, then configures the lighting so most of the illumination is up front where I'll be speaking. The clumps of talkers slowly peel themselves away from the beer tables and amble across the room to find places to sit. The noise of talking amplifies as they file into the rows of chairs, and then diminishes as the crowd settles. I'm standing at the front, and Donna is in position at the laptop.

After welcoming everybody, I run over the security precautions. Everyone present was personally invited, or otherwise vetted by invitees. The core list of people selected to attend was drawn up in consultation with a few trusted and respected names in the valley. I repeat what the written invitation they received said: they have been invited because of their reputation as important and influential figures in an industry that, according to many impartial sources, is the main economic generator for the region, surpassing in revenue lumber, mining and smelting combined, and bigger than health care and all other government employment.

"In the unlikely event," I continue, "that any police spies have been included among those invited, I'll stress that no one here to my knowledge is engaged in any illegal activity. All of you are simply local citizens concerned with the present situation and future possibilities of a vital component of our regional economy." That statement nets a big laugh.

I signal, and Donna brings up the next PowerPoint slide, a list of initiatives in US states to legalize aspects of marijuana possession or growing. I briefly summarize the info on the slide, then launch into my spiel.

"The trend is clear, as everyone in this room is aware: state after state has begun legalizing, or minimizing the penalty for, simple possession. The next inevitable step is a tax grab by cash-starved state, county and municipal governments who will legalize, control and tax the production of weed. At the moment, all this is illegal under US *federal* law. Yet how long can the feds hold out if a significant number of states and cities are rolling in money obtained by legalizing and regulating the industry? And as the US goes, so goes the True North Strong and Free."

Donna puts the appropriate slide up on the screen. "In Canada alone, as you see here," I continue, "the potential dollars at stake according to the best law enforcement guestimates indicate that, compared to pot, current government legalization and regulation of lotteries is a puny source of income."

Up comes a bar chart showing every current provincial and federal source of income. I can't resist underscoring how what is a crime today is good business tomorrow. "As you know, lotteries were once entirely illegal. For example, when I was a kid, selling an Irish Sweepstake ticket was a crime in Canada. And in the US. In fact, forty years before the Irish Sweeps were even inaugurated, the US Congress in 1890 outlawed using the mail to buy or sell any kind of lottery ticket. Today lotteries, as these charts show, are a significant income stream for governments.

"However," I caution, adopting my most serious face, "the question remains whether the small weed producer is likely to benefit from legalization. Or will you, uh, that is, will the small producer be squeezed out in favour of large corporations who are better positioned to, shall we say, bestow campaign contributions on the men and women at the various levels of government who will decide how the details of decriminalization play out? Never underestimate the speed with which a profitable free market business sector can go into the dumper due to government fiat or mismanagement." I give Donna a nod and up comes a screen with dollar and employment graphs illustrating the sad tale of the Ontario tobacco farmer and the Newfie cod fisherman over the past half century.

"You might imagine—" I try to counter an argument I've heard raised several times when the boys are chewing over the implications of legalization "—that even if the big corporations take over, you can sell your crop to them. But you'll agree with me, I'm sure, that once the stuff becomes legal, how it will be priced is not at all clear. That is, will the small grower be able to survive financially? Will the corporations not inaugurate their own production? I'll remind you that, with the rise of agribusiness, the small food-farmer is deeper in debt than ever. Most have to take non-agricultural jobs to make ends meet, if they aren't squeezed entirely off their land. If you can't make a living as a grower, what marketable skills do you have to put food on your table, never mind a new Lexus in your garage?" Dead silence at the last comment. Which is good: they're thinking. "Especially in today's depressed economy?"

I pause and survey the crowd. Rows of eyes watching me. I haven't said anything they haven't thought of themselves in the black of night. "What to do?" I look around the room, meet a few eyes, milk this pause for all it's worth, let the perilousness of their long-term prospects sink in. "What to do?"

A stir in the assembly. Nobody says anything, to me or each other, but they shift uneasily in their seats. A few take a pull on their brewskis.

"Not to worry, men. And woman: Tricia." General laughter: a tension breaker. "I've given this a lot of thought," I continue, a concerned expression plastered on my face. "I've consulted at length with various experts, as I'll reveal in a few minutes. The route out of the morass that looms ahead of us, I'm convinced, the solution to the irrelevance and bankruptcy that is likely to be the lot of the West Kootenay small producer swept aside by changes in the industry, can be summed up in a single word. Coffee."

A crescendo of murmuring starts, including a few people pointing at their heads with an index finger while they rotate their hands, indicating to someone seated beside them that I've lost my marbles. But I persevere. "I'm going to show you—" I override the increasing noise "—the benefits of starting to shift production from grass to high-end arabica coffee beans. First I want to—"

An arm is lifted and waving in the crowd, like a kid's at school. It's the chunky gatecrasher with baby face and V-neck sweater. "Excuse me," he calls, his arm still up. "Excuse me."

An adage from years in business flashes into my brain: the customer you go out of your way to help is invariably the one who causes the most trouble. No good deed goes unpunished. "Yes?"

Baby face—what was his name? Ronald? Robert? *Roger*—stands. "I'm so sorry to break in," he says, with a mirthless half-laugh, as though mocking his own audacity. "I just felt I had to correct something you said. Hope you don't mind." The thin laugh again.

"You have a question?"

"Thank you." His face swivels to take in the crowd on both sides of him. "Umm, I think maybe you painted a rather bleak picture of our industry. Possession of cannabis for personal use may be legalized here and there in some jurisdictions. But in my view, we're a long, long way away from the small grower being obsolete. I've been assured—"

Applause breaks out a couple of places in the room. I try to note who is clapping, but I'm too late. Somebody shouts, "Right on" and Bart, the treacherous weasel, yells agreement: "Totally."

Roger looks left and right, ducking his head modestly. "Thank you. I want to mention I've been assured by associates of mine who are vitally involved in the industry that no matter what any *government* does, they're interested in continuing to purchase your product. Of course, like you said, Alan, nobody here does anything illegal."

A brief laugh.

"My associates," Roger resumes, "don't only spend their time riding motorcycles. In conversations I've had, they stress that they will find a use for crops from the West Kootenay for a long, long time to come." He produces another half-laugh. "Thanks, Alan. That's all I have to say."

He sits down amid a buzz of talk and scattered applause. Somebody yells, "Good to hear, Roger."

Another voice, one of the McKay kids, calls out over the ambient chatter, "He's right, Alan. Change might be coming, but it ain't nothing we can't handle."

A few shouts of approval from various parts of the hall, and another increase in the background decibels of talk. I figure I better counter this idea fast.

"People who grow spend a lot of time, effort, money and brain power," I pronounce loudly, wishing I'd arranged to have a PA, "to try to stay one jump ahead of the cops, right? A percentage of folks nevertheless get busted and lose their crop. That's not going to change in the short term. In fact, wouldn't you agree the horsemen are getting more sophisticated? How many people still grow outdoors? Didn't overflights and colour spectrum analysis have something to do with that change? And the new smart meters the power companies are installing are directly intended, they tell us, to pinpoint power theft, a mainstay of lots of indoor grow shows. BC Hydro and Fortis claim that smart meters can tell who is stealing power, or who is using a lot of power at a time of day that isn't normal for such usage. This pronouncement might be just scare propaganda. But what if it's not?"

The room is abruptly quiet again. Faces are paying attention. "Some of you older folks like Roger here maybe are gambling you can finish your careers before the industry is substantially transformed. You might be kidding yourself. Who here can say that the new medical use legislation in California, for example, bringing in not just permits for own-use and medical cultivation, but also launching the development in that state of specialty strains, hasn't already hurt prices and demand for Kootenay product? Think back even five years."

The hall remains dead silent. "That's just short-term, too. Not that what I'm proposing can be done overnight. But those who don't start now to switch over from bud to coffee will be like those Ontario tobacco growers who were certain the drop in demand for ciggies and cigars was temporary. Which McDonald's do you think those farmers are working at today? Especially since they couldn't even get hired for factory jobs when their farms went under, because everything is made in China now."

Bill Sevastapol, a grower from Lemon Creek who has never bought anything at my store, bursts out in a voice vibrating with resentment: "Yeah, yeah, but how the fuck can we grow *coffee*? Coffee comes from Central and South America. Or Africa. You know: *hot* places?"

Big laugh. Another mocking shout: "Mountain grown." A joking voice, pretending realization: "Wait a minute, we're *in* the mountains." More hee-hawing.

Laugh it up, chuckle-heads, I don't say. "I'm glad you asked that," I state. "I'm going to explain next how coffee is grown. But first there's something else you need to be conscious of while we're considering the long-term. You think a lot of people are into weed? Millions of people everywhere, your ultimate customers? Dig this: coffee is the second largest commodity sold in the world, second only to oil. The market for coffee is hundreds if not thousands of times larger than for smoke. Many people light up, but *everybody* drinks coffee."

I nod to Donna, and in the renewed stillness the next screen shows the world's primary coffee producing areas. "Coffee is presently grown outdoors," I intone, "between the Tropic of Cancer and the Tropic of Capricorn. As for 'mountain grown,' a supposed positive characteristic of some coffee? That's a complete shuck. Arabica beans are *all* grown between four thousand and six thousand feet. The plants' prime growing environment is twelve-hour days and twenty degrees Celsius, which is why coffee is grown high up and in the tropics: that's where the required combination of light and temperature is found. The plants also like rain, and volcanic or other rich soils. You can grow robusta beans lower down the mountains, but robustas produce shit-coffees even though they generate more beans per tree. And why would anybody want to raise robustas, especially now when more consumers are used to a good-flavoured—"

"How high are *we?*" somebody calls.

Laughter again, accompanied by a hooted: "I don't know about you, brother, but I'm pretty high."

The first voice again, annoyed. "I didn't mean that. What's our elevation?"

"Nelson is about two thousand feet. Six hundred metres," Old Man McKay contributes.

"That means we're too low to grow coffee, doesn't it?" the guy sitting beside Bart wants to know.

"Hold on," I tell them. "Let me finish. The real—"

"Hurry up," a voice suggests. "I'm getting thirsty."

Widespread hilarity. "The quicker I'm done," I say over the guffaws, "the quicker you can get another drink." I gesture toward the beer tables. As if on cue, Charles waves.

"'Mountain grown' as I mentioned—" I pick up the build of my argument "—applies to all arabica coffees. The real dispute these days is between shade-grown and full-sun-grown coffee. Coffee raised in the shade of the forest canopy, in the understory, has the best taste and is the traditional way to grow. All you eco-freaks know why forests are necessary for bird life, biological diversity and all that good stuff. What's been happening, though, is—" I signal, and Donna brings up the slide of different shade categories "—extensive deforestation in order to grow coffee in direct sunlight. Coffee plants in open areas can be crowded together for better yields. But besides ecological impact, sun-grown coffee beans don't make as good coffee. Coffee raised this way also requires chemical pesticides and fertilizers that shade-grown plants don't. And you know what's wrong with—"

"So we can grow coffee on the clear-cuts?"

Laughter. Before it trails off, Bruce Sherbinin shouts, "If we're in trouble because corporations are going to take over, how is it any different with coffee? Won't Starbucks and the other mega-corporations just control everything?"

Sherbinin. An operation up McKean Road in Winlaw so small he might as well be growing on a windowsill. But I have one of my strokes of genius—an idea I hadn't thought of when I prepared my talk. "Think wine," I tell Bruce. "The wine industry in the Okanagan was just about nonexistent twenty-five years ago. A few growers started by selling grapes to the makers of plonk. Then someone realized there was a demand for estate wineries, that more money could be made producing classier, smaller volume wines. Result? An explosion of wineries and of free-standing vineyards, too. Right about when the fruit orchards were in trouble due to competition from imports, the demand for upscale BC wines stepped in to save the day. Provided, of course, you were an orchardist willing to make the shift to—"

"Screw coffee," someone suggests. "Let's all grow wine."

A surge of applause, cheers, hoots. I wait until the noise starts to taper off.

"You *could*," I suggest. Mr. Reasonable. "*If* you knew anything about viniculture. And if wine grapes would grow in our region. Which they won't. That's why—"

"Doesn't sound like coffee will grow here either." An objection from a different corner of the hall. "It's not exactly tropical outside." Much laughter. "And from what you're saying—" the voice more confident now that the room has approved of his humour —"our elevation is too low."

"Ah," I respond. "You bring me to the crux of the evening. Donna, if you please?" She gets up the slide with the greenhouse schematic.

"Gentlemen, behold the future," I declare. "Remember what I said about elevation and geography only having to do with keeping the little plants happy with twelve hours of sunlight and a steady twenty degrees? You folks may not know dick about grape-growing.

But any of you with an indoor operation, and that's most of you, do know lots about control of temperature and light. Sorry, I don't mean 'you.' Whoever is growing. But you know what I mean."

The room fixates on the drawing. This moment in the absolutely still hall is my payoff: hours and hours of research on the net, a zillion phone calls, three trips to Vancouver to meet with suppliers, big-scale roasters and more. Plus contracting with a flaky Nelson artist for this illustration: greenhouse dimensions, coffee shrub layout, irrigation and heating setup, ventilation fans.

"You'll agree this greenhouse layout looks rather familiar," I point out. "Except for the retractable cloth gizmos up top. Shade-grown coffee needs 35 to 65 percent shade for maximum effect. The experts think shade increases bean ripening times, improving the taste. Did I mention that coffee is actually a fruit? That the plants produce what are called cherries, inside each of which are two coffee beans? Anyhow, depending on the weather you can deploy the shade cloth or not."

I can almost hear the wheels churning inside the dreadlocked-and-toqued heads. Smoke is pouring out of ears as they try to assess what I'm saying, what's on the screen. Their synapses may be clogged with resin like the inside of an old hash pipe, but I can sense repeated attempts to get them to fire. Now to set the hook.

"That's it in a nutshell, boys. My beautiful assistant and myself both have handouts—" I hold one up "—providing prices for coffee plants, and for specialty products like the shade cloth. I assume you are familiar with the other indoor growing costs, though these are listed on the handout, too. The info package I've prepared also has some likely return on investment estimates, which you'll see are quite favourable. I won't bullshit you: this isn't the quick buck that weed is. But if you factor in increasing pressure from the nation's finest in the short haul, plus being bypassed by post-legalization corporate growers in the long haul, you'll see the idea makes sense. These plants take three to five years to come on stream, so the sooner you begin to shift over, the quicker you'll be making legit money. *Big* money, if I dare say so. The whole trend—"

"You're not known to be in the running for Good Citizen of the Year, Alan." Sherbinin again. He's rewarded with a huge laugh, and he grins briefly in acknowledgement. "What's in it for you, with all this? Why do I feel you'll be raking in serious dollars whatever happens to the rest of us?"

More hee-haws, and applause.

"I'm a businessman," I admit. "But so are you, or people you're acquainted with. I've done the research, I've made the contacts, I can supply you with advice, or contacts if you want to check out this stuff on your own. I'd be happy to sell you the coffee plants, and otherwise assist you to get started. You already know I offer everything you need for greenhouses. I can give you the names of processors who are interested in buying West Kootenay beans, or I can act as your agent and sell them for you. Needless to say, you're free to keep on as you always have, and be squashed like a bug as the economics of how you've made your living completely change. But, yeah, I probably understand the coffee market better than you at this point. So I have a better idea of what you should be getting for your—"

"How much per kilo *would* we get?" a voice interrupts.

"It's not that simple. Coffee prices—" I begin, but jeers erupt from a few corners of the room.

"Look, for those of you who can read, I spell out, *as* I've mentioned, likely rates of return on these handouts." I flourish one. "Coffee base prices have been on a steep upward slope since the start of this century. My estimates are based on where they're likely to be in three years and five years, since, as I say, even if you plant tomorrow you're not going to be seeing a return for three to five years. But—" I speak louder over an increasing level of talk in the room "—the coffee world is changing, too. Only in this case, to the benefit of the small producer. Some of you are old enough to remember the consumer shift from blended Scotches, which emphasized consistency of taste, to single malt Scotch, each of which has a recognizably better but unique taste."

The mention of expensive Scotch dampens the side conversations. When these folks juice, they have a fondness for pricey single malts. Most in the room are listening again. "Coffee drinking is heading the same way. Even Starbucks tells you the origin of the beans they've blended for the garbage coffees they flog. A one-off local roaster like Oso Negro in Nelson does exactly the same. The trend is—" troublesome Roger's arm is waving in the air again "—people soon are going to walk into a coffee shop and ask for a coffee from a specifically sourced bean, a named bean grown in a specific country, or even from a particular grow op, sorry, farm. Just a second, Roger. Last slide, please, Donna."

On the screen is the clincher. "Look at this. Sourced beans that customers request can sell to roasters for ten times the general market price for coffee. And the market price itself is rapidly rising, as I've said. So the price you'll get from your coffee depends on which beans you grow. Below the bar graphs, that's a photo of a new hybrid cultivar that one supplier I represent claims is perfectly adapted for greenhouse growth. When I mentioned to him my idea that I've been explaining to you good people this evening, he turned out to be way, way ahead of me. Great minds think alike. The supplier—" a universal groan fills the hall, which I ignore.

"The supplier already had been developing an arabica designed for the discriminating customer of tomorrow, yet a plant that thrives in an artificial environment. They call this cultivar 'cascadia.' They poured me a cup of cascadia coffee, and I have to say it's hard to go back to even Oso Negro's best after that. Of course, cascadia is only one of several plants I can set you up with. The others have a longer track record, although my money's on this one." Roger's hand has started pumping energetically in the air like that of a Grade 4 keener who is sure he knows the answer to some teacher's question, or else a kid who really needs to go to the can. "Roger?"

He climbs to his feet. "Sorry to interrupt again," he begins, ducking his baby face deferentially and issuing his half-laugh. "But maybe I don't understand? You say the small producer has done better as the market changed for wine, scotch and coffee? But people should stop growing cannabis because the small producer will disappear if the market for cannabis changes? Why wouldn't the small producer in our industry *benefit*, like with wine or Scotch? BC Bud is already a desired commodity among connoisseurs, I think." He sits down.

"Fucking-A," and several other shouts of approval lift on a thunderous wave of applause toward the rafters of the Vallican Whole. I have a couple of simultaneous thoughts. One is: can I identify a slight lisp in Roger's voice that wasn't there before? Hopefully an indication of stress? Did he really say, "BC Bud ith already a de-thired commodity among connoitheurth"? Could Roger's latest attempt to screw me be a product of worry, a desperate rearguard effort as he senses the boys are leaning toward adopting my idea? The second thought I have is that when this is over I am going to kill, via slow dismemberment, first this turkey and then whichever assholes invited him to attend my pitch.

"The difference has to do with effect," I manage to interject into the chatter ballooning throughout the hall. "Effect," I repeat, while I wait for the racket to fade a little. "With wine, Scotch and lately with coffee, customers have learned to tell the difference between plonk and a varietal with definite qualities that they enjoy. Everybody in this room can distinguish between a Starbucks coffee and one from Oso Negro, correct? On the other hand, to be honest, a stone is a stone is a stone. As long as smoke isn't so harsh as to burn your throat, who cares what it's called? That was true of the market forty years ago, and it's true today. I don't see any sign the situation will be different in the future."

Roger's arm is waving in the air again. I press on. "Most important, though: it's not hard to grow your own grass. Especially when it becomes legal. Tend four or five plants in your garden or apartment balcony, pluck a few leaves now and then, dry some for the winter and you're set. That's the future small grower: the individual consumer. In contrast, people are not going to distill their own single malt, or grow their own coffee. A few people will make their own wine, or, mostly, pretend to do so at a U-brew place where the owners do 95 percent of the work. But that wine isn't very good, or at least, not good enough to be a threat to the small estate wineries. Whereas people can get satisfactorily ripped on the fruits of their own labour. That's why small coffee producers have a future while small weed producers do not."

I hear applause from one source: my man, Jordan, finally springing to life to earn his grow lights. "I'm sold," he announces to the room. "How do I sign up?"

"Just come talk to me," I say, smooth as silk. "Now, I've bored everybody long enough, but there's still beer left, isn't there, Charles?"

He nods from behind the tables. Roger's hand is still madly oscillating. Is there an armpit equivalent to carpal tunnel? "Stick around if you have more questions, and please pick up one of these info sheets from either Donna or me." Donna, on cue, kills the computer and the screen goes white. "I'll have them in the store, too, of course. Thanks, everybody, for coming out and listening. And drink up, unless you're over the legal limit."

The last brings a good-natured laugh. People stand and stretch, blabbing with each other as most of them amble toward the side of the hall to see which beers remain. I'm suddenly weary. My optimism, I'm aware, is draining away. Growers are quick-buck, live-for-the-moment types, I note gloomily, and coffee requires more forward thinking. Anybody who picks up my handout is sure to grasp the required scale of the conversion project if his brain is still functioning. Multiply the pounds of beans a single coffee bush produces times the wholesale bean price, and the return is considerably less per plant than weed. You aren't going to make a living from a basement grow show of coffee. But, as I stress on the info sheet, you don't *have* to grow it in a basement hidden from the relentless eye of the law. You can build multiple greenhouses on your acreage, and don't have to worry about neighbours or jealous colleagues ratting you out or ripping you off. You don't have to hide electrical usage to heat the greenhouses. Plus there's no risk of having your whole crop busted. Still, given the brain power of most growers, my entire venture is probably doomed.

I try to shake off the negativism, to Velcro a smile on my face before stepping over to the clusters of people by the beer tables to receive some feedback. Maybe one or two of the more adventurous sort will buy into it. Which is better than nothing. "Why don't you grow coffee yourself to show them how it's done?" Marcia had asked me when I'd mentioned the idea to her. "You know, be a role model, like a demonstration forest?" That's the difference between Donna and Marcia. Donna understands that the only way to get rich is to sell those shovels, and never be tempted to start digging in search of the motherlode.

Donna can read my moods, too, and suddenly she's standing beside me holding out a beer. I take it gratefully and knock about a quarter of it back. "You did good," she says as I lower the bottle from my mouth. She leans in to peck my cheek. My frame of mind considerably brightens when I see standing behind her two young guys shifting their weight from leg to leg, fingers pulling at the labels on their beer bottles, obviously waiting to talk to me. A few seconds later they're holding copies of the info sheet, and I'm walking them through the deal one more time. I know one of them, the husband of a yoga instructor here in the valley I've taken classes from, and remember he was laid off when the sawmill at Slocan shut down. So the concept of economic changes putting your livelihood at risk isn't foreign to him.

The boys I'm talking to don't commit, of course, but when we're done I can tell they're mulling the prospect over. This evidence that my presentation didn't fall entirely on deaf ears cheers me up even more. My smile is genuine as I saunter over toward the beer drinkers.

Too late I see baby-face Roger detach from where he has been holding forth earnestly to a couple of guys taller than him. "I hope you didn't mind me asking my questions," he starts, in that self-deprecating manner which I can tell is completely phony. "You're on to an interesting scheme, though I don't quite see how it could work. But I've taken one of your handouts—" he pulls a folded paper out of a rear pocket of his slacks to show me, before stuffing it back "—to study. Oh, and before I forget." He pauses for just a microsecond too long. "Marcia says hi. I grew up in New Westminster with Bart. You know Bart, right? He knows you, anyway. His wife is good friends with Marcia, and I was over at Bart and Andrea's for supper last night. Marcia was there, too. When I mentioned I was going to attend your event this evening, she said to be sure to say hello."

Roger's face is expressionless. I can't tell if he's trying to let me know that he's aware of my fling with Marcia, that it was talked about over dinner. Is he vaguely threatening me with disclosure? Or is he just making a pathetic attempt at connection? I have a flash that he's the kind of creep who likes to have a dossier of information on everybody, especially how people are vulnerable. Just in case those details ever come in handy.

"Be sure to say hello next time you see her," I shoot back. "She's a good customer, and I like to keep my customers satisfied." The last is just in case he has the hots for her himself—she *does* have a body that won't quit. Why not rub it in that I'm getting a piece off her and he isn't? "Now if you'll excuse me."

"Actually, I do have one more quethtion," Roger begins. "How could coffee—?" But I step past him toward where Mickey Vosin and three other older growers are deep in conversation. I interrupt them with my smile and "Well, what do you gentlemen think?"

"Alan, your idea is completely full of shit. Here's why," Mickey begins, bluster being his modus operandi, especially when he's in the wrong. But I'm happy to half-listen to him repeat some of the objections I've already dealt with in the meeting, while I chew over one more time whether Roger really could make trouble for me with regard to Marcia. Or in some other way. I'm also wondering whether five years from now I'll be recognized as the far-sighted founder of the thriving West Kootenay coffee industry, or I'll still be flogging grow mixes and irrigation systems for two-bit dope operations. Also seedlings, wind chimes and plant pots for the general public.

I decide it's a win for me in either case, like with Donna and Marcia. If you can't take a few chances, step out of the well-worn path that leads ahead, you're going to end up living somebody else's dream of what your life should be like.

Graveyard

AN ICY BREEZE tugged at the edges of a flag secured to the coffin by a couple of elastic cords. The fly and hoist of the red and white cloth lifted and slapped against polished brown wood suspended several centimetres above the snow on straps attached to a chrome frame placed around the edges of the grave. Snow had been backhoed into two- to three-metre-high mounds along one side and at the ends of the substantial wooden box. Jammed into the piled snow at one end was a single lit candle. Its flame, protected somewhat by the three walls of snow, guttered from the wind flowing up the mountainside from the town and lake. Gusts soughed through the limbs of a nearby fir. In the overcast afternoon, the white was trampled flat along the remaining side of the coffin where the Presbyterian minister had said a few words and led a brief prayer, while the funeral party stood and shivered. Around the casket, a field of snow extended, broken occasionally by a snow-laden cedar or other evergreen or by stones deformed by the drifts of white clinging to them. The cemetery sloped upward to a dim wall of fir, spruce and pine that marked the edge of the forest.

Between the candle and the huge box, a woman in a gaudy blue ski jacket crouched on the snow, one gloveless hand continually patting flat the closest end of the flag as the gusts repeatedly raised the unsecured portion of cloth. A keening wail rose from her. The face of the squatting mourner was turned away from a cluster of four watchers who stood several paces back from the coffin. They could see past her skirt and jacket only a mane of long brown hair.

The slight figure's cries swelled and descended in volume, but the hand never ceased trying to hold the flag still.

"You should go to her, Gerry," one of the three women among the watchers said. "Take her out from there."

"You saw me try to get her to leave," another of the women, Elizabeth, said to the man, her face hidden under the hood of her bulky coat. "But she'll listen to you. We need to pull her away: the reception will be starting." She shifted her weight from one booted foot to the other, then back. "I'm getting cold, too."

There was a slight rueful laugh from the third woman, who rubbed the arms of her down jacket with her mitts. "It's snowing again." An occasional flake formed in the air and floated, reluctant to descend.

Another moan rose from the figure at the coffin. Elizabeth pushed at Gerry's shoulder through his coat. "Go on. I hate to see her like this," she said.

"She's not even wearing a hat," the third woman observed.

Gerry took a step forward and halted, gazing about the bleak hillside. Fear and resentment swirled through him. He saw to his left the cleared track through the cemetery where the hearse and a dozen cars, pickups and vans had been lined up during the graveside service. Now in the fading light, just his own truck and one other car remained parked on the white lane. The small corps of drummers and bagpipers who had escorted the coffin from inside the church to the hearse, and from the hearse to the casket's present location amid the snow, had departed for the warmth and conviviality of the legion hall along with the rest of the funeral attendees. To Gerry's right, above the mountain's forested summit a smudged moon had lifted into view behind the overcast.

The figure at the coffin abruptly straightened to her feet. She leaned forward. For a horrifying moment, Gerry thought she was about to climb atop the box, or embrace it, or even attempt to open the lid and climb in to join her father. He'd read of such displays of grief in stories and news reports from other parts of the world. Never had he imagined he'd be in a position where somebody expected him to intervene to prevent such madness. For a second, he struggled to breathe.

A wail crescendoed from the end of the casket. To Gerry's relief the figure resumed her crouch. Simultaneously he felt another shove, at his back. "Get her out of there," Elizabeth ordered from behind.

"This isn't doing her any good," said the woman who had spoken first.

"She needs to be at the legion," Elizabeth said. "And I'm freezing."

Gerry absolutely did not want to have to approach the coffin. The idea of being that close to the huge manifestation of death repelled him. And he felt he was being pressured to resolve a situation where the dead man's daughter was out of control. How would she react to his attempt to draw her away? Would his presence, if he moved nearer, spur her to some frenzied macabre behaviour he would not be able to thwart?

Plus, the three women he was with were her best friends. He was aware how tight the bond was between them: on the phone to each other constantly, with innumerable visits and potluck dinners in each other's homes. They had known her for years in this town, had shared triumphs and consoled each other. *They're infinitely better equipped than me,* he thought, *to end this situation, to pry her away from the coffin and convince her to accompany us down to the hall. Sure, Elizabeth tried. But maybe if all three of them approached her together it would work.*

He was only the latest boyfriend. How long had the two of them been going out: seven or eight months? Her behaviour on an ordinary day still could be a mystery when they were together. How could he be expected to understand her well enough to handle a bizarre acting-out like this?

Another push at his back.

"It'll be dark soon," Gerry heard. "We really need to leave."

The afternoon *had* become dimmer. The flickering candle, whose flame had seemed paltry to him when one of her more hippy-trippy friends had planted it in the snow, now provided most of the illumination of the scene.

These women friends of hers obviously had decided it was his duty to yank her back to sanity. The women considered the two of them deeply in love, soulmates—based no doubt on what she told them, Gerry acknowledged. He was not as convinced as she appeared to be that theirs was the love of a lifetime, the latter being her favourite expression when she described other couples she approved of. "I want to die in your arms," she had whispered to him recently in bed, which discomfited him. He enjoyed her company, was impressed with her perky energy and flattered when the whirlwind of concern and busyness that constituted her daily existence was directed toward him. He enjoyed how they made love. Her almost manic motions and demands in the throes of passion scared him a little, but her hands and mouth possessed skills she employed shamelessly to provide him moments of pleasure he had never encountered before.

Yet he was bothered by her comment about dying, had been mulling her declaration over during the month since she had uttered it. He thought of their affair, of any physical intimacy, as the most intense possible savouring of the present. For him, looking toward the finish of life was the exact opposite of why two people would want to spend time together.

Now he was aware she was mumbling between sobs, her mostly indistinct words addressed to the occupant of the coffin. The snowfall was becoming constant; the flakes angled sharply at frequent intervals toward the waiting group. Unsecured edges of the flag continued to slam against wood. The candle flame, its radiance ever brighter, wavered repeatedly.

Gerry felt he was at the mercy of forces demanding more than he was capable of providing. Anger swelled in him at her friends' expectations of him to act. Simultaneously, his conviction that he would be unable to cope with her mental state, added to his dread of approaching closer to the physical evidence of death looming in front of him, shrieked at him not to move.

Her statement about dying in Gerry's arms had also bothered him because he was uncertain whether he loved her as strongly as the statement implied. When he reviewed how their relationship began, sometimes he concluded she had insinuated herself into his life, rather than that he'd had any choice in the matter. They'd known one another for nearly fifteen years: they met when they were both members of the student outdoor club at the University of

Calgary. Each had been seeing somebody else, though he recalled how exciting he found spending time around her on club hikes and at a climbing camp at Mount Hector in the Rockies. They began to exchange a hug and kiss goodbye whenever they parted after a club function or a chance meeting on campus. He intuited she was as attracted to him as he was to her, but they lost touch after graduation.

Their friendship had been re-established when the BC Ministry of Forests accepted his application for a promotion from Kamloops to the Nelson office. Gerry was introduced to her six months later by a mutual friend at a trendy local coffee shop. He had heard years before that she was living in Nelson, working as a physiotherapist after following a boyfriend to the West Kootenay. But he forgot the information until her saw her again. Both she and he took mischievous delight in surprising their friend by announcing that they already were acquainted.

She invited him on a couple of hikes—to help familiarize him with the local area, she explained. After each of these excursions they shared long coffees in town, chatting happily. Once she suggested they canoe the wildfowl refuge over in Creston at the foot of the lake, a day that ended with Gerry spontaneously asking her to dinner at Nelson's sole Thai restaurant. Other outings were planned on the phone, and she also phoned just to talk, apparently. Yet each such call of hers concluded with an arrangement to attend a music performance at the Capitol Theatre or an art opening at the municipal gallery.

Gerry had bought a small acreage in June off Pass Creek Road at the entrance to the Slocan Valley, a fifteen-minute drive from town. She cycled out to his place one Friday after work when he invited her for supper to see his new house. After she arrived, she asked if she could take a bath and change into other clothes she had brought with her. He was astonished when in the midst of her bath she called out to ask him to bring her the bottle of shampoo she had left in her pack. When he opened the door to hand her the shampoo, she made no attempt to hide her nakedness as she leaned dripping out of the tub to accept the bottle. He tried to behave as casually as she did, as though seeing her breasts, seeing each other without clothes, was a familiar and routine event.

She stayed over in the guest room that night, declaring herself too drunk on the wine they had consumed with dinner to ride, and pronouncing him too drunk to drive her home. When Gerry knocked on her door in the morning to ask if she preferred decaf or regular coffee with breakfast, she suggested he bring his cup into the bedroom with her. "I love the luxury of having coffee in bed on the weekends," she explained, propping pillows behind her as she sat up, wearing one of his old pajama tops. Seated side by side with their arms touching, she partially under and he on top of the covers, they talked about their lives and sipped the warm beverages. After a time they interspersed the conversation with an occasional kiss. With their bodies in such warm proximity, hands strayed, and their intimate life had begun.

In the Nelson cemetery, Gerry's face began to ache in the cold wind that drove flakes against it. He had been rushed into this relationship, he decided. *I never objected when it was established,* he admitted to himself, *but I didn't choose it, either.* Gerry wasn't sure if he wanted the relationship to develop into what she evidently thought it already was. *Or should I end it?* he thought. *She obviously has misunderstood how close we actually are.*

The coffin appeared larger than ever as the light waned: an enormous ship levitated above the snow. The dead man's flag and his daughter were like storm-foam thrashing against the hull of death's vessel. Gerry remembered being taken to meet her father twice. Her mother had died several years before, and although Gerry knew the daughter did not approve of the woman her father subsequently married, the two women were civil with each other.

Gerry had liked her dad—an emigrant Englishman who owned for many years a men's clothing store on Nelson's main street. He had served in an RCAF fighter squadron's ground crew during the war and, posted to England, returned with stories about realizing how North American he had inadvertently become. The father was already terminally ill by Gerry's second visit. On that occasion he only exchanged a few words with the father, who was lying in the big upstairs bedroom. His daughter was very tender with her father, Gerry recalled: she continually touched the sick man while she stood beside the bed and talked at him, or helped him into a sitting position, or held a teacup to his lips, or assisted him to lie down again when the exertion of being vertical proved too much for him. The constant patting and stroking of her father's sleeve and shoulder—he was wearing a cardigan over pajamas—was echoed, Gerry suddenly noted, in how her fingers here caressed and smoothed the errant edges of the flag.

The candle's light streamed forth, its effect multiplied by the walls of snow surrounding three sides of the casket. Time and the thickening dark encircled the coffin. *Now or never,* Gerry thought. His stomach clenched, yet despite his terror he found himself beginning to step across the uneven snow toward the woman.

"Marlene?" he heard himself say as he approached. *Don't startle her,* he admonished himself. Just centimetres from the massive end of the coffin, he put his gloved hands on the shaking shoulders of her ski jacket. "Marlene?" This near to her, he could hear the word "Daddeee" repeated at the core of her wail. Her face turned up toward Gerry, cheeks tear-streaked and red.

"We should go," he said, firmly as he could. Every muscle and nerve in his body was tensed to restrain her, to try to grab hold if she exploded into some mad act of grief. "Everyone's gone on to the legion. They'll want to talk to you—" Her expression offered no indication she was hearing him. He blundered on: "They'll be waiting to talk to you about your dad. His friends, I mean, and your uncle." Gerry recognized he was babbling, but the sound of his voice was oddly comforting to him: some normalcy amid these seconds when he had no idea what she would do next.

She abruptly stood, despite his hands on her shoulders. Her rise knocked him off balance to his right. To prevent himself slipping sideways into the snow, he had no choice but to push with his right palm against the casket's end. A vision of the coffin toppling over flared in his mind, of the lid splintering open to spill the box's horrible contents onto the snow. His glove lifted from the polished wood the instant his hand made contact, as if the unmoving surface were aflame. Yet the momentary stabilization offered by the coffin, plus a lurched half-step backwards, kept him from falling.

Gerry's desperate manoeuvre did not appear to register with her. She uttered a cry and tilted in his direction, throwing her arms around him. He managed to hold her in an embrace as the icy wind surged. He stared over her head at the featureless wall of snow that advanced and retreated as the candle flickered.

After a while, he said again, "We should go." She snuffled but did not reply. Gerry partially untangled them, keeping his left arm around her as he turned and urged her toward the waiting clump of her friends. She clung to his body with her right arm and they stumbled forward, his arm half-guiding, half-supporting her. He marvelled at how willing, after all her histrionics, she was to be led away. *Or at least, to be led away by me,* he thought. *Like the others predicted.* The idea came to him that perhaps in her grief she had gotten herself into a place she did not know how to leave, as a child will act ever more giddy, or throw a tantrum, and lack the ability to stop unless a parent intervenes. *Is that my role now, to be the male parent?*

A moment later Gerry had delivered her to the three women, who en masse began hugging and petting her. One of them stripped off her own mitts and insisted Marlene put them on. He was conscious of a great strain leaving his body; he felt as exhausted as when he stopped to rest after hours of switchbacking up a steep trail under a heavy pack.

He heard vehicles being sorted out: she had been conveyed up the hill in one of the funeral home's sedans; she was to ride down with him. He secured his right arm around her shoulders and they descended the beaten path through the snow toward the lane.

"Let's get where there's heat, and fast," one of her friends said as the women followed behind. Gerry heard Elizabeth's half-laughed agreement.

He opened the passenger door of his pickup cab.

"Thank you for being there for me," Marlene whispered.

He bent to kiss her cheek, her skin wet and cold. "It's okay," he murmured. He grasped for the right thing to tell her. "I'm glad to be here." He was suddenly sure he and his sister wouldn't carry on like Marlene if their father or mother died. Together he and his sister, older than him, would resettle the surviving parent and tackle the details of the estate and whatever else needed to be done. He was suddenly proud of his and his sibling's self-possession, their common sense.

Marlene climbed into his truck.

He walked behind the vehicle to stand outside the driver's door, staring in at her. Her head was slumped against her side window; she looked as weary as he felt. Down the lane and through the gates he could see the lights of the houses at the top of the town. The engine of the parked car in front of him suddenly roared. Headlamps illuminated the snowy route. At a bleep of the horn, the car lurched into motion. He watched the red tail lights grow smaller.

He wondered what to do about Marlene. Was his reluctance to take charge today a sign that his attraction to her was not strong enough to overcome his fears, to let him dash without thought to her aid?

His gloved fingers on the door handle, he took a last glance around. Fuzzy moon, and the stark expanse of the cemetery's snowfield. Laughter and warmth and a drink down at the legion. Up here, though, were only the two of them. Surrounding him were acres of the frozen dead, and not one could help him.

The Three Jimmys

Jimmy

YEAH, I'M ONE of the famous three. You probably never saw it, but that was me, a cartoon of me, on the big sign for the Three Jimmys Motel out on the highway. Along with drawings of the other two, of course. I was the one behind the wheel of the Thunderbird, so we must have had the sign painted after '59. That billboard was a landmark in the valley for more than twenty-five years. Right when you drove into Winlaw from the south. By the time the sign came down, it was pretty faded. The bitch had done her worst by then, and the three Jimmys were no more.

The cars on the billboard were looking like antiques at the end—James leaning out the driver's window of his souped-up '57 Buick Special, and Jim waving from his ridiculous '54 Studebaker. That heap of Jim's was so lightweight that when you went over a bump you felt the cabin was going to float right off the chassis. And roads were a lot bumpier in those days. Drawing Jim in the Studebaker was odd anyway, because by '59 he was driving a Meteor. I don't remember who did the sign but whoever it was must have been somebody local who remembered Jim bombing around in his Studey when he wasn't steering his father-in-law's logging truck.

I was the one responsible for the motel being built. Like the sign said: "Riverside and Country Quiet. Three Times the Comfort at the Three Jimmys Motel."

My dad in the forties had bought the strip of land where the motel is. Who knows why he did? We were living then on an acreage he'd bought just past Kosiansic's, twenty miles or so down the valley. People still operated big orchards then, but after the war better refrigeration was putting the West Kootenay out of business as an apple and strawberry supplier. Kosiansic already was more into dairy and beef. You could hear their cows all the way to my folks' house. Smell them too, on the occasions when the wind was from the east. But forestry was becoming the main source of cash for everybody.

My dad sold sawmill equipment, covering territory from the border north as far as Quesnel, and from the East Kootenay west to include the Okanagan. All through the valley here was a string of mills, big and little: a good-sized one at Crescent Valley, another at what is called Koch Siding now, another at Passmore. One even was set up at Winlaw in the early days, owned by Mr. Winlaw, which is how the place got its name. His mill burned in 1937 and never was rebuilt. But my dad did all right, even during the Depression. He used to joke that I started the Depression, since I was born in 1930, around the time everybody started to realize the hard times had settled in to stay. Of course in the valley people had always scrambled to survive, so the Depression wasn't such a big deal. We had home gardens, fruit trees and venison was plentiful. Fish in the lake. Nobody was going to go hungry.

When the logging boom took hold in the fifties, my dad was in the right place at the right time. So he was able to acquire, as I mentioned, this property in Winlaw not far from where the old mill had been, between the railway and the river. He died of a heart attack in 1955: collapsed in January while shovelling snow out of our driveway. I should have been doing that chore, since I was more or less still living at home. He was fifty-nine and I was twenty-five, but to be honest I was a sort of greaser in those days. If my folks had waited for me to clear the drive they would have been snowbound all winter: my dad would never have gotten his Bel Air on the road. He had a '53, four-door, in-line six. A beautiful machine I drove after he died.

I was working in those days for John Smedlin, who had a B/A gas station on the Nelson–Castlegar road, not far past Shoreacres. Mr. Smedlin knew I was into cars, since I'd dated his daughter Patsy for a while in Grade 10. When he opened the garage he offered me a job: working the pumps, but also more and more helping the mechanic. Since I wasn't paying much rent at home, I was making enough for a good time when the day was done. I had a duck's ass haircut, black leather motorcycle jacket, drape pants, even blakeys on my shoes so they clicked when I walked on any hard surface. I was one cool cat. I had a hot rod '48 Plymouth before the Bel Air: a four-door, not exactly flashy, but a car of my own and that baby could move.

On weekend nights I'd be tearing up and down the valley, listening to CKWX from Vancouver as it faded in and out, picking up the Crew Cuts' "Sh-Boom," or Bill Haley's wild "Rock Around the Clock," or the Four Lads crooning: "When other nights, and other days, Have found us gone our separate ways, We will have these mo-ments to remember." Or me and Jim would motor into Nelson if there was a dance somewhere, just to see who we could meet. Joking about asking the girls to park along the river to watch the submarine races. Actually, Jim was seeing Lucy McCrindle off and on, and I was dating sweet Karen from South Slocan, Karen Morrow. A year after my dad passed away I remember the four of us in the Bel Air, dragging through downtown Nelson on a warm spring evening, singing along to a new pop star with a weird name, Elvis, on CKLN. Karen already knew the words and led us through it:

> So if your baby leaves
> And you have a tale to tell,
> Just take a walk down Lonely Street
> To Heartbreak Hotel,
> Where you'll be so lonely . . .

With four out-of-tune voices happily howling out the words together, we didn't sound lonely. But something in the yearning of the singer's voice, the relentless rhythm, caught us. What was going to happen to us? We weren't teenagers, either: in '56 I was about to turn twenty-six, and though Lucy and Karen were a lot younger, twenty, twenty-one, they were oddballs like us: almost all their friends by then were engaged or were married and had kids.

After my dad died my mother didn't know what to do: she'd didn't drive, had never written a cheque to pay a bill, when she needed cash for groceries or new patterns to try on her sewing machine or a new kitchen bowl she just asked my dad and he opened his wallet. She hadn't worked since my dad married her in the twenties. Had me when she was twenty-eight. Now she was a widow at fifty-four. I guess they wanted more kids, but I was the only one.

She had good friends among our neighbours. But after my dad died, she decided to move back to New Westminster, where she grew up. She had a sister there, my Aunt Edith, who came out and stayed with my mom for a few weeks in June of '56 to help her pack up. Most of what she wanted to keep from the house we shipped to Vancouver by rail, but I drove one load of breakables down to the Coast in a Chev half-ton panel delivery truck my boss let me borrow. A '52 he'd gotten in some trade, although he didn't get into really selling cars until a couple of years later. Jim came with me to Van and we had a good time. The drive wasn't like today: the Hope–Princeton wasn't paved, for example, so on a hot July day like when Jim and I drove it you spent the entire afternoon trying to avoid choking in the cloud of dust from the guy in front of you.

We sold the house and my mom used most of the money toward buying a small bungalow off downtown in New West. My dad had insurance, and, it turned out, a pile of money in the bank. My mom gave me about a quarter of what the valley house brought in, plus of course the Bel Air.

She thought we'd put the Winlaw property up for sale, too. But that's when I had this idea.

No question the valley was becoming up-to-date. Electrical power poles were slowly making their way along the valley from Playmor, where the valley road meets the Nelson–Castlegar highway, toward Slocan. Nobody much had electricity before. Up in Slocan, houses had been hooked up to the unused capacity of a local mine's powerhouse. People there were supposed to use the juice only for lamps but once a house was wired, the temptation was to connect other electrical appliances. Some nights the most anybody could get from a light bulb was a dim glow. Now, though, West Kootenay Power was busy stringing wire. Pretty soon we'd all have lights, electrical fridges and stoves, vacuum cleaners, the whole works.

Most important for my idea, the Department of Highways had begun paving the road through the valley. The announcement said the project would take a couple of years, but I knew that better highways would mean more people travelling, including tourists. Everywhere you drove in the BC Interior in those days you came across these large orange and black signs that we got a chuckle out of. The signs said, "Road Under Construction: *Sorry* For Any Inconvenience." Below that was the name of the Highways minister, "Flying Phil" Gaglardi, who was constantly getting arrested for speeding. He inevitably claimed in court he was checking the work of his contractors: "Testing the curves," he said. The judges weren't amused, but everyone else got a kick out of it.

Once my parents' place sold, I rented a small house at Playmor. One night, Jim was over to see me, this would be April of '56, and I spelled out my plan. Jim was with an army pal of his and we were having a few beers at my kitchen table.

I'd been friends with Jim since elementary school, where we were known as Jimmy 1 and Jimmy 2. I was Jimmy 2, since in the class roll his last name came before mine. We just called each other Jimmy for years, none of this "1" or "2" nonsense, although when we started Grade 7, junior high, we agreed that in public I'd be Jimmy and he'd be Jim.

Grade 7 was as far as school went in the valley. Mount Sentinel high at the junction wasn't built until 1950. Jim and I were among the handful from our class who went on to high school in Nelson. You had to board with somebody, and in my case my dad had a cousin I could stay with. But none of us from the valley got home much during the school term: so near and yet so far. No wonder lots of us never graduated Grade 12.

Jim dropped out in Grade 9 after VE Day to work for his folks, who had bought a store in Slocan Park. He didn't stick with that, though: as soon as he got his driver's licence he began working for Mickey Markin's haywire cartage outfit, hauling up and down the valley at the wheel of a war surplus truck Mickey had picked up somewhere. I don't know if driving that thing gave him ideas, but in 1950 Jim took the train over to Calgary and signed up in the Princess Pats. War had broken out in Korea, and the call went out for volunteers. Everybody told him he was nuts to go, but he said he'd been in the valley all his life and wanted to see more of the world. Remember, too, we grew up during the war, and the talk was all "our gallant soldiers," and battles, and "home-front sacrifice," and so on.

Yet we knew there was more to war than that, since eight thousand Japs had been dumped into the north end of the valley after they were kicked off the Coast. You couldn't put that many people into our area without a big impact, but to be honest where we lived we rarely saw any of them. They were kept in camps at Lemon Creek, Slocan, New Denver and Sandon, and weren't allowed to be south of Appledale, which is north of Winlaw about five miles. As a kid, I doubt I was up that way more than four times during the whole war. Gasoline was rationed, remember. I vaguely recall passing by these towns made of rows and rows of small houses you could glimpse from the highway.

Adults spoke a lot about the Japs, though. My folks and their friends at first were against the government sending them here. Why should our valley be where the enemy was locked up? But once the Jappies arrived, they turned out to be people, if you know what I mean. I remember my dad being surprised when he learned a lot of them, maybe most of them, were born in Canada and had never even been to Japan. Later everybody realized the government had seized their homes, including furniture, and cars if they had them, and also took their businesses and tools they owned for making a living, like shipbuilding sheds or fishboats. The Japs got paid nothing in return.

The first winter the trains brought them here was the snowiest we'd had in a long time. Stories started to circulate about the government having failed to plan ahead, so whole families were shivering out the winter in tents. My mother was outraged at the idea of babies and kids facing the winter weather under canvas. "Whatever the men might have done, that's not right," my mom said.

The Doukhobors were the first to befriend the newcomers, giving them loads of vegetables to help them out that winter. Being shipped over here from Russia, the Douks knew what it was like to lose everything and be forced to leave home by a government. Yet despite all the war talk, pretty soon nobody had anything bad to say about the Japs relocated to our area. If nothing else, so many new-comers suddenly here meant a lot more money to be made. The Jap-pies needed everything from lumber to jam. And before you knew it, all the towns' baseball teams from that end of the valley had Japs playing on them, since they turned out not only to be crazy about baseball but damn good at it.

Still, we kids grew up with the war all around us. We'd think it was funny to sing the takeoff on the Pepsodent toothpaste radio jingle: "You'll wonder where the yellow went, when you bomb the Japs with wet cement." That sort of thing. But to us the Japs referred to on the radio news, or always shown in the newspaper cartoons or our war comics as having buckteeth and spectacles, had noth-ing to do with the new arrivals in the valley. Yet all this war stuff from our childhood probably influenced, as I say, Jim's decision to join the army the first time there was another scuffle overseas. The cause of the new war even seemed the same as the previous one: the Krauters had invaded Poland when we were nine, and now the North Koreans invaded the south eleven years later.

Jim's dad had been in the army and came home from Europe a captain, so that might have been a factor in Jim enlisting, too. Not that I ever heard Jim's dad speak much about the war. Like the other guys from the valley who'd gone overseas, he never referred to his time in the service. He did wear bits of his old uniform when he was doing chores around the place: the pants and boots and occasion-ally his battle jacket with the three pips on the epaulettes. The odd thing about Jim's dad is that he didn't drive. Jim's mother always was the one behind the wheel. Even my dad commented on that. Jim's dad had been in the tank corps, and Jim told me when we were teenagers how his dad once mentioned this scrap in Holland where they ran their tanks over some Jerries. I mean, that's war. You're there to kill people, whether you shoot them or squash them flat.

Like everyone else, I had tried to talk Jim out of signing up for Korea, since wanting to enlist seemed crazy to me: our lives were just getting started, and it wasn't like the North Koreans wanted to invade Canada. And I guess going to war wasn't that great an experience for Jim, since when he returned he didn't say a lot more than his dad did about it. Jim wrote me in a letter that training was one screw-up after another. Apparently the regiment was overwhelmed by suddenly having to grow again after being scaled way back after '45. The Princess Pats eventually left from Vancouver in a US troopship, and landed in Japan for more training. When they finally arrived at the war zone, his outfit ended up toe to toe with the Red Chinese up along the old border between the two Koreas.

Jim did tell me once that you could never be certain which Koreans were friends or foes. If things got tense at the sharp end, outposts cut off or in danger of being surrounded, say, civilians who turned out later to friendlies, even refugees from the north, got machine-gunned if they appeared suspicious—especially by the Yanks. On the other hand, the North Koreans had a habit of shooting prisoners of war. During your time at the front, Jim said, you had a big fear of ending up in an outnumbered situation where retreat or relief was impossible. Then your only choice was fighting to the death.

So you bet Jim was glad to get back to the valley in '54. We resumed being friends right where we left off. He was a tad quieter than before, but he still had the energy to chase after chicks. This guy he met in the army came back with him: a farm kid from near Peterborough in Ontario. Jim's pal was at loose ends, and Jim talked him into trying his luck in the West. The guy was too shy or religious to accompany us on our weekend trips into Nelson or even to dances in the valley. And if you can believe it, he was yet another Jimmy. Jim said it was weird to go from being one of two Jimmys in our class at school to being one of two Jimmys in his platoon.

The new Jimmy stood a head taller than either of us, and even his muscles had muscles. One weekend the three of us were helping old Andy Soukeroff clear some of his land. Andy had a beat-up caterpillar he was using to drag the bucked logs out of the bush to where he was piling them until they could be hauled away. I'm unhooking the choker from a log behind the tractor at the cold deck, and I look up to see the new Jimmy standing patiently waiting for me to finish and get out of the way. He has a log hoisted under his right arm, another balanced on his left shoulder, and I couldn't have lifted either one. The new Jimmy didn't even rest the ends on the ground while he waited to add his logs to the deck. He told me later, when I said something about his strength, that he had the logs balanced just right and didn't want to have to set them down until they could be added to the pile.

Andy that day started referring to the new Jimmy as James, in order to distinguish him from Jim and me, although Andy still called us Jimmy 1 and Jimmy 2. The newest Jimmy had no objection to responding to "James," so we began using that name for him, too. Jim told me how handy James was in Korea, able to fix a busted walkie-talkie, unjam a Bren Gun or Lee-Enfield, build a shower when they were in camp so that the water was heated through some scavenged piping and jury-rig a fuel pump on a jeep. He was the only one in their bunch to learn much Korean, having made friends with an interpreter assigned to their company. On patrol, Jim said, James's ability to ask some farmer where they were, or about local shortcuts, or if North Korean or Chinese forces had been spotted probably saved their unit a lot of grief.

Jim was hired by Passmore Lumber where the head sawyer, a European theatre vet like Jim's dad, took him under his wing. Pretty soon, Jim was apprenticing to learn that trade. He lived at home for a while and then moved to his own place. James meanwhile got hired for the green chain at the Passmore mill, but after he stepped in to repair a machine or two gone haywire, he was more or less employed as a millwright.

This is long before James took up with that bitch, Elaine. On the rare occasion he was with Jim and me and we ran into a bunch of girls, like at some hockey game or community picnic, James wouldn't say a word. That's the way he was most of the time, anyway: he said almost nothing, but if he did speak, it was worth your while to listen to him. I learned that several times with regard to the motel. We would be hashing over some problem, and I'd have shot off my face: "It's the end unit; let's just run the pipes along the wall."

"I don't think that will work, Jimmy," James would suddenly say. "If we install them like that, they're only protected by half the insulation. In a really cold winter, they'd freeze. Let's bring them in along the floor and we can box them in and it won't look too bad." He'd be right every time.

But I'm jumping ahead. That April night at my place, as we knocked back a few smalls of Old Style, I laid out my idea to Jim and James: the Three Jimmys Motel. I had the land—well, technically it belonged to my mom, but I was sure she'd deed it to me if I asked. We'd all seen—well, James hadn't yet seen—the motels springing up over in the Okanagan. The spot by the river in Winlaw was every bit as much of a potential vacation paradise as Kelowna on Okanagan Lake. In addition to the tourists who would soon be motoring here on the newly paved highway, local people sometimes had relatives or friends visit from the Coast or the Prairies. Instead of cramming them into their houses, the locals could rent a room for their visitors at the Three Jimmys Motel. Plus folks from the north part of the valley—Silverton, New Denver, Nakusp—making the trek to Nelson to shop or see a dentist maybe didn't want to drive there and back in a day, especially in winter. So they could lay over at the Three Jimmys, too. The plan couldn't lose.

"You mean we'd be working for you?" Jim asked.

"No, no." I could see he didn't get it. "We'd be partners. We all pitch in and build the thing in our spare time. We figure out how to operate it, taking turns or shifts or something equally. And we each take an equal cut of the profits."

Silence from around the kitchen table. I jumped up to snag another round of brews from the icebox, sat down and snapped the tops off.

Jim drained the bottle he was working on and pulled a freshly opened one toward him. "We've *got* jobs. Why would we want to run a motel on the side? What if it doesn't make any money?"

"Think ahead, Jim," I said. "If this thing goes, we'll be working for ourselves, not anybody else. At worst it'll make us some extra change. I'm not planning on giving up my job just yet. But I work at a service station; I see the licence plates. Every summer there's more people on the road from the Coast, from Alberta, from Washington and Oregon. The only spot around here they can spend the night is in Castlegar or Nelson. No hotel or motel in the valley, except the Newmarket way up in New Denver and one crummy dump in Slocan. The Three Jimmys will be snazzy. Clean, reasonably priced. Happy motorists will be fighting each other to stay with us."

"I don't know," Jim said. He took a swallow from his beer. "When I work for old man Brasford at the mill, if there's a problem, it's his problem. If I'm part owner of a motel and there's a problem, it's my—"

"Jimmy, you're putting up the land," James suddenly spoke, having not said a word all this time. "What do Jim and I throw in if we're equal partners?"

"Okay, I thought of that," I replied. "We'd need an estimate of how much construction will cost, including the value of the land. We divide the total by three. That's how much we each toss in the pot. Part of my share will be what the land is worth. All of us are handy, so our contribution will include how much work on the place we each do. We'll also have to see what cash each of us can raise, and then, if we need to, we'll get a bank loan for the difference. But once we're in business, the motel guests will be paying off the debt. Eventually running the operation will be pure profit for us. Profit split three ways."

"Sounds complicated," Jim said.

"We'd have to furnish the motel," James said. "Beds and chairs and drapes."

"Plumbing," Jim offered.

"Plumbing," James agreed. Everybody took another sip.

"Who do you see manning the desk, checking guests in?" James said after a long silence. "Keeping the books? Who's going to be janitor? Would we share those jobs, or—?"

"Or would we hire somebody?" I said. "I don't mean to suggest I've got everything figured out, or that this won't take a ton of effort." Jim was staring at the beer bottle hoisted in his left hand, while the fingers of his right scrabbled at the label, peeling it off in strips. James was gazing at me, outwardly stolid as usual. But he had a faraway cast to his eyes, as though in his mind he was calculating columns of figures or weighing pros and cons.

"The motel is an investment, not a purchase," I continued. "We'll get back lots more than we ever put in. And listen, it'll be *fun*."

Jim's and James's expressions didn't alter, though Jim stopped tearing off the beer label and looked at me.

"We're young and healthy," I said. "We have jobs, like Jim says, so we're not desperate, or gambling our futures on this deal. Down the road we'll be damn glad we dared to try something other than working our whole lives for somebody else."

You might wonder why, if the motel was such a great scheme, I didn't just go ahead with it by myself. I had weighed going into business on my own. But I doubted I could raise enough money. Having a partner, or partners—I'd thought first of Jim, but had gotten to like James, too—meant that if each of us could raise a little money and pool it we'd have sufficient dough to realize the dream.

And that's what happened. My golden tongue, which would later amaze my boss when he started selling cars and discovered I could move merchandise off the lot better than anybody, finally convinced the boys. They each scuffled up their share of what we needed. First, though, the three of us spent many an evening huddled over design sketches, parts lists, price estimates. James was the one who showed us it was much cheaper to construct all the units under one roof, instead of building several free-standing bungalows each with a couple of units—the norm for motels back then. The money I kicked in over and above the land was mostly borrowed from my mother, although I talked my boss, John Smedlin, into loaning me some cash, too. He agreed, once I explained the venture to him, that this was a surefire deal. James, too, borrowed from his brother rather than get into the clutches of a bank. Since he could raise the least amount of cash, he promised to do more than his share of the construction: what we would today call "sweat equity," although nobody talked like that in 1956.

Jim was the only one who went to the Bank of Montreal in Nelson for a loan. As a result, we had to prepare mountains of paperwork, including affidavits about our contributions, and even had to pay a lawyer to legalize our partnership.

Raising the dough wasn't the only reason I didn't start the business alone. I thought it would be a hoot to do something like this with Jim. And I judged James to be a Steady-Eddie, which I figured a project like this needed to offset a couple of men about town like Jim and me. Three heads are even better than two, let alone one, and we all got along great, so why not?

Getting the motel launched and operating it for years afterwards was a gas. Even though there were a million small disagreements, from who to contract with to dig foundations, to how to pound nails, to whether or not we should hire a manager for the motel or parcel out a manger's duties among ourselves, none of us lost our sense of humour. Everybody won some disputes and lost some.

The kidding never stopped as board by board, pipe by pipe, light switch by light switch the motel took shape and then opened for business. We were a real crew. Jim's and my basketball coach in Grade 9, Mr. Sorenson, who also taught us history, said a team is more than its components combined. Mr. Sorenson also said you know you're a real team when other people recognize that each player, unique as they are, is contributing a characteristic—a *quality* he called it—of the whole. That was the Three Jimmys.

Some of our friends started to call us the Three Musketeers, but eventually everybody knew us as the Three Jimmys, especially after the signs for the motel were installed. The construction phase took up most of our free time, including summer holidays, and each of us asked for leaves of absence from our jobs for various stretches to work full-out on the project.

We still went to parties in the valley and in Nelson—or at least Jim and I did—so it wasn't all plasterboard and fir flooring and roof gutters and meetings with our accountant. James's idea of a good time during construction was to figure out solutions to obstacles we had run into, often hammering and sawing or running pipe alone on the site which he almost seemed to prefer. Maybe he'd have one helper, some guy from the mill picking up a few bucks on the side, or some other millwright he'd gotten to know. Once the motel was in operation, he constantly thought up neat ideas he made happen: we had lights in the flower beds where you turn into the motel parking lot, and an ingenious way to handle waste water from the laundry room, all thanks to James. In the fall he'd disappear for a couple of days up onto Perry Ridge or Slocan Ridge hunting, or sometimes he'd go all the way north to the Lardeau. Deer, moose, elk steaks for us all when he returned.

I won't forget opening day in June '57, when the three of us cut the ribbon to the applause of our families and friends. And even a couple of motel guests, since we already had two timber cruisers staying there. The *Nelson Daily News* sent a photographer and reporter, since as it happened they were doing a feature on the possibilities of tourism in our area. Perfect timing: they didn't usually cover news this far from Nelson, unless it was another Doukhobor protest burning or nude parade and mass arrest. The three of us were on the front page, grinning like mad, with the motel in the background, its sign proclaiming who we are.

As chambermaids we'd hired the Smedow sisters, Katerina and Grace. Grace was the younger one; Katerina had been in our class in elementary school, although then she didn't look anything like she did around the time we hired her: she had become a good-looking woman. A widow, actually. She had married Derek Scott from our class, who had been killed in a logging accident a couple of years later. A few months after the motel opened, Jim asked Katerina out on a date, and following that he wasn't too interested in Lucy McCrindle anymore. You'd see Katerina and him tearing up and down the valley in the Studebaker. They were great to be around, always joking and laughing. He got along fine with her family, even quitting the mill and going to work driving logging truck for her dad once Jim and Katerina took the plunge and got married. They had their first kid about a year later. We wanted them to call the baby Jimmy Junior, but Katerina said there were enough Jimmys in the valley already, and they called the kid Richard Nicholas after their fathers.

Katerina or not, kid or not, every Friday the three Jimmys got together after work for a late-afternoon business meeting and supper, reviewing motel operations for the week and deciding on any changes to procedures or how to handle any problems or needed repairs. We met in each other's homes, or a café that had opened in Winlaw on the highway. Once in a while we drove into Nelson to meet, if we also wanted to check out tile replacements or new plumbing fixtures at a builders' supply or hardware store.

In February of '59 I met Doreen Brown at a meeting in the Doukhobor Hall in Slocan Park that Will McGowan and Victor Rilkoff had called to see about forming a valley chamber of commerce. Nothing came of that idea, but I thought Doreen was a real looker, and sharp as a whip when she spoke at the meeting. She had started a little wholesale egg business on her dad's farm, but she had ambitions. You could say with Doreen and me it was love at first sight, although I was sort of engaged-to-be-engaged at the time to Brenda Johnston, at least in Brenda's eyes. That situation took a certain finesse to extract myself from. Luckily, Doreen was understanding about my dilemma when we started going out. We were hitched a year and a half after we met.

So now we were five, or eight if you counted Jim's two kids and Doreen's and my first, Francie, who showed up in 1961. But the Three Jimmys were a team, the three of us thick as family as we ducked, dodged and weaved year after year through a million challenges to overcome, successes to celebrate, lean months and fat months. The motel turned a small profit the first year, and never looked back.

Starting in the summer of 1963 our revenues really shot up as tourism to the area swelled. The year before, the Sons of Freedom, the Doukhobor sect that was more extreme than the majority of them, hit a high for blowing things up and burning things down. During 1962 more than three hundred incidents happened: about one a day, which scared off some visitors you can be sure, although most of the destruction was directed at fellow Douks. In March, though, the power line across Kootenay Lake was dynamited, the line that carried electricity from the dam at South Slocan over to the mines in the East Kootenay. That explosion scared everybody, because who knew what next would be blasted to smithereens? Yet the Sons of Freedom shenanigans had been occurring for decades— when I was a kid during the war they even torched one of the Douk community's financial mainstays, the jam factory at Brilliant, across the river from Castlegar.

The RCMP tried everything over the years to settle things down and bring the guilty to justice. After the war they even seized Freedomite kids and locked them up in New Denver for years, because the sect refused to send their children to school. And of course the cops arrested every adult they could justify throwing in the clink: hundreds of them. A special prison was even built for the Sons of Freedom down in the Fraser Valley at Agassiz. However, in September 1962, Fanny Storgeoff led almost all the Freedomites in a march to the Coast. Hundreds made the trek. They finally arrived at the prison early the next year. That's where most of them stayed, in a sort of shantytown they built outside the jail. But the trek pretty much meant an end to the disturbances hereabouts, and we saw an immediate big increase, as I mentioned, in tourists. In 1970 we took in so much money that we even talked about buying into a hotel in downtown Nelson that came up for sale. But the boys decided they'd rather clear their debts than have to borrow more money to acquire the hotel. Who can blame them for that?

But I don't want to stress the profits we pocketed over the fun we had. Until that bitch appeared, and the good times ended.

Elaine

WHEN I MET James, that scumbucket Jimmy and his faithful hound dog Jim were taking advantage of James left, right and centre. They called their fleabag motel the Three Jimmys. But as far as I was concerned the dive should have been named the Let's Exploit James.

My first husband and I were living in Santa Cruz when we decided to move to Canada. You'll remember in the spring of 1970 America was beginning to shoot its children: in Isla Vista at Santa Barbara, then at Kent State, then Jackson State. Nobody knew whether every protest against the Vietnam War in the future would involve demonstrators being gunned down by the authorities, like in any other police state.

My husband and I weren't kids, but we had kids, and we didn't want them to grow up under fascism. We had our kids late, since first I was working to put my husband through university, and then he wanted to get his career started. He taught high school math, and I was thirty-one when Rodney was born in 1962. I quit working as a librarian then, and two years later we had Star. Growing up in North Beach in the city, I'd always had a soft spot for the beats, for rebels—my mother was an artist, although my dad was a banker. I guess in many ways my marriage mirrored my parents', although I didn't realize it at the time: my husband was the serious, responsible one, and I was the feeling, intuitive one. Like my dad marrying my mom, I think my husband married me because not far below his starched-shirt-and-necktie surface he had a far-out side to him.

Later we became what in Santa Cruz were called "weekend hippies." By 1968 my husband was active in the Santa Cruz peace movement, and when he went to work he was dressing much less formally. His students picked up on his counterculture leanings, and said nice things about him in the yearbook, or when we encountered them at anti-war rallies or at be-ins.

I started doing dreamwork in 1970. The outside world was becoming so crazy, I felt that in order to integrate our personalities and save humanity we needed to tap the hidden powers and sacred wisdom found within each individual. Though Freud called the submerged part of our minds the *unconscious*, that entity inside us is in fact *hyper*-conscious, comprehending past hurts and how to heal them, as well as what's best for us to do despite what the rational mind insists on. Every early civilization understood that if we pay attention to our dreams, they communicate the correct course of action for us to take, and reveal the best future for us.

That May, after the Cambodian invasion and all the killings of students in the States, my husband and I began to talk seriously about moving to British Columbia. I had a dreamwork client who had visited there, and was enthusiastic about the scene in Vancouver. Then at a friend's party, we met a couple who had moved from Detroit to the Slocan Valley where they were part of a commune and loving it. The couple had come down to visit the Bay Area because the wife's brother was living in the Haight and her family back home wanted her to check on him. I can't remember how they knew our friend.

This visiting couple made the Slocan seem like paradise, and that night when we got home my husband took down an atlas and we found the place. It looked like you just drove north from Spokane for a few hours and once you crossed the border, there you were. A couple of days later he went to the city library and found addresses for school boards in the region, and wrote them about jobs. The more we talked about going, the more determined we were to raise our kids away from the madness of the US.

To be honest, we didn't know much about Canada, and nobody willingly decides to go into exile without a lot of doubts and apprehensions. About that time I had a dream. I saw a big framed painting, maybe six feet by eight feet, like you'd see on the walls of an art museum. The canvas was nearly filled by a huge yellowish-white sheet or curtain, depicted waving at a slight angle from upper right down to lower left, as though the highest edge of the immense piece of cloth was suspended from a clothesline or rope that was invisible. Although the sheet, which was also like a flag, took up almost all the space in the painting, around the edges of the cloth you could glimpse a landscape that the sheet floated above. Rolling forested hills climbed toward a line of snow-capped peaks in the blue distance. Somehow in the dream I was given the title of the painting: "The Great Year (and Others Like It)."

I was confident the landscape was a preview of where we going, so I knew the plan to relocate was right for us. In July once school was done, we drove up and fell in love with the valley. We found a small house to rent near Passmore, and a month later had settled in. Immigration in those days was not the hassle it is today, and my husband had a letter from the Kootenay Lake school district putting him on the substitute teacher list, or as they called it in Canada, the supply teacher list. When the Immigration officer at the border asked him what he'd do if there wasn't enough teaching work to support his family, my husband said he'd work as a tutor. That appeared to satisfy the border guard, and we were officially landed.

We soon were aware that dozens and dozens of other Americans were living in the valley, refugees from the war or just counter-culture, back-to-the-land types. Yet the Slocan Valley was different enough from Santa Cruz to be rather dissociating for my husband and me. Our kids, though, immediately took to the whole adventure of moving to Canada, especially after some neighbours invited us to a potluck where Rodney and Star met kids their own age. Once school started in September, Rodney in particular never looked back. But I found having to master wood heat and telephone party lines, and especially the isolation, hard. Also, we arrived too late in the year to garden. The other adults we met talked incessantly about their gardens, and I realized I had much to learn. Plus we still hadn't gotten through a winter.

Almost every social encounter involved smoking doobies, and plenty of acid was available. We were familiar with all this from California, but somehow drugs were more important in a rural area without too many other distractions. My husband was stoned more than I liked. I enjoyed getting ripped as much as anybody, but I always felt one of us had to keep it together for the sake of the kids. In addition, some of the communes in the area were into free love, and we could see that ethos was widespread in the freak community. From comments my husband made, I could tell that like all men he thought free love was a great idea. I felt our marriage was solid, though, since were in our late thirties and not as young as most of the hippies we met.

While my husband was waiting for substitute teaching gigs, he started working for a neighbour who was the local tofu manufacturer. The guy had a barn where batches were concocted, and besides helping there my husband took over the distribution route, which ran north up to Slocan in one direction, and the other way as far as Nelson. He began coming home later and later from the route, and he was evasive about why the trip was taking him longer to finish. At first I figured he was just getting too stoned to be efficient, since I learned there was often a social component to dropping off people's order of tofu. Then one night in November he confessed he'd been getting it on with a young woman who lived on a commune on a back road in Perry Siding.

Given the prevailing customs of the time, I put up with this for a while, though I was unhappy about it. After all I'd done for him, supporting him for years while he got his degree, I can tell you I was hurt by his fooling around on me. I knew the local ethics were somewhat to blame, but still I felt betrayed. When he announced he wanted to spend weekends in Perry Siding, I drew the line.

Having two kids and only a little in savings meant it was a tough winter for me. My husband needed our car for his stupid tofu job. Yet I hardly saw any financial support from him once he moved into the commune. I was happy to hear via the grapevine that his affair with the young slut didn't last more than another month, that being the way things went in those days. But after he left our family, he became more and more irresponsible about his parenting obligations. We didn't get a formal divorce for another ten years, by which time he was back teaching and being all respectable: he wanted to marry his present wife.

Meantime, I picked up some part-time work in the library at Nelson, although that was really thanks to another single mother, Lara, who I met at a community meeting of people interested in starting an alternative elementary school in the valley. Lara was originally from San Diego, and on days when I had library work in Nelson she volunteered to look after Star, and to collect Rodney from the bus after school. By this time I had borrowed money from my parents and bought a funky old pickup. The neighbour I bought the truck from, Mike Chernoff, fixed it afterwards for free on several occasions. His wife used to laugh that she encouraged Mike to sell me the thing because he so much enjoyed working on it to keep it running, and if he sold it to me he could *still* work on it. I always offered him money for the repairs but they wouldn't take any, since as they pointed out, Mike had a good job at the Slocan mill whereas I was scuffling to support two kids and myself on next to nothing. People were like that then: either they would give you the shirt off their back if you needed help, or, like my ex-husband, were complete shits.

I continued to do dreamwork, too. Since few valley people interested in that kind of personal growth had much money, I bartered for babysitting, apples, potatoes, second-hand clothes for the kids, and even some beautiful pottery dishes I still own.

I met James the summer after my husband left, at a meeting to discuss building a community hall: what became the Vallican Whole. Lara had talked me into going, and supposedly childcare was available, although it amounted to the kids running wild while a couple of teenagers pretended to keep an eye on them while busy socializing. James only spoke once at the meeting, after a lot of guys had strutted their stuff, mainly talking to hear themselves speak, to demonstrate how important they were. James quietly raised some technical construction matters I didn't understand. Yet from the reaction he sparked, it was clear his were genuine, pertinent questions. From the silence from the know-it-alls that followed his questions, I could deduce that he had set some of the bullshitters back on their heels. Different guys than those who had been monopolizing the meeting spoke in response to what James said, and the answers were serious and respectful. Much different in tone and content from the windbag rhetoric about "come together" and "family" and "community" we'd been subjected to for the previous hour. I was impressed that one low-key guy could shut down the self-important blowhards with just a few sentences. Plus I confess I thought he was awfully good-looking.

I was wondering who he was, but when somebody nominated him for the steering committee, I found out. In the social after the meeting, I saw he was chatting to my neighbour Mike, my pickup repairer. I went over and was introduced.

No question he was awkward around women, which was endearing in a way although hardly unexpected from a strong silent type like him. A non-smoking Marlboro Man, but a millwright rather than a cowboy. I persevered in talking to him, drawing him out on the issues he'd raised during the meeting. Mike's wife told me later he'd asked about me after I headed off to rescue my children, so I guess I made an impression. The next weekend he was visiting the neighbours and the two guys strolled over to inspect my truck. That's how I knew he was interested in me, but he didn't phone to ask me out for another few days. Summoning up the courage.

I really liked him when we did go out. He thought about things before giving his opinion, or, indeed, saying anything at all. In other words, he demonstrated respect for who he was talking to, and for himself. His consideration of things before he spoke might give the impression to some people that he was a little slow. But he was just weighing possibilities, looking before he leaped. When he did speak, it was obvious he was smart. He was good with my kids, careful and calm around them, taking his time getting to know them.

I have to say I found him exasperating sometimes, not knowing what he was thinking and whether we were ever going to be more than friends. Most of the summer slipped by just becoming better acquainted. But I hung in, and he did too, dropping by more and more often and helping me out first in little ways and then bigger ones.

Finally one Saturday in early August, he had been over at my house pitching in while I repainted the dingy kitchen. Which is to say he did most of the work, while I kept the kids out of our hair and passed him things. I served him supper that night by way of thanks, and we put the kids down together. We were sharing a glass of wine afterwards in the living room, sitting side by side on the couch. I took a deep breath and asked him if he'd like to stay the night. For once he didn't think the question over. I would have killed him if there had been one of his usual long pauses before he answered.

After that, he was at my place about half the week, although we didn't formally move in together for another two years, when he bought the house and acreage in Slocan Park. We figured that property was halfway between the mill at Slocan where he was working at the time, and Nelson, where I was getting more hours at the library, having completed an upgrading course in librarianship offered weekends by Selkirk College in Castlegar. Given James's manner of dealing with the world, I knew he'd never stray like that bastard first husband of mine.

James acted grateful, in fact, that I was willing to tolerate him. He was always there for us, kind and generous. He not only provided a home for me and my kids that was a definite improvement over the hovel where we'd been living, but he built a tree fort and dollhouse for Rodney and Star, and presented them with used bikes he had restored to like-new working order. Anything broken around the house was dealt with, and he constructed storage sheds, raised bed gardens and cupboards for us. He took over the ongoing repair of my pickup until for my birthday in '73, our first year in Slocan Park, he gave me a newer model used Volkswagen Beetle which drove much better on snowy roads since the engine was right over the back wheels. That's how thoughtful he could be, and you bet I appreciated it.

James had a fierce sense of loyalty once he committed to anything, whether the kids and me, the Vallican Whole construction or that stupid motel. Inevitably, he was the guy everybody deferred to at work bees for the Whole, since he could resolve just about any snag that was sure to arise when a group of clueless hippies set out to build a large hall. At the height of the push to finish the Whole in the summer of '74, he took a couple of weeks' leave from the mill and worked every day, sometimes with nobody on the site but himself on weekday mornings, to make sure the hall kept taking shape, and that the job was done right.

Erecting the Vallican Whole had a beginning and an end, despite how for a couple of years the work bogged down and all that was evident was the basement excavation, which led to the locals calling it the Vallican Hole. Once construction resumed, I was annoyed that James's knowledge and willingness to work so hard was exploited by everybody involved. Yet I was aware this situation wouldn't go on forever and at least he was giving 110 percent of himself in a worthwhile cause.

Of course, James's time and energy given over to the Whole impacted on his family duties. Especially on top of his entanglement with the motel. But, as ever, James was calm and rational whenever I became flustered and upset by how his devotion to these projects meant people were really taking advantage of him, not to mention how all the time he put in working on these schemes interfered with his home chores.

The motel was especially bad. To begin with, the owners met every Friday for supper. Most often this gathering was in Winlaw, which made sense, but occasionally that idiot Jimmy insisted they meet in Nelson. I never heard a satisfactory explanation of why they had to meet there. While I trusted James completely not to get into any deviltry in Nelson with the two irresponsible fools he was involved with, travelling all the way into Nelson to meet was a ridiculous waste of James's time.

I didn't want to nag, but giving over *every* Friday to motel business also seemed retarded. Sometimes the kids had activities or sleepovers on Friday, either at our house or at a friend's, and I could have used some help with the logistics. Try planning a week with two active youngsters where you have to work around the fact that every Friday evening your partner is unavailable to help in any way.

James was unyielding on this point. He never became angry when I noted how unnecessary it was to give up an entire evening a week for a business that virtually ran itself. The Friday meets were a commitment he had agreed to before he met me, he said. He claimed matters came up each week that had to be talked about by all the partners.

Obviously that scumbag Jimmy and his mindless follower, Jim, were misleading James. Anything to do with building repairs and renovations somehow was not only James's responsibility, but he would end up donating his Saturdays and sometimes his Sundays to work there instead of tackling what needed doing around our place. "I don't see your good pal Jimmy out there swinging a hammer," I'd point out, when James would return exhausted from a Saturday spent reshingling the roof at the motel. "He's too busy down at the car lot fast-talking some sucker into buying an overpriced clunker he doesn't really need. And what about your other so-called partner, Jim? Or did he, too, somehow 'have' to work today: sitting on his fat ass behind the wheel of his father-in-law's logging truck making money for himself when there's repairs to do at the motel?"

Of course the financial arrangement the three of them had was none of my business. Yet when James admitted how the money was divvied up, my piss boiled. On paper, everything supposedly had been equal. But Jimmy just contributed the land and cash he'd inherited, while James had to earn the money to pay back the loan from his brother, and Jim had to pay interest to the bank as well as repay his loan. One way to look at their finances, then, is that things were unfair to start with.

Then about the time the Vallican Whole project was stalled, Jimmy talks the other two into expanding the office structure into a regular house. His excuse is that instead of paying for three shifts of a front desk person each day, one of the owners can live on the property in turn and serve as night manager, meaning they can let the evening front desk clerk go home once the busy evening check-in period is done.

Guess who's free to occupy the house? Not Jim and Katerina and their two kids, and once James and I moved in together, not us either. So Jimmy really arranged free rent for himself in perpetuity. Doreen had left him in 1972, taking Francie with her, when she finally had enough of his screwing around on her. And that's precisely when Jimmy comes up with his let's-build-a-house scheme. I don't have to tell you that the majority of the work on the office expansion was done by James, with Jimmy and Jim supervising. I didn't want to say too much at the time, since James and I were still at what I call the "stinky socks" stage of two people learning to live together. But eventually I managed at least to convince James to get

Jimmy's free rent factored in when the three of them split the profits at the end of the year.

I couldn't ever persuade James, though, to bill the others for the repairs he did constantly at the motel. "If you weren't saving the day once again for free," I pointed out, "the motel would have to hire tradesmen. I can understand you volunteering your time way back when the business was just starting. But the motel is still the only one between Slocan and either Nelson or Castlegar. As long as nobody around here is intelligent enough to open another one in the valley, you guys show a good profit each year. The company can afford to pay you for work done."

James would only say, after his usual silence, that he liked working with his hands, liked coming up with a solution to the problems the repairs involved: cracks in the sidewalk linking the units or whatever. That he enjoyed the challenges of his little building projects like replacing the motel's gardening shed.

"By all means do the work," I said, "as long as you're caught up around here. All I'm saying is to bill them for it. Like anybody normal would do."

He never would, no matter how many times I brought it up over the years. Meanwhile, Jimmy had taken up with that tart Cynthia from the Slocan Park Co-op. She wasn't exactly living with him, but she had to be fifteen years younger. I was chatting with Katerina when she and her kids had stopped by the Nelson library. She told me Jimmy had started poker nights at the motel office once or twice a month, and that Jim was going to these. Apparently Doreen had been outright opposed to gambling, what with her father frequently losing his paycheque in dice and card games while she was growing up. But once she left, Jim was dropping forty or fifty dollars every time he went over to Jimmy's to play. I thought to myself that Jimmy was probably charging the food and booze for his poker nights to the motel, too. I didn't mention that to Katerina.

In July of 1979 James told me after one of the Friday night meetings that they were considering a major renovation of the motel. The dump was more than twenty years old and showing its age despite James's constant free labour. The group of them had been considering another paint job for the outside of the building, I knew, but a stoned freak had managed to set fire that June to one of the units and there was smoke damage to the adjoining units, too. Insurance covered most of the costs, but in weighing the refurbishing of these units the three of them had talked themselves into a refit of the entire place.

That would mean, James said, that all the money the motel made for the next few years would go to pay for the modernization. The trio had concocted a cockamamie plan whereby half the units would be rented while the other half were undergoing improvements. The extra money we'd been getting each year from the motel, however, was a handy addition to our household on top of James's income and my contributions. Especially given that I now had a seventeen-year-old and a fifteen-year-old who, along with the friends they invited over after school, were eating us into poverty.

The capper was that by the time James mentioned the renovation scheme to me, he had already promised Rodney that he could work as a helper on the project after school and weekends, and be paid for it. My Rodney worshipped James, but I put my foot down.

"I want Rod to do well at school," I began, when James and I were alone, "so he can go on to college. You've done okay without a high school diploma, but the world has changed. If he's fetching and carrying or whatever on the jobsite, he'll come home too tired to study and his grades will suffer." I took a deep breath. "In any event, I really think this is a good time for you to free yourself from the motel. Let the other two buy you out. You've been contributing far, far more than your fair share. Rather than take on a big reno at the motel, which I know you'll end up doing most of, why not draw the line here?"

As I expected, James didn't say anything. "The money from our share of the profits has been nice," I acknowledged. "But according to you, we're not going to see any of it for the next few years due to the reno. Whereas if the other two bought you out, that sum would be a handy nest egg for the kids' schooling. And it's a useful reserve if we ever need some of it between now and when they go off to university."

I knew James well enough not to expect an answer right away, but over the following week I kept listing the advantages to us of being clear of the motel. We'd be turning fifty next year, and retirement was looming—James needed to start to plan what he might want to do when he was finished working. If the kids buckled down and won scholarships, that education nest egg would enable us to travel, or whatever James thought he might like to get into once he wasn't employed anymore.

He allowed in a rare comment that what he had in mind for when he retired was to build us a brand new house on the property, one we would design ourselves. That was news to me. But I encouraged the idea, pointing out that the sale of his share of the motel could definitely help pay for that, once the kids' needs were taken care of.

Katerina came into the Nelson library a few days after I first talked to James about quitting the motel, and I put a bug in her ear that it might be good if Jim was free of the motel hassle, too. No more poker nights, since there wouldn't be any reason for Jim to trail around after Jimmy. And she'd have cash if their kids wanted to go on to college. Or money for whatever she and Jim had in mind for themselves. Jimmy was the one getting the most out of the business. Let him own it by his lonesome.

My mother had a saying: "You set your little ships afloat. Some come home and some don't." I didn't really care if Katerina heeded my advice, but for certain I wanted James out of Jimmy's clutches. As the next Friday meeting approached, he seemed a bit distant, which I knew meant he was thinking it over. I was patient: I just kept calmly pointing out the advantages of him not having to worry continually about the motel.

I guess the meeting where he announced his decision was quite the time. He didn't return home until after midnight. I was starting to worry when he didn't show up at the usual hour, but all he'd say when he finally walked through the door was that he'd told the others he wanted out. I tried fishing for details, but he said he didn't want to talk about it. I eventually said goodnight, and he didn't come to bed until about three in the morning. Which, again, wasn't like him.

I gathered from running into Katerina the next afternoon outside the Co-op that things were pretty tense between the partners once James gave them the news. Katerina said her Jim had always admired James, and that now that James was leaving Jim was giving more serious thought to doing the same.

Katerina also mentioned that James and Jim were old army buddies, which I didn't know, since James never talked about Korea. I had found his uniform jacket in a cupboard after we'd moved in together, and happened to mention something about war surplus gear being big among the guys in California, too, in the sixties. James, if I remember right, said the uniform was really his, and that he'd been overseas in Korea as a young kid. I waited for him to say more, but that was it, and the subject never came up again. He certainly didn't say he had been in combat, which I asked him about right after I spoke with Katerina. He just shrugged and asked which of us was going to pick up Star from her violin lesson at Mrs. Padwinikoff's.

We went through a bad few months while ending the motel partnership sorted itself out. Valley gossip has it Jimmy put every kind of pressure he could think of on James and Jim to force them to stay. Now that the chickens were coming home to roost, no question Jimmy was desperate. But despite some ugly scenes and us having to hire a lawyer, in the end everything was settled almost entirely how I'd hoped.

I like to think that I made a new friend in Katerina through all the storm and stress. We visit back and forth now like we never used to. Strangely, James isn't all that keen on us doing things with Katerina and Jim. When the four of us are together, there's some sort of tension between the men. A strained formality certainly isn't what I'd expect if they actually served in Korea together. So mostly Katerina and I go into Nelson for a girls' night out, or we meet for coffee. Or get together to trade recipes: she's teaching me Russian cooking at the moment.

That pathetic loser Jimmy managed to hang onto his dump for another ten years. I heard from Evie Stone, whose daughter Aspen worked at the motel, that Jimmy had to mortgage himself to the teeth to pay off his partners. The renovations were derailed by his financial wheeling and dealing, and didn't happen until the late eighties. By which time I wasn't the only one who referred to the place as a rural slum.

A couple of years after the reno, Jimmy up and sold the motel. He'd have been well into his fifties by then. The new owners renamed their purchase the "Starlite," fixed it up some more, and finally took down that eyesore of a sign on the highway. But the new people only had it five years and then sold it to this young couple from Calgary. Everybody was braced for the worst, but they fitted into the community real well, and decided to adopt the original name. So the place is called the Three Jimmys again, but of course it has nothing to do with us.

Jim

BEING ONE OF the bunch that built the motel was the best thing in my life. If it hadn't been for that, I never would have married Katerina, as one example. No Kate would have meant we wouldn't have had our Rick and Ophelia and Ben. Plus nobody would have thought of me as other than a mill rat. Instead, I became a respected valley businessman. *And* mill rat. It made a difference. Then I was a businessman and logging truck driver. And once Kate's dad, Nick, retired, I was motel owner and logging contractor. A big shot in our small world, and it's all thanks to Jimmy.

The motel was Jimmy's idea, and he didn't have to include me in it. So I'm grateful. We were buddies—some of the greatest times for me both before and after Korea were blasting up and down the valley in one of Jimmy's series of cool cars: his souped-up Plymouth, the Bel Air that had been his dad's and especially his T-Bird. The chicks really loved to ride in that one. I must have had my arm around a dozen chicks in the back seat of Jimmy's various bombs: either out here, or dragging the main in Nelson, or parked in the dark at Taghum Beach. My kids growing up listened to a singer called Bob Seger who has one tune about a young couple at night "working on mysteries without any clues." That was me for sure, and Jimmy too: fumbling in the dark with buttons and hooks we couldn't see, desperate to get our fingers into forbidden places.

I cut out all that when I got serious about Katerina. Jimmy and I had known her since Grade 1, but my, how she'd changed. A knock-out. Since she'd known us forever, once she started working at the motel she wasn't ever going to regard Jimmy or me as her boss. Her earlier marriage to Derek gave her confidence, too, though it gave her sadness as well. She really loved him, but she settled for me after he was gone. And she loved our kids: I'd watch her kneel down and talk to young Rick or one of the others when they were toddlers and upset about something. I'd see Kate's whole attention put to comforting the little monster, and my chest would flip right over. She's beautiful: there's no other word for her. Lots of people say it, but I'm the luckiest guy in the world. Why she puts up with me I'll never know, but we're still married.

For years I had a lot of trouble nobody was aware of except Kate. I never told Jimmy, or even James. I had these dreams, nightmares, where I'm back in the salient, Hill 677, with the Aussies somewhere on our right and the Limeys to our left. We're taking a pounding from the Reds' mortars. I'm on the ground, elbows propelling me forward, inching across chewed-up dirt with a terrible roar all around. I'm by myself, headed somewhere, and I find Bruce Littlefield on his back. He's a gapper, with the rear of his skull shot away and his brains sprayed out on the mud. To save my life, or for some other reason, I absolutely *have* to keep moving forward, I have to crawl overtop of his corpse or I'll *die*. Crazy, I know: why can't I just go around him? I'm terrified by the idea of pulling myself across his dead body but I *have* to. Other dreams, too, like that. Kate told me I thrashed around in my sleep, smacked her good a couple of times when naturally I didn't mean to. Yelling stuff. She was always patient with me when I got like this. I don't know what was wrong with me. I never heard James mention anything near to this. He came home like me and got on with living. Like my dad, though I know my dad was up at the sharp end, too, against the Jerries. He was a tanker. We had Shermans in Korea that my dad could have fought in. Whenever I saw them, I thought of him.

I'm so grateful to Kate, as well as loving her. She carried me through years of this shit, and never told a soul that I know of. I thought the bad nights would end when Rick was born, but every once in a while I would be back there, even twenty years later. Is that screwed up, or what? But you can see I owe her big, like I owe

Jimmy. Katie also knew I wasn't too happy at the mill, and probably she's the reason her dad offered me a job driving for him. She claims she had nothing to do with it, but, looking back, that job working for her old man was one of the corners I turned for the better in my life.

I liked driving truck, which took a lot more skill in those days. You always had to highball: time is money, and all that. But arriving alive took concentration on those mountain roads when you were wooded down, let me tell you. "Drive her like you stole her" was the motto, yet where other drivers are concerned, you had to weigh the stupid factor. Somebody taking a chance or not paying attention and he ends up smeared by the logs behind the cab or flattened into a tree alongside the road, or turned into raspberry jam at the bottom of a ravine with the rig piled on top of him. Bad drivers killing themselves was one thing, but when you're rolling down loaded you don't want to career around a curve and find yourself eyeball to eyeball with somebody upbound who should have been paying attention to the radio and pulled over at a turnout to let you go by. I had a couple of close calls at the landings, too. With a grapple or even a self-loader, a log can have a mind of its own. But I'm here to tell the tale.

Kate also probably talked her dad into passing the business on to me when he was ready to pull the plug and spend his days at one end of a line into Fish Lake or Bear Lake or at certain spots on Slocan Lake he thought were his big secret. The old man could have handed the reins to Kate's brother Ed. But though Ed was in AA when Nick retired, Ed had never worked steady at anything. I had to promise I'd keep Ed on the payroll, but I put my foot down and said that what we did was too dangerous to employ a drinker, so first time he showed up at work drunk, he was gone. Safety first. Nick could see the wisdom in that. Ed lasted about six months. He works for a janitorial outfit in Nelson, now.

But much as I liked the logging job, I loved more being one of the owners of the Three Jimmys. I looked forward all week to our Friday meetings. We always had lots of laughs, as well as settling dozens of problems. Both James and Jimmy were smart guys, way smarter than me, though I came up with a few good ideas myself, if I do say so. When you drove onto the property headed for the office, the first thing you saw was a big "Welcome" painted on the asphalt. That was my brainstorm. Kate suggested planter boxes under the windows that faced the drive at the office and on each unit. A woman's touch, but I talked the other guys into it and those flowers meant the building looked a whole lot nicer in summer, the height of tourist season: more homey. A couple of guests each year would tell us how friendly the geraniums and marigolds made the place seem.

Mostly, though, Friday nights were time with Jimmy and James. Once Kate and I were hitched, and especially once the kids started arriving, I didn't otherwise have time to socialize with those guys, and we'd been tight friends before. Jimmy I'd known all my life. And when you've shared with someone the boredom and bullshit of army life, as well as bullets and shells aimed your way, you get to know that person pretty good. That was James and me.

Jimmy's motel idea was lucrative, too. Some years the profit I brought back to Kate only added up to the equivalent of a month behind the wheel. But there were years where the cheque from the motel's accountant equalled half a year's wages from her dad. You couldn't live on your share, but boy, it made our life easier.

Maybe that's why Kate never minded the Friday nights. Or maybe she was just glad I was around the other six nights, and not out gallivanting around like the husbands of some of her friends. I think she *understood,* too, about people needing more in their lives than their spouse and kids, important as those are. She was close to her folks, and I was fine with her visiting over at their place a lot. I liked Nick and Agnes, even if Nick eventually was my boss. And when we first got together, I think Kate was afraid I wouldn't want her to have anything to do with Derek's parents. She was still in touch with them about once a week. But her seeing them was okay with me: Derek had been in our class, and while I didn't know anything about losing a son, I could imagine wanting to stay in touch with your son's wife, especially one as nice as Kate. When our kids came along, Derek's folks were like a third set of grandparents. I was glad they took such an interest, because my folks moved to Kelowna when my dad retired and we only saw them once or twice a year.

When Jimmy was married to Doreen, I never heard that she complained about our Friday nights. No problem, either, when Jimmy was on the loose again, or later shacked up off and on with that looker from the Co-op, Cynthia. The fly in the soup was James's partner, Elaine.

Everybody was surprised when James connected with a woman. He made good money as a millwright, and was a genius when it came to fixing anything from cars to kitchen plumbing, so he should have been a catch. As Jimmy says, the gene pool is mighty small in the valley, so it's amazing James wasn't snapped up sooner. But he was terminally shy when it came to the ladies.

Elaine, who snagged him, was one of the older hippies who came up from the States. I think she saw his good qualities the instant she laid eyes on him, and next we knew, he was taken. If James had dated a little more, and had some grounds to compare Elaine with other women, I'd have been happier. But I was glad at first for his sake that he and Elaine were together, so he didn't end up one of our old valley bachelors.

Yet the first time all six of us tried to socialize together, Elaine made it clear she didn't have any use for Jimmy and me. I told Kate afterwards that Elaine behaved as if we were a threat to her hold on James. Kate wasn't so sure that was what was going on, but promised to keep her eyes and ears open and see what her friends knew.

Almost from the start, Elaine put pressure on James to have less to do with Jimmy and me. After a while James began to miss the odd Friday gathering, claiming that he had this or that obligation to chauffeur one of Elaine's kids, or Elaine really wanted to go to a potluck or to the movie in Nelson. Yet when James did show at our meetings, he was as much himself as ever. Jimmy and I hoped Elaine would loosen up the leash when she realized we weren't any danger to her and James's relationship, or when James decided he didn't needed to abide by Elaine's every whim. But who knows, maybe James liked having a ball and chain attached to his leg?

We started to hear from third parties that Elaine was telling people that Jimmy was taking unfair advantage of James, and that I was nearly as bad. That pissed me off, since James would have had no connection with the motel, wouldn't have seen a dime of the profits, if Jimmy hadn't been willing to make him part owner on the sole strength of James being my friend. Jimmy didn't really know James when he proposed the idea of the Three Jimmys, and yet James ends up benefiting year after year from Jimmy's generosity. Tell me how that's taking advantage of someone?

Kate, thanks to a cousin of hers, Doris, scuffled up some dirt on old Elaine. Back when the hippies brought free love to the valley, when Elaine and her husband first moved here, apparently Elaine's husband left her for someone with lower mileage at one of the communes where swapping partners was the in thing.

Kate's cousin Doris had drifted into the commune life herself, what with having a boyfriend who introduced her to wacky tabaccy and all. She didn't live at the commune where Elaine's husband stayed for a while, but at a different one called Hog Heaven up the Little Slocan Road. But Doris says one night they had a party that Elaine was at, and so was Jimmy. He wasn't above checking out the young hippie chicks to see what he might find, even though he was twice the age of some of them. This was after Elaine was on her own. Anyway, before the night was done, Elaine and Jimmy got it on. The two were only a couple for about forty-eight hours, but that was Jimmy's style with lots of girls even in the days before the hippies arrived. When you think how love-'em-and-leave-'em became the norm for a while among some groups in the valley, you could say Jimmy was ahead of his time.

Despite how free that free love was supposed to be, lots of broken hearts resulted. Doris remembers hearing that Elaine was bad-mouthing Jimmy soon after their one-night or two-night stand. She couldn't remember Elaine's complaint, exactly. But hell hath no fury, hippie or not.

Elaine shortly afterwards got involved with a guy in Winlaw who had started a candle-making business with his wife in their basement before that marriage fell apart and the wife scooped the kids and went back to the States. From Doris's story I can figure why Jimmy was not Elaine's favourite person even years and years afterwards. Though why she took a dislike to me is a mystery. Once Elaine and James moved in together, I found dropping by to visit James unpleasant. Before Elaine, James and I used to just sit around the kitchen or living room wherever he was staying, suck back a beer or two and yack. At James's house in Slocan Park, besides Elaine's kids racing around, Elaine would constantly interrupt us, even if James and I were watching a game on TV, with something she demanded James do for her, from opening a jar to driving one of her kids over to a playmate's. Jimmy says James was pussy-whipped, but James didn't have a hangdog expression or anything. He looked the same no matter what she asked him to do. He'd consider the request as he always did, and then after he'd silently chewed it over he'd agree. As if the time he and I were enjoying together didn't count compared to fulfilling Elaine's latest command. It didn't appear to bother him that Elaine was about as rude to me as she could be without telling me to my face that I wasn't welcome at their house.

Kate says the reason for Elaine's behaviour could be as simple as any friend of Jimmy's is an enemy of Elaine's. But whatever the cause, Elaine was unrelenting at trying to pry James away from us. She told everybody that she knew that James should bill us for his extra time working around the motel. Which sounds fair enough, except as Jimmy says, unlike with a contractor you're paying, if James goofs up, what recourse would we have? Plus James never seems happier than when he's got some project on the go: frozen pipes to thaw out, a hole in the drywall in unit four to repair, or retrofitting fans into all the bathrooms to prevent condensation. The last was one of James's good ideas and like most of his it really worked.

With Elaine in the saddle, eventually we never knew from Friday to Friday if James would be at our meeting, or if he was, would we have to deflect some nutso suggestion of hers she would have browbeaten him into bringing up. I stopped looking forward to our Fridays. That's when Jimmy came up with the idea of a poker night at his place once a month or so: a bunch of us boys having some fun the way the three of us used to. We invited different people to play, but there were a couple of regulars, including Armand Muller, who did paint jobs around the motel when none of us were available to handle them. He turned out to be a bit of a card shark. This was low-stakes poker, but we all chipped in for food and drinks so Jimmy didn't get stuck every time with the cost. A couple of the guys, especially Armand's pals, were real boozers, and a few times Jimmy let them sleep it off in one of the units if we weren't full, rather than let them drive home drunk. I knew Kate wouldn't be keen on me paying to supply beer or rye for these alkies. So to account for my share of the drinks I would just say I lost this or that amount in the game. She already knew I'm no great shakes at cards. But, hey, the evenings were a blast, mostly: lots of jokes and kidding around, as well as some serious tussles for the pot, or I wouldn't have kept going. One night I was up seventy bucks, though I ended that evening back where I started, except for my share of the refreshments.

Jimmy finally thought of a plan to interest James in the motel again. The idea was to make James an offer he couldn't refuse, like they'd said in that gangster movie a few years before. This was the summer of '79, when we'd had the motel open for twenty-two years, amazingly enough. Jimmy proposed we do a major renovation. He and Cynthia had driven down to Los Angeles on holiday, and they'd taken photos of some motels along the road that were definitely snazzier than ours. Jimmy and I talked over how to present the list of changes we could implement, as well as how to pay for it. The next Friday meeting that James attended, Jimmy and I sprung the idea on him.

His eyes definitely lit up once he caught the drift of what we were proposing. After his usual long silence while he pored over the photos and material Jimmy had prepared, he began to suggest some modifications to our plan that were really sharp. But in the end this idea of a motel project James could really get behind backfired. The next Friday meeting, which was supposed to be a detailed planning session for the reno, James didn't have much to say, which was surprising. The following week he drops the bombshell that he wants us to buy him out. He said Elaine had convinced him this was the right time for him not to be involved with the motel anymore.

When I was telling Kate about the meeting later that night, she becomes all thoughtful and quiet and says that I should think about getting out, too. Her point was that the motel deal wouldn't be the same if it was just me and Jimmy. She reminded me how much complaining I'd done when James stopped regularly coming to the Friday meetings. Now that state of affairs was about to be permanent.

Kate was on at me the next day, too, saying she'd run into Elaine. Elaine's notion that the money from selling the motel could be used for the kids' education had impressed Kate, especially since we wouldn't be seeing any income from the motel for at least the next couple of years and likely longer if the reno turned out to be more expensive than we'd budgeted for.

I was pretty sulky about having to decide one way or another once Kate wanted me to quit. But with me realizing we'd come to the end of an era anyway, and Kate constantly reminding me that no decision is a decision, and going on about how maybe I had enough worries running the logging business, I broke the news to Jimmy the next Friday.

James was at that meeting. When I finished my little spiel, he said we had to look at whether to put the Three Jimmys up for sale, or could Jimmy buy us both out. That question set Jimmy off, I can tell you. At one point he told us to get the fuck out of his house. James, after an extra-long pause, pointed out that the house wasn't strictly Jimmy's, that he was living in a building that until we settled this matter was still owned by all three of us. The meeting got worse from there, though I can report that nobody hit anybody.

After that, Elaine got a Nelson lawyer, that asshole Duncan Locke, who really muddied the water. I spent a horrible couple of months, pissed off at James for caving in to Elaine's games, and at Jimmy for refusing to do anything one way or another, and at myself for not being able to come up with a way for us to get clear of this mess and still be friends. Mad at Kate, too, for wanting me to quit the Three Jimmys. Elaine's lawyer was constantly sending papers to us, most of which I threw straight into the garbage.

Kate wouldn't let me badmouth Elaine, either, which I couldn't understand, since she was the one stirred up all this trouble. The three Jimmys were doing fine before she came along and got her claws into James, so what was wrong with me mentioning this fact? Kate always took Elaine's side. I'd ask Kate whether she didn't think she should be on her husband's side, and she would say: "Not if he's wrong."

If you read the crap that lawyer wrote, you'd think us building and running the motel was about the worst crime ever committed. But I ask myself, would this world be a better place if the motel had never opened, if the Three Jimmys had never happened?

Skill Development

"DID I EVER tell you how I learned to drive cat?" Wayne Gillies asks his two grandkids. "Your mother says you can have a story before lights out. I don't think I've told you this one before."

The children and their parents, Wayne's daughter Sarah and her husband Al, are visiting from Kamloops for the long weekend. Sarah and Al, plus Wayne's wife Yvonne, are relaxing in the front room down the hall where Al is watching on television the Vancouver Canucks lose to Montreal. Sarah is describing to her mother a trip to Vancouver the family took the previous month. Wayne and the two kids, the latter already changed into their pajamas, are in Yvonne's sewing room, which doubles as a sleeping room for the children when they're visiting their grandparents.

"A story, a story," Samantha, Al and Sarah's youngest at six and a half, says excitedly. "I want a story and Barbie wants one, too." Samantha has been sitting on the bottom of a set of bunk beds playing dolls. "Scoot under the covers, then," Wayne says, peeling back the blankets and top sheet. Samantha scrambles obediently in.

"How about you, Tyler?" Wayne asks Samantha's brother, older by a year. "Slide all the way down." In the upper bunk, Tyler has propped his pillow against the wall at the head of the bed, and although his lower half is below a duvet, he is sitting up playing with a couple of toy cars. Being aloft in the top bunk at his grandparents' house is still a bit of an adventure. Wayne and Yvonne had bought the bunk beds only a couple of years ago; formerly, the kids slept in the sewing room on air mattresses on the floor.

"Pass me those cars, Tyler," Wayne says. "I'll leave 'em here by the sewing machine."

"Wayne, you ought to see this game," Al hoots from the living room. "The Canucks are getting *massacred*."

"What's the score?" Wayne calls.

"Four-zip . . . no, wait! Wow, great save by Padlovich! Still four-nothing. For the Habs. Come and check this out."

"Soon as the kids are down," Wayne replies.

"Everything okay, Dad?" Sarah calls. "I'll be in in a minute to kiss them goodnight."

"I'm just about to give them a story."

"Let the women put 'em to bed, Wayne," Al calls. "When hockey is on, a man's place is in front of the TV."

"Al," Wayne hears his daughter admonish her husband, "it's great that Dad helps out with the kids."

"Oh y-e-a-h?" Al drags the second word out.

"Yeah. You should be in there learning something about being a parent."

"Tried it. Didn't like it," Al responds. The dispute is ritualistic. Wayne is aware, from what Sarah says and his own observations, that Al ordinarily is very involved with raising their two.

"We're going to have coffee and dessert as soon as Wayne has the kids down," Yvonne intervenes. "Would you like a coffee now, Al?"

"Nah," Al replies. "I'll wait. We're coming up to second intermission and they'll ask some idiot to explain why the Canucks are losing. I *know* why they're losing. They should never have traded Arnie Bruce."

"How about the story, Opa?" Samantha prompts. "Barbie really wants to hear it."

"Everybody's tooths are brushed, right?" Wayne asks. A chorus in the affirmative rises. "Everybody snug? Okay, then." Wayne pauses, lowering himself into the narrow room's only chair.

"Ever since I was no older than Tyler here, I wanted to drive cat. My dad and mom, who would have been your great-grandpa and great-grandma, ran the camp commissary at Winter Harbour. That's on the west coast of Vancouver Island. Where we lived, I got to see lots of cats rumbling by. I couldn't imagine anything finer than to be up in the operator's seat to drop that blade and move dirt and rocks and build roads or clear bush for bunkhouses and repair shops and other buildings. I really, really wanted to be a catskinner."

"What's a commissary?" Tyler asks.

"What's a catskinner, Opa?" Samantha asks at the same time.

"A commissary is a general store in a logging or mining camp, Tyler," Wayne explains. "You could buy anything from work boots to lunch pails to bubble gum."

"Like Walmart?"

"On a very small scale, yes. How big the commissary was depended on how big the camp was."

"I know what a catskinner is," Tyler says.

"What?" Wayne says.

"Somebody who drives bulldozers."

"That's right. But what have dozers got to do with cats?"

Neither child replies. Wayne asks if there's another name for bulldozers. Samantha informs him that Barbie doesn't know.

"Caterpillar tractors," Wayne answers his own question. "That's where the 'cat' comes from in 'catskinner.'"

"But do catskinners skin caterpillars?" Samantha asks. "That would be awful."

"Yeah, Opa, why are they called 'skinners'?" Tyler asks.

"I'm not exactly sure," Wayne replies. "I think it's because the men who used to drive mules were called 'muleskinners,' and—" Wayne holds up his hand to ward off the question he can sense looming "—muleskinners were called that because a mule can be ornery and uncooperative. Every once in a while a mule driver would lose his temper and lash his mules so hard it looked like he was going to skin the beasts with his whip."

"That's awful, too," protests Samantha.

"You bet," Wayne says. "Though there have been times when even *I*'ve gotten so mad at a cat that broke down or wouldn't start that I've been tempted to take a wrench and thrash it within an inch of its life."

"Really, Opa?" Samantha asks, eyes widening.

"I've never actually hit one," Wayne confesses, "despite wanting to. But I'm getting ahead of myself." He shifts in his chair, crossing one leg over the other. "While I was growing up at Winter Harbour, I never lost that dream I had of driving cat. When I first went to work in the woods, I set chokers in the summers during high school. I found out the company wouldn't let you operate a cat if you didn't already know how. But there didn't seem to be any way you could *learn*. Some people had an uncle or dad who taught them, but if you didn't know the ropes you were out of luck."

"Couldn't your dad drive them?" Tyler asks.

"No. He was hurt bad logging when he was quite young, so he and my mother went into the grocery business. I guess in the early days he would have had friends who drove cat. By the time I came along, those guys were more his customers than his pals."

"He doesn't still have his store, does he?" Samantha inquires.

"He sold it a long time ago, little one, and died before you were born. Anyhow, when I quit school for good I got a job in the woods up by Holberg and that's where I decided it was now or never if I was ever going to become a catskinner. One morning I went to the boss, old Slim Connelly, and announced that I was sick of setting chokers, and that maybe he didn't realize it, but I could drive cat. I told him next time there was an opening for that work he should keep me in mind. Old Slim just grunted, because that was his way. But the following morning, when we stepped out of the crummies at the landing ready for work, Slim waved me over and told me one of the catskinners was off with a hangover and I was to take the guy's place.

"I was pretty excited at this news, but managed to stay calm. I followed Slim across the landing to where these three cats were parked. He pointed to the smallest and asked if I could handle it. I assured him I could, and he left. There I was, face to face with the machine of my dreams. And I didn't have a clue what to do next.

"It was a John Deere 450. I just walked around it, staring at it, but this turned out to be the right procedure. That's how we still start the shift: you check for leaks, check the engine oil, the reverser oil, the rad, the fuel. So the other two guys that day are doing much the same as me, circling their machines. Of course I didn't understand where any of the dipsticks were or any of that. But the other drivers just assumed I knew what I was doing.

"I climbed up into the seat. There were levers and knobs and gauges on all sides, and a key in the ignition. But I had no idea how to get it started, let alone how to steer it."

From the front room, the distant crowd noise on the television swells, and the three in the sewing room hear as well the voices of the two women coming now from the kitchen, though they can't make out the words.

"This is a good story, Opa," Samantha says encouragingly. "Barbie likes it, too."

"Thank you, Samantha," Wayne says. "Well, there I am, sitting at the controls. Completely clueless. By this time the others have their cats cranked up belching smoke. I'm aware I can't just keep fondling the various levers so I climb down and go over to one of the other guys and get his attention. I yell up at him that I've never run one of these particular *kinds* of cat before and could he help me get her started?

"He jumps down and hauls himself up onto my 450 and shows me: push the throttle knob all the way up, then back to halfway, twist the key left to turn on the glowplugs for about forty-five seconds, then twist the key right to start. Sure enough, the motor catches. He points out that the starting information is all on a plate on the dash, but I hadn't noticed it. Then the guy leaps down, and he and the other cats begin moving off up the road toward where we're supposed to begin work.

"They're getting farther and farther away. I'm still parked, trying to figure how to get her in gear, when Slim shows up. He begins barking at me for being slow. Then it dawns on him that I don't really know the first thing about driving cat. So he fires me. Not only fires me as a cat driver, he fires me as a chokerman, too. So then I had to—"

"You got fired?" Tyler interrupts.

"You bet," Wayne says. "Right on the spot."

"That's the same as being laid off, isn't it?" asks Tyler.

"'Laid off' is just a politer term," Wayne confirms. "Like 'let go,' or 'downsized.'"

"Uncle Len was laid off when the mill closed last summer," Samantha says. "He and Auntie Jill came to visit after that."

"Yeah," Tyler says.

"He's your daddy's brother, right?" Wayne asks.

Tyler nods. "Dad and Mom said it was awful that Uncle Len was laid off because he'd worked there for years and years."

"Getting fired for whatever reason is never pleasant," Wayne concedes. "A lot of guys take it personal, even if it isn't their fault they got canned. They take it pretty hard."

"Is that how you felt, Opa?" Samantha asks.

"I was young, remember. Mostly I was just thrilled to have gotten to start one of those dozers." Wayne uncrosses his leg. "I went into Port Hardy, and hired on with another outfit *as* a cat driver. First morning at that job, I manage to get the engine going, no problem. Different machine, but the principle is the same. This time I ask one of the other operators to show me how to put her in gear. I tell him I'm very familiar with a John Deere 450 but want to get checked out on this other model to make sure I don't damage it.

"He looks at me funny, but he demonstrates the whole routine: the gear shift and the blade control. That was enough to get me mobile, although I found the experience startling. A cat doesn't drive smooth like a car does. Your cat suddenly jerks and jolts when the gears engage, or if you begin to change direction. And when you make a turn, the machine pivots from about its centre, not like how a car follows its front wheels through a curve. You have to pay every bit as much attention to where your back will swing as you do to the direction you're headed. Otherwise you'll take out a tree or something alongside the trail."

"This time you didn't get fired?" Samantha asks.

Wayne laughs. "I was gone before first coffee break. I was last in line heading out to work but hoped nobody would notice my lack of skill. But the push, the foreman, was watching. When he saw my driving was so erratic, he figured I must be drunk. He comes racing after me in his pickup and flags me down. I told him I was just nervous about my new job, but he didn't believe me.

"I didn't give up, though. I went over to Campbell River and got hired there. This time I started her up fine, and did an okay job driving. But when we began work, I couldn't get the blade to do what I wanted. First I just drove the blade into the ground until I stalled out. I tried using a lighter touch and the cat lifted right up the embankment I was supposed to be punching a road through. Every attempt I made, I was doing it wrong."

"What *is* the right way to do it?" Tyler asks.

"You lower the blade to start the cut, and then lift the blade to the level of the tracks," Wayne explains. "Look here." Tyler peers over the edge of his bunk, and Samantha, too, props herself up on an elbow to watch Wayne use the flat of his hand as a blade to demonstrate. "It takes practice," Wayne says. "Okay, you kids lie back now." When the children again are horizontal he resumes.

"On that Campbell River job, I was getting suspicious glances from the other guys at coffee, but anybody can have a bad day. I lasted until noon before I got canned.

"After that I went back to setting chokers. But during the winter layoff I travelled down to Vancouver and visited a few heavy equipment dealers. I was pretending to buy a machine. I told them my dad had a road building outfit and I'd been sent to price new equipment. They let me try out a couple. I also got some operator's handbooks and read through them. I knew much more about cats by spring."

"So you never were fired again?" Samantha asks.

Wayne smiles. "Only about six more times. I hired on at Port Alberni to drive cat. Lasted a week. Then I found another job. After I was sacked there, I got another. At each place I could tell I was improving. The more experience I got, the better operator I was. I still had a few unpleasant surprises, though. One machine had a belly pan where the bolts had shaken loose. I should have caught it. When I reversed, I scooped earth into the motor compartment, doubled the pan over and trashed the engine. Boy, they were mad.

"But at every new job I lasted longer and longer before I got fired. Also, when the jobs began lasting a while, I could really talk to the other drivers. I learned plenty from them. After a couple of years, I realized I could handle any machine or job. I finally was a catskinner. And I was working in the oil patch near Fort St. John nine years ago when I met a sharp young guy driving water truck who eventually became your daddy."

"Wow," Samantha breathes.

"Every good story has a moral, right?" Wayne continues. "What's the moral in how I became a catskinner?"

"If at first you don't succeed, try, try again," responds Samantha.

"Very good, little one. That's certainly true. Anything else?"

"Hey, Wayne," Al bellows from the front room. "Cut it short and get your butt in here. It's a miracle: the Canucks just scored."

"In a minute," Wayne calls down the passageway. Then, speaking to the children, "Any other moral? There's something else very important to learn from this story. Tyler? How about you? Any idea?"

There is no reply. "He's probably asleep, Opa," Samantha explains. "He always falls asleep as soon as Mom kisses him goodnight."

"I'm awake," Tyler says sleepily.

Wayne clambers to his feet. "No other moral? What have you kids been told about telling lies?"

"We should never tell lies," Tyler manages.

"Any lesson from my story about that?"

The children are silent for a moment. "I guess, Opa," Samantha says hesitantly, "you lied when said you could drive cat? Before you really could?"

"Yes," Wayne confirms, his voice sounding pleased. "I did. You got it."

"That's the other moral?" Tyler sounds wide awake now. "It's okay to tell lies?"

"Absolutely not," Wayne says.

"But *you* did," Tyler points out.

"Yes. And it was wrong. But I'm glad I lied."

"Mommy gets mad at us if we tell lies," Samantha states. "Remember when we went down by the river and said we didn't?"

"Yeah," Tyler says.

"Telling lies is wrong, kids. But what's the lesson about that from my story?"

"If you hadn't told lies," Tyler says slowly, "you wouldn't have gotten to do what you wanted."

"Yup. It's a good thing I lied."

"Is that the moral?"

"Nope."

"This is too hard," Tyler complains.

"Yeah, Opa," Samantha agrees crossly. "You mean it's not okay to lie but it's good to lie? That's dumb."

"Once we're grown up, it's okay if we lie?" Tyler asks.

"No. It's never right to lie. But people without power . . . You kids lie to us adults from time to time, though you never should, because we have power over you. With grown-ups, sometimes . . . Maybe you have to be older to understand what I mean."

"I'm pretty grown up now," Tyler says.

"You're certainly growing up fast," Wayne concedes. "Samantha, too."

"So tell us what the moral is," demands Samantha.

"How about: when you get older you find the world isn't a simple place."

"I'm not sure that's a moral," Samantha observes.

Wayne smiles. "You're probably right." He moves toward the hallway. "Your mother will be in to kiss you goodnight in a minute. Sleep good." He switches off the ceiling lamp. He doesn't quite pull the handle closed as he leaves the room, so that the door lets in a little light.

Along the Water Line

PEOPLE GET MORE upset about their water than just about anything else. Makes sense: a house without water is like a beached ship: everything looks normal, except it can't function. Without water you can't cook. Can't wash yourself or your clothes. Can't brush your teeth. Can't use the john. City people buy a place out here and never give a thought to water. Water is something that just appears when you open a tap, right? Until one day it doesn't, and they don't have a clue how to get it back.

Country people know better. They're aware what it means to be connected, along with their neighbours, to a water system. Of course, country people as a result are more likely to flip out if there's even a hint of a problem.

Working on people's systems, I'm used to them getting all red in the face and shouting about a neighbour, or *at* a neighbour, when something goes wrong with the water. Or shouting at me if I can't find a leak or blockage right away. But calling the cops? Bringing in lawyers?

Trouble is, most water lines in the valley were constructed in the 1950s when the population was a lot smaller. Lines were added or extended when people subdivided their farms. I remember my dad and his buddies spent a month of their spare time tapping into Fulsome Creek up behind our place. My ma was so excited when she could turn a faucet handle in the kitchen and there it was. Or when dad installed a toilet and sink in what became the bathroom. A whole new world.

But that's decades ago, and some systems were sketchy to begin with. A guy would buy a load of discarded pipe from the smelter down at Trail: a real deal. The neighbours who had decided to jointly put in a water line would be pleased about the price. Nobody thought about what might have been running through the pipe year after year. Trail is a lead-zinc smelter, the world's biggest, in fact, and as you know lead isn't the best thing for you. People in Trail in those days had to garden under burlap bags because the smoke in the air killed everything green. There were no cats or dogs in Trail. They'd eat the grass and that would finish them off. It's a miracle there isn't more cancer around here than there is.

Every so often, I even come upon wooden pipes. That gives you an idea of how long ago some systems were put in. Wood slats wrapped in wire. Or I only find the wires: the boards themselves have rotted away. The water has been flowing through the space in the soil where the piping used to be. Not that people haven't tinkered with their systems over the years. In twenty feet of line I've found a couple different kinds of pipe in two different diameters, the whole mess connected with both good couplings and leaky couplings. Put your shovel in the earth and you don't know what you'll discover.

This latest job wasn't any different: I can never predict what I'll run into. That's why I like this work, besides the extra money. Every situation is a puzzle to solve, which I usually can do, and in any case trying to figure the problem is more interesting than being a yardman at Kalesnikoff's. I've worked at the sawmill most of my life and seen everything that can screw up. Which means I know how to fix anything on that job without hardly thinking.

I've had a lot of free time since my wife left, and one Saturday in April four or five years ago I was over at Slocan Park to give a pal a hand with his water. The diversion box for his system—which feeds eight homes—is on a creek that comes down off Slocan Ridge, and we were up there with a couple of his neighbours rebuilding the intake pipe. I'd helped him before change a shut-off valve on his irrigation line, and that morning as we worked he told me I have a knack for water lines. Probably he was just buttering me up, since I was helping them for nothing. But the more I thought about it afterwards, I said to myself, *Why not?*

I put an ad in the *Pennywise,* "Knack for Water: Water Line and Water System Specialists—Installations and Service." Lots of guys with backhoes list water line trenching among the jobs they'll tackle with their machine, yet nobody else hereabouts claims to be a water system expert. I guessed I'd get a job once in a while I could tackle on weekends, mainly for city folks moving into the area who've run into trouble. Most locals build or maintain their systems themselves. But the calls came in steady, even from long-settled types, and I even started doing urgent jobs weekdays after my shift at the mill.

I hire Eddy occasionally as a helper if I need one. He works with me at Kalesnikoff's, although between you and me, he's not the sharpest knife in the drawer. Worse, he likes to argue: if I say black, he'll say white. If I say Canucks, he'll say Flames. I get my fill of him at the yard so I can't say I hire him that often. Probably I should have taken him along with me Wednesday, but hindsight is 20/20 and we'd had a set-to after lunch over fixing the flat on the forklift. I was sick of his constantly taking the other side, whatever I say. It's tiresome, and I've got seniority. He ought to just shut up and follow my lead. But that's not Eddy.

I'm home by three thirty and check my messages, and a guy between Winlaw and Perry Siding on the highway has no water, can I please come right away? He's sure where a leak is on his line. My first thought is that if he's so confident about the solution to his problem, why don't he and his neighbours fix it themselves? But then I wouldn't have any business, and maybe he and his neighbours all have bad backs or maybe he isn't really as knowledgeable about his system as he sounds. As my wife learned to repeat at her AA meetings, you never know someone's story. I climb into my pickup again and head up there.

The guy says to come indoors, since the mosquitoes are bad in that area in July and get worse in late afternoon. He's younger than me by twenty years, in jeans and one of those polo shirts golfers on TV wear. Late thirties I'd say. He works in the office at Insight, the plant outside Nelson that makes parts for car and truck headlamps. I don't ask why he can't repair the line himself, since he appears perfectly healthy, but he says he has a dinner engagement: some job deal he can't get out of at his boss's place near Koziansic's on the river.

My customer's water line has two other houses on it; the line runs south from a distribution box maybe half a mile away that feeds seven other lines. He has the lowest property on this line. The house next door up his line has no water either. The woman who lives there has a toddler and can't help with the repair, though because of the kid she would really like the water restored as quick as possible. At the second house north, highest on my customer's line, the owner had to go to Castlegar for the day and his wife says they also don't have water.

My customer says he's called around, and the other lines on the system are working okay, so the problem has to be on this line. The diversion box that feeds the distribution box is up the mountain on Stranger Creek. He's been to the distribution box before he called me, and the compartment that feeds his line has lots of water. Nothing is blocking the intake to the line from the compartment. I'm a little impressed that the guy has eliminated all the possibilities I'd be checking off.

He also says he's walked the line down from the distribution box and thinks he's found where the problem is, as he mentioned on the phone message he left. He noticed a spot where the ground is wetter than it should be in the middle of July, so likely the leak is there. *Or one of the leaks,* I think to myself. With water I've learned to take nothing for granted.

Could I dig down where the soil is wet, my customer asks, and mend the leak? Only hitch is, the guy says, the ground doesn't seem as wet as you'd expect if a leak is big enough to cause water pressure to drop to zero. He's had a leak on the line a time or two before over the years, and not only was more water visible on the surface than he saw at this spot, but, unlike today, inside the house he was still getting at least a trickle.

He shows me an old hand-drawn map of the system that the previous owners of the house gave him when he bought the place. On the map, another line from the distribution box parallels his to near where he thinks the leak is. That other line then right-angles west and crosses under the highway to supply some houses next to the river. An additional line runs parallel to his as well, according to the map. Where the second line turns to cross under the road, this third line does a 180 to double back to a house north of the highest house on my customer's line. That 180 has to be a mistake. Nobody, especially not in the old days when they dug these systems by hand, would run a line a distance beyond a house and then double back. The only possible explanation is that originally a house was located where now the 180 is. But when I mention this, my customer says there's no cellar hole or any other evidence of a former house. "It's all field," he stresses. So obviously the map is wrong. It's a schematic, after all, not a survey document. Whoever was drawing it likely extended that third line too far on the paper, then reversed the line to show where it really goes.

I ask my customer if there's any indication on the surface where the second line turns west, since if that part of the map is accurate I don't want to hit that pipe when I'm digging up his. He says he's not sure, but he found an old weathered stake in the field near the leak that he figures might mark where the turn is. The location of this peg looks about right according to the map, and he can't think of any other reason why there'd be a stake in the middle of a field.

I can think of lots of reasons a stake might be there, from kids fooling around to somebody thinking of building a shed or a loafing barn for horses and then abandoning the plan. But I don't say this; I tell him we should go take a boo at the leak.

We drive in my pickup a few hundred yards north on the highway. I stop where he indicates, grab a shovel out of the box and we scramble up a steep bank and through a dilapidated barbed wire fence into what clearly was once a pasture. The high grass is intermixed with lots of bracken and knapweed, and some huckleberry bushes. Eight- or nine-foot fir and spruce trees are scattered a few places across the field, in addition to a couple of clusters of scrubby aspen and birch. Nobody has raised cattle or horses or grown hay here for years.

What this meadow still produces, though, is mosquitoes. Millions of mosquitoes. Millions of starving mosquitoes. Clouds of them find us after about three steps, and we're batting them away from our faces as we walk. I can feel their stingers on my neck, on my face and even drilling through the cloth of my shirt. I have my steel-toes on from work, but my socks aren't offering much protection. Both of us slap continually at our cheeks, foreheads, ankles, chests and arms as we push through the grass and weeds up to our thighs. I can only smack at the mozzies with the hand not holding the shovel, so I'm not as effective at defending myself as if I had both hands free.

I ask my customer, as we proceed, who owns the field we're on. He says something in a low tone that I have to ask him to repeat. In a louder voice he declares that he has an easement across the property that permits him to repair the water line. We're within our rights, he emphasizes, to be here. My heart sinks, sensing trouble, but I repeat my question. Technically the meadow is Old Lady Turner's, he says, and I learn she's half-cracked and doesn't use it for anything. She also doesn't like my customer, for no good reason. So it's best, he stresses, if the old biddy never knows we're here. You can't see Mrs. Turner's house from where we are, he says, gesturing vaguely north at a stand of tall fir and spruce her house apparently is behind. She won't notice me digging. He claims he phoned her earlier and she was out but he left a message that we'd be repairing the line.

I inform him that I'm going to be bringing in a backhoe. Besides opening up the leak, I need to excavate a place to stand while I repair it, and I'm not going to dig that out by hand. So while the old lady may not see us, unless she's stone deaf she'll hear the hoe and is bound to wonder what's up.

My customer thinks about that for a few seconds. He asks if I'll drop in at her place when I bring the backhoe, and explain to her what I'm going to do. "If she's not home," he says, "please leave her a note." I tell him I have no problem speaking with the landowner. But why, I press him, is she ticked off at him? I've witnessed enough valley feuds, and especially ones about water, to want as much information as I can about what I'm stepping into. First thing you learn about feuds involving other people is not to entirely believe either side. There's always more involved than what one bunch or the other tells you.

"She's nuts," my customer says, by way of explanation. "That's the only reason I can think of why she doesn't like me." The going is easier underfoot now, and his eyes are scanning the ground, I presume searching for the post or peg he mentioned. I keep my eyes peeled, too. Then he allows as how he's gotten himself into a beef with the neighbour highest on his water line, too, the one who is off in Castlegar but whose wife is home. Their land, according to my customer, adjoins the field we're traversing. "He and that old bag Mrs. Turner are locals. They stick together."

"What's the fuss about there?" I ask. "Is it something you—"

"A damn barking *dog*," he says, voice swelling louder before he catches himself and returns to speaking at his normal level. "Greg and Nellie let their stupid mutt out before they go to bed and the dog starts barking and it goes on and on and on. And on. It's like their hound is trying out for the dog Olympics or the *Guinness Book of Records*: the most consecutive barks without a break. I can doze off and wake up hours later and the dog is still at it. I used to phone over and ask Greg politely to bring their goddamn mutt inside when it starts to bark. Now he doesn't answer the phone at night. He claims he has every right to—"

My customer abruptly stops walking and I see a weathered wooden stake about three feet high amid the grass. A bit of faded orange flagging tape hangs in tatters from the top: the marker could be two years old, or twenty. The moment we halt, the mosquitoes jabbing at us, that up to now have been unbearable, instantly double in numbers and frequency of bites. Our hands pick up the pace of slapping at our arms and legs and faces and necks and chests. The irritating hum of the insects also crescendoes.

"So where does your line—" *whap,* I squish one on my left calf that has managed to extend its stinger through the denim of my jeans "—run?" I ask.

He raises his right arm, interrupting the motion to flatten a skeeter on his cheek, and points north. At the same time he raises his left hand, extending his arm to point in the opposite direction. "I figure about . . . " he turns a few inches to his left to align his arms parallel to where he thinks the pipe is, then moves a pace and a half east. "Here."

"And the leak?" I ask.

He takes several steps north, then stops. "What do you think?"

he calls, whacking one palm on a mosquito on the back of his other hand before gesturing toward the ground.

I join him and kneel for a better look, waving away the cloud of pests that forms in front of my face. No question the soil is damp, with a tiny puddle visible.

"Not wet enough, though, to account for us having zero water. Right?" he asks.

"Seems like a leak of some sort," I conclude noncommittally, standing again and once more flapping my hand to drive away some persistent biters hovering less than an inch off my nose. "Let's dig it up and see. It should be fixed even if it's not the main problem." A repair from three years ago in Pass Creek rises in my memory. "I've seen a break before that pointed downward, where the ground was porous enough that nothing much pooled on the surface."

"Really?"

I shrug. "We'll find out."

My customer erupts into a frenzy of slapping himself. "I hope you've got some insect repellant," he says. "I need to head home to change before dinner. Good luck."

He swivels toward the road.

"Want me to drive you to your place?" I ask.

"I can walk. Getting my water back is the first priority. I'll leave you to it."

I jam the shovel into the damp earth so the handle marks the spot, and follow him across the meadow and through the barbed wire to where my pickup is parked. I find a can of repellant in the mess on the floor behind the front seats, amid scattered clamps large and small, some rags, short lengths of PVC pipe in several diameters, a paper bag of brass and plastic connectors also of various diameters, my big crescent and monkey wrenches, a socket set, a sheaf of zap straps, a case holding a battery-operated drill on its last legs, my tool box and one of those plastic commercial milk carton containers holding a jumble of shut-off valves old and new. After spraying lots of repellant on myself, I stick the can in a rear pocket, and hoist a pickaxe out of the truck box.

I have a few minutes of blessed relief as I cross the field toward my shovel. But as soon as I begin to dig I start to sweat, and the

rivulets trickling down the skin of my face quickly dilute the repellant's effectiveness. Across the river, the sun is descending above
the summit ridge of the western valley wall. In the shadow of the
mountain over there, the temperature on the valley floor is probably
dropping to a pleasant level. Here, the sun is still blasting its heat
at the field where I'm booting the shovel blade into the rocky soil
repeatedly, and hoisting up shovelful after shovelful of wet earth
and stones.

No telling how far below the surface the water line is. Most 1950s
legal easements specify eighteen inches, but every old-timer laying
pipe knew that the deeper the line the less chance it will freeze in
winter. Normally these water lines are between two and three feet
down, so I've learned not to anticipate but just keep digging. Or, in
this case, to dig, slap, dig, flap away the little bastards, dig, spray myself with poison again and dig. At least with the increasingly soggy
soil, I'm certain there's a water pipe down here somewhere. Often
on a job I have to excavate with the backhoe a trench at right angles
to where the line is supposed to be. I'll go down a couple of feet with
the machine, and then in order to not snap the line by mistake I dig
deeper with a shovel along the trench until I find the pipe. Or don't,
and have to repeat the process somewhere else.

This time, I hit black PVC a little less than three feet down. That
may not sound like much shovel work, but with the heat and the
mozzies and having already put in a day's work at the sawmill, plus
hitting a layer more stones than earth and having to loosen that
with the pickaxe as I dig, I'm pooped by the time my shovel hits
plastic and I scrape dirt from a length of wet pipe. No question a
leak is in the vicinity, whether a pinhole or larger. I bend to try
to hear whether a rush of water is audible, but all I detect is the
whine of mosquitoes. I climb out of the pit I've created and would
have taken a breather. But I figure if I sit down on the ground for a
few minutes I won't have any blood left. I stick my shovel upright
into the pile of dirt, and set out toward the pickup to go get my
backhoe.

I used to hook up my trailer with the hoe on it and haul it to
every call. After realizing that about half the jobs didn't need it, I decided to fetch it if required and add the time involved to my bill. So

far nobody has objected. I'm in the pickup cab, feeling considerable relief at being out of attack range of all but a few skeeters I'm trying to either crush between my palms or flatten against the windshield. The thought comes to me that Duane, who lives pretty close to here across the river, owns a skid-steer loader, a Bobcat. Those things have a backhoe attachment that would be perfect for this job. Borrowing Duane's machine would save me the drive down the valley to my place.

Poor old Duane had a stroke in April, and is paralyzed on one side, so I know he won't be using his loader. Only question is whether the hitch and hookup on his trailer will fit my truck.

He's having a nap when I get there, but his wife says sure, go ahead, when I mention I'll be charging the customer for the rental of it which I'll pass on to her and Duane. Before he was knocked out of commission I'd subcontracted him and his Bobcat on a job at Shoreacres. The wife says he's making progress toward recovery, but it's slow: he can't use his right hand, although the therapist thinks he eventually will. I promise her I'll take good care of his rig, and she tells me where to find it beside their barn. I back up to the spot, and no problem about fastening the trailer. Hardly any mosquitoes in this part of the valley, too, even though as the crow or the insect flies it's only about a mile from where I've been digging. Fifteen minutes after leaving Duane's, I'm back parked beside the highway, figuring the best way to get the machine into the field, since there's a ditch and that bank between the road and the barbed wire fence.

I coat myself in repellant again, and stroll south along the highway toward the neighbour with the alleged maniac barker. From the pickup, I had thought I could see that the fence along the southern edge of the field disappears halfway up the driveway. Sure enough, a couple of the posts are on the ground, rotted out by the looks of them. Loops of rusty barbed wire are visible, but driving over them won't do any damage. I'm braced for an onslaught from a baying, slavering dog, but all is quiet from the direction of the house.

That's when I remember I promised to stop by the old lady's place to the north and advise her about digging up the line in her field. I walk back to the pickup, detach Duane's trailer, pull a U-turn and gun north to the next driveway.

Mrs. Turner's house has a couple of dormers, siding that badly needs repainting and a roof that's a successful nursery for moss. My guess is that it's the original farmhouse, from when the field where I'm digging was in use. I knock on the door. No answer, and no vehicle visible. Just me and the mosquitoes in the yard. I knock harder, then think about leaving a note like my customer suggested. But after rummaging through my glove box, and poking through the junk behind the driver's seat, I realize I don't have any paper with me other than the little scrap on which I wrote down the customer's coordinates. I worry for a second or two, then I recall him saying he'd left her a phone message. Plus I'm concerned about losing the light, and think, *Screw it.* With luck I'll open up the pipe, fix the leak, fill the excavation and be out of there before she gets back from wherever she is.

I drive the Bobcat off the trailer, very cautiously, with the backhoe attachment in the bucket. I haven't run a skid-steer for a while, but it mostly comes back to me. The machine rolls jerkily south along the shoulder of the road to the neighbour's driveway, then swivels to start up it. A woman comes to the door of the house, due to my engine noise I'm sure, so I wave and she waves back. As soon as I cross the fence line and head into the field, I can see in the mirror that she vanishes inside the house again.

Crossing the field is bumpy, but the worst is that with my hands on the controls I'm a sitting duck for the mosquitoes. A couple of times I have to brake to a halt and slap one. After a minute or two I catch sight of my shovel handle.

At the dirt pile I drop the bucket, manoeuvre the backhoe attachment out and connect it. Once I position the Bobcat, I clamber onto the hoe's seat, and begin. I stop after a while to check how deep my excavation is. I'm digging right over the line, and my plan is as usual to uncover the last few inches with the shovel to make sure I don't cut the line. As I remove soil a yard or so south of my initial hole, the ground becomes soggier the deeper I go. Further south than that, the earth isn't as wet so I've got a definite fix on the leak. I shut off the engine, climb down from the backhoe seat and reach for the shovel.

The sun has disappeared behind the ridge across the valley, but thanks to our long summer twilights, I have an hour, maybe an hour and a half before dark. A hint of dusk is in the air: that very first thickening of the light. But it's hardly a problem yet. I'm figuring I have more than enough time to patch the leak. And if this repair doesn't restore my customer's water, the rest of the solution will just have to wait until tomorrow afternoon. Meantime, the loader has lights and I can backfill in the dark if I'm done.

My immediate problem is that the loss of the sun has driven the hysteria of the mosquito population up a notch, if that's possible. They're positively berserk as they drill into me repeatedly. Cloth seems to be no barrier at all now in their desperation, so they're having a go at every inch of my body, clothed or not. Despite another bath in repellant, once I'm using the shovel I'm the target for every skeeter on this side of the river. A couple of times I lose it, drop the shovel and have a solid minute of slap-fest. No question where the expression "to bug someone" comes from. I have moments I'm certain these airborne tormentors will land me in the bughouse.

When at last I've exposed the four feet of pipe I want to access, I climb out of the pit and swing up onto the Bobcat, intending to enlarge the space alongside the stretch where the soil is wettest. I want room enough to clear under the line with my shovel, hacksaw the pipe at the leak and fit a connector in.

Without being able to shut off the water, installing one of these plastic joins is messy. Most of these old water systems don't have any shut-off valve at the top, at the distribution box. So I've gotten used to cutting the line, hammering in a temporary plug in the upstream end of the sawn pipe, then heating with my torch the downstream pipe-end. The flame expands the pipe diameter a little, allowing me to more easily insert a connector and clamp it in place. Then, as I'll have to do here, I take a deep breath, pull the plug out of the upstream pipe and try to heat that pipe-end despite the water gushing out of it into the excavation where I'm standing. Finally I jam that hopefully expanded pipe-end onto the connector's upstream half. The buzz of adrenaline I get as water Niagaras out of the upstream pipe, the flow speedily filling the pit over my boots and climbing ever higher, provides the surge of power I need to ram that pipe-end onto the connector.

I'm reviewing these procedures as I turn the key of the Bobcat. Not even a click, however, from the engine. I try two, three times. It's as if the battery is totally drained. I count to ten to calm down, take the key out, stare at it, put it back. On my next attempt, the machine fires up like nothing was ever amiss. A second later I'm sinking the backhoe bucket into the earth.

My plan is to make the floor of my larger workspace a foot or so deeper than the level of the pipe, so that the water has a place to collect when I take out the upstream plug. The work goes fast, and before I know it I'm deep as I want to be. I start to expand the hole southward a little, to give myself some extra work room, when the bucket snags on something.

I don't think about it, because I've run into a couple of good sized boulders already with the hoe, so I just back the bucket off, dig its teeth in a little lower and bring the bucket up. There's a loud pop, and a rushing sound like water, and as the boom lifts I see for a second the end of a different black PVC pipe spewing water. Then that pipe disappears while the boom lifts the bucket up to ground level.

My stomach flip-flops. I've sliced somebody else's line, one that by rights, according to the piece of paper my customer has, shouldn't be here. Unless this is that impossible line to the old woman's place that the map showed. *But it can't be,* I tell myself. *Nobody would run a line all this way past a house and then back.* More likely I've broken the line that swings under the road, a pipe whose location the map was wrong about as well. Whosever line it is, though, fixing it better be my priority.

I slap at about 150 mosquitoes, then stumble off the loader. By now dusk is a little more pronounced all around me. I jump into the pit with the shovel, poke here and there, and soon have the end of the upstream pipe sticking up, water gushing out at a great rate. Immediately a pool starts to form around my feet.

I haul myself from the excavation and make tracks across the field toward my truck, mentally listing everything I'll need—axe, handsaw, hacksaw, tape measure, propane torch, hose clamps, screwdriver. The pipe looks like inch and a half diameter, more or less the standard for these residential lines, but I'll bring a couple of inch and a quarter connectors, too. And a knife to whittle the end of a plug.

By the time I return to the excavation with my load of gear in a tote bag, the bottom of the hole is a lake, already two or three inches deep. I drop the bag, and head toward where the woods begin on the east side of the field, carrying the axe and handsaw. I step through an intact barbed wire fence, then start hunting for a branch I can make into a plug.

The light is pretty dim once I'm among the firs, scrub maple, aspen and spruce. Less mozzies in here, but my headlamp would have been handy. It's in my toolbox in the pickup. I see a likely birch branch, and saw off a plug-sized length, about a foot.

At the pit I whittle the end of the plug into a blunt point, then remember I should have brought a hammer to drive the plug into the cut end. I set out again across the field through the oncoming evening, slapping constantly at the pests that accompany me, including a tenacious specimen that won't leave my left ear alone. At the last minute at the truck, I remember the headlamp.

Ten minutes later I'm squatting in the excavation, hoping the water doesn't seep into my boots too quickly. I've successfully pounded the plug in to shut off the water, causing sprays of the stuff to jet out in all directions as I do, soaking me from bill cap to socks. The challenge now is to secure the plug with a couple of screw clamps. With my left hand I'm lifting the plugged pipe-end up above the accumulated water, but I've dropped into the drink a clamp that my right hand was trying to loop over the pipe. As I reach for a replacement from the pile of clamps I've dumped on the ground at the lip of the pit, I'm swearing a blue streak for fumbling the first clamp, and because a squadron of mozzies is opportunistic-ally and repeatedly puncturing my forehead while both my hands are occupied. Suddenly a harsh shriek interrupts my monologue.

"What do you think you're doing?"

I jump at the sound, but don't peer up from the delicate task of one-handedly flipping the springy screw clamp over the pipe, hold-ing it more or less in place with my left hand's fingers while my right hand brings the screwdriver close to the slot.

"You've broken my *water line.*" The high-pitched female voice resembles a series of yaps from one of those hideous lap dogs, upholstered rats, really, some people keep as pets.

I don't say anything. An ooze is now definitely permeating my socks, and I know I'll have wet feet for the rest of this job. My screwdriver snugs the clamp tight and I reach for another.

"I don't have any water. You've *wrecked* my water line."

I manage to tighten down the second clamp, and let the plugged line disappear under the lake's surface.

"Who *are* you? Get off my land. Right now. You don't have permission to do anything on my land."

I slosh over to the side of the pond, and, weighed down by the soaked bottoms of my jeans, get a knee up onto the edge of the excavation and hoist myself onto dry land.

"You're *trespassing.*" The decibels and pitch both are cranked higher than before. "I want you off my land."

As calmly as I can, I introduce myself, explain how I happened to be in her godforsaken bug-infested meadow at eight o'clock of a Wednesday evening after a long day's work at the mill. And that, yes, my backhoe cut her line by accident since my employer didn't know where her line was, especially since it defies all reason and common sense that the line to her house would be this far south of her place. In the ever-diminishing light, I can see she's a scrawny old hag in a frumpy dress that extends to the middle of her shins. Her face is wrinkled and scowling as a basset hound's who's just eaten something that didn't agree with him. I'm not sure she's listening to a word I'm saying.

"Get off my *land.* Now. You have no right to bring that machine here."

I'm pleased to see a gaunt arm lift a hand to slap several times at my winged friends who have decided she has just enough blood left in her to serve as a second course or dessert after what they've extracted from me.

"You're *trespassing.*"

I tell her I'm sorry about having broken her line, but I'll have it fixed and her water restored as fast as I can. I start to tell her that I'm going to wait a few minutes until the water in the pit percolates into the ground so I can reconnect her pipe without having to work under water. Already she has turned around, though, and is striding, as best her age and the lumpy ground permit, northward.

She halts a few yards away and swivels toward me. "I'm going to phone the *police*," she shrills. She spins about and resumes her retreat.

"Say hello to them for me," I call toward her receding back.

I assemble the propane torch, remember I didn't bring my torch lighter and depart another time for the pickup to retrieve this plus some extra clamps and connectors just in case. My feet squelch as I walk, though now that dusk has decidedly settled, the mosquitoes are suddenly less. Or maybe it's because I'm in motion.

The water level in the excavation has dropped considerably when I return. First I put on the headlamp for extra visibility, then hacksaw the downstream pipe-end square where the backhoe tore it. Minutes afterwards I have a connector properly fastened in, at the cost of only a few singed fingertips when I grabbed the heated pipe-end too soon. I rehearse in my mind the sequence for unplugging the upstream end and attempting to heat it even though the cold water pouring through it makes the effort more difficult. Vaseline, I remember, will help ease the spewing pipe onto the connector. I should have brought gloves before, as well. So again I cross the field to my toolbox in the pickup. Back at action central, I smear some of the goo on the upstream connector end, and ready everything else I'll need along the edge of the excavation. I suck in a lungful of air, and pick up my screwdriver to release the clamps from the plug.

"You cut into her line, eh?" My customer, flashlight in hand, is standing on the lip of the pit. He has a button-down shirt on he wasn't wearing before, although he must have changed back into his jeans.

"You heard about that?"

"The cops phoned me from Nelson. I guess when Old Lady Turner lost her water she called Greg and Nellie's to see if they had any. Nellie told her about you working here. Didn't you leave her a note? How the hell did this happen?"

I bring him up to date on the evening's activities.

"Yeah, well, the RCMP said we have to get off her property. I guess we should just leave. After a night without water, the old bat will be more susceptible to Greg or Nellie talking her into letting us fix it. Meantime the cop said Mrs. Turner is pretty upset and that if we don't leave at once we can be charged with trespassing."

"I thought you had an easement."

"I told that to the cop, but he said I still had to have prior permission from the landowner."

"Every one of those easements," I tell my customer, "says permission cannot be unreasonably refused. Asking is a courtesy, that's all. You made the effort. We're not damaging anything on the property to repair the line, except temporarily digging up an unused field. Once I backfill, and a few more weeds grow on it, no one will be able to tell I was even here."

"Jeez, these mosquitoes."

"Where were you an hour ago?" In fact, I notice I haven't been bitten for at least forty-five seconds. After making my life a misery all evening, a percentage of the little demons seem to have called it a day and gone elsewhere for a well-deserved night's rest.

"I mentioned the easement to the Mountie," my customer repeats. "I also said Mrs. Turner is the essence of unreasonableness. Senile or something. He said none of that mattered, that you would be charged with trespassing if we didn't leave the property immediately."

I recall cops I've spoken to over the years. "He's probably some dumb farm kid from Regina. I'll bet he doesn't have clue one about water law, so he's bluffing. They teach them in Mountie school to just say anything in a firm voice and the peasants will automatically obey. You have the right to restore your water. Otherwise why have an easement at all?"

"Just the same—"

"Do you think," I ask, "that cop is going to get off his fat ass and drive all the way out to the valley and get bitten by hordes of mozzies in order to chase me off your neighbour's land? Not going to happen. He's just blustering so he can tell your neighbour that he took care of the problem."

"Okay, but I think to avoid trouble we should leave. I'll pay you for your time tonight, of course. But let's pack up and get everything off her property. If Greg squares it with her tomorrow, you can—"

"I'm not going to leave without fixing her line. I caused the break, and I'm going to mend it. It's half done, anyway. I could have yours fixed in another half hour, too. At least the leak we know about."

"The police told us to get off her land. We really need to go."

I repeat that I'm at least going to restore the old lady's water before calling it a night. I tell my customer he can leave while I finish up. That I'll be in touch with him tomorrow about fixing the leak in his line, or at least dropping off an invoice for tonight.

His face appears pained, but he says he'll stay and help me reconnect her line. But then we'll get out of here.

I take the clamps off the plug, which still holds. I must have really hammered it in. The torch is lit, ready for me to apply heat to the plugged end of the pipe. The trick is to bring the flame close enough that the plastic expands, but not so close as to burn holes in it. A hole will require cutting off the newly damaged section, which likely would make the gap between the pipe-ends too long to bridge with the connector. A separate length of pipe would have to be inserted to span the gap, using a second connector. Unfortunately the torn end here is awfully jagged, so to ensure a good fit against the connector's mid-point ridge, I need to square up the end with the torch as best I can.

Gloves on, I'm concentrating on judiciously applying flame, mindful that once the heated pipe expands, the plug will shoot out ahead of a huge gout of backed-up water. My customer has squatted at the edge of the hole, watching my efforts. I'll have only seconds before the chill water rushing out shrinks the pipe diameter to its usual size. If I fail to force the pipe-end onto the connector, I'll be up to my ankles again or worse. The only remedy will be to locate the plug, pound it in and start over. At this late hour, I need to get this repair right, so my complete attention is focused on the tip of my flame.

"You two are trespassing," a male voice, harsh and authoritative, startles me. The torch jerks, and for a second I'm fearful I've burned a hole in the pipe after being so careful. "Stop whatever it is you're doing right now," the voice insists. "Leave this property. Right *now*."

I can't glance up or I'll botch the job.

"Who the hell are you?" I hear my customer say.

The wooden plug rockets out of the pipe and sails harmlessly out of the excavation in the direction of the woods. Clutching with my right hand the pipe-end that is again discharging a stream of high pressure water, with my left hand I balance the flaming torch on the lip of the excavation. Then I take hold of the pipe-end where the already installed connector protrudes.

"I'm Duncan Locke, a lawyer retained by Mrs. Turner to ensure her property rights are protected. The RCMP have been notified. You two are in serious, serious trouble. Criminal trespass, for one. Malicious destruction of property. You are on private land with no—"

"What are you talking about?" my customer says.

I'm crouched just above the rapidly rising water in the pit, lining up the two pipe-ends. Then I jam the heated pipe-end onto the connector as hard as I can. A spray of water shoots in every direction, drenching my face and the front of my clothes again while projecting streams of water into the air past me.

"*Hey*," the lawyer's voice squeaks in protest. "You did that on purpose."

"Be *careful*," my customer shouts. "I'm all *wet*."

The free pipe-end resists being attached, water continuing to spurt everywhere. I push simultaneously with my left hand and right, using every ounce that remains of my strength. As I apply pressure, I twist the upstream pipe-end clockwise and counter-clockwise. Abruptly the pipe slips over the connector enough that the fountain of water ends, though I feel multiple rivulets dripping down my face, and my soaked shirt clings to my skin. I work the pipe along until its end snugs up against the raised centre lip of the connector.

"I told you to stop," the lawyer yells. "Now look what you've done."

The water in the excavation nearly covers the pipe. I fish around in the lake to wrap a hose clamp around where the pipe is newly attached to the connector, and succeed in placing my screwdriver in the slot.

"Stop this instant," shrieks the lawyer.

I secure the clamp, wrap and tighten a second and pull myself erect to turn off the torch. I'm breathing hard, so sit for a minute on the excavation's edge and just inhale and exhale until I feel less exhausted. My stomach rumbles, and I realize all I've eaten since lunch is an apple I gnawed while driving up the valley nearly six hours ago. No wonder I'm light-headed.

"—been fixing Mrs. Turner's water," my customer is saying when I click back into the argument around me. "It's bad enough that I and Sally Bouchard and her daughter and Greg and Nellie don't have water. You want Mrs. Turner not to have any, too?"

"This damage you've done to her field constitutes destruction of her property. You're liable for a civil suit as well as criminal prosecution." I see through what's left of the light the lawyer is wearing shiny shoes, trousers with a knife-edge crease and a long-sleeved shirt with a necktie, its knot loosed and askew.

"I have an easement," my customer declares. "That gives me the legal right to restore my water line. Breaking the old biddy's pipe was an accident. Which we've now remedied, as you can see, unless you're too blind to—"

"You're attending on Mrs. Turner's property without her permission. That's trespassing, a serious, serious offense. What's worse, you've damaged her property."

"That's been fixed."

"I'm not even talking about the pain and suffering you cutting off her water has caused my client. Her *distress*. For which any court will certainly award financial compensation. Any easement . . . the standard wording, which I have no doubt applies in Mrs. Turner's case . . . permits the burying of a water line a foot and half down. You two have dug far, far deeper than that. Everything beyond eighteen inches constitutes malicious damage for which you are liable. Not to mention destroying a serviceable pasture while you—"

"That's a complete crock. It's been more than fifty years since this water line went in. Who knows how deep they actually buried it in the first place? Or what's happened to the ground here in half a century. What sense does it make if—"

"That's irrelevant. What matters is—"

"What sense does it make to pay for an easement to fix your line, if you can't fix it because it's located a quarter of an inch deeper than what a piece of paper says? It's the *intent* of the easement, not the actual wording that—"

"You only have the legal right to excavate to a depth of eighteen inches. Anything further is destruction of private property. In this instance, you're also present on the property without the owner's permission. That's trespassing, and I want you off Mrs. Turner's land immediately. The police will—"

"How am I supposed to restore my water, if I can't fix my line?"

"You're trespassing, and you've damaged my client's property. You must leave her premises at once."

The night air is cool now, but still warm enough that my clothes only feel clammy, not chilled. I struggle to my feet, standing on the lip of the pit. "Okay, we'll pack up and go," I tell the lawyer. No point getting into it with him about what an idiot he is. I turn to my customer. "You can sort this out with your neighbours, and give me a call tomorrow." I start to chuck my tools into the tote bag.

"Don't remove *anything* from the property," the lawyer screeches. "Everything stays. You don't take anything with you and you do not return unless—"

I toss the hammer in the tote, straighten up and turn toward the man. "Settle down, Sunshine," I tell him. "I'm not leaving here without my tools. And when I've stowed my gear in my pickup, I'm going to drive that Bobcat out of here."

"I forbid you to touch—"

"I'm wet and I'm hungry and I don't have time for your bullshit." I bend to place the torch into the tote.

"What you're doing constitutes removal of evidence that—"

"Give me a hand checking around?" I say to my customer. He springs to life and sweeps the area with the flashlight, then retrieves a couple of clamps and the plug.

"Good one," I tell him when he hands me the sodden piece of wood. "We can use that when we fix *your* line."

The lawyer keeps nattering at us as I squelch across the field to my pickup. Beside me my customer carries my shovel and pickaxe, and the lawyer follows us as far as the fence, still yammering. I can see he's parked his suv close behind the ramp I've lowered from Duane's trailer, where I'll need to load the Bobcat. *No doubt he'll have a reason why he won't move his stupid vehicle,* I think. *But I'll just pull the trailer ahead on the road.*

When I scramble up the bank again and move to duck through the barbed wire into the field, he shifts as if to block my way. As he does so, he lifts one hand to shield his eyes from the light from my headlamp. I straighten up.

"I'm going to retrieve my Bobcat," I tell him. "I strongly advise you not to try to stop me."

"I advise *you* not to set foot again on this property. Such an act would clearly constitute—"

"I know, I know, I'm trespassing. So sue me." I push between the strands. The lawyer backs up as I step onto the field. My customer stands uncertainly on the other side of the wire.

I point south toward his neighbour's. "Go round and up the drive there," I say. "You don't have to come onto the field if you're worried. See where the fence is down? That's where I drove in and I'll take her out through there. You can be a witness in case this moron does something more ridiculous than usual."

The lawyer sputters a dire warning as I stride past him. He trails after me toward the machine, not talking now. I'm thinking how the absence of all but a few mosquitoes is a huge blessing.

I disconnect the hoe attachment, ready to shift the Bobcat to use its bucket to carry the backhoe rig. I scramble onto the loader, but when I turn the key, the engine refuses to start.

I jiggle the key and retry several times. The only sound is my stomach gurgling. Could be a simple reason why the motor is dead, but it's about pitch black out now and all I want is to drive home, crack a beer, reheat some leftover chicken, make my lunch for tomorrow's shift and go to bed. I mentally inventory who can tow the machine tomorrow after work if I can't start it then.

As I climb off the Bobcat, the lawyer is at my elbow in the darkness, ordering me to explain what I'm doing.

"You're in luck," I tell him. "I've decided you're right. I'm going to just leave the loader here tonight."

"Everything must be restored to exactly the condition you found it in," he declares. "That means filling the trench here, and removing this machine."

"Fifteen minutes ago you were telling me to leave and not take anything with me."

"You are required by law to restore everything precisely as you found it. And that means no machine on the premises. I insist you—"

"It won't start," I say. "And it's late. I'm bushed. Some of us work for a living. I'll have it off the property in twenty-four hours."

"Not good enough—" he starts, but he's talking to my back. I head in the direction of my customer waiting on his neighbour's driveway. Soon as I get home I'll have to call Duane's wife and explain the job took longer than I thought, that I won't be able to return the Bobcat until the following evening. By then my customer should have been able to sort things out with his neighbours. Or not.

His face, when I reach him, is one big question mark. But the answers to why people take a problem and instead of solving it make it into two or three, or why people don't want to know all that's involved in keeping the world running, are, like the mysteries of water, out there in the dark someplace. And I'm too tired to look for them until tomorrow.

The Shed

WHEN YOU BOOT it down the highway through the valley, pounding your tunes, you probably don't notice toward the end of that long straight stretch west of Kosiansic's hill an old shed partially torn down. If it did catch your eye for a sec, you'd expect it to be totally demolished and gone when you gunned by a week later—the shack isn't large: fifteen feet by ten or so. But the building sits in the same half-disassembled state, day after week after month. Every time I rocket past I feel a twinge of . . . what? Uneasiness? Regret? I wouldn't say guilt.

What's left of the shed is close beside the north shoulder: the roofline sags a little and the siding is torn off along one side and one end, with just studs visible. The roof's shingles have been mostly removed, so roof decking is exposed except at the west end where a plywood sheet is missing and you can see the trusses.

It's not my fault the shack looks like it does. It belongs to Ray Waddington: the building is on his twelve hectares that run back from the highway partway up Slocan Ridge. But you could say I was responsible for tearing the shed down, and it's still standing after two years.

I'm coming out of the Slocan Park Co-op April before last, and Ray is heading inside. We start chatting. His son Donny and I met on a tree-planting contract up in the Lardeau the summer before. We weren't exactly friends—acquaintances, guys you hang with when you're both working the same job. Donny and I hung out a little when we got home, too, which is how I met his dad. I hadn't heard anything from Donny since Christmas when he was here on a break from college in the Okanagan and we ended up at the same party.

So I ask Ray how Donny is doing, and Ray wants to know what I'm up to, which to tell the truth isn't much. I'm waiting to be called to go tree planting again, and in the meantime participating in a small way in the Kootenay Economy. Just a few plants, mainly for my own use and maybe also to sell a little to friends or friends of friends. I don't mention the plants to Ray. He's some kind of manager for Nelson Hydro, though he used to be a lineman and is a straight ahead guy.

Ray says he has a small job for me if I'm interested, tearing down this shed at his place. He wants to put in a berm along the highway at the foot of his property because every year there's more traffic and the highway noise is starting to bug him, especially in summer with all the tourists. His idea is to hire a neighbour who has an excavator to put up a six- or eight-foot high mound of dirt all along his frontage and then plant trees on it. Meanwhile a shed is right where part of this berm is supposed to go. An old tractor has been stored inside for years, he says, along with some other junk. The deal is he'll clean all that out before I start, and pay me twice minimum wage in cash if I'll knock the building down and arrange to have the lumber and other shit hauled to the dump.

"Hire a couple of your friends to help," Ray says. "Somebody with a pickup or trailer if you don't have one. I'd rather not pay for a bin rental. The boards are all rotten, so just get rid of them. The job shouldn't take you more than a day, day and a half. The shed isn't that big."

He says I can offer the other guys a couple of bucks over minimum. "I realize all you young punks are getting rich off your grow shows, but maybe there's a couple of people you know who could use the money."

I was getting bored waiting to start planting. Ray's offer was a chance to make a few bucks under the table on top of EI. And since starting a season out on the cutblocks is always physical agony after a winter not doing much, I figured a day or two attacking Ray's shed might help ease the impending pain.

First guy I phone is Eric Trelawny, who is calling himself "Larch" these days. Don't ask me why; he's been a loony since I first met him on a contract in the Purcells west of Cranbrook. He's about five years younger than me, but I know he has a small pickup. I'd run into him again the previous August when I was still going out with Marian. She paid him to pick up and deliver a few loads of manure for her garden, cow shit from that farmer on the Winlaw back road who has the herd of Black Angus. Marian tells me she's hired somebody who's been getting it on with one of her best buds. I'm home from planting and over at her place to wheelbarrow the goop where she wants it. When the first load comes up her drive, who should the pickup owner be but Eric. I hadn't seen him for a few months but he was wearing the outfit he wore in camp: one of those gangsta rapper toques, like we're going to get a big dump of snow any minute even though it's so hot we're all wearing shorts. Big beard, and he's still packing this giant pig-sticker of a sheath knife strapped to his thigh like he's a gunslinger and the valley is the Wild West. Did I say he was weird?

Still, I've planted with him like I mentioned, and, strange as he is, he works hard. No ditching the seedlings in a gully, even if the side-hill is all rock or a steep mess of slash to try to plant in. He wasn't the fastest guy in camp, but he wasn't the slowest, either. When he hauled for Marian, he was on time and on budget, like they say, and I assume he'll be wanting to get in shape for planting same as me.

On the phone he starts to pressure me to hire as the third for our crew a pal of his down on his luck. Says the dude needs a break, is totally conscientious, yadda-yadda. His name is Smithski: he isn't Doukhobor, his real name is Gavin Smith, but he dated this Russian chick in junior high at Mount Sentinel where he picked up the nickname and it stuck. Larch tells me Smithski had a good-sized hydroponics setup that had been ripped a few weeks ago. The grow op was in the basement of a house he was renting along Woykin Road, and he was about to harvest when somebody cleaned him out. He and his girlfriend returned home from hearing a band at the Royal pub in Nelson and the house had been trashed. They'd been celebrating because she just found out she was pregnant. Their landlord, who had become kind of a friend of Smithski's, had bought them tickets to the Royal in honour of his tenants' impending parenthood. I'm wondering how the landlord would feel if he knew about a grow op in the basement, but I don't say anything. Around here you can never tell: maybe the landlord is a grower himself.

In any case, according to Larch, the thieves must have heard Smithski and his old lady coming up the drive that night, because as well as the crop having disappeared, their microwave and skis and other gear was piled by the back door, as though the rippers were in the middle of loading it when they were scared off. The big screen TV and stereo were missing. And three-quarters of the hydroponics equipment was gonesville. The crop itself had been intended to cover a down payment on a house and acreage, more important suddenly since Smithski and his girlfriend have a baby coming. No insurance on his household goods, so he was totally bummed by what happened. The valley is a low-crime area, if you don't count growing: lots of people never lock their doors. So getting ripped like this was a shock to Smithski, Larch says. Someone stealing a crop has been known to happen: usually kids who aren't interested in TVs and such since they don't know how to fence them. Larch is right, though, that theft isn't a problem you ordinarily worry about.

Despite this guy Smithski's problems, I'm not keen on hiring somebody sight unseen. On the other hand, I've been ripped off before myself. Not Kootenay Economy stuff, but a set of downhills disappeared from the roof of my car once in Nelson, in the days when everybody was supposed to be cool and you didn't have to lock your skis in one of those coffins everybody now has bolted to their roof racks. And years ago in Vancouver, a Honda Civic of mine was boosted from in front of my apartment building. Which was a major drag.

Growers can be the laziest people on earth, however. But Larch keeps assuring me Smithski is righteous, that they had worked together on some thinning contract up behind Silverton and Smithski had pulled his weight. After a while, I decide what the hell: the job is only for a day or two, plus I won't have to keep phoning around if I agree to hire Larch's friend. I remember this old planter from Prince George, Steve, I worked with, who used to say that for any occupation the only real qualifications you need, the only degrees required, are 98.6 degrees. We'd say 37 Celsius today, but the point is that this job of Ray's was grunt work. As long as this Smithski was breathing he could probably handle it, and I could always can him if not.

A couple of mornings later we all show up at Ray's, stand around sharing a joint and then fly at it. Smithski turns out to be a short guy, but muscular. Clean shaven, unlike Larch and me. He's wearing a toque like Larch, but also overalls with a hippie sash tied around the waist. No armament like the ridiculous bowie knife Larch is packing.

First on the list is to load some metal junk Ray had left beside the shack with a note saying we should haul this to the transfer station along with the debris from the shed. He'd left quite a pile: lengths of old drain gutter and downpipe, some angle iron, the head off the engine block of a truck or tractor, a rusty coil of barbed wire, various sheets of trashed metal roofing.

As Larch promised, Smithski positively attacks Ray's heap of metal crap. I'd brought a couple of extra pairs of work gloves with me, figuring my hires wouldn't have thought to bring gloves. Larch tugs his pair on, but Smithski refuses. I try to talk him into wearing the gloves, since lots of the metal pieces have rough edges. He tells me, "Obviously you don't know my reputation in the valley."

I'm supposed to know he's Mr. Slocan Valley Tough Guy? Or that he has a reputation for being too stupid to use the most basic safety gear? Neither he nor Larch has brought a hard hat, for instance. I expected that. And I'm pretty sure their hiking boots don't have steel toes.

Smithski dumps his first load in Larch's pickup box and trots back to the pile, bends over and tries to hoist a big chunk of cast iron—looks like a blacksmith's anvil or something. I've got an arm-load of downpipe and yell at him to wait until Larch or I can give him a hand. But he yanks the thing up to his chest and staggers to the pickup. When he's back at the pile again, I try to tell him we just came here to work and not to rack ourselves up permanently. I mention the three weeks I spent on the couch last winter after trying to load a four-by-eight board of sheetrock by myself into the rear of a friend's station wagon. Smithski is barely listening, so I drop the subject. Some guys have to learn the hard way.

Since heights aren't my thing, once we've cleared away the scrap metal I send him up on the roof to pry off the shingles. Ray had left a ladder, but I'd loaded my own onto my car-tops and Smithski and I rig that one up. Besides my toolbox, I'd brought some other stuff I figured we'd need, including a shingle ripper or ripping shovel as they're sometimes called. These puppies are way faster than trying to strip shingles off a roof with a pry bar. Smithski in no time has shingles flying in all directions. I start in on the siding with a crowbar, and Larch gives me a hand plus carries away the boards I lever off. Most of the wood is rotten and worthless, like Ray said, but a few boards aren't too bad so I tell Larch to put those aside and we'll divvy them up when the job is done. Everything cooks along smoothly, except for having to yell at Smithski a few times that the shingles he's flinging over the edge are landing too near me and Larch. Smithski really keeps ass in air and nose to the grindstone, even if he isn't paying enough attention to where Larch and I are situated below. Safety first, but I'd rather have somebody on my crew who's too much into the job than some slacker pulling his knob instead of his weight.

We stop for another joint break after a couple of hours, and I pour a coffee from my thermos. Larch and Smithski are yakking about the pluses and minuses of a video game I haven't heard of. I was never much of a gamer, but nothing makes you feel you're getting old like having the newbies in camp refer to some game you still play occasionally as being a classic. Smithski at one point asks me how long I've been tree planting, which also makes me feel my age. But I *am* the foreman on this gig, so maybe being a geezer of nearly thirty is good for keeping the drop on these boys.

We've only been back at it for maybe ten minutes when a huge pickup, a brand-new Toyota Tundra V8 extended cab with gleaming blue metallic paint and looking like it's just been washed, pulls into Ray's driveway and parks nose to nose with Larch's beat-up old F-150 with its hood and passenger door a different colour than the rest of the vehicle. Larch had turned his pickup around so when it's fully loaded he can head straight out to the dump. The Tundra now blocking the drive has a tonneau cover sealing off its box, a sunroof and one of those grilles designed to show that this vehicle eats Priuses for breakfast. I presume the monster pickup has one of those luxury package interiors with leather heated seats, Bluetooth phone, individual climate control and a high-end GPS: gear that belongs in a Lexus, not a truck.

My first thought is that this is a Regional District building inspector. I've never heard of needing a permit to demolish a building, but they're passing new bylaws all the time. The three of us stop work where we are, and stare across at the oversize vehicle towering above Larch's pickup, with its springs sagging under the load of metal and weather-beaten lumber, most of the boards split or shattered, with ragged ends where they've been pried loose.

The Tundra's driver's door opens, and a few seconds later around the rear steps a guy in shiny black leather shoes, neatly ironed slacks complete with a crease and a button-up sweater over a dress shirt. His hair is short and he has a round, baby-like face. In his left hand he's holding a package wrapped in brown paper as though for mailing.

He stops at the edge of Ray's drive. "Hello, fellows," he says, his eyes widening for a moment as he talks, making his face appear even more like a kid's. "I'm looking for Gavin Smith. His wife said he was working here. I've got something for him."

"Up here, Rog," Smithski yells.

The newcomer tilts his chin and squints at the roof. "I didn't see you up there," he calls. He shifts his gaze back toward where Larch and I are standing. "Didn't think to check the roof," he announces with a self-deprecating little laugh. There's a moment's silence and then he adds, "Is it okay if I give this to him?" His eyes widen and shrink again, as his right hand points at the package. "I know you fellows are working. This will just take a minute."

Larch bends forward to start tossing to one side a mess of shingles that have landed on a couple of boards he wants to lift.

"Go ahead," I say, indicating the ladder. "Or give it to me. I'll make sure he gets it when he comes down."

Our visitor starts moving toward us from the drive. "Thanks." As he reaches me, he extends his hand. "I'm Roger." He gives the self-deprecating small laugh again. "Gavin's landlord. Are you in charge?"

We shake hands. "You could say that," I admit. I tell him my name.

Up close I can see he's a stocky guy, about my age, but with height and build to match Smithski's. Except I get a noseful of cologne, like you'd expect from a high school kid who has just discovered girls.

"If it's all the same to you," the visitor says, "I'll pop up for a second and give this to him. It's personal, and I need to explain something to him." His eyes are round in his face as he produces the slight laugh once more. "With your permission, of course."

I shrug. "Sure. Okay."

"Thanks. I'll go ahead, then."

Smithski is waiting at the top of the ladder looking down as Roger carefully manoeuvres his shoes through the tangle of shingles and boards and scraps of wood underfoot. In a moment he's swarmed up the ladder and is on the roof looking around. "Nice view," I hear him say.

"What's up, Rog?" Smithski asks.

I could have gone back to prying off siding, but curiosity gets the better of me. I fiddle around levering a nail or two out of bits of lumber from the ground, while trying to not-too-obviously scope what's happening on the roof. I have the impression Roger's meek-and-mild, almost obsequious manner doesn't fit with his physique, let alone the truck he's driving.

Roger glances down at me, and waves his free hand back and forth. "Thanks again, Darren," he calls. I have the feeling I'm being dismissed from the presence, a broad hint not to watch, to get back to work. *But if this guy's business with Smithski is private,* I think to myself, *why doesn't he just go over to Smithski's in the evening? Did he think there wouldn't be other people on a jobsite?*

I move closer anyhow to the wall I'm in front of, pretty much out of sight of the two up top. I pretend to pull nails, yet can hear what's being said above me.

"Real sorry, Gavin," Roger begins, "to learn about your bad luck a couple of weeks ago."

"Yeah?"

"I'm happy to report, though, that through my connections I've identified the perpetrators. Some friends of mine and I went over to visit them last night, and I persuaded them to reimburse you for your loss. Here."

"What?"

"Take it. It's all cash."

"How do you mean 'reimburse' me?"

"The individuals involved were under the mistaken notion that you had insurance, so you could buy new to replace what they took. I pointed out that you didn't, that you were out of pocket and that Diane is expecting. After a little discussion, they were even persuaded the right thing to do was to share some of their profits."

"What?"

"The amount in the package there covers the costs of what they removed of yours. I wanted to give you this right away, since I don't like carrying that much cash around with me. I could have left it with Diane, except I figure you did the work and you're owed an explanation in person. They weren't supposed to touch anything but the crop. And considering your and Diane's situation, at my insistence they generously included 10 percent of what they received for the weed."

"Wait a minute, wait a minute. You know the assholes that ripped me?" Anger is discernible in Smithski's voice. "You go see them and they give you money, just like that? And what do you mean: they were only 'supposed' to take the crop?"

"They, uh, sort of work for associates of mine." The self-deprecating little laugh again. "But I look out for my friends. These guys were willing almost right away to cut you in on what they'd made. Once they understood the situation. I knew you'd be glad to have the matter rectified."

"I'm not . . . You know who they are? They just hand you some cash? Diane *thought* it was odd that we get hit when we go into town to make use of the tickets you gave us. I told her it was a coincidence. Sounds like you're telling me she was right, that you fucking set us up?"

Roger's laugh again, almost a giggle. Then, I think I hear in his voice the hint of a lisp: "They were only thupposed to take the weed. They got a little greedy, thatth all. But you'll thee in there they've more than made up for it."

"Did you fuck me over?" Smithski's voice is louder, with more rage in it: the tone that in my experience precedes something distinctly unpleasant. I back away from the wall a couple of steps to where I can see the two of them facing each other just east of the ladder on the lower part of the roof. Larch has also paused where he's been gathering shingles and straightened up.

Smithski is clutching the package in front of him, glaring at Roger. The landlord's expression is neutral, but he has both hands raised in front of his chest, palms out: a calming gesture.

"It was just business," Roger says, his tone earnest. His lisp has vanished; his enunciation is careful, deliberate. "Nothing personal. I was behind on some payments due some people on the Coast. You know how it is. As things worked out, I was able to solve that problem." His right hand gestures toward the package. "And even get you a return on your investment."

"It was *my* fucking crop," Smithski shouts. "And, no, I don't know 'how it is.' You fucking ripped me, man."

Roger shrugs, his hands still lifted, palms out. "The lease you signed? It stipulates my house won't be used for illegal purposes, right? Specifically, grow ops, right? If you think about it, you were ripping *me* off. Except I went and got you some of your money back. I doubt you were intending to give *me* a cut of what you were going to make."

Smithski is staring at Roger like he's never seen him before. "You cocksucker," Smithski finally says. "If you think you can—"

"I went to considerable trouble on your behalf, Gavin," Roger states. "I didn't have to do that. You tried to screw me. How about saying 'thank you'? After all—"

Smithski jams the package under his left elbow, squeezing the object against his body to secure it. Both his hands shoot forward between Roger's upraised palms to grab the front of the landlord's sweater.

Roger's arms don't move. "I advise you," he says slowly, "to take your hands off me."

"You piece of shit," Smithski says. "You don't—"

The flat of Roger's right hand smashes into the bottom of Smithski's chin, snapping his head back and throwing him off balance. The package drops onto the roof, skids a short distance and slides over the edge as Smithski's feet shuffle to try to keep him upright. He no sooner attains the vertical than he lunges toward Roger, who is standing apparently at ease, his baby face serene as ever, but his raised palms now don't seem benign. I've watched lots of guys fight, usually involving more shoving and pushing and grunting than punches, but never on a roof and never on a job where I'm supposed to be in charge. Before I can say "Cut that out," or something equally useful, Smithski swings at Roger. Roger jerks his head back to evade the blow, and in a second the two are grappling, feet scuffing on the sloping boards as they jockey for position, sliding downslope closer to the roof edge. Amidst the heaving and pushing, Roger's left leg hooks around Smithski's right, in what I realize afterwards must be a martial arts move. Smithski tips sideways to his right, twists his torso in midair, hands now extended as if to break his fall, and drops head first off the roof. I hear Larch yell, "Hey!"

Smithski lands a few yards to my left on a low heap of boards Larch has assembled to tote over to the pickup. An audible *crack* resounds as Smithski strikes the pile, like wood being snapped or split, followed by the rustling rattle of the boards settling after the impact. I can hear Roger breathing from above, where he peers over the lip of the roof at his opponent, who lies absolutely still. As Roger looks, his hands are smoothing his clothes into the correct alignment where they've been wrenched awry. One of Smithski's legs below the knee is bent at the wrong angle. My stomach contracts and for a moment I feel I'm going to throw up.

Then Roger is descending the ladder, while Larch scrambles over to kneel beside Smithski. I don't seem able to act. "Call 911," Larch shouts. "We gotta call 911. He's all fucked up."

I smell Roger's cologne and turn to see him standing beside me. His face has an expression like concern. "I wish Gavin hadn't tried that," Roger says, tone mournful. "I tried to warn him. I'm kind of an expert." The slight laugh. "I thought he'd be grateful I got him the money." He holds up the package, which he has obviously retrieved. "Here, you should give him this when he wakes up."

"Call 911, for fuck's sake," Larch yells. "Don't just fucking stand there."

No cellphone service this far up the valley, I'm thinking, so one of us needs to contact a neighbour or drive into Crescent Valley to a phone. My hands accept the package from Roger.

"Gavin seems to be out cold," Roger is saying. He clicks his tongue twice as though with regret. "These things happen. I'll go call an ambulance." He swivels toward his Tundra, takes a step, then turns back toward me again. "Oh." He half-laughs. "When he wakes up, would you tell him I want him the fuck out of my house by the end of the month?"

I watch as the Tundra engine squeals into life, and is gunned satisfactorily. The behemoth starts to slowly back down the driveway and onto the road.

"Did that asshole say he was going to phone 911?" Larch calls. "You know any first aid?" He remains crouched beside Smithski's body. I walk toward them. "I'd like to shift these boards out from under Smithski," Larch says. "But I heard you're not supposed to move somebody who's been in an accident. In case you snap their neck."

Smithski's face is white, and his breathing, as far as I can tell, is shallow. "He's in shock, I think," I say, trying to remember the little I've read about what to do in an emergency. "We should cover him with something."

"Okay, what?"

I take inventory for a minute. A blanket? A tarp? My mind doesn't seem to be working right, but I can't think why I'd have either of these with me. My guess is that Larch doesn't have anything in his pickup either.

"That ambulance better get here soon," Larch mutters.

As though a bubble pops in my mind, a coherent thought surfaces. "I don't know if I *trust* that guy to phone 911," I announce. My brain is replaying the fight, the sheer meanness of ripping a tenant and then kicking him out after shoving him off a roof. "What a total prick. One of *us* should go phone."

"I'll go. But isn't there a phone at your friend's here?"

I glance up the drive at Ray's house. "Nobody's home and the place is probably locked. I'll drive over to the neighbour's. Somebody will be home along the road."

"I can go."

"Your pickup is full of crap, and we haven't tied it down yet. It's faster if I take my car. I'm parked behind you, but give me your keys and I'll shift the truck over into the field so I can squeeze past. I'll be back fast as I can."

"Hurry the fuck up."

I stash Roger's package in my trunk. En route to the next property west, I'm regretting not having a first aid ticket. Each year when planting is over I think about signing up for the course, which would be worth extra pay if nobody else on a crew has a ticket. But when the last contract of the season ends, I'm in the mood to party, not study: to reward myself for having survived another year on the sidehills.

The neighbour says she'll make the call for me, so I don't get to check whether Roger contacted 911. I decide it doesn't matter: the guy is bad news no matter whether he did or didn't phone. As I approach Ray's driveway, I realize the ambulance will want to stop as near Smithski as possible, so I park on the highway shoulder.

He appears the same as when I left, though Larch says while I was gone Smithski suddenly started to moan, which freaked Larch out. I hand him back his keys and suggest he reverse his pickup further up the drive to make room for the ambulance to get close. He's stepping out of the pickup when I hear the siren.

I don't recognize either of the ambulance guys, but they tell Larch and me we were right not to try to move Smithski. Then the rest of the Crescent Valley volunteer fire crew pull in with their pumper truck, lights flashing.

I know one of the firemen, Herman the German, who has his own electrical business and who I hire a couple of times a year to replace a baseboard heater or if I can't figure out what's repeatedly tripping a circuit breaker. Herman apprenticed in Germany before immigrating to Canada, and according to him he's the only electrician in the valley able to properly wire a house, to follow the building code to the letter. You can tell when Herman has worked on a house circuit. If he removes a light switch plate from a wall to test for current, when the plate is reattached the slots in the screws are all perfectly vertical. "Anal" hardly begins to define him, but he does good work.

I nod to Herman after he and the other volunteers, who include a couple of women, leap off the fire truck carrying boxes and bags of gear and stride over to assist the ambulance duo. Finally the whole cluster of them bent over Smithski have him strapped to a device to hold him rigid, with an oxygen mask over his face. They gingerly hoist him onto the ambulance's gurney. Two of the fire crew dash to their truck again, reverse it onto the highway and park it behind my car to clear the drive. Herman asks me what happened here. When I explain, he insists I have to notify the Mounties.

I'm not keen on bringing the horsemen in on anything that's drug-related. Then, too, am I going to tell them about the package of bills Roger gave me to pass to Smithski? To distract Herman I ask if he knows this Roger guy. Herman bellows out that he's been trying to collect money from Roger for nine months for wiring up a barn. "He told me he vas going to put in a shop, yah? But I *know* it vas for a grow show. I'm not stupid." While we're agreeing on what an asshole Roger is, I see Ray's Cherokee pull into the drive and brake behind the ambulance.

The ambulance guys activate their siren briefly and flash their lights to warn Ray off, and he has to back down his drive with the ambulance following him, also in reverse. Ray waits until the first responders siren away toward the Nelson hospital, then he heads up his drive again, stopping where the ambulance had been. Turns out the neighbour had called him at work to let him know what was happening on his property. Ray doesn't hesitate about phoning the cops once I explain the situation and Herman has chimed in about procedures the law requires be followed in cases like this. Herman sounds like a cop himself.

While Ray is still up at the house phoning the piggery, the volunteer fire department bunch leave. For some reason I feel lonely with just Larch and me standing beside the shed staring at the big red fire truck disappearing down the highway. We start to half-heartedly clean up more of the shingles, but then Ray is hurrying down the drive waving his arms at us.

The horsemen apparently want everything left exactly as is. Makes sense when I think about it: I've seen *CSI* like everybody else. I can tell Ray isn't too pleased by all these developments, but I assure him we'll hang around to talk to the cops so he can go back to work. He writes down Smithski's name and says when he returns to the office he'll contact a nurse he knows at the hospital and find out Smithski's condition. Larch and I spend a couple of hours doing nothing. It's like waiting for a tow truck if your car hits a deer or conks out in the middle of nowhere.

I climb onto the shed roof and rescue my shingle ripper, and put it and my other tools back in the car. I think about retrieving my ladder, but figure the cops may want to go up top. Larch and I tie down the junk already in the pickup box, because no doubt the horsemen will complain if they think we're intending to head for the transfer station with an unsecured load.

Eventually we take my car over to the Frog Peak Café in Crescent Valley for lunch, after I find some paper in my glove box to leave a note on the pickup windshield for the RCMP. A cruiser is just steering into Ray's driveway ahead of us when we return.

Constable Goofy of the Royal Mounted, once he determines who we are, bawls us out for leaving a possible crime scene unattended. Then, like they taught him in cop school in Regina, he has us individually sit in the cruiser while he takes notes on what each of us says happened. I plan to be all "oh, yeah, I forgot" if Larch tips the cop about the package of cash. But Larch either keeps his lip zipped or hadn't paid attention to that part of Roger's visit.

Once we've both been interrogated, I ask the cop if we can leave, and he says no, so we stand around some more while he produces a camera and measuring tape from his front seat and takes a lot of photos plus determines the distances up, down and sideways around the shed and up on the roof. Then he retreats to the cruiser and spends about a half hour on the radio while I guess somebody with a brain tells him what to do. When he emerges at last, he informs us we're free to go but not to leave the area because there may be further investigation.

At home I grab a beer and sit at my kitchen table to figure out how best to deal with the package in the trunk of my car. Finally I phone Larch, since Smithski's a pal of his, to tell him he should take the money over to Smithski's girlfriend. Larch says she's at the hospital, but he has the tipping fee receipt from the dump, and how should he get that reimbursed? He agrees that handing Smithski's girlfriend the money is probably right. We decide I'll give him the package and the dump money next day on the job.

I call Ray, and he says concussion and that something snapped in Smithski's spine so they believe he'll be quadriplegic, once his broken leg heals. Of course, it's too early to tell, blah blah blah. My guts feel queasy at this news, but I inform Ray that Larch and I can finish the shed tomorrow. Ray says the cops told him to leave the site intact in case there's follow-up they need to do. He says he'll call me when we can go forward with demolishing the shed.

I take the package over to Larch's in the morning. I don't hear from Ray again. In the *Valley Voice* newspaper the following Wednesday, there's no mention of Smithski, not even in the Police Reports column. Then I'm away planting a lot of the spring and summer up on the Blueberry–Paulson Pass, then north of Edgewood on the Arrow Lakes, and after that on a contract near McBride, northwest of Jasper.

The entire business of the shed and Smithski maybe becoming a cripple nags at me off and on while I'm planting. As soon as I get back I call Larch but he seems to have moved, or at least his phone is disconnected. I phone my ex, Marian, not the easiest call to make, but she says her friend broke up with Larch in the winter, about the time Marian and I decided our relationship didn't have a future. She has no idea what happened to Larch, but promises to check to see if her friend has any information. If she does, Marian will let me know.

Nothing comes of that. I expected Ray would have hired somebody else to remove the shed while I was gone, and that the berm he had in mind would be in place, tree seedlings and all. My Plan B was to ask Ray's son Donny, if I bumped into him, whether his dad has mentioned the incident. But I learn on Facebook that Donny went to Quebec with his new girlfriend. He hasn't been back to the valley since, far as I know.

Not that I owe anything to Smithski, or Ray for that matter. Yet from time to time I consider phoning Ray to find out if he heard whether Roger was charged. And to see if Ray knows what happened to Smithski, or if he wants me to finish demolishing his shack. But I don't call, though every time I flash past the shed at the side of the road I wonder if I should.

Fenris

ONE COOL MARCH MORNING, the man rounded the corner of his house headed for his workshop, a converted small barn where he made his living as a builder of custom cabinets, cupboards, kitchen and bathroom counters and wooden toys. The lawn underfoot was still yellow and a few good-sized piles of snow remained where they had accumulated at the base of some evergreens, and where he had heaped snow cleared from the parking area beside the house. The man carried a thermos of coffee, fuel for his planned morning of chores.

Yesterday the man had seen the first robin of the season, and now he heard one call from the edge of the forest just west of the house. The scent of the woods and other foliage beginning to return to life after the winter was in the man's nostrils as he inhaled. In winter he enjoyed cross-country skiing in the mountains where he lived, so was glad each fall when the snow returned. But after four months of cold he was looking forward to the change in the year.

The man was mentally reviewing a shopping list of dimension lumber he wanted to order today. His intention was to price the wood both at Maglio's, a building supply store in Nelson, and at a planer mill nearer his home where sometimes lumber was better quality at less cost.

Delivery was a factor, too: the order would be substantial. After two decades in business, the man knew spring's arrival meant people throughout the region would begin to phone for an estimate on long-delayed house renovation projects. After the winter's lull, he would soon be swamped with commitments and would even have to turn down jobs. Stocking up with wood from Maglio's meant either a 120-kilometre round trip with his tow-behind trailer, or paying the store a hefty delivery fee. The planer mill, on the other hand, was up a side road only seven kilometres away. But the owner of the mill, Garcia, was famous locally for being eccentric. Even if his quoted price was good, something you said or did when you showed up to purchase could inadvertently offend him. A simple commercial transaction abruptly transformed into a personal matter that would have to be resolved, given the small size of this valley's population.

Garcia, a once-burly American who had arrived in the area in the late 1960s as a Vietnam War resister, now was more or less wheelchair-bound with a mysterious ailment. He appeared more overweight each time the man visited the lumberyard. From what Garcia told his customers, no doctor seemed able to diagnose what was crippling him. But whether the medicines Garcia was taking or the pain caused by his condition was responsible, his mood nowadays could shift in an instant from amiable to hostile. Which meant his customers had to walk on eggshells while they were at the lumberyard if they wished to take advantage of bargain prices. The alternative to deferring to the mill owner's behaviour was to confront Garcia about some unreasonable accusation, a tactic that most times led to a shouting match and Garcia's refusal to sell to the transgressor, at least until a phone call was made after both sides had cooled off, apologies were exchanged and the deal renewed.

The planer mill itself was a bit crazy, too: Garcia lived alone on the upper floor of the only two-storey building on the site. A customer stood below a particular second-storey window, which would eventually open if Garcia had heard someone drive into his lumberyard or noticed a prospective purchaser standing there. The mill owner would lean out and inquire what was wanted, and then verbally direct his customer to the sheds or piles of wood around the yard where the buyer could find and load his order. Sometimes an employee of Garcia's would be evident, moving lumber with a forklift or otherwise occupied in the buildings, who would assist the customer. But often the yard was deserted except perhaps for another customer also searching for the boards or skid of insulation he wished to buy. Despite the shortage of paying jobs in the valley, people seldom worked for Garcia for long.

While the customer was tracking down a desired purchase, Garcia would be preparing an invoice. When a load was complete and confirmed with Garcia, the invoice was lowered to the customer from the second-storey window in a basket suspended from a rope. The purchaser placed either a credit card, cheque or cash in the basket, which was whisked aloft. The window was closed while the payment was processed inside and the customer stood waiting. Promptly, or after an unexplained long wait, the window opened again and the basket, now containing a credit card slip to sign or the invoice marked *Paid,* descended toward the customer again.

At Maglio's, by contrast, knowledgeable staff busy in the storage sheds or out in the yard were always quick to aid and advise customers in the selection of lumber, help with the loading into a vehicle or onto a trailer, key the order into a computer in the small office adjoining the yard and accept payment. The man wondered each time he bought from Garcia whether the issue of cost really did outweigh the weirdness of the local mill owner's personality and procedures. As the man approached his workshop, this consideration was again churning around in his mind. Then he saw, six or so metres ahead of him, a large animal standing motionless in front of the workshop door, gazing at him.

The man halted, stunned by the sight. At first he thought it must be a coyote. Except he'd never seen a coyote this big. And in more than twenty years living here he'd never glimpsed one of the creatures on his acreage, nor had he ever seen one crossing the road or in somebody's field that would stand still to appraise an approaching person. Packs of coyotes lived in the valley. Nearly every second evening, summer or winter, the man could listen to them howling and yipping, either across the river or down along a loop road between the lane that the man's property abutted and the water. But any coyote observed in daylight was engaged in disappearing into the woods that edged a road, or crossing a pasture alongside the main highway that paralleled the river on the other side of the valley.

In front of the former barn, the coyote, as the man first thought it was, exhibited an unreadable expression in its yellow eyes. How it regarded him did not fit any category he could define: the eyes did not seem wary or belligerent or curious, but radiated an indecipherable, nonhuman emotion. The man recognized that his inability to read the animal's intention in its eyes, to judge what it might do next, constituted a danger. A surge of fear rippled through the man at the beast's refusal to slink away.

His dread increased as he noted that the face aimed toward him was not comprised of the fox-like muzzle and ears of a coyote. This face was blunter, squarer: more resembling a German shepherd dog. *Wolf,* the man thought, the back of his neck prickling. *I didn't even know there were wolves in the valley.* The pale brownish-grey fur was matted in spots, sparse in others, as though the animal was either moulting or diseased. An abscess or sore as large as one of its paws was visible on the outside of its left back leg. Silvery hairs around the muzzle created the impression of age, as did the leanness of its body and the ragged-edged, misshapen right ear that hinted the organ had been damaged in a long-ago accident or fight. The creature was tensely poised, looking at him.

News stories of attacks on children and even adults by old or ill bears or cougars flashed through the man's consciousness. Perhaps this wolf was similarly afflicted, ready to turn to humans as prey. The man's distress increased. He wasn't sure if he should shout at the wolf, raise and lower his arms and otherwise act aggressively in the hope of deterring it from regarding him as a meal. Or should he carefully step backwards, ceding the territory, demonstrating that he had no wish to challenge the animal? He had read accounts where a wildlife expert extolled one or the other of these responses as the sole correct way to avoid attack by a bear, cougar or other potential predator.

The man's most recent frightening encounter involving a wild animal had occurred two summers before. On a hot July afternoon he had been crouched over one of his kitchen garden beds near the house, weeding corn and lettuce rows, and thinning carrots. He had a hand cultivator with him, and a bucket in which to deposit the trimmings plus any stones that had surfaced in the soil. At one point he glanced up from tending a row of green onions, and a black bear was standing on the lawn five metres away, watching him.

The man had sensed no threat from the animal. But the man panicked—the surreal nature of the bear's manifestation on the grass so close to the house in the middle of the day, and the potential of a dangerous confrontation, felt to the man overwhelmingly scary. He had risen to his feet, clutching the bucket to his chest as if the container offered protection from an assault. Contrary to the advice of everything he had read on how to handle a bear encounter, the man had turned his back on the animal and walked rapidly toward the basement door. Just outside the house he checked over his shoulder and saw that the bear had followed him, albeit at a distance, stepping through the vegetable bed where less than a minute before he had been weeding. The beast had halted on the lawn, still looking in his direction.

Once safe inside the basement, with the door locked, the man marvelled at his behaviour, including his determination to carry away the bucket which he continued to hold. After a few minutes, he steeled himself to return outside. He cautiously peered about, but the bear had vanished.

The rest of that summer the man had been jumpy each afternoon when he attended to garden chores. He would stop whatever he was doing every few seconds to scrutinize the landscape surrounding him, especially the edges of the lawn and each opening into the forest.

The apparition of the wolf instantly resurrected the anxiety that the unexpected arrival of the summertime bear had caused. The man noticed he was grasping the coffee thermos to his chest, as if, like the bucket, the thermos could defend his vital organs should the beast lunge toward him. Yet because the wolf was smaller than the bear, the man, despite his fear, resolved to challenge the wolf's presence. "G-g-g-go on, get out of here," the man tried to shout. As in a nightmare where a cry for help cannot be articulated despite the urgent need to pronounce the words, the man heard only a soft squeak emitted from his mouth. He tried again with the same result: "G-g-go."

I am Fenris. The man registered the calm declaration in his mind. The voice vibrated with confidence; its tone was both measured and heavy with import.

Panic flooded through the man. His knees felt shaky. "Wh-what?" he heard himself say.

The country silence answered his question as man and animal stared at each other. In the stillness, broken only by the chittering of a squirrel somewhere in the woods on the far side of the workshop, the man desperately dismissed what he imagined he'd heard. A trick of the brain brought on by stress, he reasoned—subconsciously he must be anticipating and, yes, at some level dreading the whirlwind of projects he'd be called upon to undertake in the next weeks, juggling customers, suppliers, preparation of estimates, figuring out how to build and install specific orders. The absurdity of his situation struck him: awful enough that a wolf had materialized between him and the workshop, but now he was imagining that the monster could communicate with him. A giggle almost escaped his mouth.

I am Fenris, he was sure he heard the statement again.

As if to emphasize the implications of the utterance, the animal slowly seated itself on its hind legs without breaking eye contact. Its stance even on its haunches remained taut, as though at any second it could explode into motion.

I am the devourer of the sun and moon, the creature informed the man. *After so many years, the space between you and me is thin.*

"I . . . I don't . . . " the man managed. Then his near-hysteria overcame his terror. "Go. Get out of here." His voice regained some strength on the final phrase, but his words, breaking as they did a couple of times, sounded unconvincing even to himself. Despite this failure, he attempted to reinforce his command by lifting his trembling hands over his head, thermos clutched in his left, and waving his arms around in accordance with the advice to make yourself look as aggressive, as big as possible.

After all, the wolf was even smaller than the deer he ran off his property. Deer were the animals most often present around the man's home, grazing on the lawns in season: commonly a doe and fawn, or two or three does and a fawn or two. The man diligently sprayed a deer repellant of milk and eggs on his flower beds and the unfenced kitchen garden. The omnipresent threat of the ruminants' hunger for rose leaves and radish greens goaded the man, despite the general effectiveness of the spray, to chase after the animals, shouting curses and waving his arms, whenever he was working outside on the grounds and deer emerged from the forest.

That thought now gave him a tiny spark of courage. "Scram," he tried to shout, as he did at the deer. "Leave. Go." He recognized that his voice was more muted than he'd intended.

The wolf remained seated, but its body seemed to relax.

"I have to *work*," the man continued in what he hoped was a more assertive tone. "I've got a full day today and I need to get at it." His arms felt tired, so he lowered them. He took a breath. "Fuck *off*," he suddenly bellowed.

The wolf continued to stare at him, not budging.

Each day we are closer, the deliberate voice was in his mind again. *Yet I will be here even when you are gone. There is an end to your busyness.*

"Just *leave*," the man spoke aloud. He was conscious that under his shirt, sweater and parka, sweat trickled down the sides of his torso, over his ribs.

The creature's mouth opened, and a long tongue extended and licked left to right along its lips. As the tongue passed along the muzzle, the man could see jagged ivory-coloured incisors. The tongue retracted.

I visit here often. You will—

The man's mind registered the words, but he listened to himself interrupt: "You're not wanted. *Go*."

The animal abruptly lifted itself onto all four legs, and the man took a step backward.

—You will see Fenris again.

The wolf swung its head away from the man to gaze to its right at the forest. In an instant the animal had leapt in that direction, and bounded with the speed of a deer through the tangle of winter blow-down of fallen hazel, pine and fir limbs at the wood's edge. A second later the creature had disappeared into the forest's evergreens and just-budding underbrush.

The man stood paralyzed for a moment, staring after the wolf. Then he strode quickly to the shop door, locking it behind him with shaking hands. He collapsed onto the stool at his workbench and succeeded in unscrewing the top of the thermos and slopping coffee into the mug he had rinsed and left on the bench at the end of the previous afternoon. Both his hands were needed, he found, to steady the trembling mug in order to bring it to his lips.

Wolves, he thought, *aren't supposed to be as dangerous as what the myths say about them. But one-on-one, they're still spooky.* The man felt the hot fluid slip down his throat. *Yet animals don't talk,* he told himself. *Why would I imagine I could hear one speak?* Through the shop window he saw his house's cedar siding opposite. At one corner of the dwelling was a hazel tree, its leafless branches a maze. A low mound of snow remained on the lawn near the trunk, where house and tree shadowed that location from direct sun.

He reviewed the wolf's supposed utterances. *"Destroyer of the sun and moon." Give me a break. Sounds like an evil-doer from a superhero comic.* The man felt chilled, and poured more coffee into the mug. Some of the fluid spilled on the workbench and he wiped at it with a sleeve. *If I'm making all this up, why such a corny line? And why am I making this up?*

The man rose, swivelled and squatted in front of the wood heater behind him. *Isn't running into a wolf so near the house enough? And what did it mean by "You'll see me again"? Pure Arnold Schwarzenegger: "I'll be back."*

The man scrunched up newspaper from a pile in a box near the stove, and added some wood chips and small bits of kindling from a heap propped up against one side of the box. He located the match-box on a small shelf nailed to a nearby support post, and with fingers that continued to vibrate struck a match. As the paper ignited, he snagged some larger pieces of wood from a discard box under the workbench. He stood staring into the flames, prepared to add the variously sized board-ends when the kindling had sufficiently caught.

The wolf, or whatever the voice in the man's head was, had said something about the space between itself and him being thin, he recalled. *Something about time: after years . . .* The voice also claimed to be around the property often, he remembered. Which was nonsense, since he'd never seen the animal before. *This is like trying to puzzle out a dream,* he thought. *Or else I'm cracking up. Except the wolf looked real, whatever I imagined it said.*

The man judged the fire was ready and tossed in the wood he was holding. He turned to pick up another few pieces from the discard box, and laid these on top of the blaze as well, mindful of the roaring flames. He shut the stove door and slumped back onto his seat at the workbench. He felt warmth radiate from behind him, and sipped the coffee, gazing through the window.

Maybe this episode is one of those getting-old things, he thought. *I'm fifty-eight, healthy: I cycle, ski, hike, canoe, all that. Yet I consider my age often: how long can I keep living this life out here in the boonies? There's plenty of old-timers around the valley, but I can picture being too sick or frail to keep this place going.* A bout with the flu in January had kept him mostly bedridden for three days, almost too woozy to occasionally stumble downstairs to the basement to replenish the wood furnace, or into the kitchen to heat soup for a meal.

He remembered the wolf had declared it would remain after the man was gone. *Is the wolf supposed to be* time, *then? Or did my mind make the wolf be death? Time and death* are, *in a scientific sense, the killer of the sun and moon. The sun will eventually expand as it uses up all its fuel and dies. The sun's death will burn up the moon along with the earth. Also, everything ends for you when* you *die, including the sun and moon. The death-wolf eats them up along with you.*

The man felt a wave of gloom overtake him. Even if a person could somehow live forever, in time he would have to find a new planet since this one will be destroyed. The man tried to shake off his bleak feeling. He poured out more coffee. He liked the life he had built in the country, but sometimes lying in bed at night he experienced a sense of panic at his certitude that the price of being born was that all he had ever experienced, knew and enjoyed, all he had done and planned to do, would wink out of existence. At his age, too, the death of everything—the abolition of his personality— was nearer rather than further. He would lie coated in sweat and slightly dizzy at the thought of ceasing to be. He imagined himself on his deathbed in that very bedroom, consciousness cutting in and out for the last time. To break the spell of his thoughts he sometimes would turn on the light and pad into the kitchen to brew a cup of herbal tea. Reading something to divert his mind from his sentence of death helped, too.

Now in the wood shop he was aware he was in the grip of the same dread. He attempted to distract himself by lifting his shopping list of lumber from a shelf and reviewing what he intended to order today. But images of the wolf, and a replay of his fear of the creature, and of dying, interrupted his attempts to concentrate on what he wished to buy. The idea struck him that if the wolf was death, or fear of death, then indeed, as the wolf had stated, it frequently hung around his property. Even if it hadn't taken tangible shape before.

Never mind death; is my life *worthwhile?* the man asked himself, taking a sip from his mug. *If I have to die, did how I spent my years have value?* He climbed off the stool to feed more scraps into the heater. *I build things with wood that people find useful or enjoyable, at least for a time. I'm competent; I do an adequate job. But I'm not going to win any design awards. I haven't exactly set the world on fire.* He smiled mirthlessly at his choice of metaphor as he shut the stove door on the revitalized blaze.

Who determines whether someone's life has worth? he asked himself. He swung back onto the stool and had another swallow of coffee. *The media takes some low-talent starlet or pop musician and describes her or his every whim and stupid escapade repeatedly for years as though this person is one of the most significant inhabitants of the planet. By any objective measure, though, the person is a complete parasite. Does such a life have importance?* Probably an objective measure of value, of meaning, doesn't exist, the man corrected himself. After all, he mused, the world contains both the precision of cutting a countertop from a sheet of Arborite, and also Garcia's nutty lumberyard. And his own mind was apparently capable of concocting a telepathic wolf. *Surely,* he reasoned, *only* I *can decide whether my life is creditable.*

He reached to remove the cordless phone from its base on the wall and ran his finger down a posted list of frequently called contacts for Maglio's number. *And what about someone who's depressed?* he thought. *The person might be making a solid contribution to people's lives around him, but because of a chemical imbalance in his brain he's convinced he's worthless.* The wares of the potter who had built the man's mug were, he knew, highly regarded by area residents. Yet whenever he visited the craftsman's studio, the owner always declared he was about to give up creating with clay, due to his failure to be selected for some juried show in a False Creek gallery in Vancouver, or inclusion in a forthcoming book on contemporary BC artisans. The potter was equally morose about any topic the man introduced to try to shift their conversation to a more cheerful subject.

The man put the phone down, stood up for a second, looked around the shop, sat again.

I've got to think of something else, he told himself.

He remembered a late afternoon several weeks before. The snowy valley had been silent except for the river fluttering over shallows near the trail he skied along, the hiss of his skis travelling in the set track, and the steady heartbeat of his poles meeting snow and pulling him forward effortlessly as he kicked and glided through chill air. A mist or cloud had settled low over the route, and icy pinpricks of snow now needled the skin of his nose, forehead, cheeks. The visible world had shrunk to riverbank, woods and the bottom slopes of the forested mountainsides. All about him was a variegated grey perceivable through the falling snow, except for the mass of dark moving water, the distant unbroken white patch of a barn roof across the river, and the ivory of the trail that curved ahead.

His passage through the sleet's sharp shards in the failing light had purged him of every belief, every idea except the experience of his float through the desolate beauty of the landscape, of the harsh weather he was alive in. He was no more or less than a body journeying across the wonders of the snowy mountain, and a mind comprehending the beauty through which it travelled, a mind and body that were the product of the luck, the happenstance that had set him here, in motion in a storm as random as the hidden sun, the hidden moon, the planet he now navigated beside a glacial river amid the exalting and terrifying snow.

Acknowledgements

MANY THANKS TO the editors and staff of publications in which some of these stories, often in earlier forms, first appeared:

The Dalhousie Review: "Dwelling"
Existere: "Skill Development"
Grain: "Fenris"
The Nashwaak Review: "Many Rivers," "What We Know About Our Neighbours"
New Orphic Review: "Green Hell," "Mountain Grown," "Respect"
Overtime (Blue Cubicle Press): "Along the Water Line"
The Prairie Journal of Canadian Literature: "Graveyard"
The Windsor Review: "Clouds"

It takes a village to write a book—*this* book, anyway—and I very much appreciate the help (often in ways they do not know, and sometimes with regard to specific stories) of, among others: Jeremy Addington, Ben Aubin, Fran Brafman, Victoria Carleton, Rod Currie, Dymphny Dronyk, Bouk Elzinga, David Everest, Nina George, Bruce Hayes, Ernest Hekkanen, Mabel Kabatoff, Anna Ling Kaye, Sharon Lang, David Lawson, Raynald Losier, Peter Martyn, Diehl McKay, Rita Moir, Steve Mounteer, the Nelson Nordic Ski Club, Greg Nesteroff, Margaret Parker, Capt. Brian Plummer (CMSG), Verna Relkoff, Melanie Schnell, P'nina Shames, the Slocan Valley Heritage Trail Society, Joanne Taylor, Wolfgang Teiner, Fred Wah, Judy Wapp, Ron Welwood, Victor Woods.

My gratitude to the Canada Council for the Arts for a Grant to Professional Writers in 2013–14 to assist completion of this manuscript. Many thanks as well to editor Jennifer Day for her highly perceptive and helpful reading of the MS. And I'm grateful to all the Harbour and D&M crew, including Anna Comfort O'Keeffe, Marisa Alps and Nicola Goshulak. Special thanks to the latter for her astute and judicious eye.

"The Shed" is for Fred F. Dutoff, because he asked.

Names, characters, locations and events portrayed in these stories are entirely fictional. Any references to actual places or individuals, or descriptions of landscapes, are for fictional purposes only and are not intended to represent reality. Any inadvertent accuracy is coincidental and unintended.

About the Author

TOM WAYMAN HAS published three books of fiction, as well as more than a dozen collections of poems, six poetry anthologies and three collections of essays. His previous short story collection, *Boundary Country* (Thistledown Press, 2007), was shortlisted for the Danuta Gleed award. His 2012 poetry collection, *Dirty Snow* (Harbour Publishing), won the Acorn-Plantos Award; in 2003, *My Father's Cup* (Harbour Publishing) was shortlisted for the Governor General's Literary Award. He has taught widely at the post-secondary level in Canada and the US, most recently (2002–10) at the University of Calgary. He has been a resident of BC's West Kootenay region since 1989.